A NEW EXPERIENCE IN HORROR
FROM ONE OF TODAY'S MASTERS

Bridging many centuries and realities, John Coyne's newest bestseller blends ancient magic and contemporary horror to produce an experience as terrifying as it is unique. With the bestselling success of THE LEGACY, THE PIERCING, THE SEARING and now HOBGOBLIN, Coyne affirms his place among the writers who are making the horror novel today's bestselling literary sensation.

"A DIFFERENT AND INVOLVING CHILLER . . . HIS PROTAGONISTS (ARE) AS BELIEVABLE AND FAMILIAR AS HIS HORRORS ARE FRIGHTENING!"
—*Publishers Weekly*

"HORROR FANS AND D'n'D AFFICIONADOS WILL WANT IT!"
—*Library Journal*

JOHN COYNE
HOBGOBLIN

BERKLEY BOOKS, NEW YORK

HOBGOBLIN

A Berkley Book / published by arrangement
with the author

PRINTING HISTORY
G. P. Putnam's Sons edition/January 1981
Berkley edition / July 1982

ISBN: 0-425-05380-6

A BERKLEY BOOK® TM 757,375
Berkley Books are published by Berkley Publishing Corporation,
200 Madison Avenue, New York, New York 10016.
The name "BERKLEY" and the stylized "B" with design
are trademarks belonging to Berkley Publishing Corporation.
PRINTED IN THE UNITED STATES OF AMERICA

To Peter Lampack

hob-gob-lin (hob/gob/lin), *N*. 1. anything causing superstitious fear; a bogy. 2. an evil spirit. 3. a fantasy war game based on Irish mythology and folklore, played with dice and a deck of cards.

One

Christmas, 1980

Barbara Gardiner swung the family station wagon off the avenue and into the cul-de-sac. As always, she immediately felt safe. She was home.

It had snowed earlier in the day and a few inches of heavy wet snow clung to the bare branches and wooden fences. A perfect Connecticut Christmas card, she thought, with the houses laced in colored lights and children building snowmen on their front lawns.

Barbara slowed, drove carefully on the icy street. The children were everywhere, dark figures slipping out from behind parked cars, running from lot to lot. They were like characters from Scott's fantasy game, she thought, all elves and goblins.

"You find yourself in an enchanted forest, Brian Ború, lost somewhere in time." The Dealer paused to shuffle the deck of blue *Hobgoblin* cards. Scott glanced quickly at the other four players circled around the dormitory rec-room table, and then down at the Battleboard where the miniature figure of Brian Ború waited for the next round.

Scott had painted the one-inch-tall lead figure himself.

Whenever he played *Hobgoblin* Brian Ború was his character a twenty-fifth-level paladin whom Scott had kept alive through dozens of adventures in the ancient land of Erin.

"Pick a card, Brian," the Dealer instructed, spreading the blue deck out on the table.

Scott tensed. The start of a new *Hobgoblin* game always made him nervous. So much depended on the card selected, so much of Brian Ború's fate depended on chance.

"Hurry up, Gardiner, for chrissake," one of the other boys demanded. "We have less than an hour to play."

Scott glanced up at the wall clock at the end of the lounge. Twenty to five. At five-thirty they had PE and then dinner. They wouldn't be able to play again until eight o'clock, after study hall.

There were other fantasy war games in progress around the rec-room, students playing *Dungeons & Dragons, Traveller* and *Runequest*, but most of the boys had *Hobgoblin* cards on the table and were running an Adventure.

Scott smiled. It made him feel good knowing that he had introduced *Hobgoblin* to Spencertown Academy, knowing too that his classmates at the prep school considered him the best player and his Brian Ború unbeatable.

Barbara had a moment of concern thinking of Scott. He would be home within the week and she still hadn't found him the right Christmas present. Perhaps, she thought, she should go into the city on Friday and find him something at the hobby shop. A new game perhaps. Something more realistic than *Hobgoblin,* she thought, less megalomaniacal, less devoted to vicarious slaughter.

Then she saw her husband's MGB parked in their driveway and she swung behind it, wondering why he was home from work so early, and she forgot about her son.

"All right, Brian, draw the first card," Mr. Speier, the Dealer, instructed. Scott inhaled deeply. On the exhale, he reached out and impulsively pulled a blue card from the deck.

He did not look down at the card. It was a superstition with Scott. He thought it would bring bad luck to Brian Ború. He waited until Mr. Speier dealt the other players their game cards.

HOBGOBLIN

McNulty's monk/dwarf, Saint Finn, was entrapped in a "labyrinth in the land south of the mountains of Connaught." Rob Evans's banshee, Boobach, had been sent on a fool's errand to the Isle of Skye, and Rick Wenzel's troll, Billy Blind, still guarded the pot of gold at the bottom of the lake called Lough Neagh.

"Here," explained Mr. Speier, reading from the *Hobgoblin Dealer's Manual*, "at Lough Neagh can be seen—if you have the gift of fairy vision to see under water—columns and walls of a beautiful palace where once inhabited a fairy race that some called the gods of earth.

"Now below these waters when the full moon is shining, it is said that boatmen, coming home late at night, can hear music rising from beneath the waves, hear laughter, and see glimmering lights far down under the sea.

"Your Adventure," the Dealer said, glancing at Scott, Evans and McNulty, "is to find your way out of your present situations, then rendezvous on the marshy shores of Lough Neagh and locate Billy Blind in the underwater palace. If you can free him from this fairy race of gods, you may divide their gold among you." Mr. Speier closed the *Hobgoblin* guide and added carefully, "Should any of you happen to survive."

Scott edged forward in the chair, eager to begin. He loved the way Mr. Speier dealt the game, built up the story. Of all the teachers at Spencertown Academy who played *Hobgoblin*, Mr. Speier was the best Dealer. He was always able to create another world, to help Scott let his imagination roam.

"Everyone ready?" Mr. Speier asked. He glanced at the four teenagers circling the table. "All right, let's begin."

"Warren?" Barbara Gardiner unlocked the front door and stepped into the foyer. In her arms she carried several Christmas packages which she dropped on the sofa as she quickly crossed the room. Where was he? What was wrong?

"Barbara . . . ?" His loud voice carried clearly through the house. "I'm out here."

Barbara sighed. "Thank God," she whispered, and followed his voice into the kitchen.

"Why are you home, honey? It's not even five o'clock."

He was sitting at the breakfast table drinking coffee with

3

the morning *Times* spread before him. He seemed the same as when he had left for work, except that he had taken off his jacket and tie and rolled up his sleeves, but in the bright fluorescent light of the breakfast nook he looked grayish.

He glanced up from the paper and smiled.

She saw the fatigue in his eyes, the sadness on his face. He was working too hard, she had told him. If owning his own business was going to drive him into the ground, then the business wasn't worth it.

"Are you all right, Warren?"

"I'm fine." He pushed the sports page away and leaned back in the chair. "I just wasn't feeling so hot and decided not to go back to the office. Where have you been, shopping?" He kept smiling.

She went over and touched his forehead. "You have some fever," she said, and her tension began to subside. "You may be coming down with the flu. It's around. Do you want anything? An aspirin?" She wanted to do something for him, something to ease his discomfort. She hated it when he or Scotty was ill. She felt so helpless.

"No, I'm fine." He stood up, dismissing her concern, and went to the stove to pour another cup of coffee. She followed after him, as if she were afraid to let him get beyond her reach.

For the last few weeks he had not been sleeping well and several times she had awakened to find him reading downstairs, saying he was too uncomfortable to sleep.

"Warren, I think you should see a doctor about this. You haven't been getting any rest. You're not eating at all. Just look at yourself. You're losing weight."

She stopped to appraise her husband. He was a big man with the thick neck and forearms of someone who made his living from manual labor, although nowadays he did not. In college he had been a football player and it was his brute strength that had first attracted her.

"I did call the doctor. I'm seeing him tomorrow." Warren stepped away from the stove and turned toward her.

The coffee cup was trembling in his hand. Oh, God, she thought, he really was sick.

"It's all right, Ba. Everything is all right. I'm fine." He kept talking, watching as her face filled with fear.

4

HOBGOBLIN

* * *

Scott flipped the blue card, laid it face down on the table. In capsule form it described the giant which BrianBorú had to defeat in battle before he could reach Lough Neagh.

Type: Brobdingnagian
Frequency: Very rare
Armour Class: 10
Moves: 10 feet
Size: 52 feet and staunch
Intelligence: Low
Alignment: Chaotic evil
Magic Resistance: Standard
Weapons: Fangs
Special Attack: Poison sting within 20 feet
Special Defense: Amphibian
Language: Gaelic

Scott sighed. It was worse than he had feared. The Brobdingnag was a new card in the *Hobgoblin* game and BrianBorú had never faced one before. Scott sat back in the chair, trembling with nervousness, realizing that it might happen today. BrianBorú might be killed.

"Well," Barbara said, turning to the positive side of the problem as she always did when troubled, "let's first see what the doctor says. There's no need to get too excited. After all, you had a physical two years ago."

"Three years ago."

"Three, then, and everything was fine." She had taken off her coat and boots and begun to straighten the kitchen, to wash the few dishes in the sink, to keep herself busy. "But, darling," she went on, "you just have to think about cutting back."

"Ba, you know I can't just work nine to five. When the factory is in operation, I have to be at the plant."

"Sell the plant! I'd rather have you do that than die on me at forty." She began to cry, leaning against the sink, looking out at the backyard and terrace, all under a smooth blanket of pure white snow.

"Ba, come on, please," Warren whispered. He was behind

her, his arms around her tightly. Sometimes he hugged her so hard it hurt. He was careless with his strength, she knew. He thought it would last forever. "I'm not feeling well, honey—that's all. I've had a few restless nights and naturally I'm exhausted. Who wouldn't be? But I'm not selling the plant. Granddad started printing in this town. We employ eighty people now and by the time Scotty takes over there's going to be a lot more."

"Scotty is only sixteen, honey, and he's told you he's not interested in the printing business."

"Oh, he'll feel different when he gets older." Warren released her, as if he didn't like her disagreeing with him.

"He's not like you, Warren—or like me, either, for that matter," Barbara continued. "He's not interested in sports, as you are, or art, as I am. He's really a missing link in our gene pool. Some days I don't even think he's ours." She turned and smiled wryly at her husband, but he had gone back to the table and sat there looking pensive.

"I suspect he'll stay in academics," she went on, "become a teacher. You see how he is on vacations. He'd rather stay up in his room reading *The Chronicles of Amber*. He's just not gregarious the way you are. I can't imagine his going to the country club, making contacts, getting business for Gardiner & Sons."

She had never confronted Warren this way about their son and her directness surprised even her. It was not her way. She had always lived in her husband's shadow. He was so forceful, so sure of himself that she had just been carried along on the quick tide of his energy.

Warren did not respond. He was thinking of when he had driven Scott back to school after the Thanksgiving vacation, and what a good time they had had, the two of them together. Scott had wanted to know what it had been like in Vietnam during the Tet Offensive, and he had talked for nearly the entire two-hour drive, describing how they had fought from street to street, flushing out the Vietcong.

The boy had been mesmerized, Warren recalled, and he smiled thinking how much pleasure it had given him, bragging to his son as if he'd been some kind of war hero. It was a story he would never have told Scott if Barbara had been around.

Scott had a brave, tough side that his mother never saw, or didn't understand when she did see it. But Warren understood it, saw it in Scott's love of science fiction adventure books and that war game he was always playing—*Hobgoblin*. Scott was his father's boy, and the two of them knew it, even if Barbara didn't.

"Well, we can't worry about that," he said. "Let's just wait a year or so, then we'll know what will become of Scotty." Warren planted his huge hands on the kitchen table and stood. "I'm going outside and shovel off that front walk."

"No, Warren, don't!"

"Honey, at least two inches have fallen since I got home, and the Beavens will be here in a couple of hours. They'll be up to their ankles in it by then."

"I'll shovel it!"

"Ba, don't be silly." He laughed at her concern as he took his parka and boots from the hall closet. "It's ten minutes' work. My God, I carried a ton of paper this morning and didn't even lose my breath. You're talking to the old nose guard, honey, twenty-eight games without an injury." He sat down again at the table and began to put on his heavy boots, breathing hard as he leaned over, struggling with the laces. It was twenty years since he played football, and his bulky body was no longer in condition. It wasn't that he was fat, Barbara thought, just huge. Whatever room he sat in, he filled the space like a monolith.

"There!" He sat up. He was smiling, satisfied. His face was on fire.

"Darling, look at yourself." She laid her cool palms on his cheeks and was frightened by the heat.

"Ba, it's ten minutes. Besides, the house is stuffy." As he passed, he leaned down and kissed her lightly on the cheek, as one might a child. There was always that element in their marriage. Often Barbara felt as if she and Scotty were both his children.

"You're just being reckless with yourself, Warren," she called after him.

"If I'm going to have a heart attack over a few inches of snow, honey, there's nothing I can do about it. I'm not going to sit around worrying where my next breath is coming from."

Then he was gone, out of the kitchen and down the hallway. She could only see his huge back, lumbering along, as she sat in the kitchen chair, filled with the sense that she would never see Warren alive again.

He had been the same in college. He was never happier than after a game when he had been bruised and cut up from playing. She hadn't worried either, back then. She had found him daring, this wonderful, battling knight of hers.

"Brian Ború, what is your wish?" the Dealer asked.

Scott had moved his lead miniature one square on the Battleboard, placing Brian next to the Brobdingnagian. Mr. Speier had built an enchanted forest at one edge of the table, carving styrofoam packaging into trees, ruins and small mountains. These he had painted in somber colors, and Scott could almost feel this enchanted forest, smell the vegetation, see the heavy mist surround the valleys beyond Lough Neagh.

"The dice," Scott announced.

"The dice? Oh, God, Gardiner, no!" Rob Evans protested. "It's too risky."

"The dice," Scott demanded. "Brian Ború is ready to attack."

Evans leaned across the Battleboard, gesturing with both hands as he talked. "Brian Ború is our only hope, Scott. Christ, Boobach is off in the Isle of Skye, and McNulty's dumb monk is all the way south of Connaught." He gestured at their positions on the Battleboard. "We're spread out all over the fuckin' landscape!"

"Rob, will you control your language?" Mr. Speier asked quietly. Already their table had attracted the attention of the other students who were leaving their own games to circle this *Hobgoblin* round.

"Mr. Speier, you tell him!" Evans appealed to their teacher.

"I'm merely the Dealer, Rob, the referee. It's Scott's decision. What will Brian Ború do . . . ? Take on the Brobdingnagian?"

"If Brian Ború is killed, Scott, we're finished," Evans warned. "There is no way Boobach or Saint Finn can get Billy Blind out of Lough Neagh." He was angry, challenging.

"Well, what am I going to do, Rob? I'm within range of

the poisonous sting. If I turn my back he can kill me before I even have a chance to retreat. Besides—" he looked back at the Battleboard, at his finely decorated paladin—"Brian Ború never loses."

Around the tables shouts of encouragement went up from the other students, urging him on.

"Brian Ború, what is your decision? Dice or an evasion card?"

The English teacher stared across at the tall, good-looking blond teen-ager. By the rules of the game, the Dealer should have been getting a time limit, insisting that Scott make a quick decision. *Hobgoblin* was based on the laws of nature. By now these two fighters would already have joined in mortal combat or parted. Still he hesitated, giving Scott time to reconsider. Speier liked the boy. In the sophomore English class Speier taught, Scott was the best writer. His papers were always original, often bizarre and fanciful, as if somehow Scott saw the world in four or five dimensions instead of the usual three. It was not surprising that Scott was so good at fantasy games.

Hobgoblin had made Scott popular at Spencertown. He was not a natural athlete or a leader, but his skill at the game had given him the edge, a way to make people notice him, and by the end of his first year everyone, even some of the teachers, was playing the new game. And for almost two years Brian Ború, his twenty-fifth-level paladin, had survived all the Adventures, all the attacks and melees in the ancient land of Erin.

Still, Scott had never come up against a Brobdingnagian. No one had. The new blue challenge cards had just arrived that day, and Speier had decided to add them to the deck immediately for one last big game before the Christmas holidays.

Scott glanced over at Mike McNulty who nodded back, saying simply, "You're good with the dice, Scott. Go ahead. We can't have this Brobdingnagian tracking us into Lough Neagh. He's amphibian, remember! He could attack when we're beneath the water."

"Let Brian at him, Scott," shouted several of the boys surrounding the table. They were pressing closer, waiting for Scott to make his decision.

"The dice," Scott said again and a cheer went up.

Speier handed the three pyramidally-shaped dice to Scott

who cupped both hands and shook the dice rapidly, tossing them up high so they spun in the air before hitting the Battle-board.

"Oh, God," he whispered to himself, "let them roll in the 100s."

"Ninety-eight point six," someone shouted, quickly reading the numbers.

"I told you!" Evans spoke up, already angry. "I mean, the odds were against you."

"Shut up, Evans, will you!" McNulty ordered. He too was nervous.

"What's it mean, Mr. Speier?" Scott asked politely, disregarding the others. Only the Dealer could interpret the rolls of the dice; his Dealer's *Guide* told him what the various percentage points meant.

"Ninety-eight point six attack points means you missed a surprise hit on the Brobdingnagian. And he's seen you, of course. Brian is within the twenty-foot range." The Dealer picked up the pyramidal dice and tossed them down again on the Battleboard.

"Eighty-three point four." Reading the result in the Dealer's face, Scott relaxed. Eighty-three point four meant the Brobdingnagian had struck at him and missed. BrianBorú was okay; he had survived the first round.

Scott knew everything about BrianBorú, his strengths, weaknesses and special skills. In Scott's first year at Spencertown the Celtic knight had started out as just a first-level fighter. But with each attack he survived, Brian had grown in power and abilities until in the deck of *Hobgoblin* cards he could only be defeated by treachery, or by the introduction of a new monster like the Brobdingnagian.

Only once had BrianBorú been seriously challenged. Early in the fall semester several seniors with Scottish bestiary characters had rallied together, attacking BrianBorú while he was crossing the Twelve Pins hills. It had taken Brian three games to kill off the half-dozen blue hags of the Highlands and the Boobri, gigantic web-footed birds that hid in passing storm clouds and swooped down on Brian while he slept in the valley of Connemara.

Yet he had won, using the sacred sword given to him by

the king of Erin when Brian had freed the king's daughter from the giant of Loch Leín.

For a second Scott thought of using the sacred sword again, but according to *Hobgoblin* rules Brian could use his sacred weapon only once in an Adventure, so he had to calculate his chances carefully. Scott glanced at the blue card which described the Brobdingnagian. It stated that the giant had only standard resistance against magic, which meant, Scott knew, that any throw of the dice over twenty-five meant an instant kill with the magic sword.

He could easily throw that high, Scott reasoned, yet he resisted the easy solution. Brian Ború would be handicapped without the sword, and Scott knew there would be greater dangers closer to the bottom of Lough Neagh, once they got nearer Billy Blind and the pot of gold. The Brobdingnagian was surely not the only new threat among the blue cards.

The giant had missed him. Now it was his turn to attack again. Scott threw the dice. "One-hundred and twelve!" he exclaimed. He always tried to keep calm while playing the game, to seem above the fate of his Brian Ború, but 112 attack points meant a direct hit on the Brobdingnagian. It could mean that Brian Ború had killed the giant. Scott shifted nervously in the chair as he waited for the Dealer's verdict.

Barbara stood behind the bedroom curtains, looking down at her husband. First he shoveled, then he went back and swept away the remaining patches of snow, doing it meticulously, as if a perfectly swept sidewalk really mattered. It was the way he did everything—a maddening obsession with detail. Barbara had told him he had the mind of a proofreader.

Barbara left the window. She couldn't bear watching him. She knew she was being obsessive herself, watching, waiting, fearing that he'd keel over.

And she was tired. Her sudden panic had been exhausting. She went to their bed and, slipping off her shoes, stretched out, pulling the comforter up and over her. The house was not cold; it was only her fright that chilled her. She felt as if she was standing in an open doorway, exposed to the weather.

"Darling?" Warren was standing at the bottom of the front stairs, shouting up at her.

"Yes, dear . . . ?" She rolled over on the bed but otherwise did not move.

"The front walk is clean and I'm still alive."

"Warren, don't kid around!"

"Well, it's done and I'm fine. Can I get you anything?" He sounded energetic, as if he wanted to keep busy.

"Nothing, dear. Why don't you just relax? We're both going to be up late this evening." She smiled, hearing his voice.

"Yes, I think I will. I'm going to get a drink, then watch the news in the den. You sure you don't want anything? I'll bring a glass of wine up to you."

"No, sweetheart, but thank you. I'm going to take a nap." And she rolled over and drew the pillow to her, still smiling as she cuddled it close. Everything was fine. Warren was safely inside the house, and she had time for a long nap before preparing dinner. She fell asleep thinking of how happy she was with her husband and son.

Mr. Speier flipped through the Dealer's *Guide,* searching for the attack points. He was going slow, Scott saw, building tension while they all waited. What did 112 attack points mean against a Brobdingnagian? Had Brian Ború killed the giant?

"Brian missed," the Dealer announced.

"Missed!" The outcry was in unison. They all knew that in *Hobgoblin* a roll of over 100 on the pyramidal dice usually meant a direct hit, most often an immediate kill.

Mr. Speier raised his hand, silencing the students, then read from the new supplement to the Dealer's *Guide.* "Brobdingnagians have existed for thousands of years, but the world first learned of them in 1703 when Lemuel Gulliver was shipwrecked on their native land. He said they were 'as tall as steeple spires.'

"The Brobdingnagians are not native to Erin and their presence in the land of *Hobgoblin* is curious."

Scott smiled. For a moment he forgot his fear of losing Brian Ború as he lost himself in the story of how the Brobdingnag came to Ireland. This was what he liked best about *Hobgoblin:* all the details, so much physical description of the locations, all the background information on ancient times.

"We suspect," Mr. Speier went on, "that the first Brobdingnagians came from an extensive peninsula on the coast of California. Gulliver, the only westerner to visit the place and return, is embarrassingly unclear about its exact location, but then again, he was shipwrecked and we can't expect him to be precise.

"At the time of the first great California earthquake their thin elbow of land was cast into the sea, and a handful of them managed to survive by setting sail in long ships. They were carried around the world by the North Atlantic drift and their ships arrived in Erin before the time of Tara, approximately 200 A.D.

"These long ships were wrecked on the rocky coast of western Ireland, and to this day their remains can be clearly seen in the shallow waters of Blacksod Bay.

"Despite their great strength and size—Gulliver said they could cover ten yards with every step—few of the Brobdingnagians were able to survive the cold and hostile climate of Erin's northern latitudes.

"Those few who have survived are rare beings, easily provoked to battle, but nevertheless faithful and trusted friends, as worthy as any knight of Erin, if treated with respect and camaraderie." Speier stopped reading.

"You shouldn't have attacked, Scott." It was Evans finding fault again. "If you had talked to him instead, he could've been your friend. He could've helped us."

"Fuck off," Scott answered back.

"Come on, you two," Mr. Speier interrupted. "I'll call a fault in this game if you keep it up. What if Dean Campbell comes into the lounge and hears this language?" He took in all the students with his glance.

"All right," the Dealer went on, picking up the dice. "The Brobdingnagian has seen BrianBorú, has taken the full force of the paladin's blow and survived. Now he attacks!" Speier checked his *Guide*. "I need to throw only a 34 to hit BrianBorú. And any number over 100 means a mortal hit."

A howl went up from the crowd of students. Several of them leaned down to catch Scott's eye, to shout that BrianBorú had finally met his match. Even Evans, whose character couldn't rescue Billy Blind without Brian's help, seemed perversely pleased that Scott's *Hobgoblin* supremacy was about to end.

"Wait! Wait!" Scott shouted over the noise. He raised his arms for silence, and yelled loud enough to be heard. "Brian Ború has something to say. Brian Ború humbly requests everyone's attention. Brian Ború will not die."

The silence woke Barbara Gardiner. She knew she had heard a noise. A crash. A heavy thump, as if someone had pushed a grocery bag off the kitchen table. She was jerked fully awake out of her brief, deep sleep.

"Warren?" she asked. Then louder, "Warren, do you hear me?"

It was a large house and if he was in the kitchen or study she knew he would not hear her. She tossed off the comforter and went to the doorway, her footsteps silent on the thick carpet.

From the top of the stairs she shouted his name into the house. Now she was frightened. She raced down the steps and at the bottom she nearly fell in her panic, her stockings slipping on the polished hardwood floor.

She kept shouting his name, shrieking it. She could hear the television in the den, hear the voice of Walter Cronkite say, "And that's the way it is on the four-hundred-thirteenth day of captivity for the American hostages." The sentence stuck in her mind, stayed with her forever, as if burned into the membrane.

The den was empty. The television played to an empty room. Warren had probably turned on the set, then gone into the kitchen to fix a drink. A perfect Manhattan—always a perfect Manhattan. He made them himself. No one else knew how, he insisted.

"Warren!" She wailed like a lost child, but she was thinking furiously as she headed for the kitchen. He had taken out the trash. Gone out the back door and dumped the garbage in the cans by the drive. That was it. That was why he wasn't answering. Her body shook. She could barely wait, trembling now from relief.

HOBGOBLIN

* * *

Scott Gardiner waited for silence. He had their attention. He saw the puzzlement in everyone's eyes. Even Mr. Speier frowned, unsure of what Scott was planning.

"I know what BrianBorú is capable of, Scott," Mr. Speier warned, picking up the Dealer's *Guide*.

Scott grinned. It was so simple. BrianBorú would not die. Scott had kept him alive for another attack.

"Well, what is it!" Evans demanded.

"Mr. Speier, you said this was an enchanted forest, right?" Scott asked, knowing the answer.

The English teacher nodded.

"All right," Scott went on, "it is already established that BrianBorú, because of his attacking victories, is a twenty-fifth-level paladin. And he comes into this game with over 400,000 battle points."

Scott had already pulled out the computer listing of Brian's achievements. The result of all the *Hobgoblin* games were stored on the school's computer and Scott displayed the readout as if it were evidence.

"That means," he continued, speaking quickly, excited by the knowledge that he was right, "that my paladin has arcane powers. Right?" He hesitated a moment to wait for Mr. Speier to agree, to let everyone realize what BrianBorú was about to do.

Mr. Speier nodded, still unsure of what was happening. It was true, according to the guide: a paladin at the twenty-fifth level had secret knowledge and magical powers.

"Okay. According to *Hobgoblin* rules, if I roll higher than four on the cube dice I am granted one wish. And because I'm so proficient, I can roll for a wish at any time. It doesn't constitute my taking any extra turn." Scott glanced up at the other students and added, "If you don't believe me, it's on page 108 of the Player's guide."

Mr. Speier looked up from his book and gestured to Scott to proceed. "You're right," he said. "Roll the dice."

Scott took his time. He held the small cubes loosely in his cupped hands and shook them slowly. He knew he could roll a four, but he heightened the suspense by making them all wait. A moment ago the other students had thought Brian Ború was finally finished, about to be killed by a Brobdingnag. Scott ducked his head, grinning with pleasure. It was so easy, he thought, and still they hadn't guessed how he could outsmart the giant.

The Battleboard was an enchanted forest—a Brigadoon world where time stopped and could be played again. If he won the right to make one wish, he would reverse the game, bring it back in time to the moment before Brian Ború attacked the Brobdingnagian. Then he'd have Brian negotiate with the giant instead, win him over as a comrade. It was within Brian Ború's power to sway the Brobdingnagian. Brian had enough charisma points to influence humans and nonhumans alike.

"Come on, Gardiner!" Evans yelled. "Brian Ború can't miss. Roll the dice!"

Scott glanced at the other boy and casually, confidently tossed the dice onto the Battleboard.

"Read 'em and weep," he said smugly.

At the door to the kitchen Barbara saw Warren. The sight puzzled her and it took a moment for her to comprehend why he was sitting upright on the floor with his eyes open and staring off across the room, as if he were trying to recall what he had wanted. His hand still clutched the glass of ice.

"Oh, darling," she whispered, falling against the doorjamb. In an instant she visualized what must have been the last moments of his life.

The rye was on the counter, the cabinet door was open. He had walked across the kitchen to the refrigerator and placed the glass under the ice dispenser. The cold ice tumbling into his glass must have been the last sound he heard. When he turned his heart gave out. He fell back against the refrigerator. That was what she had heard. Her husband's body sliding down the length of the refrigerator as he died in silence.

The dice spun to a stop on the Battleboard.

"Snake eyes!" Evans shouted.

A roar went up from the students crowded around. Scott had not made enough points to gain a wish. The paladin could not reverse time. The giant would attack. Brian Ború would be slaughtered.

While Scott sat stunned, the Dealer inexorably threw the dice. The Giant's twenty-foot sting pierced the armor of Brian Ború and the legendary knight arched his back, crying out silently against his fate, then slowly crumpled to death on the floor of the enchanted forest.

Two

Fall, 1981

The boy who called himself BrianBorú stood in the glen and waited for the Bugganes, the small, headless ogres that lived in the marshy creek below the castle. The creek ran diagonally across the sloping hill, and its course left a ragged scar in the carpeted lawns as if the rocky mansion were a craggy face, and the long green grass a neck with its throat cut.

In his hands he held firmly the leather slingshot the Irish blacksmith had made, carving the handle from one solid piece of black walnut and using a strip of cowhide for the long strap.

"Here," he had said, giving it to the boy. "The king of Ireland himself killed the giant of Loch Léin with the selfsame weapon."

Brian placed a small hazelnut in the deep pouch, as the old man had shown him, and whipped the sling about his head. It whistled in the wind, frightening the golden finches from the oak tree.

The boy spotted the headless Bugganes, watched the little ogres crawl from the rocks, scamper across the creek, and pause again by the thick woods. He kept whirling the sling, holding fire, seized with both fright and pleasure as the cruel creatures metamorphosed into snarling dogs, then screaming goblins.

The evil fairies kept changing shape, but Brian tracked them to where the creek disappeared into the oak woods he called Lough Mask. It was to this very spot yesterday, after school, he had tracked the giant Gorm, killing the stupid creature with his battle axe, hacking away bits and pieces of the twenty-foot giant until finally he had chopped it down to his own size. In a single swoop he had lopped off the monster's head, severing it like a sunflower top.

He had the Bugganes in sight and he edged forward carefully, getting into range, keeping downwind from them. He was dressed for the hunt, camouflaged in gray leggins and a leather vest made from the skin of a young elk. In his other hand he carried a knobbed shillelagh.

The shillelagh had magical powers, Conor had told him, but Brian had not yet tested it. He would wield it in battle someday, he knew, but for these weasellike demons he needed only his courage and the singing slingshot that whistled near his ear.

On the rocks the fairies popped up, looked alarmed, searched the woods until in the morning fog they spied Brian Ború, heard his footsteps ruffle the thick bed of yellow maple leaves, and they scampered off, running like gray squirrels across the open lawn.

Brian Ború's sling whipped around once more, and the hazelnut shot from the pouch with the force of a crossbow bolt. He had aimed at the leader, but the hazelnut missed and smashed against the rocks, scattering fragments in a fine spray, and the woods were silent. The boy stood at the bottom of the landscaped lawns, breathing deeply, thrilled by the near hit, the sense of adventure. His leather sling hung loose in his hand and he sighed, exhausted by the early morning hunt.

The autumn sun had reached the fields and was shining against the facade of the mansion, burning away the mist with the smooth, even hand of warmth.

He was late. It was time for school. His mother would be calling him soon, and he ran up the hill toward the guest house, his sneakers leaving a straight path in the wet dew as if he were marking his way through a magic world.

HOBGOBLIN

* * *

"You just have to control your imagination, Scotty," she insisted. Barbara returned to the kitchen table and sat down across from her son, pausing for a moment, as if to invite a response. She never ate breakfast, but while she waited she lit another cigarette and glanced up at the kitchen clock to see just how late she was. The mansion would be open soon.

"It's only a game, Mom," the boy answered nervously. He knew he was delaying her.

"It's more than that, Scott. It's not healthy, especially when you're out at dawn tramping through the woods, dressed up in that weird costume and chasing after squirrels." Barbara glanced at her son. She would have to call Dr. Frisch long distance, she decided; he might have something to suggest.

"Bugganes, Mom. I was hunting Bugganes, the evil fairies that live in the wood of Lough Mask." Scotty tried to explain, taking a certain pleasure in detailing the nuances of the game. It would be smarter, he knew, to keep quiet, to let her yell at him and get it over with, but he couldn't stop himself. He wanted his mother to understand. But she just shook her head impatiently.

"You're too old for cowboys and Indians. You're sixteen. You have your driver's license . . . you'll start going out with girls soon. It's absolutely ridiculous to be playing children's games."

"Adults play *Hobgoblin,* mother. Grown-ups. Doctors and college professors. People like you play this game. Old people."

"Thanks, darling." Barbara smiled curtly. "I didn't realize I was already a member of the geriatric society."

"Ah, Mom, you know what I mean. Look—it's a game. Everyone at the academy plays it." He was leaning forward, gesturing with both hands. "Even Mr. Speier played. You didn't mind when I played with him. You never told me I had to stop."

"In Connecticut you didn't play all by yourself." She hesitated. "In Connecticut you didn't refer to yourself as Brian Ború."

"Mom, for cryin' out loud!"

"I'm sorry, but it's true." She kept shaking her head. "Besides, I thought you told me BrianBorú died in your last game at Spencertown. How can he still be your character?"

Scott didn't answer. His mother was right. According to the rules of *Hobgoblin,* a dead character could in fact be resurrected. But he had to begin all over again, at the first level, and Scott couldn't bear to do that to BrianBorú. He couldn't stand to lose both his father and his mighty, twenty-fifth-level paladin.

That had been the wrong question, Barbara saw, watching her silent son. But she had to get through to him.

"You're just too involved in that game, Scotty. I've seen you spend endless hours painting those silly miniatures."

"You're never home long enough to see me spend endless hours working on anything," he answered quietly, not looking up.

For a moment Barbara didn't reply. She stamped out her cigarette and studied her child, thinking. Then she said softly, "That's unfair, Scotty. I explained to you already that this is a difficult time for me. We only have this nine months at Ballycastle and I have to finish the report." She could hear the frustration in her own voice, and she stopped talking. It was only ten months since Warren's death, and she had promised herself that she wouldn't burden Scotty further by talking about her career problems. She had upset his life enough by taking him out of the academy and leaving Connecticut. But she had had no choice. Warren had borrowed against Gardiner & Sons to buy new plant equipment. His death had left her with a lot of debts and little savings—certainly not enough to keep Scotty in private school. This job didn't pay much, but it was the only one she'd been able to find. Women with M.A.s in art history were not in great demand.

"Let's not fight, Scotty." She reached across the table to hold his hand, but the boy moved his arm beyond her reach. He did not like to be touched. Even as a child, he had resisted her hugs. He just wasn't very affectionate. Beyond his clean, blond looks, his quick, effortless smile, there was a coldness to him, as if his heart were packed with arctic ice.

"I'm not fighting," he insisted, but tears flashed in his eyes. She always misunderstood him. "Just because you don't like

Hobgoblin, you think it's silly and stupid and anyone who plays it is crazy. Well, it's not fair!"

He pushed back his chair and stood, rushing into his bedroom to find his book bag. He wanted only to get out of the house, to get away from his mother's voice.

"I'm sorry," Barbara shouted after him. "I'm sorry to upset you, but these games are just fantasies, and you have to begin facing reality—you know what Dr. Frisch said."

"Mom! For chrissake, that was months ago!" He was back in the kitchen doorway, a tall, slim boy who looked out of place in the cottage, too big for the small rooms.

At times it seemed to Barbara he was a stranger in her house, an intruder she did not even know. He had grown so quickly in the last year that she no longer recognized him. I have to buy him new clothes, she thought, seeing how uncomfortable he looked in his old corduroy jeans.

"Dr. Frisch didn't blame my problem on *Hobgoblin,*" Scott went on. "He said I was emotionally disturbed about Daddy dying. I was experiencing a psychic seizure, a disassociation from reality, and I was acting out violently." He tossed off the psychiatric jargon sarcastically, knowing she didn't understand half of it.

Barbara shrugged helplessly. She had never thought much of psychiatrists and knew very little about them. It was only her desperation over Scott, in those first nightmare weeks after Warren died, that had led her to seek out the best psychologist she could. Dr. Frisch had saved Scotty, she knew, but still she feared she had lost her child forever.

"Scotty, you're too upset. Let's talk about this later," she asked, backing away from the confrontation.

"I'm not upset!" he insisted.

"All right, you're not upset!" Barbara sighed, exasperated. "But it's 7:20. You're late. And I don't want you racing the car to school," she added, feeling the need to exercise some maternal control.

"I have football practice after school," he said calmly. "I'll be home late."

"Fine." The crisis was over. She picked up his breakfast dishes and went to the sink, stacking them with the unwashed dishes from the night before. She would come back at noon, she promised herself, and straighten up. But immediately, at the thought of housework, she felt depressed. She needed help. The house was getting out of control.

"Are we going to eat at home tonight?" he asked.

"Yes, Scott, we are eating at home. Don't we eat at home most nights?" She turned to see what he was implying.

"I mean, are you going to cook? You never do anymore."

"Come on, Scott, give me a break. Stop this whining. You know that's not true." A hot flash of anger swept through her.

"Well, it is true," he answered. "We had pizza last night, and the night before that. . . ."

"I think we've had enough family discussion for the moment." She glanced again at the wall clock, thinking she had to be careful with Scotty. His transferring schools was turning out to be just as difficult as his doctor warned her it might be.

"I've gotta go," the boy said, moving toward the kitchen door.

They confronted each other at the doorway; she blocked him from hurrying outside. Close up he towered above her, taller by at least six inches. His body was all long arms and legs, and he moved with the quick, jerky motions of a puppet on strings.

"Let's not fight," she asked, trying to be conciliatory, whispering as if she were his lover. She slid her arm about his waist, hugged him briefly. She expected him to pull away, but this time, tentatively, he wrapped his arm over her shoulders and made an awkward gesture at an embrace. They went outside that way, walked across the small patch of lawn to where he had parked his small MGB the night before. The car had been Warren's, a present to himself after one particularly successful year. Barbara knew she should have sold it, but it meant so much to Scott that she'd let him keep it and sold the last of their stocks instead. A businesswoman she would never be, she sighed.

Beyond the car the lawn swept up to the mansion itself, to where the huge Gothic castle was built across the hilltop. Like a dark cloud on the landscape, it dominated the countryside. Barbara did not like the mansion. She found it ominous and grotesque, out of place on the river.

It had been a rich man's perversion. In the 1920s Fergus

O'Cuileannain had imported the old castle from the west of Ireland, then rebuilt it stone by stone on the bluff overlooking the river.

The castle was at the summit of two thousand acres of woods and farmland and several curved roads led up to it, cutting through maple woods, pine forests, and natural fruit groves. The thick foliage had a way of concealing the massive castle from anyone driving up, and it wasn't until a car came out of the woods, reaching the crest of the hilltop, that the castle suddenly appeared, as if conjured by magic.

The guest houses were below, tucked away in a white birch wood between the mansion itself and the river. From the Gardiners' house, Barbara looked up at the facade of the castle and could see the full length of the front side.

The castle was a massive collection of towers, turrets, buttresses, bays and pinnacled roofs. Seen from the disadvantage of the lower lawn, the building seemed hostile and impenetrable. It only lacked, Barbara thought, a moat and drawbridge.

Yet the castle did not create a sense of awe or wonder. She had expected more from the mansion, when three months before, an Irish genealogical foundation contacted her through a friend at the Metropolitan Museum of Art who was helping in her job search. The Foundation asked if she would come to Ballycastle and write a history of the estate, including a catalog of the art and furnishings.

She hadn't wanted the job. Driving up from the city that spring, she had spotted the castle from several miles away, looming like a vulture, blotting the horizon with its gray turrets and towers. She had slowed down, stopped at the entrance gate, thinking she didn't want to spend nine months of her life inside such thick, depressing walls.

But Warren was dead. And she needed to get on with her life.

"Do you want me to stop off and pick up a pizza on my way home?" Scott was asking, trying to make amends.

"No, sweetheart. I'll cook veal scallopini," she offered, naming one of his favorite dishes. She hugged him tightly and let him go.

Everything was all right again. The crisis had been averted. She would just have to be more careful, she realized, less

judgmental. She was forcing him to react, upsetting him need-
lessly.

"It's okay, you know, if you want to ask someone from the
Foundation over for dinner," Scott said offhandedly, folding
himself into the tiny English sports car.

"Why, Scotty, aren't you nice!" Barbara smiled, pleased
by his suggestion. "Thank you, but I think the two of us should
have dinner together."

"No, it's okay." He glanced up at her. He was worried, she
saw. His gray eyes showed the fear. It was as if he had swum
out too far into the deep water and realized he couldn't save
himself.

"Another time," she suggested, and she leaned forward on
impulse and kissed him on the cheek. It had been awhile since
he had allowed her to kiss him—not since the funeral, not
since the terrible last moments at the grave site.

"Have a good day at school," she said, smiling down at her
son, then she stepped away to let him drive off.

A third-level Barrow-Wight, he thought, looking up at his
mother and listening to her voice. An inhabitant of rivers and
seas. A subterranean monster capable of magical powers and
psionic abilities. That was what she reminded him of.

"And when are you going to ask some of your new friends
home?" she asked, suddenly feeling secure enough to intrude
into his private life.

"I don't have any friends," Scott answered flatly. He reached
over and turned on the engine. But as a knight, as a fourth-
level magic-user, he ought to be powerful enough to outwit a
Barrow-Wight, he thought, and extract two wishes. He hesitated, deciding what to demand of her.

"Oh, Scott, I'm sure you have some friends. What about
your football buddies?"

"They're all assholes," he stated, gunning the engine. He
would make her grant him the ability to cast spells.

"And girlfriends?" Barbara asked, trying to sound jilted.

"They're all dumb, Mom. The girls, the boys, and the teachers. Everyone at that crummy high school." He shifted into
first and popped the clutch. The small green sports car shot
off, tearing up gravel as it raced onto the drive. The second

wish, he decided, would be to make his mother invisible, to get her out of his life.

Barbara watched the car as it followed the curving drive below the castle and disappeared into the woods. The morning sun swept across the edge of the woods, spotlighting the blaze of fall leaves. It made the hillside a canvas of bright colors sweeping down to the river in straight, clean brush strokes.

What a strange child, she thought in a moment of dispassionate appraisal. She wondered if all teen-age boys were that difficult. He needed a girlfriend, she decided. A girlfriend would persuade him to cut his hair, help him with his manners. Best of all, a girlfriend would get Scott away from his daydreams, away from *Hobgoblin*, and warming to the idea, Barbara Gardiner walked uphill, following the cinder path to the castle, feeling better about herself, feeling better about her son. She would find Scotty someone, she decided. She would find him a girl.

Three

Just waiting for him made her nervous. Yet still she watched, standing in front of her locker and fiddling with the combination. She had unlocked the metal door several times, gotten out her books, put away her jacket and lunch, and even attempted to straighten out the top shelf. It was only the sixth week of school and already she couldn't find anything in there.

"Hey, Dunn, let's go."

She glanced over her shoulder at the two girls.

"Go ahead, I'll catch up." She kept busy fishing in the messy shelf.

"What's taking you so long?" one of the girls demanded. They were both shorter than she and wore their hair in the same short, curly style.

"I have to find my geometry homework," she explained, still searching. "Go on, I'll catch up." Now she was afraid he would come while those two were there. She would never have the courage to say anything to him then.

"We'll wait," one of the two said, leaning with a thump against the row of lockers.

"Don't! I have to check in with Tinko. She wants to see me about something."

"About what?" the girls asked, almost in chorus.

"I don't know. Something." She didn't look at her friends.

"Jesus Christ, more bullshit," one said, and turned to the other. "Come on, Tracy, let's go."

"See you in class, Val," Tracy said, following her friend into the thick pack of students who crowded the hallway on both sides, opening lockers, getting ready for first period.

Valerie sighed. Then she spotted him, coming toward her down the length of the hallway. His head bobbed above those of the other students. He was moving quickly, weaving his way through the crowd. Not speaking to anyone. Not even nodding hello to classmates.

She jerked open her locker again and picked up a small mirror, concealing it in her hands. She caught her reflection, looked to see if her hair was all right, that she hadn't smudged her lipgloss. Then she glanced around the open locker door.

He was hurrying, realizing that he was almost late. The first bell had already rung. Reaching back into the locker, she pulled tissue from her purse and blotted her lips. The lipgloss had been a mistake. She shouldn't have tried to look older. He would only think it was dumb. He wasn't the kind of boy to like girls who wore lipstick.

"Hey, excuse me."

Valerie looked up, trying to sneak the mirror back into her purse inconspicuously.

"You're blocking my locker," he said.

"Oh, sorry." She stepped away to give him room, slamming her own locker shut.

"That's okay." He slipped the green backpack off his shoulder and set it on the floor between his feet while he twirled the dial of his lock. She noticed the pack had come from L. L. Bean; so had his navy-blue down vest.

"How did you memorize the combination so fast?" Valerie asked. She held her books for first period clutched against her chest.

Scott shrugged. "I don't know. I've always been good with numbers." He jerked open the lock, slipped it off the metal latch, doing it all with one hand. He was trying to be casual about it, effortless, but the Yale lock slipped out of his grasp and hit the concrete floor.

"Shit!" He reached down quickly and grabbed it, embarrassed by his clumsiness.

"You're new, aren't you?" Valerie asked. She took a step closer, watching him.

"Yeah." He opened the locker door and began transferring books, trying to remember which class was first period. In his shirt pocket he had a schedule, but he didn't want her to see him checking it.

"You'll need the geometry book," she said, seeing him shove that one back into his locker.

"What?" Scotty glanced at her.

"You have geometry first period. Mr. Schwinn. We're in the same class." She smiled. "I'm Valerie Dunn."

Her smile was lopsided. It seemed to spread to one side of her face as if there was too much of it. And she was tall. Taller than his mother, though not as tall as he was, and skinny. He could knock her over with a shove.

She was wearing jeans and a Michigan State football jersey. The jersey was enormous on her and she kept pushing up the sleeves, bunching the folds at her elbows. He thought she looked cute.

"What's your name?" she asked when he didn't respond.

"Scott. Scott Gardiner."

"Hi." She kept watching him, still smiling. Her eyes were bright and very happy, as if she didn't have a care in the world. He wondered why he hadn't noticed her before. He liked tall girls. Short girls made him nervous; it was as if he couldn't trust them.

She inched closer, still leaning against her locker. Down the length of the hallway only a few students were still at their lockers; most had moved into classrooms. Nervously, he wondered why she was hanging around. The second bell would ring any second, and they'd both be late. He began rifling through the shelf again, searching for his notebook.

"Missing something?" she asked. She still sounded cheery, as if she were having a terrific time.

The bell rang.

"Oh, Christ!" He slapped the metal door in frustration.

"What is it?" she demanded, concerned now.

"I can't find my goddamn notebook, that's what!"

"Is this it?" She reached out and lifted a spiral binder from the zipper pocket of his pack.

"Oh, yeah, thanks." He grabbed the notebook from her, slid it under his arm, and hurriedly locked his locker.

"Well, how do you like Flat Rock?" she asked conversationally, falling into step with him as they walked toward the classroom.

He shrugged. "It's okay. I don't know." He walked fast, trying to shake her off, but her legs were almost as long as his.

"Where did you go to school before?" she asked, keeping pace.

"In Connecticut. Spencertown Academy."

"Boys only?"

"Yeah." They had reached the doorway of the classroom and Scotty paused. He did not want to walk in with her.

"Thank you." Valerie beamed as he paused at the door, giving her room to enter first. Inside the classroom, in the wide space at the front of the room, she glanced back at him and grinned. He liked her smile. It made her pretty face seem slightly out of whack, a little less perfect. Then Scott spotted Nick Borgus watching him, saw the big senior lean across the aisle and nudge Hank Simpson, nod toward him and Valerie.

Scott kept walking. He went around Mr. Schwinn's desk and down the far aisle, away from the two seniors, away from Valerie Dunn. He dropped into his own seat and slumped down immediately, as if trying to hide behind his books.

The two seniors were the first students he had met at Flat Rock High School. It had been the opening day of school and his mother had wanted to drive him. It was a new school, she had said, and he might get lost, but he wouldn't let her come.

"I'm a junior, Mom. I don't need to be led around like some little kid."

He had driven the car himself, arriving just as all the school buses were coming from the rural areas. The buses had blocked off the drive to the front entrance and student parking, so he cut across the section marked Faculty Parking, circled the one story building and came up behind the school on a dead-end drive.

There were a handful of students standing outside, smoking by the trash cans. They watched him drive toward them, shouted at him to stop, that he was going the wrong way. Scott wheeled the car around, using one hand and handling it easily, showing off a little. He hit the brakes and the MGB squealed to a stop.

"Hey, where's student parking?" he shouted, keeping the engine running.

There were half a dozen boys standing near the huge trash containers and none of them answered. They glanced back and forth, snickered, as if his question was funny.

"Who is this turkey?" one of the boys finally asked, not moving from where he stood, leaning against the trash containers.

"Shit, I don't know," another answered. He was taller than the others and he slowly went into a deep knee bend, so as to bring himself down to the level of the low-slung MGB. "Hey, Nick," he drawled, "let's give this asshole some shit."

For a moment Nick, the shorter one, said nothing. He had a small, round, smooth head, shaped like a bullet.

"New guy, huh?" he said to no one in particular.

"He's wearing a fuckin' tie!" the taller boy exclaimed, as if startled by the sight.

"Hey, you want to just tell me where should I park?" Scott asked again, trying to sound unimpressed. On the steering wheel, his hands began to sweat.

"Nick," said the big student, "this is some fuckin' new kid. Some rich kid with a fuckin' MGB."

"Shut your mouth, Simpson," Nick said. He sounded annoyed. He, too, had seen that the new kid was wearing a tie and a blue blazer. Who did this fucker think he was, Nick thought, coming to school dressed like that?

"Come on, Nick, let's just ride this wimp's ass," Simpson pleaded.

Nick glanced at him. "Keep it cool," he ordered.

Scott saw the two of them exchange glances, then move toward him. They walked slowly, taking their time, as if time itself belonged to them. Scott knew their kind. He had seen them at the Academy. Seniors. Football jocks. Assholes.

The two boys were wearing jeans, football sweatshirts and

sneakers. Self-consciously Scott jerked at his tie, loosening

"Now, what did you say you wanted?" the one called Nic asked. He was not smiling.

"The parking lot. Where do students park?" He was almo whispering, embarrassed and afraid.

Simpson sat down on the MGB's hood, as if claiming th car. He leaned over the windshield and grinned. "You ne here, preppie?"

Scott nodded, not wanting to speak. He had to get away It would only get worse.

"Where you from?" Nick asked.

"Connecticut." He kept his answer short so they wouldn see how nervous he was.

"Well, preppie, usually you can park anywhere in the bac. lot," Nick answered, speaking quickly, as if he wanted to b helpful. "But they use the lot on Tuesdays for band practice so you'll have to park on the side street." His face was withou expression, as if it were paralyzed.

"But there are No Parking signs . . ." Scott turned around pointing to the side street at the end of the football field.

"It doesn't make any difference on Tuesdays. The cop: know kids put their cars on the street."

"Yeah, we all do," Simpson added. He got off the hood as if ready to let Scott drive away.

They were lying, Scott knew. And they knew he knew What they wanted to see was how he would handle it. At Spencertown, Scott would've known what was cool. But here he wasn't so sure. Was their violence just a pose, or would they beat the shit out of him if he challenged their word?

For a moment they all waited. Then the shorter guy said, "My name is Nick Borgus." He extended his hand. "And you're . . . ?"

"Gardiner. Scott Gardiner." He reached to shake hands and saw what was so strange about Nick Borgus. The boy's eyes were the color of shallow water, pale and nondescript, dead in his face.

"What year?"

"Junior, but my schedule is pretty messed up. I've got some senior courses, and for some courses I'm only taking the final exams." He kept talking, explaining how he had been in the accelerated program at Spencertown.

"A smart prick, huh, preppie," Simpson said. The MGB's canvas convertible top was down and he leaned into the front seat intimidatingly.

"Hey, Simpson, lay off!" Borgus interjected. "Don't bother about Simpson here," he said to Scott. "Everyone knows he's a dumb fucker." Borgus grinned, shoving Simpson away from the car. "He gets weird around anyone who has an I.Q. over ninety-five."

Simpson shoved back and the two of them struggled noisily, but Scott could see it was all a put on, that they were just playing at having a confrontation.

"Hey, go park it on the side street," Nick said, suddenly turning back to Scott. The game was over. "You never have to worry about Tuesdays at Flat Rock," he added, grinning.

Scott moved fast. He nodded okay and wheeled the tiny car around, shifting rapidly as he accelerated down the short drive, and out onto the side street. He didn't look back. He was afraid they might be watching him and laughing. He felt stupid driving through the big empty parking lot, but he knew Borgus would make an issue of it if he disobeyed. So he parked the car on the side street, under a No Parking sign, and shut off the engine. Then he held onto the steering wheel, as if for his life.

He hated Flat Rock High School. It was a crummy place, full of Neanderthals like Simpson. He should have stayed at Spencertown; he shouldn't have let his mother make him move to Ballycastle. He reached up and closed the canvas top of the convertible, then got out of the car and locked it.

She had given him his father's car as a bribe to make him transfer, and he had fallen for it. He had left his friends and *Hobgoblin* and now he was an outsider. He knew it already, had known it the minute he saw the way they acted and the way they dressed. They would never accept him nor did he want to be like them. They were all hicks, he thought, country crackers. Farm boys.

He glanced again at the No Parking sign. "Ah, fuck it," he swore out loud, spun around, and walked back across the football field to the school. That afternoon when he came back to the car, a parking ticket had been slipped under the windshield wiper.

What other trouble were they planning for him now, he wondered, as he glanced across the classroom. The two seniors were whispering to each other, and as Valerie went down the aisle, Nick Borgus grabbed her arm and pulled her closer.

"Hey, do you actually know that creep?" he asked. He had hold of her coat, had pinned her against his desk.

"Let go, Nick!" Valerie jerked free of his grip.

"Hey, cool it, Dunn." He softened his voice and glanced around, searching for the teacher, but it was okay; for some reason the teacher was late. "Do you know that preppie?" he asked.

"What if I do?" She glanced nervously between him and Hank Simpson. She had been in school with the two of them all her life, rode the bus with them every day, but ever since classes had begun that fall, things had seemed different. Now she was frightened of them, of their size and strength.

"Where does he live?" Simpson asked, whispering, as if the information were a secret.

"At Ballycastle. . . ." Immediately she felt as if she had betrayed Scott and she glanced across the room and saw he was watching her.

"See, I told you he had money," Simpson said, leaning across the aisle and slapping Borgus hard on the shoulder. "Is he related to that crazy old fart?"

"His mother just works at the castle, that's all," Valerie answered, pushing past the two seniors. "Quit picking on him. He hasn't done anything to you."

"Yes, he has," Borgus whispered, staring across the room.

"Like what?" She moved between the two, blocking Nick's sight of Scott, and making him respond to her.

"He looks funny. I don't like funny-looking assholes. And he's got money."

"No, he doesn't. His mother, I told you, only works there. She's writing a history of Ballycastle, or something. My sister is a tour guide there; she told me all about it."

"Have you seen his car, that MGB?"

"So what?" Valerie was puzzled, unsure of what Borgus meant. "It's just a tiny little car."

"It's an MGB, for chrissake. Do you have one? Do Hank or me even have a car? Fuckin' no. We've got to ride the goddamn school bus and this preppie tools in here every day." He was growing angrier as he spoke.

"Borgus, you're crazy." Valerie started to laugh at him.

"You don't like him because he's tall and makes you look like a shrimp." Laughing, she dodged quickly down the aisle, getting away before he could reach out and smack her on the bottom.

"Bitch," Scott thought, watching her. First she's nice to him out in the hall, then she stands there laughing at him with Borgus and that cretin Simpson. He flipped open his spiral binder and skimmed through the clean pages until, hidden in the back, he found his list of names, and at the bottom, in his most flowing script he added hers: Valerie Dunn.

"Coffee?" Derek asked, raising a cup. He stood in the archway to Barbara's small office off the main hall.

"Yes, thanks." She smiled, pleased at his gesture. As director of the Ballycastle Foundation, Derek Brennan had a spacious office upstairs, in what had formerly been Fergus's master bedroom, so his visit to her first floor niche was flatteringly premeditated.

"And how's Scott?" he asked, coming in and setting the cup on her desk.

"God, I wish I knew."

"I saw you by the car earlier." He spoke carefully. "I was a college professor, you know, before I joined the Foundation, and I dealt with a lot of kids not too much older than Scott. It's tough being a teen-age boy."

"Yeah, well, it's tough being a teen-age mother, too. If Scott were a girl, I wouldn't feel so inadequate. At least I would have some empathy. But Scott! God, sometimes I feel like we're in the middle of *Invasion of the Body Snatchers,* and his body has been taken over by alien forces." She laughed, and Derek smiled too, watching her. He liked her best at moments like this, when her face relaxed and the tight, controlled lines around her mouth and eyes slipped away. Her laughter made her seem younger and more reckless.

"Do you think it might help if I talked to Scott?" Derek suggested. He was sitting on the edge of her desk with his legs hooked over the corner. His closeness, the way he casually took command, made her wary but also secretly pleased. She liked having him concerned, offering suggestions, but still she resisted. It would not be good for Scotty. It would not even be good for her. She didn't need any other man in her life.

"I don't know if Scott would appreciate having another adult telling him what to do just now. As things are, he can barely tolerate my telling him what day it is."

"Oh, he seems like a good kid," Derek ventured.

"He is really, but with his father dying, and having to leave school and move here . . ." She shook her head and for a moment she looked lost, overwhelmed by events. Her fingers were gripping a pencil, squeezing it hard.

"Yes," Derek whispered. He touched her, brushed her cheek lightly with the back of his hand. "You okay?"

Barbara nodded, blinked away a flash of tears. "Yes, thank you. Just sometimes, you know, I suddenly get self-pitying and start asking myself: why me?" She smiled wryly.

"I'm for that," he said firmly. "After what you've been through this year, you're entitled to all the self-pity you can generate."

Barbara laughed, realized at the same time that he had a nice voice. It was soothing, like his touch. She had forgotten how relaxing it could be, talking to another adult.

"How about dinner tonight?" he asked. "Why don't you and Scott come over? Nothing fancy, just hamburgers or something. It's Monday night, we'll put on the game. Scott plays football, doesn't he? I thought I saw him in the school uniform."

"Well, he went out for the team, but that was more my idea than his. Mine and the school counselor's. We both thought it might be a way to get him involved, meet some friends. He's not very sociable. Since his father died, all he cares about is *Hobgoblin*."

"Hobgoblin . . . ?"

"You haven't heard of *Hobgoblin?*" She looked up, surprised. "It's the rage among teen-agers, especially boys. Scott played it at Spencertown."

"What is it, exactly?"

"A fantasy war game. I'm not really sure how it's played. They use a deck of cards and each person makes up his own character. It's all based on Irish mythology. The characters go on an adventure together, and they do battle in some sort of make-believe ancient world.

"It all depends on imagination, Scott says. The more a player becomes his character, the more fun the game is. But it scares me."

HOBGOBLIN

"Why?"

"I don't think it's healthy for Scotty, not now. When his father died, Scotty changed. There were days when he wouldn't even leave his bedroom. He'd sit on the bed playing *Hobgoblin* by himself for hours. I couldn't reach him."

The thought of her son as he had been after Warren's death sent another tremor through her, brought back her strange, almost primeval fear that she would lose him, that he would slip permanently into a private nightmare.

"These are stages, Barbara," Derek said, trying to reassure her. "He'll forget all about hobgoblins once he starts getting interested in girls."

"That's the real problem," she laughed. "The only way I can keep Scotty normal is to lose him to another woman."

Derek stood and moved away from the desk, put a few feet between them before he commented. "Do you mean Scott is my competition?"

"No, that's not exactly what I mean. Scotty isn't . . ." She laughed, realizing she had placed herself in a predicament.

"How about lunch?" he offered, making it easy for her. "We can talk about your Jocasta complex over a Big Mac." Then he smiled and sauntered off, not waiting for her reply.

He had left her emotionally ragged. His sudden approach had unnerved her. She was not prepared for anyone reaching her feelings, making her care. It was not on her timetable. She had Scotty to worry about, to take care of. She didn't need a man. Yet she had felt defenseless before his eyes, the way he looked at her, and she found herself growing weak when he came close. He had some power over her, she realized. And she recognized the source. It was the way Warren had affected her. The same basic drive of nature. She was reponding with the pure instinct of a female. And it delighted her. She was thrilled that another man could touch her. That she could respond with such desire. That she might again have someone in her life besides Scotty.

*F*our

"Hey, you! Number seventy-two! What's your name?" the coach shouted. He was pacing up and down in front of the junior varsity players, all spread out along the length of the forty-yard line.

Scott stepped forward. He hated to be singled out; hated even more the thought of the other kids seeing his awkwardness.

"I said, what's your name, kid?" The coach was short, much shorter than Scott, and built like the stump of a tree, with no neck and a flat, squat head. He looked, Scott suddenly noticed, like a Grampus, one of the ugliest mongrels in the *Hobgoblin* manual of demons and monsters. "Seventy-two! What's your goddamn name?"

"Gardiner, sir," Scott murmured.

The coach rushed up, planted his legs apart and leaning forward, shouted again, his broad face inches from Scott's chest.

"Gardiner, what the fuck are you doing wearing glasses? This is football, for chrissake."

Down the length of the line Scott could hear the other kids snickering, turning away to laugh. The coach went on shouting, and Scott felt the hot breath of the man, smelled his sweat.

"Get those glasses off!"

Scott pulled off his helmet. It was too tight for his head and the thick padding hurt as he forced it over his ears.

"How do you expect to play ball wearing glasses?"

"It doesn't matter," Scott admitted, clutching his helmet. "I can't play football anyway."

"What do you mean, you can't?" The coach backed off and squinted at him, judging his size. "A big guy like you. You played at the prep school, didn't you?" He remembered now who this tall aloof student was.

"Yes, but everyone had to play something. It was a school rule. I was only a sophomore; I never played in any league games." Scott spoke quickly, feeling his voice going out of control. It began to squeak, as if the sound was being squeezed from his throat. Along the forty-yard line, the rest of the team began to snicker again.

"Well, Gardiner, at this school you either play ball or get off the field. I don't have time to pamper little preppies." He turned away, blew his whistle, shouted at the varsity. "Okay, you bums, get your asses moving. Five laps on the track. That's everybody. Spruce Pine is going to run your butts off tomorrow night."

Scott moved onto the track with the other junior varsity players. In the anonymity of the pack he felt safe. He would run to the far end of the field, then off the track and back into the locker room, change clothes and get away. He didn't have to play football. He didn't have to put up with that shit. Or with the coach, that Grampus.

"Hey, preppie!"

Scott glanced at the outside lane of the track and saw Nick Borgus gaining on him. The heavy linebacker was pushing himself, running full out.

Scott picked up his pace.

"Slow down, for chrissake," the senior shouted, breathing hard.

"Hey, Gardiner, wait a fuckin' minute," Hank Simpson shouted. The other senior had come up on the inside, sandwiching Scott between them. He was as tall as Scott, and as fast. Scott slowed, knowing he couldn't outrun them both.

"Listen, don't let Tagariello get to you," Nick said, coming alongside. He spoke between quick bursts of breath. "He's always giving new guys a lot of shit."

HOBGOBLIN

Scott glanced back and forth between the two seniors who now matched his pace. He had reached the end of the track, where he had planned to run off the field, but the two kept him between them as they talked.

"Listen, Gardiner, don't worry," Borgus went on. "New guys never get to play except when we scrimmage. Don't worry. You're in our homeroom; we'll take care of you." He glanced over and smiled as if he really meant it, then clapped Scott on the back reassuringly. "Don't worry. Hank and me, we'll make sure no one gangs up on you."

Scott sat on the sidelines for the next twenty minutes with a handful of others, mostly sophomores, extra players not needed for the scrimmage teams that kept taking turns on offense. He didn't mind. At Spencertown he had gone out for football only because of his father. Scott had never liked the game, the tackling and hitting, but he hadn't wanted to disappoint his dad; hadn't wanted him to know he was afraid to play. Now at Flat Rock he had signed up again because of his father, because he thought he owed it to his Dad to try, at least. Warren Gardiner would have loved to see his son a football star.

For a while Scott stood and followed the practice, moved up and down with the play action, worried that he might have to join them, but when he saw the bench cleared several times and he wasn't called, he relaxed and sat down, forgetting about the game.

Instead he imagined that the scrimmage was a battle melee from *Hobgoblin*. One team he named the Kelpies; the other were the Spriggans. He labeled both ends Groundbats, monsters capable of fighting only within a handful of yards, and gave them a class five rating and the ability to use paws like hands.

The backfield for the defense he called the pit, and filled it with sprites and demons. The offensive quarterback he fixed as a Ghent, a fourth-class ghoul, and the big, heavy black fullback was an Azmara, a cleric with the ability to cast spells, unlock doors and heal villagers. A positive force for good in the football melee.

Hank Simpson and Nick Borgus were on the defensive team, playing halfback and linebacker. Scott named them last, reviewing the dozens of possible races in his mind before decid-

43

ing. Hank he cast as a Giant Troll, because of his size, and classified him as sixth level with limited ability, brain dysfunction, and shortsightedness.

Nick he made a Banshee, a wailing woman with long, streaming hair and a gray cloak over a green dress. Banshees had the ability to do magic and use spells and poison. But Scott added a handicap, making it impossible for her to see during the day.

Scott wished he had his *Hobgoblin* cards with him. He could have played a real game then, and worked out a battle melee. Yet even without cards he still had his imagination. He made himself the Dealer and concentrated on how these football players might battle, what adventures they could undertake. He let his mind work out all the possibilities.

In the woods and field of Knock an Ar the two armies battled. Scott closed his eyes and listened to the rush of fighting men, heard the thud of leather and the groans as the men came together, fighting hand-to-hand for territory.

He opened his eyes and there on the field was the medieval melee. The Kelpies and Spriggans, crashing, swinging pole axes and halberds, charging with lances. On the flank a small Barquest ripped into the Spriggans; its teeth and claws grabbed flesh, tossed over the taller creatures. He watched the Giant Troll sweep past him, followed by the screaming Banshee.

In his mind, Scott rolled the *Hobgoblin* dice, read the revenge points: twenty-seven plus. That meant one of the Spriggans had scored a direct hit. The Giant Troll was down, his legs hacked off below the knees.

Scott flipped a *Hobgoblin* attack card. It gave the Banshee a chance to retaliate. Seizing the Giant Troll's mace, she swung out, shrieking, striking at the Azmara. Scott flipped another card. The Azmara withstood the strike, fended off the blow with his shield, then dealt his own return: a blow to the Banshee with his lance, driving it deep into the leather shoulder armor of the wailing woman.

Scott mentally rolled again: eleven plus. More than enough to kill the Banshee. Yet she had magical powers, Scott knew. Powers that could revive her, bring her back to life to fight again.

"Hey, Gardiner! Gardiner, goddamn you!" The coach's

44

voice broke through Scott's concentration. "Get your ass out here."

Scott bolted to his feet, grabbing his helmet. He could see Tagariello standing with Simpson and Borgus. They were taller than the coach, dominating him with their size and heavy equipment.

"Come here, kid." The coach moved out of the cluster of players, still shouting as he came toward the sidelines. He was wearing cleated shoes and tore up the turf as he rushed toward Scott.

"Get on offense, Gardiner. Play right end." He was pointing toward the second team. "And get your ass moving!"

Scott ran through the defense team to the huddle. Envisioning the game as a melee had revived his interest, and now he was psyched up to play.

"Go get 'em, Gardiner!" Hank Simpson shouted, clapping his hands together as Scott ran past. He sounded encouraging, but when Scott glanced over, he saw Hank looking back at Borgus, and both of them were grinning.

The first play was an end run left. The play action was away from Scott. He did not even have to block and his team gained three yards. On the next down, the quarterback Kohler called a short pass to both ends. Scott was to go down five yards and then out toward the sideline. The pass would be into the flat.

He set up a few yards off tackle and glanced across the line, watched the defense develop, saw Hank Simpson move over to cover him. But Scott knew better than to think the quarterback would throw the ball his way. He was the fourth string end, the last player called off the bench. They needed him to fill a position, and the quarterback hadn't even looked at him in the huddle. He had called the left end's number and told him to look alert.

"Watch Gardiner!" Nick Borgus shouted from his linebacker position as he jumped around behind the center. Scott grinned under his helmet, pleased that they were including him.

At the snap he jumped forward, sprinted the first five yards, ran right at Simpson, who kept backing away, not letting Scott get behind him and into the open field. Scott kept grinning. It suddenly felt great to be running, to be playing football, to have the senior under control, to know that Simpson had no idea which way he would turn.

At the fifty yard line, Scott planted his left foot, pivoted, and spun off to the right. He took three long strides before glancing over his shoulder toward the quarterback. The football was already in the air, sailing smoothly toward him through the afternoon sky. He raised his hands almost in self-defense and grabbed the spiral, pulled it effortlessly into his arms as he stepped out of bounds.

Behind him Scott heard the team cheer his catch, and as he ran back to the huddle, spotted Simpson and Borgus together, whispering in the backfield.

"Let him get the pass," Borgus instructed Simpson. "Give him a yard maybe, then hit him high. I'll get him from behind."

"What if he drops the ball? The fucker isn't any good."

Nick Borgus looked up the field, toward the offensive team huddle. "I told Kohler to send it sailing up like a balloon. No one will rush him. He'll have all fuckin' day to throw it nice and easy so even Gardiner can't miss. And if he still misses it," Borgus shrugged, "hit him anyway."

Scott's number was called again on third down. They won't be expecting Gardiner again, Kohler, the quarterback, said, and Scott ran back to the line of scrimmage. They were going for long yardage this time. He was to fly straight down fifteen yards, then buttonhook, turn into the middle of the field. He could outrun them, he began to think. He was faster than Borgus, faster even than Simpson.

At the snap Scott put down his head and raced, getting the jump on Simpson who had played him close to the line. It was only when he was ten yards into the secondary that he realized Borgus had dropped back and was racing across the open field, cutting him off.

Scott crossed the third chalk strip, fifteen yards downfield, and cut left, buttonhooked into the field. The football was there. A soft floating pigskin. He leaped up and gathered the ball into his body, smothered it with both hands, holding tight.

He could hear his team cheering. He would score, he thought, turning downfield. There were less than thirty yards to the goal. He shifted his hips, moving toward the end zone.

It was wide open, an empty field before him. He could lope across. The second team would win. He would win. He laughed, unable to contain his pleasure, and then they hit him.

Hank Simpson, coming from his blind side, caught Scott as he turned and hit him in the face with both forearms. The force of the blow popped off his helmet, left him dizzy. Nick Borgus caught him low and from behind, knocking his legs out. He was whiplashed between them, jerked off his feet as if he were on a string.

At first he did not feel the pain. He was flying, tumbling in the air. He lost the football. It floated off, as if in slow motion, and he flipped over, then hit the ground with a flat thud, losing consciousness.

He was stretched out on the field, surrounded by faces.

"What's your name, kid?" the coach asked.

"Scott."

"You got a last name?" Tagariello grinned, realizing the boy was okay.

"Scott Gardiner," he whispered and tried to sit up. Now he felt the pain. It enveloped his body, wrapped the hurt tightly around his legs and up his spine. He could not find his tongue.

"Welcome to Flat Rock, Gardiner," Tagariello said, still grinning. His whistle dangled around his neck and Scott tried to locate it, to grab hold and tighten it around the coach's throat, but his eyes kept seeing double.

"You're okay," Tagariello announced, "just shook up." His voice did not register any concern.

Scott nodded, but when he lifted his head, the pain shot across his chest. "Aw, shit," he exclaimed.

"Easy, Scott." Bill Russell, the assistant coach, put his hands on Scott's shoulders and held him down. His voice was gentle. Scott nodded. Mr. Russell was his social studies teacher.

"Take care of him, Bill," Tagariello instructed. "I'm going to run some field goal drills." He spoke in short bursts of speech, as if he were farting, Scott thought.

"Nice catch, Gardiner," the coach said. "See what you can do without glasses?" He laughed, adding, "But Borgus and Simpson really stuck it to you, didn't they? Well, this isn't

47

Pansy Prep. We play football at Flat Rock." Then he walked off, blowing his whistle, shouting to the other players.

"Fucker," Scott whispered.

"Easy, Scott," Bill Russell said. "You got pretty shook up on that catch."

"Those fuckers."

"It's football, Scott. You have to expect to get banged up."

Scott shook his head. "They set me up. They had it all planned. Let me catch one going out of bounds, then get me in the middle of the field where I couldn't get away."

"They weren't ganging up, Scott. You caught the pass and you were wide open. They both were covering you deep. I saw how the play developed. Both of them happened to get you at the same time. Remember, they're first team. They're two of our best players. And listen! You're not bad yourself. That was a hell of a catch."

Scott had managed to sit up and could see the two teams at the other end of the field. Tagariello was still shouting, and his sharp voice, like a dog's bark, carried clearly in the cold late afternoon. He was nothing but a small, fat Grampus, Scott thought. He looked back at the social studies teacher. "They *were* ganging up," he said quietly.

He had calmed himself down, and he took a deep breath even though it hurt his rib cage. The game didn't make any difference, but he wanted this teacher to know he wasn't a fool. "Simpson and Borgus and that second string quarterback, Kohler, all of them are seniors, all of them are buddies. They let me catch that first pass just so they could get me the next time deep in the secondary, out by myself, and then hit me." He knelt for a moment, gathering his strength, then pulled himself to his feet. He swayed dizzily, and the teacher steadied him.

"Look, if you think it might do some good, I could mention this to Coach Tagariello . . . if you really think they did go after you." The social studies teacher was young and unsure of what to do. This was his first extracurricular assignment and he was uncertain of his authority.

Scott waved off his suggestion and walked toward the locker room. "I can take care of them myself," he answered, not believing that he could. Well, maybe it had been his imagination. Scrimmage wasn't *Hobgoblin*. Football wasn't really a life-or-death war.

From the far end of the field he heard several of the seniors shout, their voices in unison, and he glanced over his shoulder. They were waving at him and from the end zone he heard them shout, in falsetto, "Bye, bye, Preppie."

He raised his arm, as if to wave back, then gave them all the finger.

Five

Barbara Gardiner worked late at the castle. Scott would not be home before six, she knew, and she enjoyed the quiet of the building after the tourists had gone and the office secretaries left.

Derek appeared in the doorway while she worked. In his shirtsleeves, cuffs rolled up, he looked like a campaign poster of Bobby Kennedy. As a graduate student Barbara had worked on Kennedy's last campaign and at his death had felt herself orphaned.

"Want to drive down to the Crossroads for a drink?" He smiled and pulled his tie loose, strengthening the Kennedy resemblance.

She smiled, shaking her head. "Sorry, but I've got to go home."

"Home? Come on, Rapunzel, let down your hair. Everyone deserves some time away from this mausoleum, even the resident princess of the tower."

"Very funny, but I'm not the princess. I'm the Queen Mother, and I promised the crown prince that I wouldn't feed him anything frozen tonight."

"Well, maybe the prince will turn into a frog and you can feed him some fresh flies." He continued to smile, but she could see he was disappointed.

"Can I have a rain check?" she asked, trying to be nice, trying to show him that she did care.

"Sure. Any time." He seemed nonchalant again, and for a moment she almost weakened, wanting to recapture his attention. But the moment was over. "Good night. See you tomorrow." He waved good-by.

She listened to his footsteps disappearing down the long marble corridor. It was quiet then. She could hear the building settling down. A few more doors opened and closed, then silence, and she returned to her report, an opening section on why Fergus O'Cuileannain had selected this particular site for Ballycastle.

For a dozen minutes she concentrated on her report, re-working the last few paragraphs once again, and it was only when she looked up, ready to type out the final draft, that she felt the full silence of the massive castle and a quick shiver of fear. She heard nothing. She felt nothing. Yet she was frightened. It was as if a cold hand had reached out and touched her flesh. She tried to relax. It was nothing, she told herself. There was no one to fear. She was safe in the castle.

Barbara slid white paper into her typewriter and began to type.

Why Fergus O'Cuileannain selected this site for Bally-castle is unclear. In the 1920s, Ballycastle was far from New York City (over three hours by train) and the piece of property too hilly for the ambitious farm we know he wanted to develop here on the western banks of the river.

We do know that before reconstructing the main castle he ordered twenty-five feet of topsoil removed from the crest of the hill so that the foundations of the mansion could be built on solid rock, a construction device used earlier by John D. Rockefeller.

Barbara stopped typing. Now she heard footsteps overhead, heard the opening and closing of doors, then the distinct tumbling of locks and more footsteps on the cold marble staircase.

Oh, God, she thought. She realized she had never before been alone in the huge house, and at once the stories Derek had told her about Ballycastle, all the folklore and rumors about the mansion, came rushing back to mind like cobwebs catching in her hair.

Barbara stood immediately and walked out into the main hallway, thinking, this is foolish. She had been through the house; there was nothing at all to be afraid of.

There were not many rooms in the old castle keep, where the office was located, and they were grouped around the wide entrance way and a second-story wooden balcony. The vastness of Ballycastle was in the newer north and south wings, two long halls that contained the ballroom, an art gallery, the library, a billiard room and guest quarters.

Again Barbara heard sounds from the second floor. It was as if someone were dragging a metal chain along the length of the long hall. Derek had told her the rumor of how Fergus O'Cuileannain had kept an insane niece locked away on the third floor for years, and it was rumored the young girl had been chained to her bed. This is ridiculous, Barbara decided, forcing herself to keep her imagination in check.

"Hello?" she shouted, wanting at least to hear the sound of her own voice in the silence of the huge building.

There was no response, but at that moment the metal being dragged stopped, as if someone was listening.

She called out again.

Now there was nothing. She sighed, relieved, then turned toward her office. She reached the doorway when again she heard the dragging metal.

Oh, God, she thought. She glanced at the office phone. She could telephone security, or try to locate Conor, the caretaker. Perhaps she should just leave, go home to the guest house, and phone Derek from the safety of her own kitchen.

This was silly. How could she explain to Derek that she had been chased from the castle by her fear? The Foundation would expect her to be responsible, to investigate what that noise was. After all, the niece was dead; Fergus was dead. And there was no one, she told herself, upstairs.

Barbara went into the main entrance hall and slowly up the stairway, her shoes soundless on the thick carpet. At the top of the stairs, she hesitated and called out. In response she heard only the clanking of the chain. She could locate it now; it was coming from the end of the north wing. In spite of her rising panic, she tried to think clearly. What was in the north wing that could create that sound?

The armor, she realized. It wasn't a chain. It was the sound of armor moving. The long north hallway was lined with weaponry from the fifteenth century, suits of plate armor, basinets and armets. She had catalogued this weaponry already, the armors from Lombardy, swords from Cologne and Milan, the long steel *Ahspeiss* spike and the Flemish sallets used by English knights in the War of the Roses.

How could suits of armor move, she asked herself, and peered down the length of the hallway. The only light she had to see by was that which slanted through the high, narrow notches in the stone walls, small rectangles of sun splashing on the marble floor and the hallway rugs, but it was enough for Barbara to know that the hallway was empty.

She called out once more, but now her own fright clutched at her throat. She could hear her heart pounding in her ears. Someone had to be there, she told herself, hiding behind the ancient armor. There could be no other explanation. She had to leave, she ought to run away, but even as her mind whirled with that thought, she moved forward, going cautiously from one suit to the next, peering on tiptoe into the darkness behind each piece of weaponry. To do so, she had to get up close to each one—put her face near each fierce-looking eyeless visor, resist the fear that the mailed arms would reach out and grab her.

By the time she reached the end of the hallway her silk blouse was ruined with perspiration but she had found nothing out of place.

All right, she told herself. She had done her duty. She had been responsible and now she could go home. She had started back along the hallway when again she heard the chain. This time it was being banged against a wall.

There were rooms off the hallway, guest bedrooms and a small study used by Fergus O'Cuileannain during the last years of his life. The study was not opened to the public and the door was supposed to be locked at all times. Still, Barbara hesitated before the room and listened. She could not hear anything from behind the massive wooden door.

Tentatively she pushed down on the medieval latch and

shoved. The door did not move. She sighed with relief. Then the door gave way, swung silently open on the force of its own weight.

No one was in the tiny room. Silent. In perfect order. Barbara stepped inside the doorway and glanced around. The study was one of her favorite places in the castle, filled with art objects and furniture that Fergus had collected from around the world. It was a cluttered room, but Barbara's trained eye could see everything was in place. The Oriental tapestries on the walls, couchant jaguars by the leather sofa, the teakwood desk from Beirut, two Moorish inlaid chairs, the ivory tusks from Mombassa, two small Hindu coffee tables, and his collection of Etruscan cooking pots.

Barbara reached for the latch to pull the heavy door closed behind her when from the corner of her eye she saw the edge of the heavy tapestry move slightly as if rippled gently by a breeze. She flipped on the room lights.

"Come out," she demanded, raising her voice.

The heavy tapestry stirred, but no one emerged from the corner. At that end of the study, she recalled, there was a doorway and back staircase to the first-floor kitchen.

She waited. Her heart beat like a child's fist against her chest. Now she should run downstairs and telephone for help, she realized, but instead, against her common sense and her fear, she went further into the room, forced herself forward as if she were a tightrope artist compelled to step into space.

She called out and again the thick Oriental tapestry stirred, as if beckoning her toward the dark corner and entrapment. She heard nothing. But fear grabbed her throat and tightened around the jugular.

Yet she moved effortlessly, slipping behind the sofa, moving easily past the shelves of Etruscan pots and, with the strange fascination that attracts people to danger, pulled back the tapestry and revealed the hidden corner of the room.

No one was hiding in the bare space, but the stairway door was open and Barbara could feel a cool breeze from the first floor whip around her legs.

"Oh, Christ," she whispered and reached out to close and lock the entrance.

In that instant, while she was reaching out, leaning slightly forward and feeling in the shadowy corner for the knob, the door flung back and a figure appeared, his arm already raised, holding high the long-bladed knife.

"No, please!" She threw up her arms, attempted to shield herself as she scrambled to get out of the dark corner, but he had seized her elbow and held her tight.

She struggled free of the man's grip, wrenched her arm from his and then turned as if to strike back, and saw that it was only Conor, the old caretaker of the estate.

"What in God's name are you doing here? Why didn't you answer me, damn it?" She was trembling with rage.

"I was fixin' the dagger, ma'am, and moving that chain mail hauberk down to my shop like I was told by Mr. Brennan. I always use this back way to the castle. It keeps me out of the way of them tourists." He sounded helpless and afraid, as if he had done something wrong.

"Oh, for God's sake," she laughed, seeing then that the old man was carrying the Rondel dagger. She had even been in the office when Derek had spoken to Conor, asking him to fix the disc-shaped guard of the dagger and, while he was at it, to clean up the rest of the thirteenth-century knight's armor.

"I'm sorry I frightened you, missus." He came into the room and edged around Barbara, as if he thought she might retaliate.

"Well, what was all this sound of dragging chains I heard?" she asked at once, trying to reclaim some sense of authority.

"Ah, well, that would have been the hauberk. It was too much for me to carry all the way to the shop, so I dragged it along behind me and the chain mail made a terrific clatter." He darted a glance at her, then looked down and away.

Barbara did not like the man or his looks. He was small and slight with hard features, long, thin limbs and bulging eyes that distorted his face. He reminded her of a weasel with his quick, secretive ways.

"And how's the lad, Mrs. Gardiner?" Conor asked, going about his work. He took the dagger over to the teakwood desk and set it down carefully, beside a half dozen other medieval weapons.

"He's fine," Barbara replied curtly.

She was not that way usually. She always felt intimidated by service people, waiters and taxi drivers, employees like

Conor. But she knew Scott had been befriended by the old Irish caretaker and their unlikely comradeship worried her. She would have thought her son would have been put off by the meddling old man, but until school had started they had been inseparable. It was the stories, she knew. Conor told endless tales from Irish myth and folklore, which fed into Scotty's passion for *Hobgoblin*.

"I've made the lad a little thing in the shop," Conor went on, smiling.

"Conor, I've seen his slingshot and I don't want my son having such dangerous objects around the house. Please don't give him any more weapons."

"Aah, they aren't nothing at all, Mrs. Gardiner."

"A shillelagh and slingshot are dangerous, Conor; at least I think so, and I don't want Scott having anything like them." She spoke quickly, as if summing up, and walked out of the study.

"There's no harm in an old shillelagh," he called after. "'Tis just a plaything. The boy can't hurt himself." There was now a sharpness to his voice, as if he were fighting back. Barbara stopped in the hallway and turned to face him.

"Nevertheless, Conor, I don't want my son having one." She knew she sounded blunt and disagreeable, and she hated it, but she couldn't let the caretaker influence Scotty. She had to protect her son from his own imagination.

Conor nodded obediently, then tipped his black cap and turned away without a word. Barbara watched him return to the study and lock the door behind him. He now seemed harmless, and she felt guilty. He was just an old man, she thought. The last surviving employee of Fergus O'Cuileannain, brought over from Ireland in the late twenties to care for the horses. He had worked his whole life on the estate, and the Foundation had kept him on as the caretaker. She guessed he resented her and the other Foundation people who had come onto the estate, into his world, and turned the castle and grounds into public property.

He wasn't at all threatening, she realized. He was only an old man, poorly dressed and not very strong. One of his shoulders was slightly higher than the other, and he shuffled his feet when he walked. He resembled Chaplin's little tramp, and her fear of him was swept away by compassion. As she moved back along the north wing and then down the staircase she debated whether she should go after Conor and apologize.

At the bottom of the stairs she caught sight of him in the main dining room, walking toward the pantry. She called out, her voice shatteringly loud in the empty building, and went after him, running across the room, then through the swinging pantry doors.

He was neither there nor in the kitchen. She kept calling as she searched, looking in the ballroom, the laundry and the housekeeper's office. At the rear of the castle she looked out the windows toward the stables but did not see him in the yard or walking downhill to his apartment.

"Damn," she said out loud. It was impossible for him to vanish that quickly. And she was certain he had heard her voice.

Then she realized he might still be in the mansion hiding somewhere, spying on her, and again she was frightened, not for Scotty this time but for herself.

She rushed from the kitchen, ran back across the main hall to her office and, without putting away her work, grabbed her coat and purse and left the castle.

In the bright sunshine she immediately felt better. Derek was right, she thought. The castle was a mausoleum, full of ancient furniture and past lives. But it contained nothing threatening. It was her imagination, she thought, not Scott's, that was creating phantoms, and she giggled at the absurdity of the situation. And in her pleasure at being outside and alive on such a beautiful day, she began to kick up the deep blanket of fallen leaves, forgetting Conor Fitzpatrick, the last Irish serf of Ballycastle.

Six

Conor Fitzpatrick kept on the lookout for the boy. He stayed away from the castle, worked near the stables and paddock. There was little hard work to be done. Only a few horses remained on the estate, and no one rode them anymore. His only other regular responsibility was going up to the main kitchen once a day to pick up the meals, but that he usually did in the evening. Most of his days he spent in the tackroom, sitting by the open doorway that looked east from the building. In the horseshoe valley beyond the river, farms and houses made a patchwork pattern of green and brown. He found it a comfort to sit in the sun and look across the river toward the horizon. The sight reminded him of Ireland, of when he was a lad growing up on the shores of Lough Mask.

He felt in his trouser pocket for the pebbles. When all five were gathered in his palm, he shook them out on the dirt before the tackroom door, letting the stones cast their own spell.

The old man smiled, then sat back in his chair and watched the afternoon sun cross the valley. Before nightfall, the stones told him, the lad would come, find him waiting in the blacksmith shop below Ballycastle.

* * *

59

"Did I ever tell you about Sluagh Sidhe, lad?" Conor asked. He went back to the forge to pick up a small ballpeen hammer and worked it over the metal.

With evening it had begun to rain and Scotty had moved inside the open barn door. It was warm there by the forge fire, and he knew he was safe. His mother would not come looking for him in the barns.

"The what?" Scott asked.

"The Sluagh Sidhe of Ireland. The people of the hills." Conor paused to glance over at the boy. He never looked directly at him but kept glancing sideways, always on the sly.

"I told you I don't believe in leprechauns, or fairies or wee people," Scott answered, grinning.

"Ah, well, and that's a shame, for the Sluagh Sidhe are a true enough people, so help me God, but they live in the hillocks, you know, not in the barrows." He paused as he went back to work, banging out the hot metal on the forge fire. The ballpeen hammer struck with a clean, clear hit like a clapper striking a bell.

"It's just a story," Scott laughed. "There's no such thing as wee people. No way!" Scott liked the old man and his strange tales of Ireland. Of all the people at Ballycastle, Conor had been the only one to spend time with him, to be nice and listen to him. They were alike in some ways, Scott knew. They shared the same love of Ireland.

"Well, now I wouldn't be so sure." The small man kept working as he spoke, moving around the forge, handling the hot iron with a long pair of tongs.

Scott had found a place to stand behind the forge, deep in the shadow so the fire flickered on his face and made him sleepy with its heat.

"I was only thinking that this game of yours is full of goblins, and so you might be curious about the Sluagh Sidhe." Conor peered up at the tall teen-ager for a moment, then went back to his work, moving the length of metal off the forge and quenching the hot iron in a bucket. The metal sizzled when it hit the cold water.

"*Hobgoblin* is just a game," Scott said at once. He was used to defending himself. "You know there's nothing real about it. You just imagine the characters."

"Aah, well, I don't know about that. The Sluagh Sidhe are real enough. I saw them once myself in the old country. I was hardly a child myself." He nodded once, then gathered the peak of his cap and reset it on his head, twisting the peak as if corking a bottle.

He did not go back to the forge, but set the long tongs aside and walked to the wide doors of the shop, stood there looking toward the fields. Away from his tools, he seemed less sinister, fragile almost, as if he really wasn't fit for work.

"What about these Sluagh Sidhe?" Scott asked, following the old man. "When did you see them?" He was curious, and also he wanted to be nice to Conor.

"Well, I was only a child as I said, and though many's the time I remember hearing about the wee people, I only saw them once, on Slieve Gullion. They were no further away than that brook. They'd lit scores of fires and there were hundreds of them; I saw them plain as yourself right here. Some of them were mounted and rode their horses straight through the flames, I swear to God. But there's stranger tales than that," he went on, not pausing to let Scott question the story. He sat down in the chair by the open doorway and Scott pulled the small stool over, closer to him. The two sat looking out into the cold fall rain.

"There was a story I heard as a boy, much younger I was than yourself, told to me by Liam MacMathuna, an old grave digger in our village. It was a story about a man who crossed Slieve Gullion one night, before my time of course, and before Liam's time as well, I am sure. This old crony lost his way and wandered for hours up in the hills before he saw a big house, bigger than this here Ballycastle, and all lighted up, with the doors open and people going in and out.

"Well, he went inside, you see, to find out where in the hills of Gullion he was. And what did he see but scores of grand ladies and gentlemen in silks and satins and velvet, and all the tables and chairs and dishes were of gold and silver, shining fit to blind you, and there was grand food and drink all set out. It was as if Himself were alive today up at the castle having a grand party.

"He walked right in, you see, Scotty, and not one of them fine ladies and gentlemen seemed to see him, so he thought he'd take a rest and watch them for a bit, and he did, sitting quiet in a corner. And he helped himself, would you believe, to both the food and drink, and it wasn't long before he fell asleep. And the next morning when he woke the house was gone, and so were the people, the fine ladies in their silk gowns and the beautiful gentlemen, and he was lying in the fern up on the very top of Slieve Gullion."

Conor stopped. He had been leaning forward in his chair, whispering as he told the tale, and now he simply nodded and sat back, looking again out into the driving rain.

"And you expect me to believe that?" Scott demanded, embarrassed that he had listened to the story so raptly. "That's nothing but bull—"

He stopped as the old man stood and hitched up his trousers. "Well, don't be too sure, lad." He sounded disappointed. "Liam MacMathuna was a fine man, God rest his soul." He went back to the forge and stirred the coals again, brought up the flame quickly and began to work on the metal bar. "Strange goin' ons happened in those mountains. And they happened here at the castle as well."

"Like what?"

"Well, I'm not sure I'll not just be wasting my time telling you stories. You think you know it all."

Scott moved closer to the forge, watched the old man hammer on the hot stake.

"I don't think all stories are fairytales." He was afraid he had hurt Conor's feelings but wasn't sure what he should say. He never knew when to apologize to adults, or how to say he was sorry. "Hey, Conor, what sort of thing used to happen at Ballycastle?" He tried to sound eager to know.

For a moment the old man kept working, shaping the metal, hammering it, and then without a word he quenched it in the water and set aside his tools.

"It was years ago, of course—before you were born, long before, and Himself was very much alive. It was a grand place in them days, Scotty. Ah, you wouldn't believe it. I was only new to Ballycastle myself and caring for the horses. I had forty horses in the stables then, pacers and jumpers, and ponies too, for the children.

"We had nearly a thousand acres of farm land in them days.

We had two hundred milking cows, a dozen plow horses, over a thousand chickens and ducks. We grew three hundred tons of hay on the land and enough vegetables to sell through the market down in town.

"And there were over a hundred of us doing the work—all from the old country, too—taking care of the animals and the lawn and running the farm. Twenty people worked in the greenhouse. Himself had over six thousand different types of orchids, two thousand of the azaleas. Ah, it was a lovely sight in the spring what with the flowers blooming."

He stopped for a moment, remembering, looking out over the valley as if trying to draw back to mind the past. Scotty had seen him get this way before. He seemed lost, as if his mind had slipped permanently into another age.

"What else?" Scott asked, trying to bring the old man back to his story.

"Down there by the river," the old man said quietly, continuing, "Himself had built a glass ballroom, would you believe. It's gone now. Those Foundation people tore it down because some lad from hereabouts fell through the roof and killed himself, but that's another story. And besides the ballroom there once was an indoor swimming pool, and a lifeguard worked twenty-four hours a day, keeping it open so guests could swim at any time and in any weather. And would you believe, the pool was so big the lifeguard used a rowboat in the water."

He wasn't smiling. He didn't wink and nod knowingly. It was a true story, Scott could tell.

"We had telephones everywhere, in every building. From one place to another. One extension here, of course, connecting the barns with the castle. An extension, as well, at the gatehouse, in the carriage houses, the superintendent's home—Mr. Burley, a fine man, God rest his soul—and a phone down at the pool, one in the guest house where you're staying, one even on the boat mooring on the river.

"You could summon help, you see, quickly, for there was always trouble here, prowlers and burglars and people from town who would come up and hide in the shrubbery, just to see what was going on.

"Himself had his own people, of course, to guard him. Oh,

it was a common enough thing, you know, for someone of his wealth during the Depression. The times were full of anarchists, bomb-throwers.

"So we couldn't be too careful, none of us, for Himself or ourselves, if the truth be known. Those left-wingers could have killed all of us with one of the bombs. And especially because of Himself owning so many companies without trade unions."

"You mean the fairies of Ireland were after Fergus because he didn't run a union shop?" Scott smiled wryly. "Come on, Conor, what's all this got to do with those Sluagh Sidhe?"

Conor thrashed the air with his open hand, silencing the boy. "I'm tellin' you lad, but I'm telling you in my own way. Now did I stop you when you were tellin' me about *Hobgoblin?*"

"Okay! Okay!" Scott sighed. He had gone through this before with Conor and knew he couldn't rush the old man. Conor would tell the story his way, wandering from point to point.

"There was a party up at the castle, a grand party," Conor went on, picking up again. "We were always having parties, of course, when Himself was at home, and it was in the summer of the year.

"I had some horses grazing in the north fields, beyond the woods, and coming back in the late evening from looking after them, I could follow the music from the ballroom, hear the women laughing, even the sounds of silverware and glasses clinking together.

"It was a lovely night, I tell you. A real joy to be out in the woods. I hadn't a torch with me, but there was no need. I could find my way across every inch of Ballycastle, and besides it was a bright night, what with the moon shining on the path through the birch woods.

"And up there on the hillside I could see the glass ballroom and the castle itself, all lit up and blazing. The doors and windows were open, and the light spread across the lawns. You could see the guests as well, the women in beautiful gowns, and men wearing white suits. It was like a movie, you know, one of those grand Hollywood affairs with hundreds of actors and actresses. The dancing had spread onto the terrace off the ballroom and when I got to the river I stopped to watch a moment, standing in the dark there beyond the boat mooring."

He stopped to point toward the birch woods beyond the river. "It was a thing I'd often do," he said, then paused, staring own at the river, at what was left of the wooden mooring, the attered posts and planks still remaining in the muddy water.

"Ah, it was a wonderful life we had in them days, and I njoyed myself listening to the music, watching them dancing n the stone terrace." He stopped again, his voice sliding into ilence.

Scott glanced over at Conor. He was staring off, his eyes ow wet and glazed. There were tears on his face; they slid own the old man's rough brown cheeks and Scott looked off, mbarrassed at seeing Conor cry.

He looked across the fields, toward the river and the birch voods. A fog had moved into the valley with the cold late fternoon rain. It was a dismal day.

He had to go home, he realized. His mother would be earching for him soon, and he had homework waiting to be lone. Without looking at the old man he got up and said nicely, 'Hey, Conor, I guess I better be getting home. I'm late, and Mom will only get after me."

Conor did not respond. He was remembering evenings spent with Carmel Burke on the mooring. It was dark there at the end of the landing and they would dance to the ballroom music carried across the estate on waves of wind.

"I had only been there a moment, you understand," Conor continued, picking up again the loose thread of his story, "when I saw them."

Scott sat back on the stool. "Saw what?" he asked impatiently.

"I wasn't sure, you see, at first. I was standing in the dark of the woods, leaning against a birch tree and looking across the river, up toward the castle. The ladies and gentlemen were coming out on the lawn, carrying glasses of champagne down to the river where it was cool. And then a dozen yards from me, I saw something move in the shrubbery."

Conor paused, turning away from the river to fix his gaze on Scott. His eyes were bright and alert, as he went on with the story, speaking louder now to be heard over the driving rain.

"I thought at first it might be one of the lads, out like myself to watch the party. I couldn't see the figure clearly, you see, what with them being in the shrubbery.

"Then I realized it wasn't one of us, and I thought it was

prowlers, anarchists for God's sake, and I tell you, Scotty, was frightened, thinking of how I was in danger.

"Yet I couldn't tell for sure. The bushes were thick at the river, and I was, to tell you the truth, too frightened to get closer. I couldn't move at all. Sure as God is in His heaven they would have seen me run from the trees, killed me before I reached the telephone at the mooring.

"I was frightened for them across the river, too. They were close enough that I could hear them whispering to themselves, as people will, thinking they were alone by the river's bank. Whoever was out there could have killed them without even coming out of the bushes. If you look yourself tomorrow, go down to where the mooring was, you'll see they were that close.

"But Himself was up at the house, so I figured they'd want to go to him and there wasn't but one way to do that. There wasn't a bridge nearby except at the mooring, and they had to come by me to get there. I said to myself, 'Well, so help me God, if they do come this way, I'll have a go at them.' In my day I wasn't bad with the fists, you know.

"To this day I don't know how long I stayed flat against the birch trees, but, my God, it felt like an eternity. Then one by one they came out of the bushes, pushed their way into the clear and stood by the river in plain sight of me."

He stopped and stood, going over to the forge where he pulled a pack of cigarettes from his pocket and shook one out, lighting it from the hot coals.

"Who was it?" Scott demanded, jumping up so quickly he overturned the stool.

Conor puffed rapidly on the cigarette, as if it were poorly packed and he couldn't light it. Then the end was glowing, and he coughed from his inhaling.

"Come on, Conor! Who was it? Stop teasing me!"

Conor walked to the open barn door and stood looking out at the rain. Scott followed, leaned against the doorjamb and watched the old man.

"It's hard to see at night, you know," Conor started up again, beginning casually, taking his time, "unless your eyes are used to the dark. Well, by then my eyes were. I could see as well as I might at midday, or else I wouldn't have believed what I did see, by God."

He moved closer to Scott, as if about to share some great secret. Standing beside the boy, Conor looked smaller, an old man needing help. Scott had to bend down to hear his whisper.

"There on the banks of the river, as sure as there are saints in heaven, I saw half a dozen Nuckelavees."

"What?"

"Ah, and I had only been told stories of them in the old country, but thanks be to God up to that moment I had never seen one myself."

"Conor, what are you talking about?" Scott slapped his thighs, frustrated by the old man and his long story.

"You don't know?" Conor cocked his head, glanced sideways at the boy. "Why, the Nuckelavees are the foulest hobgoblins of them all." He shook his head and moved away, shuffled his feet in the dirt of the barn door.

"They weren't but three feet high ... matted hair all over their bodies, and pale, flat eyes. And they smell, you know, the odor of dead pigs. Why, to this day I can still choke on the memory of the stench.

"I had never seen one, as I told you, but I knew at once they were Nuckelavees, what with their heads like men, only ten times larger, and pig snouts for mouths.

"They were as big as dwarves and I could have knocked the lot into the river with a backhanded slap, they were that near to me, but I didn't dare move, not a muscle. And, good God, I was frightened I might sneeze or cough, for I would have been a goner for sure."

"Why?" Scott asked, caught up unwillingly in the old man's story.

"Well, they say in Ireland that if a Nuckelavee sees you spying on them, you'll be cast into stone, for the Nuckelavees have a real affinity for stone and rock and crannies. And I've seen those stones myself in Connemara, shaped they were like human figures."

"Come on, Conor, how could there be Nuckelavees here? This isn't Connemara!"

The old man stepped back from the boy and pointed off to the house, the castle up on the hill. His thin hand was only a shadow in the glow from the forge.

Scott moved out of the cold and closer to the fire, away from the blacksmith, as the old man spoke softly, his thick brogue full of warning.

"Oh, 'tisn't Connemara we're in, more's the pity. But I told you those evil hobgoblins, those Nuckelavees, are partial to rocks, to cold stone, to the cracks and crannies of old castles." He cocked his head and turned slowly, looked back at the boy.

"And where do you think Ballycastle comes from, every rock and stone of it, but from the mountains of Donegal, from Erin Isle, and who would be there living between the rocks, but such a thing as evil hobgoblins like those I saw on the river years ago, with heads ten times the size of yours or mine, and only pig snouts for mouths?"

Scott shoved his hands into the pockets of his jeans. The old man had kissed the Blarney stone, that was for sure. Yet Scott wished he had gone home when it was daylight. Before the fog crept in. Before the rain enveloped them. Now every flickering shadow on the shop walls was a monster figure from his *Hobgoblin* bestiary.

"Do you believe me now, lad?" Conor asked, thrusting his face forward, as if into the flame.

Scott nodded, unable to speak.

"That night long ago, a woman was killed on the banks of the river. The blood was sucked from her veins. I know that for a fact, I found the girl myself down by the mooring.

"Ah, it never made the papers. Himself saw to it. It was an Irish girl, one of the maids from Donegal. Her name was Carmel Burke. A lovely lass, I recall, but when I found her that day, at dawn, she looked as if she had been attacked by the devil. Her body was like stone, and may the devil rob my mother's grave if that isn't the truth. I saw it all. I was there. And I'm the only one left who remembers the day."

"I've got to go home," Scott whispered. Over the hot flame his hands were trembling and cold with fear.

The old man nodded. "Your ma'am will be out searching, and it's not safe, you know, being out after dark about here, especially if you're as young and pretty as your mother is. The hobgoblins, you know, they love a lovely lass."

"Conor, stop!" Now Scott's body was trembling.

"You have nothing to worry about, lad, they won't touch

you." He winked at the boy. "Off with you now and tell your mother she's a fine lady. I'll be bringing her some soda bread once I get time enough to make a few loaves."

He had Scott by the arm, moving him toward the barn door. "You'll have to run the whole way, lad, it's a real downpour," and with that he shoved the boy forward, out into the driving rain. "Keep away from the river, though." Then he rolled the barn door closed and the light of the forge disappeared, leaving Scott to find his way home in the dark.

For a second the boy blinked in the darkness, groping for his bearings. Then he took a deep breath and ran, first up toward Ballycastle, then down across the lawns and formal gardens to the guest house, bursting into the kitchen.

"My God, what is it, Scotty?" Barbara asked, jumping up from the table at the sight of her son, soaking and trembling with rain and fear.

Scott shook his head, still unable to speak. He could sense the hobgoblins around the house, peeping into the windows, crawling into the stone walls, hiding in the crevices of the rock foundation.

"Hobgoblin," he whispered and fell into his mother's arms.

Across Ballycastle the old man dampened the forge and shut off the lights. At the door he paused, squinted into the storm. He could no longer see the river or the mooring, but he thought again of Carmel Burke and the nights they had danced at the edge of the woods, in the soft light of the great glass ballroom. He had told the lad too much, he realized; he had gotten carried away with his tale. The boy might talk, say something that would start again the rumors. Then he shook his head, as if to reassure himself. They were all dead, he thought. All of them—Carmel and Peggy Connolly, Monica Healion and Nuala O'Neill, everyone who might know a thread of the truth. All that remained was the tombstones, and the cabin, and Conor himself, who had known it all and said not a word.

Seven

"You should have telephoned me," Derek said. He got up from his desk and began to pace about the office, as if her story had upset him.

Barbara shrugged. "I didn't think of bothering you with a family problem." She was across the large room, sitting sideways in the small seat of the high, narrow windows. From this second floor vantage she could look across the fields toward the main gate. When Fergus had built Ballycastle he had banned cars from the property, and guests were met with a horse and carriage at the main gate.

It was less than a mile across the fields to the castle, but Fergus had landscaped the property so that the drive curved through the trees, going deep into the woods. His goal had not been to impress people, Barbara had been told, but rather to give them a sense that they had come upon a Brigadoon sort of world, an enchanted place lost in time.

"But from what you say, it sounds like the Foundation's problem," Derek replied. "I'll have a talk with Conor, put the fear of God into him and warn him to stay away from Scott. But I can't fire the man. According to Fergus's will, Conor must be employed as long as he can work and taken care of until his death. He's even to be buried on the estate. There's really no way of getting rid of him." He sounded worried, as if he had let Barbara down in some way.

"Oh, I don't want to have him fired. Actually, it isn't Conor's fault. Scotty is just so impressionable."

"How is he now?"

"Fine, but it took hours to calm him down. First I had to talk through the story Conor told him, find out about the hobgoblins. Then I gave him a Valium and put him to bed. He slept for a solid fourteen hours. That's why I wasn't in yesterday. I stayed home just to be around when he woke up."

"He's okay?"

Barbara nodded. "I went home at noon. He's up and around, watching television. I kept him home from school just to be on the safe side."

"Why don't you take the rest of the day off? I mean, there's nothing around here that can't hold," Derek said casually, fighting his desire to go to her, to wrap her in his arms. His weakness, he knew, was for women like her—women who needed caring for. But he stayed away from where she was perched on the window seat like some rare and fragile bird. He kept the distance of the office between them like an expanse of water.

Barbara shook her head. "It's better that I give him some time alone. I don't want him to think I'm afraid to let him out of my sight."

"Are you?"

She nodded reluctantly. "Yes, I'm afraid so. And I keep checking in by phone. When I called a few minutes ago he answered, 'Yes, mother, I'm still alive' and hung up. I can't blame him. Even I'm feeling like a pest."

"Why play it so close? He's not suicidal, is he?"

"No, of course not. After his father died he did make one flamboyant attempt to asphyxiate himself with carbon dioxide, but he was simply acting out, feeling this enormous guilt that he was alive and Warren was dead." She smiled again, the same sad, wry smile. "I didn't blame him. I wanted to kill myself then, too. Warren was only forty."

"But Scott's all over that now," Derek stated carefully, still feeling his way with her, as if he were in a room full of unexplored emotions.

"Yes, he's over that." She looked up and caught his glance and added quietly, "We're both over it, Derek."

"And what's next?" He smiled, attempted to change the atmosphere.

"I think we should get back to work, both of us." She slid off her perch, as if taking flight, and came across the office toward him.

She had her eyes on him, as if he were a beacon light and she was tracking her way home. He looked apprehensive as she moved closer.

"Barbara?" he asked. He reached out and touched her arm, pulling her to a stop.

She turned her head slowly to one side and her eyes widened.

He had stopped her impulsively. The way she had slid off the window seat—the gracefulness of her moves—had made him decide to kiss her, to play his hand. Now he saw, as if reading the thoughts behind her brown eyes, the fear she felt, her uncertainty, and he realized for the first time how alone she surely felt in her life, without a husband, with only this strange son at home.

"I'll help you," he said. It was not what he had meant to say, or do, but her vulnerability stopped him. He couldn't tamper with this woman's life. She needed his friendship more than his love.

"Thank you," Barbara said. She moved her arm away and smiled quickly, once. She felt let down, but did not know why. It was only when she went into the hallway, into the cooler breeze of the building, that she realized what had happened between them. Her pace slowed as she kept playing back the brief exchange, seeing the expression on his face, then seeing the doubt cloud his eyes like cataracts.

It hurt her. Feeling betrayed, she ran all their recent exchanges through her mind, trying to document her growing sense that he was interested in her. She could clearly hear him saying, "Do you mean Scott is my competition?" There—she was not crazy. That was certainly flirtation.

She reached the main floor and went slowly toward her office. It was Scotty, of course, and her hysterical story of the hobgoblins. That was what had scared him off. What normal man would want to get involved with her and Scott? And office affairs were always messy, especially at a small place like the Foundation; she should have had more sense herself. She would be crazy to jeopardize her own work by getting involved with the director.

She sighed, tucked away her bruised feelings the way a sleeping cat curls his paws beneath him. She was all right, she realized, reaching her office. Their encounter upstairs had been like a near accident on ice. Both of them had spun out, but in the end they'd each skidded safely to a stop. And she walked into her office briskly, smiling, feeling sure of herself again.

"Mrs. Gardiner?" The girl's voice came at her from the corner like a sniper's bullet.

"Yes, I'm Mrs. Gardiner," Barbara answered sharply, then softened her voice. "May I help you?" She kept smiling, seeing that the teen-age girl was nervous.

"I'm Valerie Dunn," the girl said, rising from the chair where she'd been huddled. She had an armful of books and when she stood, several of them tumbled from her grasp.

"Oh, God!" she exclaimed, mortified.

"Here, let me help," Barbara offered. Bending quickly she picked up a few books, noticing their Flat Rock High School jackets as she handed them over. Town people rarely ventured near the Foundation, and as she took her seat behind the desk Barbara wondered what had brought the girl to Ballycastle.

Barbara rarely met young girls and the way they dressed always astonished her. She couldn't imagine what could have possessed this girl to wear such a collection of items: tight jeans and cowboy boots, a long-sleeved blouse, bright pink, with a man's narrow plaid tie knotted at the neck, and topped with a brown leather vest.

She was a girl whose figure was still boyish, Barbara saw, and she was almost as unkempt as a boy. Looking at the girl's loose black hair, Barbara had to keep herself from rushing to the child and combing out the tangles. Still, Valerie Dunn was cute. Her smile was large and lopsided, and it made her look fresh and trustworthy. And she had lovely eyes, very bright and arresting, swatches of sea green velvet.

"I'm a friend of Scott's," Valerie announced.

"Oh, I see." At that, Barbara reappraised the girl. "Scotty didn't say . . ." She kept scanning the tall teen-ager, as if searching for faults.

"Well, we're sort of in the same class. The same homeroom. And when Scott missed two days of school I thought . . . well, I knew he lived here at Ballycastle, and . . ." She sighed, exhausted by the tension of explaining. She shouldn't have come, she realized. His mother would think she was some kind of creep.

"It's very nice of you to stop by. Scotty wasn't feeling very well on Monday, so I—he decided to stay home for a few days."

"I thought he might be sick or something, and I live out this way anyhow, at Nolan's Corners, and I always cut across the grounds, you know, after school." Valerie tightened her hold on her textbooks, and edged toward the office door, as if planning to run.

"Did Scotty tell you I worked at the castle?" Barbara asked, halting Valerie with the question. The girl's explanation hadn't told her any of the things she really wanted to know. Was she just a classmate, or someone with a crush on Scott? Barbara couldn't imagine Scotty having a girlfriend without telling her. But this Valerie Dunn was, in spite of her nervousness, curiously appealing, and Barbara found herself pleased to know the girl existed.

"No, Scott never talks about the castle. I knew you worked here because of my older sister, Karen DeWitt."

"Oh, Karen, yes."

"She handles the Foundation tours," Valerie went on.

"Yes, I know Karen; I just didn't realize she was your sister." Barbara smiled. "Now I see the family resemblance." She was disappointed that it wasn't Scott who had told the girl about her.

"Well, I guess I better get along. I just wanted to stop, you know, and see if Scott was okay, not sick or anything. A lot of kids have been catching the flu."

"Valerie, if you like, why don't you stop by the house and say hello to Scotty . . . since you're here," Barbara suggested, thinking quickly. "I'm sure he'd be pleased. He's been by himself for two days, and you could also tell him what homework he's missing."

Barbara stood and moved around her desk. Now, standing next to Valerie, she realized how tall the girl was. She and Scotty made a good match. Perhaps that was what had happened at school; they had been thrown together because of their height. But they were bound to have noticed each other eventually, Barbara thought; they had the same rangy style and intelligent eyes.

"Scott won't mind, will he?" Valerie asked, sounding apprehensive.

"He'll be pleased. I'm the only one he's seen since the weekend. I'm sure he'll be thrilled that you were nice enough to drop by. We live in..."

"Yes, I know. The guest house. I was around Ballycastle a couple of times during August. I saw where you were living."

"Well, just tell Scott I'll be home at five o'clock." Barbara put her arm around the girl's waist and walked her out into the entrance hall. "It's been very nice meeting you, Valerie, and I hope to see you again soon. Tell Scott he shouldn't keep you hidden away."

Valerie glanced sideways at her, then took a deep breath, as if she'd just decided something.

"Mrs. Gardiner, you know, Scott...he and I...well, we're not exactly going out together or anything. I mean, I don't want you to get the idea we've been sneaking around or something. I mean, I'd like to go out with him." She grinned, embarrassed by her own forwardness.

"Well, maybe we can push him along, Valerie. You know, the two of us. Scott was in a boys' school before coming here. He didn't have much of a chance to meet girls his own age."

"I think he's really cool. I mean, he's not like the other kids at Flat Rock. They're always showing off, getting into trouble. Drinking and stuff. But Scott...he's sort of above all that. It's all kids' stuff to him, juvenile." She had not talked to anyone about why she liked Scotty. She had not said anything to her girlfriends, even her best friend, Tracy, knowing what they'd think, and she found it a relief to be telling someone her feelings, even if it was Scott's mother. She liked Mrs. Gardiner. She was beautiful, Valerie thought; it would be great to look that way, trim and cool, and always in control.

"Thank you, Valerie, I think he's pretty neat, too. And so are you." She hugged the girl briefly. "Now go down to the house and cheer him up. He needs a friend like you."

When she returned to her office, Barbara thought of telephoning Scott so he could straighten up the house before Valerie arrived, then decided against it. It was better to leave them alone to work it out themselves. She couldn't force them together. She just hoped it would work out. And she went back to her work, typing out rapidly:

> Ballycastle, like all great houses, reflects the lives of the people who lived in it. Fergus O'Cuileannain changed little of this ancient castle, and destroyed less, so that it can be presented as an almost pure example of its style. It is a living memorial to this strange man who lived here all his adult life.

Barbara paused a moment to look through her rough draft, read again what she had typed. The page seemed to blur before her eyes. She couldn't concentrate. Something was wrong. She closed her eyes and tried to let whatever it was float to the top of her consciousness. She saw Scott. His figure flashed into her mind. Something was wrong with Scotty. Reaching for the telephone, she dialed quickly. She would just hear his voice, she thought, and hang up. He would think it was a wrong number, and not suspect that she was checking up on him.

She counted out five rings. Two more, she decided, and she would go down to the house. No room in the guest house was that far from a phone. She could picture the extensions: one on the kitchen wall and another in her bedroom, a princess phone on the night stand.

One.

Two.

"Hello?"

Barbara pressed her palm across the phone's mouthpiece and said nothing. Her hand was shaking with her intense relief. He was all right, nothing was wrong.

"Hello?"

He sounded angry and upset. She must have woken him from a nap, she realized.

"Shit!" He slammed the phone in her ear.

Slowly she replaced the receiver. Barbara smiled wryly, thinking this time it was she who was being irrational, not Scott. He was all right, she told herself once more. Besides, a pretty girl was on her way to visit him.

She turned back to the typewriter. That was another worry: two teen-agers together in an empty house. Well, whatever happened, she thought, at least it would be normal and healthy. She shook her head and went to work.

Scott sat trembling beside his mother's bed. The ringing phone had upset him, broken his concentration. He had been in the upstairs bathroom, kneeling beside the tub with the water running. He had been there for almost twenty minutes, waiting for the right moment, waiting for the courage to rip the razor blade across his upturned wrist and get it over with.

He knew it had been his mother on the phone, calling to check up on him. He jerked the telephone plug from the wall and went back into the bathroom, knelt down again beside the tub.

It was harder than he had expected. That morning when he'd made up his mind it had seemed easy, even restful. Lying in bed, he had planned how to do it. There would be no mess. She wouldn't be able to blame him for leaving blood on the bathroom tiles. He would simply fill the tub and submerge his wrists, numbing the pain with the soothing warm water.

He liked the idea and he imagined how she'd react, finding him slouched over the bathtub, his face white, his eyes wide open, his mouth gasping. The way a fish looked washed up dead on shore.

For awhile he thought about who she would telephone first. The police? Conor? Mr. Brennan? He knew she would be calm and controlled. Scott remembered how she had reacted when his father died.

Scott turned on the water again, measured the temperature so it wouldn't be too hot, then, taking one of her hand towels, he looped it around his right arm and held the ends in his teeth. The veins in his right arm popped up, clearly defined and pulsing.

In his left hand he held the straight blade, pressed it gently to his wrist. He could feel the cold metal of the blade, like a piece of sharp ice on his skin. It was so easy, he told himself. Just press hard and the blade would cut into the vein before he felt the pain. He could already imagine the warm blood squirting his face as the vein burst open. Then he'd douse his wrist in the water, let the blood flow freely until he weakened and lost consciousness.

Still he couldn't cut his skin. His knees began to hurt from kneeling on the tiled floor. He pulled the bath mat under him and repositioned himself against the tub's high side. All right, he told himself. Get it over with. Make her be sorry for how she had treated Dad. He leaned forward, his ear inches from the rushing water, and closing his eyes, squeezing them tight, he thrust the blade's edge into his flesh.

Eight

Valerie stepped up to the front door of the guest house and knocked. Scott couldn't be angry at her, she told herself. She was bringing him his homework. She was doing him a favor. And for a moment she almost believed that was the only reason she was at Ballycastle.

Valerie knocked louder and listened for a moment. She heard the phone ringing. Perhaps he was out on the grounds somewhere, she thought, but then abruptly the ringing stopped. She stepped back, away from the door, and looked through the bay window of the living room. The television was turned on and the color picture was rolling. The room was empty.

Valerie followed the stone path around the building. She liked the guest house. It was small and elegant, like an antique doll house. When she was a little girl she had often come to the estate with her father when he delivered hay. And while the hay was being stacked, she would sneak away to see the tiny cottage tucked away in the woods below the mansion. She never had liked the castle, never even looked up the hill toward it. All of the kids in Flat Rock thought the huge building was haunted.

But not the guest house. She had even promised herself as

a child that someday she would have a home like that, a small cottage just for her and her husband.

Valerie stopped at the screen door to the kitchen. The inside door stood open, and she could hear the television set from the living room, the quiet, melodramatic voices of a soap opera. Yet when she called his name, no one answered. She opened the screen door and went inside. She would leave him a note, she decided, just tell him the page numbers and the problems that had been assigned, and then leave.

Valerie piled her school books on the table and searched through her shoulder bag for a pencil and notebook. Then she heard the sound of running water.

She walked slowly out of the kitchen and into the short hallway, stopped and looked around. There was a tiny room under the staircase. It was his room, she saw. The bed was unmade and boy's clothes were scattered across the floor. That surprised her. He was always so clean at school, so neatly dressed. The room was a shambles, like one of her own brothers'.

"Scott?" she asked softly, peering behind the door. He was not downstairs.

Now she was sure he was nowhere in the house. He had seen her coming and run out the back, leaving the kitchen door open as he fled.

"Oh, God," she whispered, feeling awful. She had ruined everything by coming here. He thought she was just chasing him, embarrassing him by running after him.

Well, she wouldn't leave the homework. She wouldn't even talk to him at school. Let him be all alone, if that was what he wanted. She was the only one at school who had even been nice to him.

She hesitated at the bottom of the stairs, enjoying her own self-pity for a moment, letting it seep through her like water dampening a sponge.

The water, the running water. What a creep, she thought, so turned off by her that he had left the house with the water running. She hurried up the stairs.

There were only three bedrooms upstairs and off the largest was the bathroom. Valerie walked toward it, into the room that she assumed was Mrs. Gardiner's. She felt like an intruder, but nevertheless she was tempted to stop, to open dresser drawers and see what clothes Scott's petite, elegant mother wore. Next to Barbara, Valerie had felt huge and awkward, helpless in her size.

But Valerie was afraid to stop, afraid she would be caught upstairs. She went straight to the bathroom and turned toward the tub. It was only then that she saw Scott, slumped over the bathtub side.

Her screams startled him. He spun around on his knees, slipping on the wet mat and losing control of the razor blade. It flew off, hitting the wall with a tiny ting.

She only saw blood. A fine rivulet of it on Scott's arm and more blood dripping to the wet tiles, making a shallow puddle under the tub. It was something she had read about in books and seen on the news. She thought at once of Terry Miller, a girl who had killed herself two years before at Flat Rock. Valerie had often sat next to her on the school bus and for months she had blamed herself for the suicide, dreamed of it in nightmares.

Scott was swearing at her, trying to find his feet on the slippery floor, and in his haste he stumbled when he stood and his long body fell against the tiles, as if he were sliding head first into the doorway.

His forearms struck Valerie, shoved her into the bedroom where she went tumbling, tripping on the rug, falling against the bed. She hit her head and began to cry, not from pain, but fear. He grabbed her, seized her right ankle, and she kicked out at him as if he were a tanglement of weeds.

"What are you doing here?" he yelled over and over. He had grabbed her leg with one hand and was pulling himself forward, crawling on his knees after her.

"Let go!" she screamed, kicking frantically to free her leg from his hand. She felt as if she was drowning. She hit him in the forehead with her free foot and he cried out and let go.

"Goddamn you!" He swung wildly at her with both hands, hysterical in his pain.

"Stop it!" she demanded. "You're bleeding all over me."

He stopped abruptly and looked with surprise at his wrist.

"I'm not bleeding," he insisted, examining the small slash marks on his wrist.

"You were," she declared. "Look at yourself."

There were dark stains on his T-shirt, blood on his face and in his hair. He had taken off his glasses and she had not seen him before without them. He looked tired, as if he had not slept, and his face was pale. She wanted to hold him.

"I cut myself. I was trying to fix something in the bathroom."

"You were trying to kill yourself," she said flatly.

"I was trying to clean out the drain. It's all clogged up."

She looked away, as if bored with his explanation, then said, "I don't care what you were doing. I have to go."

"Why are you in my house anyway?"

"I came by to give you your homework, that's all. I told your mother and she said it was okay to come here, and then I heard water running. Oh, never mind!" She was on her feet, tucking her jeans back into her boots.

"Now you're going to run tell my mother that you found me slitting my wrists." He had gotten up along with Valerie and stood with both his arms hugging his sides, hiding the marks.

"You know, Scott, sometimes I think you're really a creep." She looked sideways at him, as if from a new angle.

"Well, am I wrong? Isn't that exactly what you're in a big rush to do? You and mom, all girls together."

"Oh, God, don't be such a squirrel." She marched from the room and downstairs, her boots banging on the hardwood.

He caught up with her in the kitchen. "Hey, I'm sorry I yelled at you and everything."

"You don't have to be nice to me, Scott. I have no intention of telling your mother." Valerie caught her books up in an untidy pile, hurrying, trying to escape. She felt foolish and dumb, as if she were to blame for all this.

"I wasn't trying to kill myself," he said again.

She stopped and stared at him. Her long, lopsided smile was gone. She looked older and a hard edge had come into her green eyes. "You know, you're not the only one who's ever tried it. It's no big deal. Lots of kids do it."

"What do you mean?"

"What I said—it's no big deal. It's quite common." The tone of her voice had changed. No longer frightened, it was lofty and condescending. She clutched her books firmly and went toward the kitchen door.

"Wait!" he asked, catching her sleeve.

"You're bleeding again." She nodded at the bracelet of blood on his right wrist.

"Oh, shit!" Now he was embarrassed, conscious only of looking like a jerk.

"Here," she said, taking command. She dropped her books on the table. "Where are your bandages?"

"I don't know. Maybe in the downstairs bathroom." He stood in the middle of the tiny kitchen, holding up his arm, baffled by the sight of his own blood.

"You're getting it on the floor. Go over to the sink." She took him by the arm, leading him across the room. "Is it your job to wash the dishes?" she asked, clearing away plates from the sink.

"Yes, why?"

"Because they're not done."

"I've been busy."

"Yeah, we know, killing yourself."

"Hey, come on, lay off." He tried to pull away from her, but she had hold of his elbow.

"I'm sorry. I'm sorry," she said, her voice softening.

"I don't pick on you," he went on, attacking now that she was retreating.

"You never say anything to me at all," she responded. "I mean, you won't talk to me at school and we're in the same classes, and your locker is even next to mine." She did not look up at him, but she was aware of his closeness. "I better get some bandages or something," she said, moving away. "Keep your wrist under that warm water," she went on, giving orders. It made her feel more secure, telling him what to do.

"I don't like this school," he shouted after her. "It's crummy. I don't want to go there."

"Then why are you?" she called from the bathroom.

Scott could hear her moving bottles in the medicine cabinet, searching for bandages.

"Because of my father," he answered. He would make her question him, and then tell her about how his father died. It would make her feel terrible.

"Your father?" She was back with her hands full. "Is your mother divorced or something?" As she talked she began to wrap his wrist in gauze. She had taken first aid in school the year before and took a certain pleasure in using what she had learned for the first time. The blood had stopped and she could see that the two razor blade cuts were slight, they had barely marked the skin, but she wrapped the gauze in lengths around his wrist, enjoying the sight of its cleanness on his tanned arm, enjoying being next to him.

"My father died last Christmas of a heart attack. My mother found him on the kitchen floor two days before I was due home for Christmas vacation."

"Oh, God!" She looked up from what she was doing. He had spoken so calmly, without raising his voice, and she wanted to cry for him, to show him that she understood.

"I tried to kill myself after Dad died. That time I went out to the garage and turned the car on. I was going to asphyxiate myself." He began to grin, as if now his behavior seemed amusing. "I was only out there five minutes before Mom came looking for me. Our doctor had told her I might try something stupid like that."

"If it was so stupid then, why were you trying to cut your wrists today?" Valerie asked. She had finished taping the bandages, but she did not move away from him. They stood together by the kitchen sink.

Scott shrugged. "I don't know. There doesn't seem much sense, you know, being alive."

"You think being dead is more fun maybe?" Her eyes widened.

"Come on, don't give me that. You know what I mean. I haven't been feeling good lately."

"Everyone gets down, Scott, big deal."

"I don't mean down, I mean crazy. I keep having this nightmare and waking up screaming." He shook his head. "After awhile, you know, you figure it's better if you're not around, if you're not waking up your mother in the middle of the night, crying like some dumb little kid."

"What kinds of nightmares?" she asked, her green eyes soft and worried.

"Different things. After my dad died, I kept dreaming about Brobdingnagians."

"You dreamed about *what?*"

"Oh, it's just a game. Have you ever heard of *Hobgoblin?*"

She shook her head.

Scott smiled wryly. "That figures. A bush school like Flat Rock won't know anything about FRP games."

"What are you talking about?"

"FRP—fantasy role playing."

Valerie shook her head, frowning.

"Well, have you read any books like *The Lord of the Rings?*"

"I tried once, but it didn't make sense. I mean, it's not real."

"Of course it's not real!" He was angry again. Why was he wasting his time trying to explain *Hobgoblin* to someone who'd never appreciate it?

"What about these Brobdingers, or whatever they're called?" she asked quickly, seeing his reaction. He tensed up fast, she noticed. She could almost see his muscles contract.

"Never mind." He moved away from her.

"Hey, just because I don't know anything about this *Hobgoblin* stuff isn't my fault. Okay, we're backward up here. I'm sorry. But at least I don't go around killing myself. Jeez, you sure are moody. One moment you're fine and the next, you're a turkey."

"What do you mean, turkey?" He was sitting on the other side of the room in the window seat. From there he could see the path through the birch woods, uphill to the castle, and everything inside the kitchen. It gave him a sense of control, having that kind of look out.

"You're a turkey," she said again. "It means, you know, dumb. Odd."

"Because I play *Hobgoblin?*" He still sounded angry.

Valerie nodded. She was frightened again. The way he kept watching made her nervous.

She glanced at her books piled on the table and her leather vest where she had dropped it on the chair. She should have left the house right away. She shouldn't have come to see him in the first place. "I think I better go," she said, going for her books.

"Hey, wait." He sounded disappointed. "Why are you leaving? Because I'm a turkey? Because I'm strange?"

"Look, don't get all excited over nothing."

"Well, you called me a name."

"Oh, God, it's just an expression. It doesn't mean anything. I mean, kids say it to each other all the time."

"Not at Spencertown. I never heard it at Spencertown."

"Jeez, you know, you're really something." Her fear was gone. Now she was angry with him. "You never heard the word and I never heard of *Hobgoblin*. So we're even." She had her vest on and again she snatched up her pile of books. The geometry text hit the floor.

"You need a book bag," he suggested. The tone of his voice had changed and he sounded chatty, as if he were having a good time.

"And you need a new head," she said, stooping down for the book.

"Very funny."

"Well, it's true." She moved toward the kitchen door, walking backwards, as if she wanted to keep him in sight.

"Hey, you didn't tell me the homework." He scrambled off the window seat.

"First half of chapter five and do the questions at the end, but only up through number six."

"Hey, I was just thinking. Do you want to play *Hobgoblin* sometime? I'll teach you." Scott had followed her outside into the sunlight. It was still a warm afternoon, full of bright foliage and sunshine.

She stared at him, puzzled.

"What's the matter?" he asked, grinning.

His smile surprised her. She realized then that she had never seen him smile and it changed his looks. He suddenly seemed handsome.

"A minute ago I thought you were going to hurt me and now you want to teach me this silly game."

"Hurt you? I'd never do that." He sounded scared himself. "Why did you say that?"

"Well, maybe not hurt me, but you seemed so strange in there, and you were trying to kill yourself."

"Oh, come on, let's forget that." He moved nervously around. "You really won't tell my mom?"

She shook her head.

"Thanks," he whispered, nodding.

"I got to go," she said but did not move away.

"So would you like to learn *Hobgoblin?* I mean, even from a turkey like me."

She smiled. "I don't know. I'll think about it." She began to move off, to cross the lawn toward the river below the mansion.

"It's really a neat game," Scott added quickly, following after. He was excited, thinking he could convince her. They would have to get other players, of course, but she had friends. At school she was always with a crowd.

"If I agree, will you promise not to run this kind of number again?"

"What number?"

"You know—upstairs."

"Come on, give me a break. I said it was stupid. I said I was depressed."

"Why were you doing it anyway?" Outside in the safety of the sunlight, she felt she could ask him again.

"I told you—because of my nightmare. Because of those dreams I had."

"Of this Brobdingnag?"

"No, not this time. Now I'm having nightmares about Nuckelavees."

"What kind of game is this anyway? All the names are unpronounceable."

"They're Irish hobgoblins," Scott went on, explaining, telling her the blacksmith's story of the girl found dead by the river's edge. "He said she was killed by evil hobgoblins with heads like men, only ten times as large, and mouths like pig snouts."

"Do you believe all that?" Valerie asked. She had continued to walk downhill toward the river and he had tagged after, walking with his hands in his pockets, his long stride matching hers.

"Oh, it's just a story. But Conor, the blacksmith, made it seem so real, I believed it. That's a problem I've got. I'm too impressionable. My imagination gets out of control." Now in the bright sunlight, with a slight breeze off the river and the smell of fresh cut grass, Conor's tale did seem ridiculous. Nuckelavees in the niches and crannies of Ballycastle. He shook his head at his own gullibility.

"Well, people have been killed here," Valerie said solemnly.

She glanced at Scott, surprised he didn't know.

"Oh, they say that about all castles and old mansions." Scott turned around, looked up the hill at the gray stone building.

Valerie did not turn her head.

"What's the matter? Are you afraid to look?" he asked, teasing.

Valerie shrugged. "I don't like the place."

"You mean you won't even look at it?"

She nodded. "Not unless I have to. I never look at Bally-castle. I think it's evil."

"Come on, it's just a big house on top of a hill." Scott grinned. "Maybe there's something wrong with your imagination too."

They had reached the creek and Valerie turned left, following a narrow path into the woods that flanked the long sweeping lawns below the castle.

"Where are we going?" Scott asked, surprised at how far from the house they had walked.

"I'm going home," Valerie answered, still leading the way into the woods. "This is a short cut to my house. We live off Route 12 below Ballycastle."

"Is it far?"

"Oh, I don't know. Maybe ten minutes from here. There are several paths from the castle through the woods." She glanced over her shoulder. "Have you been into the woods?"

"Nah, I don't like forests. They make me nervous. I don't have much sense of direction, so I'm always thinking I'm going to get lost. I like the suburbs best. You know, concrete side-walks and streets with name tags on them." He tried to make it seem funny, but he was afraid—of the stillness of the woods, and the way thick trees and bushes closed off the sky.

"Then you've never been to the graveyard?" she asked.

"No. What graveyard?" The path widened and he came up beside Valerie. He would have to turn back soon; he did not want to have to find his way home alone.

"There's a graveyard here, started by the man who built Ballycastle."

"Fergus O'Cuileannain?"

"Yes, Fergus. He built it for his employees, and himself. It's on a hill called Steepletop. It's my favorite spot in the whole world. When I was little I used to go up there all the time. Would you like to see it?" She stopped on the path. She was smiling and looked excited, as if this was a sudden and unexpected pleasure.

Scott glanced around, into the thick trees.

"Well, how far away is it?" he asked.

"Up there." She gestured.

"We'll get lost. There's no path or anything."

"Scott, I've been playing in these woods since I was six years old. We're not going to get lost." She sounded irritated at his caution. "Besides, everything is downhill from Steeple-top. All you have to do is walk." She turned her back and took a few strides, then stopped and faced him again. "Here, take some of these books. They're heavy." She dumped several textbooks into his arms and struck off, going immediately off the path and into the trees.

The climb was straight uphill through second-growth trees. It was easy to walk, without heavy underbrush. The sun was on that side of the hill and the late afternoon light seeped through the leaves, falling in patches.

"Look!" Valerie said, stopping abruptly to point out the pattern of sunlight on the forest floor. "It looks like a checkerboard, doesn't it?"

Panting, Scott stopped and caught his breath, glanced around to where Valerie was pointing. He didn't see the sunlight but the shadows, the dark clusters of brush. In *Hobgoblin* the Fear Dearg lived in such places. They were little men, about two and a half feet in height, and wore scarlet sugarloaf hats and long scarlet coats and had long gray hair and wrinkled faces. They always waited and watched for stragglers tracking through the forest.

They were deceitful creatures and cunning. Once in a game at Spencertown, BrianBorú had been tricked by two of these red men who magically changed form on him, appearing in the woods of Glastonbury Tor as lost children. His righteousness as a paladin knight had obliged him to aid the children, and it was only because of his skill as a sixth-level magic-user that he'd managed to overcome their trickery. Scott had pulled a green saving card from the *Hobgoblin* deck, giving BrianBorú an escape route from Glastonbury Tor.

"Isn't it lovely?" Valerie whispered. She was smiling, enchanted by the silence and beauty of the place, the moist and earthy smell. It felt like being inside a terrarium.

"Come on, where's this graveyard?" Scott was frightened, but he couldn't tell Valerie. She wouldn't understand. It was just that he saw more and, he realized, imagined more. Beyond them, a hundred yards further away, the remains of an old stone fence crossed through the trees. Nuckelavees would be in those old stones, hiding in the fissures. "Let's go," he demanded, moving up hill, rushing to reach the top, to be back again in the full sunlight.

"Boys!" Valerie exclaimed. "They never appreciate *any*-thing." And she fell into step behind him, rushing to keep up with his long stride. "Easy," she complained. "Quit running! You can't enjoy nature if you're just going to rush straight to the top."

"I'm not interested in woods," he shouted, "and besides, we're looking for graves, not trees!"

It was only another few minutes to the crest of the hill, to where the cemetery was fitted into the slope above the tree line. It was a small site, with fewer than a dozen graves, but a high metal fence had been built around the cluster of tombstones, and someone had been there recently to cut away the grass and plant fresh flowers.

"See!" Valerie said, pointing off to the setting sun and the flat horizon. From Steepletop they looked away from Ballycastle and could not see the mansion. The river was below them, though; it curved around the hilltop and then, beyond the woods, widened as it crossed the long valley, flowed toward the horizon. "I love it at this time of day. See how the sun shines off the water? Isn't it incredible?" She was smiling, wanting him to share the pleasure. "In spring, you know, you can actually smell the earth after plowing. There's my house to the right, the blue one with white shutters. And there's my dad. See the tractor? He's trucking feed out to the Holsteins. We keep them in the big field until the weather turns."

Scott was not following her directions, nor did he find the sight incredible. It was only the river and miles of farmland. He looked back at the graveyard. It had been a mistake to follow her up here. The sun had descended to the horizon and already he was cold, and still he had to walk back down through the woods.

"Come on, let's go," he said.

"Wait! You haven't seen anything." She put down her books by the graveyard gate and swinging it open went inside. "You have to look at the tombstones. They're all weird." She was excited again, anxious to impress him. "Most tombstones have angels and saints, but these are strange."

Scott saw what she meant. Coming around in front of the first grave site he saw what the carved stone figures were.

"They're gargoyles," he whispered, "standing upright." Each headstone was an elaborately carved figure, a wild animal's shape, with ugly and distorted features cut boldly into the stone.

"Aren't they something?" Valerie exclaimed, pleased that he seemed impressed. She began to rush around, reading off the names and dates on the gray stone scrolls that each gargoyle held forward, as if in offering. "What do you think these ugly statues mean, Scott? I mean, why would anyone want these guys standing over their graves? And why do you think only girls are buried here?"

But Scott was not listening. He had stopped in front of one grave and read the name spelled out on the stone scroll. Carmel Burke, 1912–1931. It was true, Scott realized. Conor Fitzpatrick had not told him a tale, as his mother had claimed. There had been a Carmel Burke and her body had been found as cold as stone.

Nine

"You wanted to see me, ma'am?" Conor whispered, standing behind Barbara Gardiner's desk.

She jumped at the sound of the old man's voice and hit her knees against the typewriter stand.

"Conor! My God, what are you doing sneaking up on me?" She spun her chair around and the old man scurried back, clutching his cap in both hands. He left behind the odor of his body.

"I got a message, ma'am, you wanted to see me." Conor stood at a respectful distance, looking fearful, as if he expected her to pounce on him.

"Yes, Conor, I did." Barbara turned her chair around again and began to search through files piled on her desk. "Conor, some information is missing from Fergus's personnel files and Mr. Brennan thought you might have an idea of where to look." She looked at the old man and waited expectantly.

"Well, I wouldn't be knowing for sure." He moved forward, his farm shoes shuffling on the floor. "I only took care of the horses, ma'am." He grinned, as if it were foolish to question him.

"I realize that, Conor." She answered patiently, trying not to rile him. She was tired of treating Conor with kid gloves, as if he were a visiting sheikh. "Nevertheless, you were a trusted employee and you do seem to know where everything is on the estate." Barbara smiled, attempting to flatter him. "And I thought—Mr. Brennan and I thought—you might have some idea where other filing cabinets might have been stored. Fergus was a very meticulous man; we have detailed records of every piece of property, of everyone who worked here at Ballycastle with the exception of the ten years from 1929 to 1939."

"Oh, the Depression years, ma'am."

"Yes, the Depression."

"Ah, those were hard times for most people. Even for Himself, would you believe." Conor was edging closer to the desk, still clutching his wool cap in his bony hands.

"Yes, Conor, I know they were difficult times." She recognized what was coming. Unless she could deflect him, Conor would be off again on one of his stories.

"The Depression was why I came to America in the first place, did you know that, Missus Gardiner? 'Tis true." He cocked his head, making the point. "It was worse in Ireland, you know, in '27 and '28. Ah, you couldn't find a day's work in the land. We were all starving to death in Galway. And then Himself came home for the racing, and I met him by chance. Did I ever tell you how I met Himself?" He stopped and winked at her.

"No, you didn't, Conor, but actually I don't have time at the moment. I'm behind in my work and I need to find those files." Barbara hated being rude, but she knew his way. Unless she kept talking she'd be there for hours, listening to stories of the old country. "Would you mind, Conor, looking around for the files? Perhaps they were stored in one of the farm buildings when the Foundation moved into the castle. It would be a great help to me if you would do that." She smiled sweetly, trying to show the old man that she'd appreciate his efforts.

"Oh, I'd be happy to look for you, ma'am. 'Twouldn't be a bother at all. Files, you say?" He cocked his head again and seemed attentive.

"Yes, like those old wooden cabinets." She pointed to the long row of them in her office.

He studied the wooden cabinets as if they were a new disovery. "Well, to be truthful with you, ma'am, I've never seen he likes of them anywhere on the place."

"Perhaps the files aren't in cabinets. Perhaps they're just stored, you see, in boxes." She picked up an old gray file and showed it to him. The old man was getting on her nerves. Sometimes she suspected his denseness was just an act, useful when he wanted to be uncooperative.

"Ah, well, that could be true enough." He nodded agreeably. "I'll have a good look myself and see what I might be finding. But, tell me, ma'am, just what would you be needing a lot of old papers for?"

"It's for a history of Ballycastle, Conor. I need to know who worked on the estate."

"Oh, I'd be glad to tell you, ma'am." He came forward again, shuffling his old shoes on the marble floor. "I was here myself in them days. I came over from the old country in the summer of '27."

"I'm sure you could help me, Conor, and I appreciate your offer, but I need the files. I need the official records of all the employees."

He nodded, disappointed, and backed away. Again Barbara felt guilty. He was an old man who'd worked hard his whole life and now all he had left were his memories. She hated to seem as if she were dismissing them.

"I do want to speak to you soon, Conor, and write down all your experiences. You're very important to my study, but before I can ask you to sit down with me I have to at least see what the records say about the rest of the staff." Barbara heard herself rambling on apologetically and decided enough was enough. "See what you can find, then," she added, bringing the whole discussion to an abrupt close.

"And how's the lad?" Conor said brightly. "I haven't seen him about the place these last few days."

"He's not been feeling well." For a moment Barbara thought of settling things with Conor, of asking him not to talk to Scotty any more. Derek, she knew, had not had time to take this up with him. But the sight of the old man stopped her from confronting him.

He was so pathetic-looking, standing patiently, like an old dog waiting for a command. Barbara felt another wave of

compassion. Conor was so frail; every move he made seeme
to require all his strength. She would just have to be nice
him, she told herself. Kinder. Just raising her voice, she r
alized, intimidated Conor, sent him cowering.

"Well, I'll be off then, with the help of God," he sa
finally, moving toward the door, still clutching his black cap
"and I'll have a good look for them files, ma'am."

"Thank you, Conor. That would be a great help to me." Sh
tried to sound pleased.

At the door he hesitated, as if caught by a thread of though
then looked back, saying, "The lad seemed a little upset whe
I saw him the other evening. I was telling him a story, yo
know, about the old days here at the castle. There wasn't a b
of truth in the tale, but the boy got a little frightened, I'n
thinking." He sounded apologetic, as if he realized it was hi
fault.

"Yes, Conor, he was upset, and now that you mention it
I was upset as well. Scotty has a very active imagination an
your stories, I'm afraid, do frighten him. I would appreciat
it if you didn't tell him any more of them."

"Aah, there's no harm done."

"Yes, Conor, there is harm," she answered, insistent now
"My son hasn't been well lately. His father died suddenly las
year and he has had nightmares ever since. Maybe stories abou
hobgoblins and girls murdered right here at Ballycastle migh
seem innocent enough to you, but not to Scotty."

She stopped abruptly, trembling. The depth of her own
anger surprised her, but she wondered if the old man even
understood what she meant. He simply stood meekly at the
doorway.

"Well, I didn't mean to do the lad any harm," he said
remorsefully. "I won't say another word, so help me God."

"Thank you, Conor." Barbara saw the worry in the small
man's eyes, saw his obvious concern. "I know you've tried to
be friendly to Scotty, and I appreciate that. He doesn't have
many friends, not here at Ballycastle or at school."

"Aah, he's a fine lad, that one." A spark of pleasure lit
Conor's eyes. "I was meaning to ask you, ma'am. You
wouldn't be Irish, yourself, or your late husband?"

Barbara smiled. "No, I'm afraid we're Scottish and English on both sides."

"Well, you know, he has the look of an Irishman about him." He had put on his black cap. "I won't say another word to the lad, of that you can be sure." He cocked the cap's bill and winked. "Don't you worry a thing about it."

"Thank you, Conor." In that moment, the old man looked almost grandfatherly, and Barbara had the impulse to invite him home for dinner. They were the only people living on the estate and it would be, she realized, the neighborly thing to do. Yet she hesitated.

It was irrational, she knew, but nevertheless she wanted to keep her distance from Conor. Her early warning system alerted her that something was wrong about this old man, and she had come to trust that instinct.

"And I'll have a good look for those files," Conor went on.

"Thank you again." She kept smiling, standing behind her desk, as if it were a barricade. It was only when Conor was out of sight, gone from her office, that Barbara found she had been holding her breath and trembling.

The ring of the telephone startled her, and shaking off her apprehensiveness, she lifted the receiver with relief.

"Mrs. Gardiner?"

"Yes?"

"Mrs. Gardiner, this is Valerie Dunn." Barbara could tell from the girl's voice that something was wrong.

"What's the matter, Valerie?" she asked quickly. "Is it Scotty? Is he all right?" She was already shouting into the phone.

"Yes, he's okay, I think. But maybe you should come home . . . now."

"My God, what happened? What's the matter?" Barbara was on her feet and pacing.

"Nothing happened. We were just up on Steepletop, you know, at the graveyard, and Scott was looking at the tombstones and everything and then he got all crazy about someone who is buried there and started telling me this weird story and then he was afraid to walk back through the woods, so I came home with him. Anyway, he asked me to call you and see if you could come home right away." She paused a moment. "Mrs Gardiner, I think maybe you should."

"I'm on my way. Please stay with Scott until I get there."

"I will, but it's getting late, and I . . ."

"I'll drive you home, Valerie, but tell me, did Scott hurt himself?"

"No."

"Has he tried to do anything?"

"Like what?" Now she was puzzled.

"He hasn't tried to hurt himself in any way, has he?"

"Oh, no, we're just sitting here in the living room."

"Please, Valerie, until I get home, don't let Scott out of your sight." The panic was again in Barbara's voice. The fear, like a hot iron against her heart, was that she wouldn't get home in time. Grabbing her purse she started for the door, then remembered Derek. She went back to her telephone and buzzed his office. This time, something told her, she couldn't handle Scott alone.

Valerie hung up and went back into the living room. Scott sat on the couch, and she stayed carefully on the other side of the room.

"She's coming," Valerie reported.

Scott nodded.

"Do you want anything? A drink of water or something?" Valerie sat down on the arm of the chair. She spoke softly, afraid that even her voice might upset him again.

He shook his head. "You don't have to hang around here," he said without looking at her.

"That's okay. I told your mother I'd stay until she got home."

Scotty grimaced. "You must think I'm some sort of fruitcake," and he chanced a glance across the room.

She shrugged. "I don't know. I mean, I don't know why that name on the tombstone upset you. Was it because of your father or something?" She was curious, yet still afraid of Scotty, of the violence of his reaction. On Steepletop she had only wanted to run away, but she had known she couldn't leave him.

"I don't want to talk about it."

"Sorry," she whispered and took a deep breath. If he got out of his chair, she told herself, she would just run, get out the back door and run up to the castle. Karen was still working; she would take care of her.

"I didn't mean to yell at you," he said next, as an apology. He shifted positions on the couch and began to relax. Valerie could see he was no longer trembling.

"That's okay."

"I'm always yelling at people," he admitted, "and I guess I usually don't mean it. I just seem to be angry a lot of the time."

"You got angry up on Steepletop?" she asked, surprised.

"I got scared. I just freaked out when I saw that tombstone."

She kept herself from asking why. That was the trouble with her. She never knew when to keep quiet.

"Remember that story I told you? About the girl found dead down by the river? Well, her name was Carmel Burke. The same name on the tombstone up on the hill."

"Scott, that doesn't mean she was killed by hobgoblins." Valerie was no longer afraid of him. He was just wrong. He was only inventing monsters, making up stories to frighten himself. "Scott, everyone knows there's no such thing as hobgoblins. I mean, they're just fairy tales! Little kids believe in them, the way they believe in Santa Claus and the tooth fairy."

"Yeah, I guess you're right."

"What do you mean, you *guess?* I mean, have you ever seen a monster? A leprechaun, even?" She couldn't believe that he believed in the bogeyman. At school he was the smartest student in all their classes.

"Look who's talking," he said. "You won't even look at Ballycastle."

"That's different."

"Only to you."

"The castle looks evil," she said, defending herself. "People always told ghost stories about it when I was growing up. And when Fergus was alive he was always acting weird."

"Like how? Did you ever see him?"

"No, silly. He died a long time ago. My aunt saw him once though, when she was really little. Before my mother wa born."

"Did she tell you about it?"

"Yes, but she doesn't remember much. My grandfather use to deliver hay for the horses and she'd come with him some times." Valerie kept talking, seeing how her story was pulling Scott out of his depression. "She had wandered off and wa walking through the woods, out by the arboretum, when she saw him."

"What was he doing?"

"He had his little hammer, this little gold hammer, and he was going around marking trees that seemed diseased. Some-body would come along later and chop them down. That way he kept track of every single tree planted on the lawns. He saw to each one himself."

"Well, did he say anything? Did he see her?"

"He asked her name. She was afraid he was going to get mad at Granddaddy because she was off alone, but he was very nice. He was wearing a white suit and a tie. He looked pretty, you know, like he was at a garden party."

"Did he say anything else?"

It wasn't until then that Valerie remembered what the man had said to Aunt Theresa that summer afternoon years before. He had been bending over, inspecting a patch of discolored bark, but when he saw her he straightened up and smiled. He was wearing a wide-brimmed straw hat and he took it off, then bowed gently, smiling. He was younger than Theresa's father, and his body was straight and strong. His eyes were a very bright blue that sparkled like the sea in the sun.

"What did he say?" Scott pressed quickly, seeing the re-action on her face.

"Oh, nothing. I can't remember."

"Yes, you can." He got up and came toward her.

"He said that she should watch out for hobgoblins."

"See! I told you. I told you," Scott shouted, pointing his finger at her.

"It just doesn't mean anything. Jeez, it's just something any adult would tell a little kid." Now she was out of her chair and after him as he kept backing away, circling around the furniture.

"I told you!" Scott was laughing as he dodged Valerie. She was trying to slap him, swinging wildly.

"Stop it!" she shouted back, and now she was laughing because it felt good to be hitting him, getting even.

"Watch out for the hobgoblins," Scott shouted at her. They had circled the small room once, Scott darting between the furniture, then doubling back to keep out of Valerie's long reach.

She was breathing hard from the pursuit and she could feel her arms growing weary from her ineffective assault when he caught his foot on the rug and tumbled over the sofa's arm, falling in the middle of the room.

Valerie dove for him, landed across his body and quickly straddled him, pinning his arms.

"Get off me."

"No." She was leaning down, grinning, her long black hair falling in his face.

"Valerie, come on, goddamnit!" He twisted his head. "Get your hair out of my eyes." He was laughing, giggling under the touch of her fingers. "Please get off me," he begged.

"Not until you stop making fun of me," she demanded.

"I'll stop! I'll stop!" Then he gathered his strength and rolled to one side, spilling her onto the floor beneath him.

"What in the world is this?" Barbara Gardiner stood looking down at the two of them. She had run into the house through the kitchen to find them sprawled out on the living room rug.

"Oh, hi, Mom." Scott rolled away from Valerie and sat up.

"Scotty? Valerie?" Barbara leaned over the back of the sofa. "What's going on here? Valerie, you said Scott wasn't feeling well."

"I wasn't before, Mom, but I'm okay now." Scott got up off the floor. "It isn't Valerie's fault. I asked her to call you—I mean, I wasn't really feeling good, but . . ."

"Scott, you're not making much sense." She spotted the fresh gauze bandages on his arm. "What happened to you?"

"Oh, nothing. I just . . ."

"I was showing Scott what we did in first aid today, Mrs. Gardiner. We were just practicing wrapping a bandage, that's all." Valerie, too, was on her feet, tucking in her blouse.

Barbara kept glancing back and forth between the two. They

weren't telling the truth, but she did not press them. Through
the front bay window she saw Derek's car wheel into the drive.

"I better go home," Valerie said quickly, seizing the moment
of silence in the room. She moved around behind the chairs
as if ready to make a quick escape.

"Valerie, please. If you could just wait a minute, I'll drive
you." Barbara smiled to show there was nothing to worry about.
"Now, both of you, please sit down." She gestured toward the
chairs and waited while the two of them slid slowly onto the
cushions.

Derek came through the front door without knocking and
walked over to Barbara. "Is everything all right?" he asked
softly.

"Well, I think so, but I'm not sure. Sit down, Derek, and
let's find out." She moved around the sofa and sat down opposite Scott and Valerie. "Okay, what happened?" She kept
smiling, trying to sound cheerful, positive, as if the two did
not have anything to worry about.

"It's my fault," Scott admitted at once. "I sort of freaked
out earlier and got Valerie all scared and everything." He was
staring at the rug, afraid to look at his mother.

"Freaked out how, Scotty?" Barbara asked.

"Oh, we went up to that cemetery on the top of the hill."

"Steepletop," Valerie added.

"And there's these tombstones, see. All these weird-looking
tombstones shaped like gargoyles or something, and one of
them was marked 'Carmel Burke 1912–1931.'" He glanced
at his mother.

She saw then the fear in his eyes. A moment before he had
been laughing, carried away with excitement in a way she had
not seen since before Warren died. Yet still he carried this
unexplained terror inside, locked away like some secret.

"Yes, I've seen those tombstones, Scott." Derek spoke up.
"They are strange, and now that you mention it, they do look
like gargoyles." He was leaning forward in his chair, his arms
braced against his knees. Scott hated having Derek agree with
him.

"It wasn't the tombstones," he said scornfully.

"Then what was it?" Barbara asked quietly, sensing his
hostility.

"It was *her*," he burst out. "You said Carmel Burke didn't exist, that Conor had only made her up." His voice flared up as he accused his mother.

He had so little control of his emotions, Barbara realized. The slightest provocation set him off.

"The name isn't important, Scott," she replied calmly, trying with the softness of her voice to ease his tension. "I'm sure Conor just used it for the purposes of his story. What matters is that he said she was killed by Nuckelavees and you know they don't exist, don't you?" She had to hear her son agree with her, to reassure her that he could still separate reality from his fantasy world.

Scott nodded reluctantly.

"Then why were you so upset?" Barbara pressed.

"Oh, God, I don't know. Seeing it, I guess." He stood up and began to pace.

"Please, Scotty, can't you sit still for a moment?" Barbara blurted out. She could feel her nerves begin to fray. This was foolish, fighting with Scott in front of strangers.

Across the room, Scott dropped into a straight back chair.

"You're not upset now at finding this tombstone, are you?" Derek asked. He, too, spoke softly, like a guidance counselor.

Scott looked away, not responding to Derek.

"Scott, you were asked a question," Barbara said, seeing her son's reaction. He was getting into one of his sullen states, she realized, and it made her furious. She couldn't stand it when he began to sulk.

"No, I'm not upset," Scott mumbled.

"Scott, no one can understand you," Valerie said.

Barbara glanced at the girl, surprised by her remark, and pleased, too, that she was reacting to Scott's surliness.

Slowly, hesitantly, Scott pulled his hands away from his mouth and sitting up, said again, "No, I'm not upset."

"There's nothing malicious about old Conor, Scott," Derek continued, earnestly, "he's just a story teller. And I'm sure that, since he knew you played *Hobgoblin,* he just figured he would work these Nuckelavees into his story."

"Well, everything's all right now," Barbara interjected, trying to end the discussion. "I think we should just drop the whole thing. Derek, would you mind driving Valerie home?

I'm afraid we've kept this poor girl here past her dinner time. Valerie, would you like me to telephone your mother?"

"No, that's okay. Mom knows I sometimes stop by here to see Karen. And you don't have to drive me home, Mr. Brennan. I can just cut through the woods."

"Oh, no, Valerie. It's on my way home." Derek turned to Barbara. "Everything all right?" he asked softly.

She nodded.

"I can drive back later, if you like."

She shook her head.

"I'll call you this evening, then." He could see the tension in her small face, see how her jaw was already set against the pending encounter with Scott.

Barbara nodded, only half-aware of his offer. Already she was debating with herself how to handle her son, whether to chastise him for his behavior or to console. Obviously, he had had another brief psychotic episode. Mr. Frisch had warned her to expect them, while at the same time saying that Scott would eventually grow out of his illness as he became an adult and left his fantasy behind.

Barbara walked Valerie and Derek to the car.

"Thank you for being Scott's friend," she whispered to Valerie.

"Oh, that's okay. I was having a good time and everything until we got up on Steepletop. I'm sorry. I mean, I didn't know it would get him all upset."

"That's all right, Valerie. It's not your fault, and Scott is fine." She hugged the girl, trying to reassure her. "He needs a good friend. He needs someone like you."

Ten

Conor Fitzpatrick had had a bad night. Twice he had gotten up in the dark of his small room to make a pot of tea, to sit at the kitchen table and worry about the files Barbara Gardiner had asked for. There was no reason why she should want to know about those years, about Maeve and Peggy Connolly and all the others. It had been a mistake to say anything to the boy, even to have mentioned Carmel Burke.

His hand trembled, lifting the cup of tea. Well, he'd put a stop to it. He'd get rid of those papers. It had been a mistake to keep anything at all. Himself had warned him as well, telling him in those last days to take the files from the office, to remove everything about the girls. "Let me vanish in peace," he had said, speaking in Gaelic as he had so often once his mind was not what it had been. "They'll only pry into our lives once I am gone."

Conor went to the wooden locker in the corner, the one he had brought with him from Ireland. It had been his only piece of luggage, hammered together by his father out behind their cottage in Clooncoorha, and over the years he had filled it with the secrets of Ballycastle. Lifting the lid, he looked down once more at the weapons used, the passports and working papers, the meager items he had stripped from their rooms. He spotted a corner of yellow cotton, and reached to the bottom to retrieve the blouse. Nuala O'Neill, he thought. He still could remember folding away her clothes. And when was that now? He paused, remembering—1940?

He replaced the blouse and picked up a rosary. It was made of olive wood, and was from Rome, he knew; a cousin of Peggy Connolly's had mailed it to her. Pope Pius XI had blessed it, Peggy had claimed. God rest her soul, he thought, kneeling beside the locker. He moved several more items. A shoe box of old letters belonging to Monica Healion. Her fella had mailed them to her from Dublin. Conor glanced at the date on one— 1933. Aah, that was right. She had been with them only that one summer. A lovely lass, he remembered. Himself had been especially fond of her.

In one corner of the locker, stacked separately and neatly, were his memories of Carmel. Again, as he had often done over the years, he took out these few possessions, among them the pearl-handled mirror and brush he had given her that first Christmas at Ballycastle.

"Oh, Conor," she had whispered, unwrapping the silver tissue, "they're lovely." She raised the glass to her face, turning it slightly so he could see her reflection in the oval shape. They were sitting before the fireplace and the yellow flame glowed in her eyes, licked its reflection across the mirror. Her image glowed.

Then she had unfastened the clasp, letting her hair fall in a waterfall of locks. He had never seen her with her hair loose before and it left a lump in his throat. She glanced coyly at him as she brushed and he could still hear the sound of the brush sweeping through her hair, still see her tilted head, the smooth, soft flesh of her neck exposed.

He had kept only one garment, a blue dress she had worn on their last night. They were to have gone to the movies, and she had dressed for the evening. Conor remembered how she had come down from the house in the late summer afternoon, the sun catching hold of her dress. She had taken her shoes off and was running to him, her feet sailing over the smooth lawns. She was so happy, so young, he remembered, and he was crying by the time she reached him.

"What is it, Conor, my love?" she asked in Gaelic, bewildered by his tears. He held her tightly to him, weeping on her shoulder. How could he have explained to his darling what Fergus O'Cuileannain wanted him to do?

"Good morning!" Derek knocked lightly on the door of Barbara's office. He had not yet been to his own office and he was still carrying his Burberry trench coat and his attaché case. "How's everything on the home front?" he asked cheerfully.

He had a little boy's smile, appealing and shy, as if he had been up to no good. She had to suppress the desire to cross the room and hug him.

"Everything's fine. I sent him off to school. Actually, he was in a good mood this morning. As you have probably gathered, his emotional equilibrium is on a rollercoaster."

"He was just frightened."

Barbara shook her head. "I wish it was that simple." She was holding a pen in her hands and she twisted it rapidly. "He hasn't really been normal—whatever 'normal' is for a teenage boy!—since Warren's death."

"Was he very attached to his father?"

"Not that I was aware of, but I've learned since then that Scott really idolized Warren in a certain way. Between football and Vietnam, Warren seemed like a hero to Scott, and the therapist, Dr. Frisch, even thinks that all this *Hobgoblin* stuff might have been one way for Scott to try to measure up to his image of his father. Anyway, I've called Dr. Frisch in Connecticut to see if he can recommend someone up here for Scotty to see. This is going on too long, his inability to separate reality from his fantasy world."

Derek came into the office and set his attaché case on her desk.

"Is there anything I can do to help you?"

"Well, yes, I would ask one favor, if you have the time." She paused, as if deciding whether to trouble him. "Could you take me up to Steepletop? I'd like to see this grave site."

"How about having lunch on the cliff? It's a lovely day."

"I don't know if I could make the time today. I'd have to go home first and fix some sandwiches. And all I have is white bread, which is the only kind Scott will eat. And besides, I've got to do some serious work if I'm going to have a preliminary report ready for the board meeting. . . ."

"Stop!" he said, laughing. "Don't worry—this is my invitation. I'll handle it all. I'm going into Flat Rock for a meeting at ten and I'll stop by the delicatessen and pick up some food. On whole wheat or pumpernickel. Now, what do you want to drink?"

"A Tab."

"Why? Don't tell me you're dieting?"

"Always."

"But you have a wonderful figure." She blushed, but he was smiling, flirting with his eyes. Whenever he focused them on her, his eyes brightened, flashed as if with some secret amusement.

Barbara nodded. "Thank you. But you haven't really had access to all the necessary information."

"Well, no." And now he blushed.

She laughed. "See you at twelve," she said, dismissing him, getting down to work again. It was only when he was gone from her office that she allowed herself the luxury of daydreaming about him, of imagining him beside her, touching her body, moving his palm over her breasts and down to her navel. She could almost feel the lightness of his fingers against her bare skin and she shivered at the thought. Then she forced her mind back to the far less appealing prospect of searching Ballycastle for Fergus's missing files.

It was called Times Square, the intersection of the two main corridors of Flat Rock High School. Nick Borgus and Hank Simpson stood there, as they did every morning before the bell, leaning up against the metal lockers, waiting to grab a little ass. The four corners were controlled by football players, but it was Borgus who dominated Times Square, and the girls feared him the most. Borgus did more than just pat their bottoms when they had to pass through in the rush to first period.

This morning, however, Borgus let the girls go by as he watched for Gardiner. It had been several days since he had last seen the preppie, and Nick wondered if he had quit school because of what had happened at football practice. That disturbed him. Harassing the new preppie was fun. School was boring and having Gardiner around created a diversion, gave him something to do.

Then he spotted Scott, down the length of the hall, head and shoulders taller than most of the other students.

"There's our boy," Nick informed Simpson, nodding to the right.

"And look at who the fuck's with him," Simpson added.

Nick stretched to see, hooking his heels over the concrete base of the locker which gave him several inches of lift. Holding on to the locker handle to keep his balance, he could see that Scott was walking with Valerie, that he was listening attentively to what she was saying.

"Yeah, you're right," Nick answered. "She wasn't on the bus this morning, remember? She's got the preppie picking her up in his MGB. What a shit." The idea of Valerie Dunn being picked up in a sportscar, of being free of the bus, enraged him more. "That cunt," he added. "She'd hang around with a squirrel like him just because he can ride her ass to school."

"You think she's laying him?"

"He wouldn't know how even if she unzipped his pants. Come on, let's get the fucker."

Valerie saw them. She had suspected they'd do something once they saw her come into school with Scott. In fact, when he'd telephoned that morning to offer her the ride, she'd almost said no. She didn't want them giving Scott more trouble just because of her, but the thought of being alone with him, of riding in his car, close beside him, had made her say yes. She could protect Scott, she told herself. She could handle Nick Borgus all by herself.

"Scott, come in here," she said, and pushed him toward an open classroom door.

"Val," he protested, "I've got to go to my locker first."

"I only need a minute. This is the journalism classroom. I want you to meet someone if she's here."

"Why?" Extricating himself from the student traffic, he let himself be led into the room.

"Because I think the paper should do a story about *Hobgoblin,* and you can write it for them."

She had dreamed it up as an excuse, but as she thought

about it, it was really a terrific idea. If Scott wrote about the game, kids would understand it better and get to know him, too.

"I don't want to write about *Hobgoblin*. Nobody here cares."

"Well, maybe they would if they knew about it. Besides, what's the big deal? You can do the whole thing during sixth period."

"Sixth period? You mean study hall?"

"Yeah. You're supposed to do homework, but if you belong to a club or have a hobby or something, you can work on that instead." The journalism room was furnished with long, narrow worktables and Valerie hopped up on the nearest one, so she was looking directly into Scott's eyes.

"Come on," she urged. "It'll be fun. Jackie Schlenger, the editor of the paper, is a friend of mine. I'll ask her to run your picture with the story, too. Everyone will know who you are then. You'll be the most famous person at Flat Rock," she teased.

"I don't want to be famous. I don't even want anybody to know me."

"Come on, Scott! If you start that again, even I won't talk to you." She was angry with him now, and showed it.

"I'm too busy to write something," he hedged. "I've missed two days of school, don't forget."

"Oh, give me a break," she said impatiently. "You could miss a whole week around this place and still be smarter than everyone else. And you know it."

"Yeah, well, tell me something—why are you so mad all of a sudden? What did I do?"

"Nothing—but everyone treats you like you're about to break apart or something. Your own mother is afraid to disagree with you, much less yell at you."

"So?"

"Well, it's boring. And besides," she said, smiling again at last, "I know you're not all that fragile. You won our wrestling match yesterday, didn't you?"

Scott grinned. "Because you let me." When she smiled at him he couldn't help grinning back. She made him feel good. "Maybe I'll fall apart unexpectedly," he went on, then made a big act of crumpling onto the bench opposite her.

She giggled at his routine, thinking, he was all right, and she felt immensely better.

"All right, let's start working on the article." She glanced at the clock over the door. It was fifteen minutes before first period. They could wait until the first bell, and still have time to get to their lockers. And by then Times Square would be empty. "I'll help you write it." She already had paper and a pen out.

"Okay, pretend I'm Barbara Walters. Why do you play this game, Mr. Gardiner?"

Scott shrugged. "I don't know. Because it's fun."

"Why is it so much fun? I mean, is it the joy of winning? If I played with you, would you try to beat me?"

Scott shook his head. "No, we'd probably be on the same side, unless you were a terrible character. Brian Ború doesn't associate with thieves or dishonest people."

"Brian Ború? Who's he?" She wrote the name in her notebook.

"Brian Ború is my character. I created him two years ago at Spencertown. We used to play every day at Spencertown, after classes, then for an hour before Lights Out. And no one could touch Brian. He was a twenty-fifth-level knight.

"Once, you know, when I was running a game, Brian was given a secret challenge by the Dealer—he's the person who directs the Adventure. Mr. Speier was our Dealer at Spencertown. Brian Ború was given this secret challenge to rescue the daughter of the king of Erin—you see, the game is played in this mystical land that is based on Ireland but a long time ago. Anyway, Brian Ború, who then had earned only enough points to be a sixth-level, got dealt this challenge card and he had to go rescue the king's daughter. She was being held by . . ."

"Wait, Scott, wait." Valerie was shaking her head. "I don't understand what you're talking about. Stop it. It doesn't make any sense. Okay," she said, beginning again. "How many players are there on each side? Is it like baseball—nine to each team? Do you do it that way, choose up sides?"

Scott sat back, shaking his head. It was no use. She didn't understand him. None of them would. He felt as alone as he had during the first days at Flat Rock. As if he were Brian Ború, lost in an alien land.

"Come on, Scott, don't get like that," Valerie demanded.

"Like what?"

"Like I was some kind of idiot."

"I never said you . . ."

"I can see the look on your face. Well, never mind, forge I was trying to do you a favor."

"Favor? What kind of favor is it, making me do this stupid article."

"You call it stupid, letting everyone here know how good you were at *Hobgoblin?*"

"I wasn't good. It was Brian Ború. Look, you don't un derstand the first thing about what I'm talking about." He opened his book bag and took out his *Hobgoblin* manuals.

"That's because you don't want me or anyone else to un derstand. You think it's really cool that you're this hotshot *Hobgoblin* player and we're all country bumpkins." She watched him begin to leaf through the guidebooks.

"Didn't I ask you to play *Hobgoblin* yesterday?"

"Yeah, but you didn't mean it. If I had really wanted to play, you would have made it impossible."

"Valerie, you know something? You're full of shit!"

He picked up his book bag, preparing to depart. "I said I didn't want any article in the school's crummy newspaper."

"Everything, everyone is crummy but you. You know, you use that word in every other sentence. Crummy. I'm crummy. Flat Rock is crummy. Well, you're crummy, too."

He gave her the finger and she gave it back to him, glaring.

"Hey, that-a-way, Dunn."

Both of them flinched. They had not seen Borgus and Simp son standing in the doorway.

"This isn't a lover's quarrel, is it?" Borgus went on, coming into the room. He was grinning, and with a blue wool cap pulled down over his forehead he looked, Scott thought, like a small Billikan.

"It's none of your business, Nick," Valerie answered. She began to put away her notebook.

"What's this?" Borgus said, intrigued. He had sauntered up to the table to look at the *Hobgoblin* books lying there.

"They're mine," Scott said, reaching for them.

Nick slid the two guidebooks away from Scott, ignoring him. "Hey, look at this shit, Hank."

"Nick, give back the books or I'm going to call Mr. Farley. He's right out there, on hall duty."

"Go screw yourself, will you, Dunn? Scott, you don't mind me looking at your books, do you?" He looked up, grinning.

"I have to go to my locker. The bell is going to ring." Scott made another gesture at getting back the books, but Hank raised his arm, fending him off.

"Hey, Hank, catch all this weird stuff. Look at this dude. What's a Jilly Do, or however you say it?"

"A *Ghillie Dhu*. It's a harmless spirit, but wild. It dresses in leaves and green moss."

"This is kid's stuff! All these fairy-looking characters," Simpson said. He was leaning over Borgus's shoulder, looking down at the picture books. "This is a book for queers, Nick. You see all these fairies?"

"Is that true, Gardiner? Do you have to be queer to play this game?" He looked at Scott and waited for an answer.

He was really looking for trouble. Valerie sensed it.

"You don't have to be queer, Borgus, just smart. Which lets you out." She reached for the manual, tried to snatch it from his hands.

"Goddamnit, Dunn. Get the fuck out of here. I'm not talking to you." He came half out of the seat, reached over and tried to swat her away.

"I'm going to get Mr. Farley." Valerie picked up her books and went around Scott, keeping away from the two football players.

Simpson stopped her at the doorway, blocking the exit with his body.

"Hank, I'm going to kick you in the balls if you don't get out of my way." She shifted the books in her arms.

"Hey, Dunn, cool it. We're just asking about his game," Nick said reasonably. "Look, I'm interested." He was grinning. "Hank, let her go. Get Farley, we don't give a shit." He turned back to Scott, saying in a friendly tone, "Sit down, will ya. Look, what's all this stuff, anyway? You know, I'm curious."

Scott dropped onto the bench across from Borgus. It was

better this way, he reasoned. Talk to him. Humor him. It was only ten more minutes to the first bell.

"Who's this?" Nick asked, pointing to another full page *Hobgoblin* illustration.

"That's an Afane. They're water demons who live in the River Conway and drag humans into their den. They turn up a lot in *Hobgoblin* games. Their chief weapon is treachery, and their special defense is that they're amphibians." Scott kept talking, detailing the qualities of the Afane. It gave him a sense of power, realizing the football players were baffled by the game.

"And what's this?" Nick flipped the page.

"A Black Annis. She kills mostly lambs and small children and lives in a cave near Groagh Patrick. A Black Annis has unusual magical powers. I mean, she can change herself into a tree or a rock, and disappear into the woods."

"Hey, Nick, this doesn't make any fuckin' sense."

"Shut up, Simpson, and listen to the man. This game isn't no fuckin' *Monopoly*. Right, Gardiner?"

Scott nodded, reluctantly.

"Okay, how do you play it?" he asked, as if suddenly eager to learn.

"Well, it's complicated."

"You think Hank and me can't learn?" An edge of anger slid into his voice. "Okay, we're not preppies, and this is a big preppie game, but try us." It was an order, not a request.

Scott shrugged. He didn't care if Borgus taunted him. He would be indifferent, bored with both of them.

"This is a game where you construct your own characters. These characters are all fantasy. It's like having a Monopoly piece on the board, but the piece has a personality of its own, different from yours, and you have to play by *that* personality. I mean, the character could be just like you, but that's not as much fun as making up a new person, and besides, they tell you it's not a good idea to make your character yourself."

"Why?"

"Well, because in *Hobgoblin* mostly everyone gets killed. It can be weird, you know, seeing yourself get killed.

"Anyway, you create a character. He could be a warrior of some kind, or a dwarf, a magician, or maybe a druid. My character is a paladin."

"A what?"

"A paladin. A knight, Brian Ború. He's a legendary king of Ireland, which is where *Hobgoblin* takes place. It's all based on Irish mythology."

"This is stupid," Hank commented, standing. "Come on, Nick, let's go."

"Shut up, Hank. Go on, Gardiner, what else?" He kept listening, closely. This was all stuff he could use against the preppie.

"Well, there's a Dealer. He runs the game. He controls the *Hobgoblin* deck of cards and uses them to create the Battle-board, and the Adventure that the players take."

"Who do we play against?"

"Monsters, usually. Giants or even, for example, Sheens. They're cave-haunting spirits. You can't see them or anything, but if you're on an Adventure and you take refuge in a cave where Sheens live, well, they can kill you."

"How do you know they're in the caves? How do you protect yourself?"

Scott shook his head. "Lots of times you can't." He took the *Hobgoblin* guide from Borgus and flipped through the stiff pages until he found the drawings of the Sheens. "See, they show them as mist. In the Slieve Gamph mountains where they live, you wouldn't know whether you were surrounded by the morning mist or Sheens—until they killed you. The Sheens seep into your ears and up your nostrils, and down your throat when you inhale. Once inside they eat your heart out, you know, like ants."

"Oh, fuck!" Simpson slapped Borgus across the shoulder. "No wonder he can't play football."

Borgus swung back at Simpson. "Goddamn you, shut your fuckin' mouth."

Scott jumped at the violence. Borgus and Simpson were as short-tempered with each other as they were with him. But instead of consoling him, that knowledge only made him feel more in danger.

"What else?" Borgus asked, the tone of his voice pushy, demanding.

"It just gets more complicated. I mean, you'd have to play the game, or watch someone play, to really understand how it works. Just to start with, I'd have to throw dice for each of

117

your characters to see how strong they are and what their charisma is.

"Then I'd have to make a Battleboard. That's where the Adventure would take place. Maybe I'd have to go look for gold, or rescue someone from, say, a Jenny Greenteeth. She's a water fairy. You know where she is by the green scum on the water."

"I want to play," Nick demanded. He reached across the table and grabbed the books back from Scott as the first bell rang.

"My books," Scott said, almost apologetically.

"It's cool. I want to read 'em," Nick answered, smiling. "Hey, man, don't worry," he continued, standing up and tucking the two *Hobgoblin* manuals under his arm. "I want to play. I want you to teach me." He kept grinning as he walked with Simpson to the classroom door.

He wouldn't return them, Scott knew. And he wouldn't be able to buy new ones, either—not up here where nobody had even heard of the game. He wanted to rush the senior, rip the manuals from his stubby little arms, but he couldn't make himself move. He was afraid of Borgus, afraid of getting hurt, and that made him feel shitty and unworthy of Brian Ború, unworthy of his ancient paladin.

Derek used the firebreak road to reach the cemetery, racing one of the Foundation jeeps up the steep incline. Barbara clung to the dashboard with one hand and held on to her seat with the other. When they hit a big bump she yelped with pleasure, as thrilled by the rough ride as a schoolgirl.

"God! That was wonderful!" she exclaimed as the jeep bounced to a stop at the crest of the hill. Breathless and flushed from the ride, she stood in the open cab and scanned the horizon. "Why, you can almost see forever," she remarked, and jumped down to survey Steepletop.

"It's lovely, isn't it?" Derek said, calling after her. "Fergus took the best site at Ballycastle for his graveyard. Some sense of values, right?"

"Oh, I don't know. It brings the deceased closer to heaven, doesn't it? I can understand why Valerie is so fond of this spot."

Barbara stepped to the edge of the cliff and stood quietly

for a moment, taking in the vast view. Below was a section of the property that she could not see from the mansion, and it reminded her again of the wealth of Ballycastle.

"What's that?" she asked, pointing off to the far corner of the hilly terrain.

"Where?" Derek picked up the picnic lunch and came to stand beside her.

"There!" she pointed. "That house. I don't remember ever seeing it on the landscape map." She turned to Derek, frowning, afraid she had made a mistake in her work.

"Oh, that." Derek set the picnic basket down and began to spread a blanket on the grass. "It's nothing," he said.

"It looks like some sort of log cabin. Derek, I can't remember any mention of a log cabin on the property." Barbara had raised her hands to screen out the bright sun and she squinted into the distance, trying to decipher the structure.

"That's what it is, a log cabin." Derek stretched out on the blanket and began unpacking sandwiches. "Fergus had several on the property. He used them as hunting lodges, I guess. The others have been torn down because of disrepair, and that one is next. We'll get around to wrecking it next year.

"Now, how about a sandwich? Let's eat," he suggested, sounding eager. "I'm starving."

"Wait." Barbara turned away from the view. "I want to look around for a minute." She stepped through the open iron gate and went inside the graveyard, walking from one tombstone to the next. "They are unbelievable, aren't they?" Barbara laughed, shocked by the grotesque shapes of the headstones. She moved from grave to grave, silently reading the out-thrust scrolls and searching for Carmel Burke's headstone.

The graveyard was small and in the second row she spotted it:

Carmel Burke
1912–1931
Adieu ma cuisette folâtre

Strange, Barbara thought, carving an obscure French epitaph on an Irish housemaid's grave. She glanced at the other headstones. They, too, bore similar lines:

Adieu, ma gorgette
Adieu, mon sein
Adieu, mon oeil
Adieu, mon coeur
Adieu, ma délicate main

And so on, down the line of headstones.

Barbara's French was rusty, but a few of the words came instantly to mind: *ma main,* my hand; *mon oeil,* my eye; *mon coeur,* my heart. It struck her then. When Fergus's people died, he bade them goodby, not as servants, or even as family members, but as parts of his own body.

"Farewell, my delicate hand. Farewell, my eye. Farewell, my heart."

She couldn't recall the meaning of "gorgette," "sein," or the others, but she imagined they would fit the pattern. How creepy, she thought—and how like Fergus. What he owned he owned totally.

Barbara took out a small pad and pencil and jotted down the names and dates on each headstone. Maeve Donnellan's was the last, and Barbara noticed that this particular maid had not been honored with an epitaph.

"Fergus must've run out of good parts," she thought wryly. "At least he had the good taste not to say, 'Adieu, my elbow.'"

She circled around then to the front of the cemetery, to the only monument in the small graveyard—a giant bronze angel of death hovering over a raised slab of Connemara marble. She stepped closer to read the name on the stone.

Fergus O'Cuileannain
1900–1945

There was no French or English epitaph beneath the lettering. No words of mourning. She backed away, suddenly uncomfortable. The gargoyles, the epitaphs, the strange black figure of the angel—the whole graveyard, she realized, made her nervous.

"Fergus was a young man when he died," she commented, quickly stepping through the gate and joining Derek on the picnic blanket. "What happened to him?"

"An accident on the steeplechase field," Derek said. "It was right after the war and he had just begun having house parties again. He was killed the first grand weekend after V-J Day— thrown by his favorite jumper, Nightfall, and dragged clear across the steeplechase."

"Oh, God, how ghastly."

"I guess it was even worse than that. The body was all mangled and mutilated and he was buried at once, in a private service. He had no living relatives, or so they thought at first."

"What do you mean?" Barbara settled down with her back to the cemetery.

"Well, his will established the Foundation, worth thirty million in trust, to do good works here in America. When they read the will—"

"How did he make all that money, anyway?" she interrupted.

"Lots of ways. Like many poor boys, he started young and took a lot of risks. In his teens he went out to South Africa to look for gold and ended up smuggling diamonds instead. After the First World War he came back to Europe and put the money he'd made into buying and selling scrap metal. He even had oil wells in the Middle East before Mobil."

"And he died without any heirs?"

"So it seemed, but before the Foundation could be put into operation, some distant cousins from Galway hired an American lawyer and tied up everything in Irish and American courts. That's why it has taken so long to establish the Foundation.

"I was only hired myself shortly before I interviewed you last spring. In the interim Conor lived alone at Ballycastle, except for people hired by the estate from time to time for repairs and upkeep. You should have seen the place when we took over. Wild dogs living in your house, bats hanging from the ceiling of my office, junk and garbage everywhere. Conor isn't much of a caretaker, but he is, of course, our sole link with Fergus and Ballycastle as it was then."

"And as we well know, Conor can be maddeningly oblique on the subject."

Derek glanced across at Barbara, registering the frustration in her voice.

"I know," he said understandingly. "But you're really making it harder for yourself. You can write your report so that the history of the castle is general rather than detailed. That would be fine with the board of directors. What they really want to know about is the art and furnishings—what's there and what it's worth. Don't forget, that's the bottom line."

Barbara nodded, as if agreeing. But then she said, "I'd feel cheated if I didn't make one last effort to locate all the missing files. After all, that's how you recreate history—by piecing it together, bit by bit. I want to know what it was like to be an indentured servant here in the thirties. I want to get to know Fergus." She took a gulp of her diet soda. "That's the real fun of this job—finding out what Fergus was all about."

That afternoon Barbara found Carmel Burke. Recharged with energy, she returned from lunch ready to tackle the task of cataloguing several storage rooms of furniture. It was there, in the cellars of Ballycastle, that she found them—a set of black payroll ledgers, stashed away in an old cabinet. As she turned the thick, stiff pages, she spotted Carmel's name almost immediately, between Bernadette Comerford and Ray Mc-Manus, the name entered in the vertical, almost backward-slanting script of a European.

Barbara sat down on the nearest old armchair and slowly turned the pages of the ledger, picking out Carmel's name in each month's listing from the year 1930 through the summer of '31. In September 1931 Carmel disappeared from the list.

Barbara closed the book. It was a beginning, she realized. The personnel files were still missing, but Conor was searching for them, and now she had what looked like a meticulous listing of all of Fergus's employees for the period in question. Collecting all the remaining ledgers from the cabinet, she carried them excitedly upstairs, as if she had discovered buried treasure.

"Have you checked to see if the others are listed?" Derek asked.

"You mean the others from the graveyard?"

"Yes. I wonder how long each of them worked for Fergus." He set the ledgers down on the conference table and rolled up his shirtsleeves. Pulling over a pad, he said, "Okay, let's go over your list. Start with Maeve Donnellan."

Obediently Barbara produced the list she'd compiled on Steepletop and consulted it. She was glad that Derek now seemed much more interested. "Maeve Donnellan... let's see.... Here it is. She died in 1939."

Using the dates of death to establish which ledger they should consult, they were finished in less than fifteen minutes. Then Derek listed the information on a large white poster pad and they both stood back, away from the standing pad, and studied the findings.

"All women," Barbara said at once.

Names	Length of Employ-ment	Date of Death	Age
Peggy Connolly	eight months	1934	18
Maeve Donnellan	six months	1939	19
Nuala O'Neill	seven months	1940	19
Carmel Burke	eleven months	1931	19
Anne Kilferick	four months	1937	20
Eileen Manning	three months	1936	18
Peggy Condon	twelve months	1935	16
Maura Ward	fourteen months	1938	19
Maureen Leahy	two months	1932	17
Monica Healion	five months	1933	16

"And all but one of them worked here less than one year." He indicated the length of employment. "Every year from 1931 to '40."

"This doesn't make much sense. How could so many young girls die like that?"

"It might have been tuberculosis. TB was still fairly common at the time, and these girls were straight from the bogs of western Ireland."

"I can't believe it. Ten young girls dying one after another within one decade. It isn't natural. What did they make of it in Flat Rock? There must have been some notoriety."

"Ballycastle was a closed corporation when Fergus was alive. There are plenty of stories of how the local people were kept away from here. Fergus was always afraid for his life, I'm told, so he employed a private army of bodyguards to patrol the place. And during the war years, just before he died, he refused to see anybody."

"What about all those lavish Great Gatsby parties?"

"They were in the '20s and '30s, and his guests certainly weren't from Flat Rock. Fergus chartered special trains to bring people up from New York. But after the war began even those parties ceased."

"Yes, you're right." Barbara nodded. "So no one really knows what life was like at Ballycastle. Except, of course, for Conor."

Eleven

The boys' locker room was jammed with football players when Scott came downstairs after school. Already the team had spontaneously begun to chant, "Kill 'em! Kill 'em! Kill 'em!" as they dressed for the afternoon game. Scott ignored the shouting as he pushed his way along the aisle to reach his locker. He did not want to play ball, especially not on the home field, not with everyone from school in the the stands. Still, he suited up, put on his shoulder pads, pulled on his Flat rock jersey, doing it slowly as the noise reached a crescendo around him. He kept his face to the open locker, avoiding the rest of the team, realizing again how lonely he was at Flat Rock, among all these strangers. It made him feel sick.

"Hey, Gardiner!" Nick Borgus smacked him hard on the shoulder pads with the thick *Hobgoblin* manuals. "Your books," he said, shoving them into Scott's hands. The senior was already dressed and walking off toward the football field.

Scott nodded, but did not say thanks. The two manuals were a surprise. He hadn't expected to see them again, and he handled them carefully, like a prize. Only after Nick had walked by did Scott notice that something was odd about the books. The pages weren't lying right. Flipping one of the manuals open, he saw the reason—all the color illustrations had been torn out.

"Hey!" Scott slammed down the aisle after Borgus, pushing everyone out of his way. "What did you do that for?" he demanded, grabbing the linebacker's jersey.

Borgus swung away, tore himself free. "Hey, man, get your fuckin' hands off me."

"What did you do to my manuals?" Scott shouted, too angry to be afraid.

"Nothing. I didn't do nothing to your books."

"Like hell you didn't. You cut them to pieces. Every color picture has been cut out—and that's more than half of each book."

"Ah, I was just showing them around in study hall so I ripped a few out. I mean, it's no big deal. They're only pictures, for chrissake."

"Only pictures?" Suddenly Scott was quiet, his voice how but fiercely intense. "They're the best thing about the books. You can't buy *Hobgoblin* manuals in this town, Borgus. I'm going to have to wait till we go to New York or Boston. And even when I get them, they're going to be expensive. I just want you to know, Borgus, because you're paying."

"Oh, shit, forget it." Borgus waved at him in disgust and turned away to leave. "It's a silly game, asshole." Scott grabbed him from behind and shoved Nick into the nearest locker. The chanting had stopped and the crowd of students pushed back, expecting a fight.

"How would you like it if I ripped your fuckin' jersey, Borgus?"

"Hey, man, get out of my face." He pushed at Scott.

"It's a silly game. It's a silly game," Scott chanted, using his arm to brace Nick against the lockers. "Hey, Nick, how would you like it if I ripped the numbers off your jersey? Maybe I could show them around the study hall."

"This is my football uniform," Borgus answered, not sure what Scott was getting at.

"Sure, I know, but who cares?" Scott said sarcastically. "I mean, everybody knows that football is a *really* silly game."

Nick shoved him then, bounced Scott off the row of lockers opposite them. "I told you to get your face away from me," he yelled, angry now that he understood. "This is football, Gardiner, not some kids' game full of fairies. You keep away from me, understand?" He was pointing his finger at Scott, ordering him to listen. "If you give me any more shit, I'll cream your ass, do you hear?"

Scott went for him then, lunging toward Borgus, but the senior ducked, then swung his padded shoulder into Scott's middle, hitting him hard. The blow doubled Scott over and he fell across the bench as if he'd been totaled deep in the backfield. A cheer went up from the football players, and again the chant began. "Kill 'em! Kill 'em!" they shouted in unison as they followed Borgus out onto the field.

Scott pulled himself off the floor. He could hear the kids cheering in the stands and he said quietly in the empty locker room, "It's only a game, Borgus. It's only a silly game."

Back in her own office, Barbara buzzed her secretary and asked if she had seen Conor. She hadn't, not all morning or during lunch.

"Call around Ballycastle, will you, and see if you can find him," Barbara said. "I'll be downstairs finishing up the storage inventory. If he turns up, send him down there. Before the day is over I want to pressure him again about those missing files."

Taking her keys to the cellar she left her office and headed for the stairs. In the late afternoon the main floor of the castle was always crowded. Tourists moved through all the rooms, looking and chattering, the sound of their voices bringing the huge building back to life. The afternoons, Barbara had come to realize, were the only times when she felt comfortable in the mansion. The presence of others, even strangers, relaxed her, made her feel secure. The castle needed crowds of people, she thought. It was no wonder Fergus had held so many parties: to keep back the gloom of the endless rooms, the long dark corridors, the sounds of doors being opened and closed somewhere deep in Ballycastle.

Sidestepping one last tourist, Barbara reached the heavy oak door that led below and heaved it open, struggling for a second with the weight. Stepping onto the landing beyond, she let the door swing to and flipped on the fluorescent lights. Then she began her descent.

Of all the castle's rooms the cellars were the most ominous. In their damp, dark caverns she felt the secrets of the castle lying in wait for her. The darkness around her was deep, and the lights overhead did little more than cast her shadow gigantically against the cold white stone walls.

She had not been particularly nervous earlier in the afternoon, before she'd discovered the ledgers. But now, after her brush with Fergus and the mysterious deaths of his house servants, she felt much more uneasy. The cellars were like catacombs in which every sound she made came back to her, magnified one hundredfold.

Still she kept walking, plunging deeper into the depths of the building. The superintendent's furniture was stored under the south wing, at the far end of Ballycastle, and she forced herself to continue. She would not let her imagination make her leave.

When she reached the storage area itself she felt better. The task at hand began to occupy her mind, and she remembered thinking earlier that the light way back here was insufficient. There was no track lighting, only a single naked bulb hanging from the low ceiling, and the furniture had been stacked directly below the light, almost swallowing it up. Her first job, then, was to move the furniture over toward the walls so she could get a look at what she was uncovering. The heavy work was distracting and she kept at it, forcing herself to concentrate, to see what remnants of Fergus she could find in that dark and chilly room.

Scott was the last player to reach the field, where the team was already circled around Tagariello. Scott glanced up and saw Valerie high in the stands. She had been watching, waiting for him, and when he looked up toward her she smiled and waved.

He looked away quickly, as if he hadn't seen her, and rushed into the crowd of players.

He would not be asked to play, Scott knew. It had been almost a week since he last practiced and he didn't even know all the plays, so when the game started he went to the end of the bench, sitting as far as possible from Borgus and the first string players. He was alone there, his face hidden behind his helmet. He didn't look around to see if Valerie was watching him. He knew she was. She had been waiting for him after last period, waiting to wish him good luck.

"They won't put me in," he had informed her as he put his books away in his locker.

"They might. You're not that bad."

"How do you know?"

She shrugged. "I saw you a couple of times at practice. I mean, you're as good as that halfback, Marty Burns. I saw Burns—he's all butterfingers. You're better than him. At least I think so." She said that with certainty, and then she grinned.

For a second Scott sat on the bench and daydreamed of playing, of racing down the field, of catching the ball in the open field. He could imagine Valerie on her feet, urging him on. He was flying, sidestepping tacklers, stiff-arming the defensive backs, running effortlessly.

Then Flat Rock kicked off and all around him the team stood, cheering. Scott stood with the other players, then glanced around to the bleachers. Valerie was still watching him, and she raised a clenched fist in encouragement.

"Hey, Gardiner, are you ready?" Nick Borgus yelled down the length of the football bench. "We're going to need you, preppie. Keep that helmet ready." He was laughing, nudging the others. Scott looked away, stared out at the game.

After an hour of working, Barbara glanced down at the list of furnishings she had compiled.

1 Maple bedroom set: bedstand, wardrobe, dressing case,
2 Chairs (Victorian)
1 Box spring for bedstead (Victorian)
1 Hair mattress for bedstead (Victorian)
1 Hair bolster
1 Feather pillow
1 Square walnut table (Victorian Gothic)
1 Side lounge, covered with figured blue reps
1 Lot of rugs, Smyrna and Persian
2 Chairs covered with blue striped figured reps
1 Rattan rocker
1 Wooton patent desk

At the bottom of the page, Barbara jotted down several notes of her general impressions. "It is curious that subjected to storage were several fine examples of English Gothic—an octagon table, for example, by A. W. Pugin, as well as the wheel back chairs for the former reception room. While the additional furniture reflects a 'worldly' taste (the Wooton desk, etc.) the house was mainly filled with Victorian Gothic furniture. Few American pieces can be located either in the main castle or among the other small houses on the estate."

Barbara paused and looked over the vast collection of beautiful antiques. It was true, she thought. Fergus had lived nearly all his life in America, but had never been part of the country. He surrounded himself with Irish servants, European furniture, and foreign guests. He was barely touched by America, yet he wasn't Irish or European either. In Ballycastle Fergus had deliberately created a kingdom in which the only distinct personality was his own.

She closed her notebook, pulled the cord on the overhead light and left the darkened storeroom, heading for the lighted hallway.

She had reached the storeroom door when those lights too went out, leaving her corner of the cellar entirely dark. She reached out and felt along the wall until she found the switch. A string of fluorescent lights ran the length of the hallway, and she flipped them on. They blinked on slowly and in the bluish glow Barbara saw Conor coming toward her. Then the lights went out again.

"Hey, coach." Scott tagged after Tagariello as he stomped up and down the long sidelines. "Let me play. I'm faster than Burns."

Tagariello didn't even turn his head. "What are you talking about, Gardiner? Get out of here, will ya?" He pushed by Scott and paced off several yards, following the game's action.

"We're already winning, Coach, by one touchdown. I mean, we can't lose. Let me go in for one series of plays."

Tagariello stopped and glanced back at the tall student. He liked it when the kids were eager, anxious to get into the game. Perhaps he'd been wrong about Gardiner.

"Okay," he grunted. "On the next down take Burns's place. Seventy-two-flat, got it?"

"What's seventy-two-flat?"

"Jesus H. Christ. And you want to play!" Tagariello stomped back toward him and rapidly diagrammed the pass play. "Go down five yards, turn out, then Hanlon will hit you with the fly. Got it?"

Scott nodded as he pulled on his helmet.

"Then get your ass out there!" Tagariello slapped him across the back.

Scott ran back along the sideline to where the defensive team was standing, and found Borgus in a cluster of players.

"It's only a silly game, Borgus," he shouted, then ran onto the field and into the huddle.

Oh, God, Valerie thought, seeing Scott appear on the field. Now she was frightened for him. Something would happen, she knew; some way or other he would make a fool of himself. She should never have encouraged him to play, especially with the seniors. He would only get hurt. She jumped to her feet.

It was cold at the top of the bleachers. The late October wind blew across the open fields and she kept tossing her head to keep her long hair out of her face. Her eyes never left Scott. She saw him spin out of the huddle and take Burns's place at halfback, watched as he set up for the play. They wouldn't throw to him, she thought. He didn't know the plays. She held her breath.

At the snap Scott dug his feet into the hard dirt, sprinted ahead two yards, let the quarterback fake to him and then he spun off, running parallel to the line toward the wide side of the field.

Valerie watched the pass float into the cloudy sky, saw it ride the wave of the wind. It hung as if motionless and Scott easily picked it off. She jumped up again, cheering with the others, as he spun in the air like a basketball player, then cradled the ball and drew it safely into his arms.

"Oh, no, Scott!" she shouted. "Stop! Stop!" Everyone shouted. She saw the quarterback running after him, yelling, waving his arms, trying to catch him.

But no one could. He was faster than anyone. His long legs tore down the sidelines. The other team had begun to cheer, to run after him, seeing, as everyone else did, that Scott was scoring a touchdown for the wrong team.

"Oh, Christ." Barbara worked the switch again, flipped it several times, but the lights kept blinking off. "Dammit, Conor, what's wrong?"

"Oh, these are old lights, ma'am. I'll have to be getting to them soon," he said, approaching through the dark. Barbara tried again, apprehensive now at being with the old man in the dark cellar. The fluorescent lights came on again. "Thank God," she sighed.

"They told me I could find you down here, ma'am." He held out a set of green folders. "The files, ma'am." He smiled, showing his yellow teeth.

"Thank you, Conor." Hiding her surprise at his sudden cooperation, she took the files and moved around him, starting toward the basement door. Again the lights gave out. "Not again! Conor, you'll have to see to these lights right away. I can't work down here in the dark." She kept walking, reached the wooden stairs and climbed them quickly. At the top she found the switch and snapped it back and forth. The lights blinked on again. "There! This one works, Conor," she said, turning around, looking back into the basement.

The old man was gone. His disappearance had been soundless and swift, as it had been the day she'd encountered him with the dagger, and it frightened her all over again, the way he could suddenly disappear from sight inside the castle. It wasn't right. Then the lights blinked off again as if on cue. Barbara pushed open the heavy oak door and rushed into the sunlight and the friendly crowd of tourists.

"Scott! Don't drive so fast!" Valerie ordered. She sat curled up in the right front seat of the MGB, her legs braced against the padded leather dashboard, Scott's school books and her own piled in her lap. He was speeding up the parkway, had been speeding since they raced out of the high school parking lot.

"No one asked you to come," he answered, shifting down

and changing lanes, passing three cars before cutting back to the right. They were traveling at eighty miles an hour. Valerie kept checking the speedometer.

"I missed the bus."

"That's not my fault."

"I missed the bus because I wanted to talk to you after the game, and you took forever to come out of the locker room."

"Why?"

"Why what?" she yelled. He sped by another car, passing it on a hill, then cut back into the right lane, just missing a car coming against him.

"Scott," she screamed, "you're crazy!" Now she was scared he would kill them both. "If you're going to commit suicide, then let me out."

He slowed slightly, bringing the car under control. "Why did you want to talk to me?" he asked.

"I don't know—because I knew you'd be upset about that touchdown."

"Upset—hunh! I'm not upset." He glanced at her, grinning.

She managed to turn sideways in the seat to look at him. "You weren't? Why not?"

"I ran the wrong way on purpose."

"But we lost the game!"

"So what? It's just a goddamn silly game." He grinned happily as he raced the car.

"Oh, shit, Scott. They're going to get you. They're going to kill you. I mean, what did you do a stupid thing like that for?" She was near tears.

"Because of Borgus. Because of what he did to my *Hobgoblin* books." He told her to open up the manuals, showed her how the pictures had been cut out. "Borgus said it was only a silly kid's game." Scott shrugged. "Well, football is only a kid's game too, and it doesn't matter who wins." Ahead of them were the south gates of Ballycastle and Scott shifted gears, slowed down.

"But you're only hurting yourself, Scott. I mean, all the kids are mad because we lost."

"I don't give a shit."

"That's your problem, you don't give a shit about anything."

"Goddamn you, Dunn, get off me." He hit the brake, skidding the small car on the gravel. "Did I ask you to hang around my locker? Why don't you go off with your friends if you think I'm such a shithead?"

"Maybe I will."

"Then get out of my car."

"No."

"Dunn, I'm going to beat the shit out of you."

"Is that going to make you feel better, picking on girls?" She was crying, searching through her bag for a Kleenex to wipe her eyes.

Scott shifted into first and pulled the car back onto the road.

"You want to go home? I'll drive you if you want me to."

"No, I want to go see my sister. She'll take me home after work."

"Well, you can come by the house and stay there until she's ready to leave. Unless you think I'm too much of a shithead."

He spun through the open gate and speeded up. At this corner of the estate the drive crossed open fields, bare and brown in the late fall. Higher up was the tree line, the stand of trees that blocked the view of the mansion from that side of the road. He liked to race the car on this stretch. It was a rollercoaster of hills and the MGB flew over the slight rises, turned abruptly into the tight corners. He would race for the woods, the darkness. He always felt like Brian Ború, charging back to the king's castle, riding his stallion across the Irish hillside.

At the woods he slowed and let the car coast. That was another game of his, to see how far the MGB would travel without power. He was always making up little games like that, ways of entertaining himself. It was because he didn't have friends, he knew, because he was an only child. He had read an article in one of his mother's magazines about only children, how they were more creative, more imaginative than other kids. He took a secret pride in that; it made him feel unusual and special.

"What's the matter with the car?" Valerie asked.

"Nothing. I'm seeing how far I can go without gas."

"Boys," Valerie sighed.

"I'm not hurting anything. I'm just playing a game, that's all."

"I know. But you're just like all boys. Always playing some silly game."

"I'm not like *all* boys!" he snapped, glaring at her.

"All right, you're not." Valerie backed off at once to appease him. She had come to learn his moods and knew when he was really angry.

"I'm not like those creeps at Flat Rock."

"Well, some of the kids aren't so bad," she said, defending her own.

"Those assholes."

"Come on, Scott. That's not fair. Do you think I'm an asshole, too?" She leaned forward to catch his eye and then she saw the figure back in the woods. It was running, trying to keep up with the slow-moving car.

At first she thought it might be a deer. The woods were thick with them below the mansion, and they were hard to spot, dappled as they were to blend in with the leaves. But then she caught a glimpse of the figure standing upright, peering at them.

"Scott, stop the car! Look!" She pointed through the small window.

Scott turned and looked left out the window.

"Where?" he asked, seeing nothing.

"There! There!" she shouted, striking the air, pointing, following the creature. "Oh, God, what is it? Oh, Scott, let's get out of here. Start the car, please!" She grabbed his arm, digging in her nails.

"Quit it, Val! Where? What do you see?" He kept scanning the thick wood beside the drive, watching for the animal. Then he saw it move. It was closer than he'd expected, less than twenty yards from the car, and hidden partially by the trees and thick foliage, but he saw the small head covered with yellow hair. It raised its arm and brushed back a branch, moved closer to the road, coming at them.

"Scott, please, hurry."

It was a Black Annis. The old hag who devoured lambs and young children.

"Scott! Hurry." Valerie was beating his shoulder. "It'll kill us. It will kill us."

Scott lowered the window. He was frightened, too, but he

wouldn't leave. He wanted to see the Annis. It was quiet in the woods. Valerie's fear had caught in her throat. She was now too petrified to scream.

The Black Annis kept coming forward, brushing back branches. Scott could hear the rustle of leaves as the heavy animal tramped through the trees. It stopped once again, closer now, and Scott caught its scent. It smelled like rotten eggs, like their sulfur experiment in the chemistry lab.

"Scott, please," Valerie whispered.

He kept watching the creature, but reached forward to start the car. Still he did not drive away. The Black Annis was watching them. It raised its head, stretching to see through a cluster of bright yellow and orange leaves. Then it disappeared from sight. He could hear it retreating, stamping on the bed of leaves, disappearing into the woods.

Barbara showered, then, naked, walked into her bedroom. She carried a towel and as she walked she dried her hair. Holding her head to one side, she let the dark hair hang free as she rubbed the ends briskly with the towel. She glanced at the bedroom clock. Scotty ought to have been home by now, she thought, and then she remembered the football game. Well, she would do her hair and take a look at the personnel files before cooking dinner.

She sat on the bed and leaned down to plug in the hair dryer. But before she could turn it on, she heard the clattering sound of the garage door rolling up.

Scott, she thought. And then a second thought: how could it be Scott when she hadn't heard his car? Besides, Scott never voluntarily put the MGB in the garage.

Feeling vulnerable in her nakedness she snapped off the lamp of the night stand, casting the bedroom into darkness. Keeping away from the window, she slipped into her robe and hurried down the hallway to the guest bedroom, hoping it was Scott after all.

In the second bedroom she went to the windows, moving along the wall so her shadow could not be seen from below. Carefully, without touching the curtains, she looked down at the yard behind the guest house. Back in the trees, concealed by darkness and the heavy foliage, she caught sight of someone moving.

She would have to go back to her bedroom and phone the castle, she realized, get hold of Derek or security. Someone was trespassing, looking around for something to steal. But before she could move Barbara saw who it was, saw the strange, old woman run out of the trees and toward the house.

The sight of the woman, so inappropriate and inexplicable, paralyzed Barbara. She couldn't move from the window; she stood still in the dark house, listening as the old woman disappeared around the corner of the cottage. She was leaving, Barbara thought, and sighed. She walked back into the hall and toward her bedroom, but at the top of the stairs she heard more noise and she hesitated again, listening. Then she identified the sound. The woman was trying to open the front door of the house; she was frantically turning the doorknob, but it was locked, as it almost always was.

The back door wasn't. The screen door was unlatched and so was the inside door. The woman would go there next, Barbara thought, circle the house and get in through the kitchen. The front door rattled as the woman pushed against it, harder this time. She was old but she was strong. Perhaps she had escaped from some local institution—Barbara shivered at the thought of being trapped in her own house by a madwoman with hands powerful enough to pummel the door, as this one was doing.

Barbara forced herself down the stairs, keeping to one side so the woman couldn't see her in the dark house.

The rattling stopped. Barbara heard footsteps on the path, heard leaves being rustled. The woman was going for the back. Barbara ran.

At the bottom of the stairs she grabbed the newel post, spun herself around and hit the hallway running, her bare feet soundless on the wooden floors. In the kitchen there was no light and Barbara streaked across the linoleum. She spotted the woman outside, saw flashes of her stooped shoulders passing the windows, saw, through the glass panels of the upper door, the woman opening the screen. Barbara dove forward, felt for the lock and tumbled it closed. She collapsed onto the floor, cowering behind the wooden lower half as the old woman shook the knob, banged against the door. Barbara could feel her outside, feel her body pressed against the panels, only inches away from her own.

Barbara crawled away to the farthest corner of the kitchen, away from the door and windows. Now she could see the old woman clearly, her distorted face pressed against one of the glass panels, one milky white eye searching the kitchen, the bruised lips moving as if she could see Barbara and was trying to tell her something.

Then the face disappeared, melted into the night. Barbara lay shaking in the corner, listening to the receding footsteps. And then, like an earthquake's aftershock, she felt the fear. The invader was gone, but she was still in danger. Scotty was in danger. Something was being kept from them. There was a secret here at Ballycastle that she and Scotty did not share.

Twelve

"Scott mustn't know," Barbara ordered, pacing around the office. As soon as the pounding of her heart had become bearable, she had crept to the phone and called Derek, then dressed in the dark, upstairs, and gone downstairs to wait while he and the two security officers searched the woods around the guest house. Now Derek sat quietly at the conference table in his office, listening to her instructions. "It will only convince him that his fantasies are real."

Derek nodded, then answered bluntly the question he knew she was afraid to ask him. "Barbara, I've been here for eight months, since the Foundation opened the castle, and I'm certain that there's no Mrs. Rochester hidden away in the attic. Don't you think you're being a little irrational about this?"

She quickly glanced at Derek, as if sizing him up, as if assessing his loyalty.

"Do you think I just made this up, her trying to break the doors down?"

"I believe you, of course, Barbara. I just question whether this woman was really out to get you, personally. You know, a wide variety of people visit Ballycastle. It could have been someone from one of the mental hospitals."

"Well, were any groups here today?" Barbara asked, accepting the possibility. All sorts of organizations made day trips to the estate, where they were welcome to tour the house and then picnic on the grounds. Perhaps this woman had gotten separated from her group and, by evening, was frantically trying to find her way back to someone.

"I'm not sure. I'll ask Karen tomorrow. But this woman might not have come with a group. She might have been on her own. Barbara, a bus from Flat Rock stops at the gate. There's free admission to the grounds. I'm surprised we don't get more crazies here at Ballycastle."

He had been sitting on the corner of the small conference table and now he got up and went to the window, stood looking over the fields, as if imagining what might be lurking out there.

"This woman was bizarre, Derek. Her face was disfigured, but that was actually the least of it. Her clothing was odd—I couldn't really say *how*, but I remember it was—and her whole demeanor was weird and violent. If she had been around the castle, people would have noticed. I mean, she wasn't exactly the suburban matron."

Derek came away from the window, smiling wryly, and sat next to Barbara on the leather couch.

"Okay," he said, "You say she was in the woods, hidden at first by the trees." His tone had shifted, become deliberately patient and rational, as if he were dealing with a cranky child.

"Derek, I'm not imagining this," she said, furious at being patronized. "I saw the woman. She was standing under the porchlight when she pressed her face up against the glass of the door." Her voice rose and caught on edge. "Her complexion was blotchy red in some places, almost blue in others. And her left eye was milky white, as if she were blind on that side." She gestured angrily. "Derek, you're just not taking me seriously. You don't believe me."

"I do believe you. But you've got to admit, it's a strange story."

"I have to leave," she said, realizing there was no way to persuade him. "It's late. Scotty will be home, and I have to get dinner started."

She picked up her down vest and slipped it on, moving toward the door. The phone rang before she reached it.

"Wait!" Derek asked. He moved to the phone. "Let me

explain myself." He picked up the receiver and said hello, then listened a moment.

Barbara stood with her hand on the doorknob, debating whether to leave. It would be childish, she knew, to just walk out while he was tied up on the telephone. But Derek deserved it, and she anticipated the satisfaction she'd have when he came after her, wanting to apologize.

"Thank you, Ted," Derek said into the phone and hung up. "Well, our mystery's solved." He came away from his desk and toward her. "That was Ted Ward from security. The highway patrol called him. They found a woman wandering around on Route 12, across the road from the south gate, and they wanted to know if she belonged here. Ted said the police described her as a shopping-bag woman. She acted incoherent and hostile."

Barbara nodded, "Fine, that explains it. Now do you believe me?"

"I never doubted you."

"Sure."

"It's true! And to prove my good faith, let me buy you dinner."

"I can't. Scotty's at home. But how about having potluck with us?"

"You're sure Scott won't mind?"

He was being nice, she realized, giving her a way out. "I think it would be good if Scotty began to realize I have certain rights."

"Yes, but the other night he wasn't very pleased to see me."

"The graveyard upset him that day, not you. Speaking of which, I forgot to tell you: I saw Conor. He found the personnel files from the Depression. They're at the house but I haven't had time to look through them."

"Good, we can go over them this evening. I'll bring what documentation I have at the office." He had walked with her out into the wide second-floor hallway. "It will give me a good excuse for Scott."

"Derek, you don't need any excuses. I'm sorry I've created that impression. Scott isn't some kind of monster."

"I know. But if I were Scotty I'd be overly protective too." He was leaning against the door frame with his arms crossed.

His long hair was rumpled and a lock had fallen down across his forehead. Barbara felt a surge of attraction toward him, then firmly suppressed it.

"I'm the one who's being overly protective," she said. "But that's about to stop. I'm not doing Scotty any good trying to keep him from facing the world. And it's not doing me any good either. Tonight when that woman was attacking the house, I suddenly realized I couldn't protect myself and that I had no one, really, to turn to. It wasn't a very happy feeling."

"Well, you have Scott."

Barbara shook her head. "Not for a few more years. And once he's old enough to count on, he'll be going off to college. I can't expect him to stay at home for my sake. He has his own life to live." She shrugged as if to say: that's the way it is.

At that moment, he thought, she did seem lost and helpless. She looked like a kid herself, dressed in tight jeans, a leotard top and a green down vest. Her long black hair didn't help. It made her look even younger.

"What time shall I come by for dinner?" he asked, avoiding a real answer to her problem.

"Give me an hour to get the kitchen under control." She brightened up, as if putting a good face on things. "How about spaghetti and meatballs? Not fancy, but it's one of Scotty's favorites."

"Fine. I must have a bottle of red wine around here somewhere."

"All right, but don't worry if you don't. See you soon."

Barbara ran down the stairs lightly and he slowly returned to his office, closing the door behind him. Only the desk lamp was lit and it spread a bright circle of light over his papers, leaving the rest of the room dark. He liked the effect, the contrast of shadows.

It was a lovely office, he thought, and a good job. He just had to stay in control. Most of the time it was easy. Only at moments like this did he worry about letting the Foundation down.

He slid back into his leather chair. Swinging his legs up onto the desk, he reached for the phone and tapped out the phone number.

"Conor? It's Mr. Brennan. Has Ted telephoned you? She got out."

"Scotty isn't home," Barbara said, opening the front door as Derek approached. She had heard footsteps on the gravel drive and rushed to the living room, thinking it might be her son.

"Well, you said there was a football game."

"Yes, but they play in the afternoon, right after school." She stepped back from the door, letting him enter. "He's usually home by six. And, besides, he's not supposed to drive after dark."

"Maybe he's in town. You know kids. They're probably celebrating the game at some fast food place."

Barbara was shaking her head. "He would have called."

"Okay, we can call the school." This was the sort of crisis he could handle easily, and he took a certain pleasure in showing Barbara she could count on him.

"I've already telephoned the school," she said. "No one answered."

"The state police?"

She shook her head. "There have been no accidents."

"Do you have any idea who he might be with?"

Barbara shrugged. "He doesn't really have friends. I should telephone Valerie Dunn, the girl you drove home the other day. It's possible he's gone to her house. But still, he would have called and told me." Her voice trailed off.

"He may have tried to call, Barbara, but you were over in my office for at least an hour." He went to the hall phone and dialed information, taking charge. "If he's not at Valerie's, we'll start looking. We'll take my car and drive into town. He could have had car trouble."

Barbara dropped into the sofa. The thought that something might have happened to Scott immobilized her. She kept thinking of Warren, of how he had died while she lay upstairs, unaware. She wouldn't be able to stand it if something had happened to Scott.

"He was with Valerie," Derek reported, returning to the living room. "I spoke to Mrs. Dunn. He dropped Valerie off about half an hour ago. Valerie was upset about something, but all she would tell her mother is that Flat Rock lost the football game."

"Half an hour ago?" Barbara looked out the picture window. "Then where is he? Goddamit! I'm going to take that car away from him."

"Barbara, we'll give him another twenty minutes, then we'll go look for him, all right?"

"Let's go now. I can't stand just sitting here."

"Wait!" He put his hands on her shoulders, halting her. "The three gates are still open. They will be for another twenty minutes. He could come home any which way off Route 12, but once security closes the gates he has to come in from the north side."

Barbara nodded, understanding his point. "It's just that I hate waiting here for him."

"Let me make you a drink."

She shook her head.

Derek still had her, still held her firmly in his hands, as if balancing her slight body, keeping her steady with his grip. She was looking past him, out the windows to the drive that swept up the hill and through the white birch woods.

For a second she glimpsed the headlights of a car coming up from the north gate, but then the woods were dark again. It had to be him, she told herself. In a few minutes he would be home.

She felt Derek tighten his grip on her shoulders, felt herself being pulled toward him. Still she did not look away from the dark frame of the picture window. It was as if she were being tugged by mysterious forces. For a moment, she wasn't even aware of who held her. Her consciousness was adrift. She was aware only that she needed this, needed to be held securely in someone's arms, even a stranger's. To feel the warmth of a human body. Her eyes were still open, still watching for the headlights.

Her head was pressed now against Derek's shoulder, but she was not responding. It was as if this embrace was happening to someone else's body, not hers. Her arms hung loose at her side. He tilted her head, raised her chin, brought her eyes in contact with his. She didn't focus. Her eyes never found his face. When he kissed her lips it startled her.

"Don't," she asked, breaking away.

"Why not?" he asked, still holding her. She fitted against his body like a child.

"God, why?" She pulled away slightly and found his face. Her dark eyes were watching him, evaluating. She had returned to the present. "Do you want this?" she asked.

"I'm not sure what I want. That question may be a little premature."

She was shaking her head as he spoke and she pulled herself from his arms. "Are you ready for an office involvement?"

"You're a very beautiful woman, Barbara."

"Don't change the subject. Do you think we can keep something like this quiet?"

"Why should we? Neither one of us is married. We're roughly the same age and we're not the same sex. Compared to most people I know, we constitute a model couple."

She didn't laugh, didn't even look up, and he went to the couch and sat down beside her. She was leaning back against the arm of the couch, with both her legs pulled up, making herself into a tight, unapproachable ball.

"Derek, we both know that you have been flirting with me for months. First you'd come on, and then you'd back off, as if you were testing the water with your toe. Now, when I can least afford to complicate my life, when my sixteen-year-old is out there somewhere in the dark with his sports car, you decide to make a move." She was shaking her head, trying hard to hold her emotions in check. "Derek, really, I don't need to have my life jerked around any more."

"But you find me attractive," he protested. "I mean, you've been flirting with me too."

"Come on, Derek, don't be a jerk. My finding you attractive has nothing to do with getting something going with you."

"Well, it's a beginning," he replied, trying to lighten the exchange.

"Derek, I'm thirty-six years old. I have a growing son, and I'm a recent widow trying to establish herself in a fairly esoteric profession. Really, no offense meant, but I'm not interested in a casual affair."

"Is that what you think I'm suggesting?"

She shrugged. "I don't know what you're suggesting."

"You're making up your mind about whatever might transpire between us before we get beyond a few handshakes and one kiss. Christ!" He stood up and moved away from the sofa, running his hands through his hair. "How do I know I won't get hung up on you, and you'll treat it all like some casual affair? Jesus, Barbara, that's why you get involved with someone. To find out what happens. You know, you take a chance!"

"I can't take chances," she said from her couch.

Derek shrugged, nodded. He couldn't think of what more to say.

"It would be hard on Scotty, bringing on another father figure so soon after his father's death."

"Barbara, the boy is almost an adult. He's old enough to handle it."

She tilted her head sideways, as if contemplating that notion, then replied thoughtfully. "That's one of my great fears, that he can't—that he isn't in control."

"You have to let him grow up. Trust him."

"I do trust him. And look where it's gotten me." She glanced at her watch, then looked out up the window, searching for the headlights that had never reappeared.

"You also have to have a life of your own." Derek came back to sit down next to her. "A half hour ago you were telling me that Scott had to begin recognizing your rights. Well, is one of those rights some sort of relationship with another man? You're still young, Barbara. Do you want to go through life alone?" He was leaning forward, whispering, trying to catch her dark eyes. He could see they were sparkling with tears already.

"I don't know what I want, Derek," she admitted. "All I seem to do is worry. I worry constantly about Scott. I worry about my job—whether I'm good enough even to call myself a professional."

"Barbara, I told you, what I've read of your initial report is first rate."

"Thank you." She reached out and took his hand, cupped it in both of hers as she continued. "I haven't worked full time for so long, since before Scotty was born, so I just can't judge how I'm doing. And then, topping all that, I rented our house in Connecticut and moved away. I had a pretty secure world there, all in all. At least I knew where to get my clothes cleaned and where to buy meat."

She was laughing now with her tears, at the absurdity of her complaint. Yet when he tugged at her arms, tried to pull her into an embrace, she said good-naturedly, "Wait, there's more. I mean, this is important. It took me nearly two months to find someplace where I could get fresh fish."

"Why didn't you ask me? It's Miller's Market in Flat Rock."

"Thanks, but I know that now."

"But this was all good for you, leaving Connecticut and coming here to Ballycastle. You saved your own life. I mean, what would have become of you if you had stayed there, living comfortably off Warren's estate?"

Barbara shrugged. He didn't know that there had been no estate, to speak of. "I would have improved my bridge game, and lowered my golf handicap to a seven or eight. I might even have won my flight at the Country Club Championship."

"And it would have killed you. You would have been bored out of your gourd."

Barbara nodded. "Perhaps, but at least I would have felt safe. I haven't felt safe since I arrived at Ballycastle. I don't know whether it's me or the place."

"It's the place," Derek stated. "I felt the same way about the castle when I first came here. It's the way it looks, I'm sure. The dark dreariness, all those turrets. But look, you'll only be here until spring. It's not as if you're condemned for life."

Barbara smiled wryly. "Some days I don't think I'll live till spring. I'm already dreading the winter up here. I have the vision that we'll be snowbound till April."

She moved then, uncoiled herself from the corner of the sofa, and Derek reached out and took her into his arms. It was simply done, without effort, as if it had been rehearsed.

He kissed her again. This time she did not hesitate. Her body melted against his, and she ran her fingers into his thick hair.

"I've been wanting to do that for months," she admitted.

"What? Kiss me?"

"No, run my fingers through your hair. You have gorgeous hair, do you realize that?"

"Well, here, do it again." He took hold of her small hands.

"No. The gates are closed. We have to find Scott." She swung her legs off the sofa. "And when I do," she added, half in jest, "I'm going to break his neck for putting me through this worry."

The telephone rang before they could leave the house.

Scott had turned into Ballycastle through the south gate and driven up through the woods, back to where they had seen the Black Annis. There he stopped. In the early twilight he could still peer into the trees for several hundred yards. Weeks before, Scott had looked down on this section of the property from one of the turrets of the house. There was over two thousand acres of land, sloping upward and to the east in a solid expanse of trees. From the top of Ballycastle, it looked like a small foreign country.

Now, in the twilight, he could not see anyone on the hillside. He drove the MGB slowly along the drive, scanning the slope, then pulled the car over and glanced at his watch. His mother would not be home before six. She wouldn't have dinner ready until after seven. He had time. From the crest of the hill he might see the Annis, or find her cave.

Scott slammed the car door and ran across the road and into the brush. For a moment he felt his old fear of the woods. It would be dark soon and he might get lost. He looked back at the green MGB. He would be able to see the car from the ridge, he decided, and then he would just walk downhill to the road.

Scott ran straight up the hill. The trees on the slope had already begun to lose their leaves and he was able to move fast, dodging the bare, black trunks. There were deer paths on the slope; they criss-crossed through the grass, and in several spots Scott noticed trees whose bark the deer had scraped away.

Halfway up the hill he ran out of breath. He stopped, leaned back against a tree and gulped for air. Below him he spotted the car, the emerald green a solid patch among the kaleidoscope of fall colors. It made him feel better knowing where he was on the hillside.

He began to climb again, walking this time. It was steeper here near the crest, and he needed to pull himself forward on branches to get over rocks. At the top he found there was no clear spot, no peak from which he could see in all directions. Trees blanketed the top of the rise that now stretched out into a smooth plateau.

It was easier walking here. It was almost like an orchard. The trees were spread out evenly, as if they had been planted, and the ground was thick with moss. Scott walked toward the setting sun that was flat ahead of him, a huge bronze, blazing ball. He had to keep his eyes down and away from the horizon.

It took him five minutes of steady walking to reach the edge of the plateau, where he had a clear view. A few of Ballycastle's turrets pierced through the canvas of tree tops, and he could see patches of lawn, then part of the river and the boat basin.

But no Black Annis.

The sun had reached the far horizon beyond the castle. For a few moments, Scott watched as it spread out on the land, like a wedge of butter melting.

It would be dark soon, he realized, and he had to cross back over the ridge. He watched a moment longer, wishing Valerie were with him. He would bring her up here, he was thinking, and surprise her, and then he saw the Black Annis.

There was a rustle in the dry leaves right below him where the slope dropped away precipitously. He saw the birches sway as she ran away from the ledge, and at first he thought it was probably a deer. Then, as the path broke for a few yards into the open, he saw the yellow hair, the powerful body, dangerously strong. She was running from him, he knew, racing into the valley.

"Wait," he shouted, but the creature kept moving, stumbling forward, bending branches and scattering red leaves on the forest floor.

Scott went after her. He plunged forward, straight down the hill, but lost his balance in the thick bed of leaves and slid down the embankment.

Indifferent to his bruises, Scott hit the bottom of the slope running. He had lost sight of the Annis in the trees, but he ran in the direction he had seen her go. Here in the valley, at the base of the hill, Scott's view was limited by the nightfall and the trees. Here, too, the soil was soft. Mountain streams flowed down toward the river. The mud sucked at his sneakers, and he tripped in the marshy ground.

He stopped to catch his breath a second time. His side hurt and he doubled over and let the pain subside. When he straightened up, he took off his glasses and wiped away the sweat on the lenses.

Nearsighted without his glasses, Scott gazed a moment into the distance. The vista was misty, unclear. He hooked the wire stems over his ears and looked again.

Now he saw the mist clearly. It hung at eye level, a thin cloud woven between the black trees. Most of them were tall, straight pine or elm; their topmost branches created a high cathedral ceiling in the deep, narrow valley.

For a moment Scott thought he had come upon Inisdoorus, the fabled valley of the Kilcourse clan. Brian Ború had once gone into that valley on a hazardous quest.

Inisdoorus was a land where the sun rose and set one day a year and only on that single day were visitors allowed into the fertile valley. At night the cliffs guarding the valley came to life and destroyed strangers on horseback, attacking the defenseless. Brian, who had been sent by Matholwch, the king of Ireland, to find the golden cauldron, had to fight a giant named Llassur Llaesggvnewid.

Scott smiled, remembering how Brian had tricked Llassur and his giant wife and children. He had been dealt two treachery cards and, rolling five hundred on the pyramidal dice, he had got the giant and his family to follow him outside the valley, distracting him with games of draughts until the sun disappeared and the guardian cliffs fell upon Llassur and his family. Brian saved himself by using the second treachery card. It changed him into a Ghillie Dhu, the green moss that grew against rocks, and he rolled down the long valley, escaping from the highland cliffs and from the land of Inisdoorus.

Scott could hear the woods. The silence was broken with the sounds of birds flying nervously overhead. He looked straight up and spotted them, small blackbirds in coveys, darting from tree to tree. There were other sounds from the brush itself, of wildlife moving away from him and deeper into the trees. Deer, he thought. In the open fields beyond the castle he had often seen herds of a dozen grazing. As he slowly turned his head, keeping his feet stationary in the soft earth, he could not see deer or anything else.

Yet the woods moved beyond the clearing. In the stillness Scott listened as the wind picked up with nightfall. It brushed the heavy fall leaves, sent a ripple of sound down the length of the long valley. Scott scanned back and forth, searching both hillsides for sight of the Black Annis.

Now he was scared. From everywhere noises broke the stillness. Branches cracked overhead. The wind picked up. It whistled above his head. From behind there was an explosion. He spun around, stumbling in the marshy soil and falling. Two small golden deer broke from the underbrush, crossed the narrow clearing and leaped up the steep slope, their white tails bouncing in the darkness.

Then Scott saw the Annis. She was crouched higher on the hill, behind where the deer had been hiding.

"Wait!" Scott pleaded. He ran for the old hag, his feet sinking in the earth, slowing him.

She didn't wait. She skirted over the rise and disappeared from sight. Scott scrambled after her, going up the slope. The ground here was hard and he used the branches to pull himself forward, turning his sneakers sideways to gain an edge on the hillside.

At the crest there was level ground and a smooth deer path that slipped into the trees, ran straight for twenty yards. The trees were sparser here and even in the gathering dusk Scott could see pretty well. He began to relax a little. The castle was ahead of him, he knew, straight toward the setting sun.

He took off, racing along the deer path. The Annis would go for higher ground, Scott guessed. In his *Hobgoblin* guide it said the old hags lived in caves above the tree line, in barren patches. This one's cave was probably someplace nearer Steepletop. It was the only place in ballycastle above the trees, with a clear view of the county.

Already the path was rising, Scott saw. It had lost its straight course and was twisting in the trees. He lost his breath and slowed to a walk. Still he kept climbing, searching both edges of the wood. The hag could disguise herself. Perhaps she had already, was hiding behind him, waiting to strike, to creep up on him on the path.

He glanced at once over his shoulder, saw that the thin ribbon of a deer path was empty. Again he had come to an opening in the wood. A high, level spot as if a slice of trees had been cut from the forest, giving him a panoramic view of Ballycastle.

Below him was the mansion. He was closer, less than a half mile, and from there he could see the barns, the house itself and the guest house. The house was all lit up, which meant his mother was there and waiting for him. He would have to stop soon and go home.

He looked ahead. Now he knew where the Annis was headed. From where he stood he could tell that the deer path kept climbing, right to the crest of Steepletop. It would go by the graveyard, then toward the river beyond Steepletop.

And now he knew where to find the Annis. He would go as far as the graveyard, Scott decided, then start down. He knew the path home from the top of the hill.

Scott started moving again, back into a thick stand of trees. He had gotten another twenty yards higher, keeping his head down and both arms up before him, brushing back branches, when she came at him.

He saw her yellow hair, the wildness of her eyes, and she was on him, stunning him with a two-handed blow to the side of his head. And then another, whipping him from side to side. Losing his balance, he fell back a few steps, slamming into a tree trunk, and before he could recover himself, she was coming again. Throwing up his arms to protect his head he went into a crouch and, terrified, smelled the foul odor of her breath. With a grunt of effort she threw her shoulder against his own, sending him flying off the ridge and into the heavy brush.

Scott rolled for several yards, gaining speed on the sharp slope, bouncing over the hard, rocky ground. He came to a stop against a tree, breathless, unconscious, his long, thin body wrapped around the tree trunk.

Security found the MGB on the south gate drive and telephoned the guest house.

"The engine is cold," Barbara said, hanging up the phone and grabbing her down vest. "He must have left the car a while ago."

"Would he take a walk in the woods?"

Barbara shook her head as she went to the front door. "Scott isn't a nature lover. He hasn't been near the woods all fall."

They were outside, walking quickly toward Barbara's station wagon. She had the keys out and went around to the driver's seat.

"What about a class assignment?" Derek slid into the front seat beside her. "He could be doing field work for biology."

"He isn't taking biology or zoology." She wheeled the heavy car around and gunned the engine, spewing gravel. "Which way?" she asked, confronting a network of interlocking drives below the castle, and realized she had never been on the south drive.

"Left," Derek instructed. "Go behind the superintendent's house, where we park the tour buses. The south drive links up there. In Fergus's time it was used for deliveries and farm equipment, but we don't need it. There are too many accesses to Ballycastle as it is." Already he had decided to send a memo to Ted, ordering him to seal off the south gate.

It was less than a mile to the gate from the main building. Ted Ward had parked his jeep beside the MGB and stood with two of the maintenance staff in the center of the drive.

Barbara slowed and came up beside them, rolling down her window as she approached.

"I got Lou and Rick here," Ted began at once, gesturing to the young men. "They're willing to help out if we need them." Ward was stooped down, looking through Barbara's side window, but he looked past her and directed his remarks to Derek Brennan.

Barbara glanced at Ward. He looked like a cop, she thought. His face was square and sullen. She suppressed an urge to remind the man that it was her son who was missing.

"We don't have much time," Ted continued. "If the kid went into the woods, we got maybe a half hour to find him."

"My son's name is Scott," Barbara put in.

The big man tipped his baseball cap and grinned, as if her remark were amusing. "Sorry, ma'am. Scott. Your boy Scott could get himself lost in these hills. We got maybe six hundred acres of woods. And he's a city boy, ain't he?"

Barbara looked away from the fat man, her neck muscles contracting with her anger. Quickly Derek intervened.

"Ted, go on up there with Lou and Rick. Spread out along

the south drive and walk west toward the big house." He spoke quickly, having formulated his plan on the drive from the guest house. "I'll drive your jeep around to the north drive. We'll meet you at the pond."

"We ain't got much daylight, Mr. Brennan," Ted began to protest, looking toward the high ridge.

"You have time enough to walk through the woods and into the pasture," Derek stated, making it an order. "Go ahead. You're wasting the little light we have." And then, in a softer tone, he added, "You can use the exercise, Ted. A hike through the woods will do you good."

"What about that old woman? The shopping bag woman who was trying to break into my house?" Barbara was glancing back and forth, from Derek to Ted Ward, and she caught the silent exchange between the men, the initial frown on Derek's face. Then Ward spoke quickly, nervously.

"We caught that lady, Miz Gardiner. I told Mr. Brennan that."

"Yes, but what if she came back here and Scotty encountered her? It's possible. We don't know how long the car's been here." Barbara could hear the panic in her voice. That crazy woman had gotten to her son. Scotty was hurt somewhere in the woods. That premonition was so powerful it sent a shudder through her body. Shivering, she began to get out of the car.

"Wait!" Derek instructed.

"I have to look for him," she insisted.

"Ma'am, over that ridge is hollow, marshy land. It's pretty thick going in those woods. I know, ma'am. We hunt this property come November."

"We'll take the cars back to the north road, Barbara, and come in from that side." Derek had his hand on her shoulder, restraining her.

"Please," she insisted. "I know where he is. I know he's been hurt." She shook off his hand.

"All right!" he said angrily. Let her go. For a moment he took perverse satisfaction in knowing that she would soon find out how dark and difficult the woods could be, each foot of progress a triumph of will. Then he thought of Scott, of how frantic she must be, fearing for his life. And there was a chance she was right. Perhaps the woman *had* gotten to the boy, done something to him. She was certainly strong enough. Oh, Christ.

He got out of the station wagon, went after Barbara who stood before the car, looking toward the woods, the steep slope. Already they had lost the sun and the temperature had dropped. Derek felt the approaching winter, and he wished he had worn a jacket.

"There's no need for you to go too, Derek."

"Barbara, I'm not going to let you go by yourself. The light's almost gone, and I don't want to have both of you lost on me."

"This is my responsibility, not yours." She was still angry at his attitude. "There is no reason for you to tear up your clothes tramping through the woods." She heard her own voice rising, lecturing him, and she stopped speaking. She could not treat him like her son.

Derek did not respond. Instead he asked Ted for his portable CB and told the security chief to go around the hill and meet them by the pond near the north gate. He turned to Barbara.

"All right. Let's go." He stepped off into the woods, leading the way through the brush and up the steep hill. Barbara charged after him, angry at his presumption. He was humiliating her with his show of strength. She kept after him, like a terrier.

At the crest of the hill he lost his breath and stopped. They had reached a plateau where the trees were not quite so thick.

"This way," she said, breezing by him. They crossed to the far end of the plateau, then Barbara struck off downhill into the deep hollow. She moved on impulse, striding forward, slipping at times on the wet bed of leaves, but always moving, following her instincts into the dark ravine.

He came after her, silent now, but she could hear him breaking branches, pushing his way through the trees, following her like a heavy, silent, brooding animal.

She was lost now and no longer so convinced that Scott was hurt and needing her. She stepped forward into the soft marshy soil at the bottom of the gorge.

"Wait!" Derek asked, gasping. He burst into the clearing at the base of the hill and stepped into the marshy grass beside her, immediately engulfing his feet in mud.

"Oh, Derek, your shoes." She felt guilty, knowing she had goaded him into following her down the hill.

"Yours, too," he answered. His anger faded with her obvious concern.

"I'm sorry I got upset with you." She leaned against him, felt the strength of his body. Then she added, "If we go up the other side, we can get out of here."

"Sure?"

Barbara shrugged, smiled wryly. They both knew she had no idea.

"All right, you've convinced me," Derek laughed. Taking her hand, he led the way up, climbing through the second growth of trees on that side of the hill.

"Oh, we're here," Barbara said, reaching a second hilltop and seeing the castle.

"Yes, we're here and it's there," Derek answered. He pointed ahead, down the hillside. "The pond is below us. If we go through the woods, we'll reach the pasture land by the north drive."

"I don't think that's the way." She pursed her lips, as if summoning up psychic skills, waiting for that same flash of recognition she had had down on the road. Nothing happened. She opened her eyes and saw the narrow deer path that followed the ridge line.

"Barbara, it's almost dark. We're going to get caught without a flashlight."

"He went this way," she insisted, pointing to the path that went up, away from the castle.

"All right, we'll follow it to the firebreak. I'll call Ted on the CB and have him meet us with the jeep."

"Tell him to bring blankets."

Derek flipped on the CB and picked up the security jeep.

"I was just about to radio you," said Ward, his voice hearty even over the radio. "We've got the kid."

"Is he all right?" Barbara asked, grabbing Derek's arm.

"How's Scott?"

"He's okay. Been cut up some, but okay. Conor found him up on the ridge, near the firebreak road."

"What happened to him?" Barbara leaned closer to Derek and spoke into the CB.

"Ma'am, I don't know. He didn't talk much. He's pretty

upset. Kept saying he was looking for someone named Black Annis and she attacked him on the ridge."

"Black Annis?" Derek looked at Barbara. "Who does he mean?"

"*Hobgoblin.*" Barbara turned away from Derek. The wind blew up out of the valley, whipped around her as she stood exposed on the tip of the ridge. She looked toward the castle, toward the guest house.

Like a boy possessed, he had plunged into these woods, pursuing a danger that existed only in his mind. But he *believed!* Barbara felt sure that Scott had been chasing the same madwoman who had attacked the guest house. But the shopping bag lady, terrifying as she was, was not what frightened Barbara most. It was knowing that Scott had seen a Black Annis in the hills of Ballycastle, if only for an afternoon.

Thirteen

A date. Barbara found herself smiling into the mirror as she applied her lipstick. This was silly. She was too old for dating. But Scotty was right; what else could she call it? Derek had invited her over for dinner. She wasn't driving there herself; he was picking her up at the house. She couldn't even pretend it was a Foundation function, something that was social on the surface but business underneath. No, it was a real date. She had had to admit it when she found herself going back to her closet to change outfits for the second time.

Well, it didn't matter. Whatever the terminology for this evening—date, dinner, or social engagement—she knew she would enjoy it. Her mistake, if she had made one, had been in allowing Scott to invite Valerie over for the evening.

Initially she had refused his request. "Tonight wouldn't be a good time, Scotty," she had said.

"Why not? You're going to go have a good time and I'm just supposed to sit here," he complained.

"I don't know if it's a very good idea, leaving you two alone in the house."

"Why?" he had asked, baiting her.

She gave him a look. "You know why."

"What about you?" He followed her into the living room.

"You're going out with Derek. You might go park someplace and make out."

"Scott! What a thing to say to your mother!"

"Well, what a thing to say to your son!"

She paused. It was true. It was unfair to assume that he would automatically get into trouble if she left him alone with Valerie. As Derek said, she had to start trusting him.

"All right," she answered. "You can ask Valerie over, but no one else. I don't want a houseful of kids here without an adult."

"Nothing is going to happen, Mom. We're not delinquents or anything."

"I know you're not. And let's keep it that way."

When she came downstairs, Scott and Valerie were sitting on the floor with the coffee table between them. He had even gone outside and brought in firewood, a task he had managed to avoid all week. It was not cold for October, but he had lit a fire anyway. It blazed brightly, making the house too warm.

Open on the table was the *Hobgoblin* handbook, and beside it Scott had already set up his Battleboard and miniatures. Well, it hadn't taken him long, she thought.

"Good evening, Valerie," Barbara said, coming down the stairs. Her heels tapped loudly on the bare wood steps, like the short repeat of a handgun.

"Oh, hi, Mrs. Gardiner." Trying to stand, Valerie began to extract her long legs from beneath the coffee table. The girl was all legs and arms, Barbara realized; she hardly had any torso.

"Please, Valerie, don't get up." She appreciated Valerie's manners, but was afraid she'd overturn the table and send *Hobgoblin* flying.

"You look great, Mrs. Gardiner. That's a beautiful blouse."

"Why, thank you, Valerie. That's just what I wanted to hear."

"Mom always looks good when she goes out," Scott said. "Dad and her used to go to the country club. Boy, she really looked like a movie star. Everyone said so. They were the best-looking couple at all those parties. Dad, too. He was really a big guy, you know. In college he played guard. No one could mess around with him. By the way, Mom," he finished up, "what time is Mr. Brennan coming?"

This was deliberate, Barbara realized. He was getting even with her now for Derek. She should have expected that and played down her date, not let on that it was a big thing. Scott didn't want to face the fact that another man could be important in her life.

"Seven-thirty, Scott. You know, Valerie," she went on, without giving him a chance to resume, "Scotty told me you wrote about him in the school paper. That was very nice of you." She was standing at the mirror, her head tilted to one side as she worked on an earring. She could see both of them in the reflection.

"The article is about *Hobgoblin,* Mom. Not about me."

"Oh, no?" She frowned, as if disappointed.

"Well, actually about *Hobgoblin* and Scott, Mrs. Gardiner." Valerie spoke up quickly.

"I think it's very nice of you to go to so much trouble."

Valerie shrugged. "Oh, it's okay. I mean, it's no trouble, and I am a reporter for the paper."

"And you're even going to learn the game." Barbara came away from the mirror. She could see a car approaching, its lights moving like the eyes of a cat through the dark woods.

Again Valerie shrugged. Barbara suppressed a smile. She knew what girls would endure in order to charm boys. At seventeen she had spent months shivering on rainy river banks, just because of a boy who liked to crew.

Barbara stopped trying to be talkative. They didn't want to chat, they wanted to be alone, free of such adult persecutions as polite conversation.

"Scotty, I'll be home early, but if I'm not back by nine I think you should take Valerie home." She was being officious again, like all parents.

"Mom, you know I can't drive after dark."

"Oh, I'm sorry, that's right. I forgot."

"Mrs. Gardiner, my brother Billy will pick me up. It's okay. He does it all the time."

"What time do you have to be home?"

"I can stay out until ten on weekends. But it's not *critical.*

My mother knows I'm here, so it's okay. She'd get upset if I were in town. She doesn't like it when I'm with a gang of kids, you know, driving around, or hanging out at the Bay."

"The Bay?"

"It's a hamburger place, Mom, near school. It's called Hudson Bay and everybody goes there."

"They do? Have you been hanging out at the Bay, Scotty, and not telling me?" She had wanted the question to sound funny, but as she said it, she realized it sounded more like prying. Even Valerie hung her head.

"I've been there a couple of times, yeah."

"You have?" Valerie blurted out. She, too, was surprised. Then she realized Scott was lying, to impress his mother.

At last the doorbell rang, rescuing them all.

Barbara picked up her purse as she went to the door. "I'm leaving Derek's number here, Scott. Call if anything happens. Good-by, you two." She would not invite Derek in. The less Scott had to do with him at this point, the better. "Don't leave the place a shambles," she added, and immediately regretted it. It was just her nerves talking, she thought. Her "date" was worry enough, but leaving Scotty home with a girl was worse. She ought to be the one staying home by the fire, and her son the one going out.

Barbara opened the front door.

"Hi," she smiled, trying to shift emotional gears. It was hard to be cool and charming when what she felt was hectic and scattered. Why did she always have such difficulty talking to her son? It was as if they were broadcasting on two different radio bands.

"Hello—you look great," Derek answered, then paused, waiting for her to invite him in. When she didn't, he stepped around her, into the overheated living-room. Something wasn't quite right, he thought, and his eyes went to the two teen-agers before the fireplace. Valerie Dunn was smiling up at him. Scott was looking away, studying an open book.

"Hello, Valerie."

"Hello, Mr. Brennan."

"Hello, Scott."

"Oh, hi." Scott glanced up briefly.

"Say good-by, Derek," Barbara said. "We're late."

Outside, circling the car to open the door for her, Derek asked, "How can we be late? We're eating at my place."

"Oh, Scott was just getting impossible again. It's best for the time being if he doesn't have to deal with you."

Derek did not say anything more until he had turned the car around and they were out of the drive, going back across the wooded estate toward the main gate.

"It's natural, I guess. He sees me taking you away from him."

"I think it's more than that. He sees you as an interloper, someone taking Warren's place in my life and, of course, in his. And that he doesn't want."

"And what do you want, Barbara?" They were in the midst of the woods, sealed off from the world by corridors of trees. They had only the lights of the car ahead of them, blazing through the darkness.

"Oh, God, what do I want?" She laughed slowly, amused by the notion. "It's been so long since I had the privilege of deciding. For so long it was, what does Warren want? And now, what does Scott want?"

"Yes, but be honest, Barbara. Isn't that just another way of saying that it was easier to let Warren have his way?"

Surprised at his directness, Barbara retreated into silence for a moment. Then she said, "Yes, I suppose that's true. Making Warren happy was a lot simpler than deciding what it would take to make *me* happy."

He said quietly, "Well, are you ready to figure it out now?"

"Oh, no," Barbara said lightly. "I think I'll let it come as a surprise. We can all dress up and go to the Santa Monica Auditorium, like they did for the old Academy Awards. And Anne Bancroft can come out on stage and say, 'And now, Barbara Gardiner, the suspense is almost over. *This* is what you've always wanted—the envelope, please!'"

Derek laughed, acknowledging her unwillingness to be cornered. "Sounds like a good plan," he said, reaching over to touch her knee lightly. "Just be sure you let me know in time to borrow a shirt with French cuffs."

"You'll be the first," she whispered, barely aware of what

she was saying. She was still registering his touch, the feel of his warm hand on the black velvet of her slacks. At that moment, all she wanted was for him to touch her again.

"Your mother is really neat," Valerie said in the silence that followed Barbara's departure.

"Yeah, she's all right, I guess." Scott had gone back to rearranging the *Hobgoblin* Battleboard, setting up cardboard forests and caves.

"I don't think you know how lucky you are. I mean, she's nice to talk to and pretty and just *everything*. I wish my parents were like that. All they do is work on the farm and stay home and watch television. My mother is fat. And I can't talk to her about anything. That's why I'm always over here seeing Karen. She's the only one in my family that understands anything."

"If she were your mother you might not think she was so neat. She's friendly to you, all right, but it's not like that all the time. And at least your mother is at home, not going out to dinner with what's-his-name. I had to eat at six o'clock just so she had time to get dressed."

"Well, what's so weird about that? We always have dinner by six. What time do you eat, usually?"

"Oh, I don't know. Whenever she can get the food cooked. Maybe seven o'clock."

"What do you do?"

"About what?"

"Do you cook or anything?"

He shook his head.

"Do you wash the dishes?"

"I'm supposed to."

Valerie picked up the *Hobgoblin* handbook and began to flip through the pages.

"You're spoiled," she commented.

"I'm not."

"Yes, you are." Her green eyes were angry and disappointed. "Your mother does everything for you, and you can't even be nice to her."

"I am nice."

"Not tonight, you weren't. You were awful to Mr. Brennan and that hurt your mother's feelings."

"Brennan is a wimp."

"He is not! He's cute."

"My dad was twice as big as him. Dad could have broken him apart with one hand. My dad played football for Syracuse!"

"You told me," she said.

"Well, it's true. I've got a picture of him when he made All East. Do you want to see it? I've got it in my bedroom."

"No."

"I'll get it, I'll bring it in here."

She shook her head, not looking at him.

"Why not?" He was mad at her now. She was doing it on purpose. She was just trying to be mean.

"I thought we were going to play *Hobgoblin,*" she said. She leaned forward across the low coffee table, as if to get started with the game.

Scott grabbed hold of her wrist. "Why don't you want to see Dad's picture?"

Valerie had learned that when he got angry, his face changed. His skin turned white and his eyes widened. He was no longer looking at her, but through her, as if his eyes had fixed on some spot at the base of her skull.

"Let go," she said nicely. Scott had never hurt her, but she felt uneasy, not knowing what he would do next.

"Tell me why you won't look at my dad's picture."

"I don't want to." She jerked sideways suddenly, surprising him and pulling her arm free.

He reached after her, scrambling around the table which she had put between them. She began to crawl away and he dove for her, his hand grabbing for her waist but glancing off her breast instead. She wasn't wearing a bra and the warm softness surprised him. His anger disappeared.

Still he didn't let her go. Stretched out on the floor, trapped between the sofa and coffee table, they touched along the entire lengths of their bodies.

"Please move," she asked. Scott lay above her, barely touching, supporting his weight on the palm of one hand.

"Come on, move!" she asked again, but for the moment, she did not want him to move. She had never been embraced before by a boy and her whole body felt the pleasure of his closeness.

"Only if you tell me why I can't show you Dad's picture."

"Scott, this is boring and you know how I am. If you make me mad, you'll have to kill me before I'll look at it."

Planting his weight firmly on his one hand, he began to tickle her stomach with the other. "Stop it," she squealed, squirming under him.

"Tell me."

"No. No. No."

Pretending to be tickling, he let his fingertips wander higher.

"Scott, let go." This time she meant it.

"Only if you tell me."

His face was above her; it filled her vision and suddenly she was angry at him for using his strength against her.

"Scott, damn you."

He kissed her then, found her lips with his open mouth, clicking his teeth against hers in his inexperience.

She hit him hard on the side of the head and slid out from the confined space in which she'd been trapped.

"Goddamn you, Scott Gardiner. Did I tell you to kiss me?" She wiped the back of her hand across her mouth. "If you try to do it again, I'm going to call my brother and go home." She tried to sound upset and furious, but she wasn't. She had not wanted him to take her by surprise, that was all, before she was ready and expecting it to happen.

"Why can't I show you the picture?"

"Scott, you know, you're such a bore. All right. Go get it." She sat cross-legged on the floor, strands of black hair loosened from her clip and falling across her face.

Now he did not know what to do. Without looking at him she bent her head and opened the clasp, shaking out the rest of her hair. There were dark circles of perspiration under her arms and perspiration on her forehead. The second button of her white blouse was open and he could see the beginning curve of her breast.

"Go on," she demanded, "get the picture."

"It's in my room. I don't think I can get it off the wall. It would be a lot easier if you would just go see it."

Valerie gave him a brief, speculative glance. Then she said flatly, "Let's play *Hobgoblin*."

HOBGOBLIN

* * *

Derek's house was across the river and high on a bluff, looking back toward Ballycastle. While he went to open a bottle of wine, Barbara drifted toward the casement windows, searching for the mansion in the distance. She could feel the castle, sense its presence, but all she could see on that clear, cold night was the river, like a bar of silver in the moonlight.

She stood at the windows, hypnotized by the sight. Derek was talking, but she heard only his voice, not his words. Never since her marriage to Warren had she been alone like this with another man. Never since his death had she been anywhere without Scotty. She felt, at that moment, like a new woman, a young girl even, with only her fantasies to guide her.

Derek was ready with the wine. Coming up beside her he placed the glasses on the window seat, then filled them. He was telling her about the house, how once it had been a hunting cabin, then later a weekend place for wealthy people from New York City. She stood listening, motionless, as if paralyzed at the window.

"Here," he said, "a glass of Pouilly Fuissé. I've been saving it for a special occasion and I think this evening qualifies. It's only taken me months to lure you away for an unchaperoned dinner."

She was afraid to take the wine, afraid that in her nervousness she would spill it, but when she touched the thin stem of the glass it brought her at once to reality. She felt the heat of the fireplace on her cheek, could smell his after-shave lotion when he stepped by her to return the bottle to its bucket of ice, twisting it into the ice cubes. At the sound of the ice she thought immediately of Warren, of the last moment of his life. Oh, God, she thought, am I going to be consumed by guilt forever because I'm still alive?

"There are tears in your eyes," Derek whispered.

"I'm sorry." She brushed them away, hoping her mascara hadn't run.

He turned and stood beside her, sipping his wine quietly for a moment. Their shoulders were inches apart, but they did not touch.

"Sometimes at night," he began, "when I'm in the house alone, I stand here and look toward Ballycastle. During the summer, when there was more light, you could see the tower and the top floor. That was all you could see over the treetops, but I kept trying to spot the guest cottage. Once the leaves fall I'm sure I'll be able to."

She turned away from the window to look at him curiously. "Why?" she asked.

"Because I miss you. I leave the office and drive home and immediately I miss you. I keep imagining how you'd look in this house, sitting by the fireplace, making coffee in the kitchen. Silly, I know. But this house seems made for you. It's a perfect fit, a perfect size . . . eight?"

Barbara laughed, touched and pleased by his confession. "How sweet," she answered and touched his arm. At once he turned to her, setting both their glasses down and burying his fingers in her silky hair. She snuggled closer, fitting herself against him, her fingers slowly massaging his strong shoulders. She smiled at him and his hands went behind her, curving around her tiny bottom, gently pressing her body even closer. Breathless from tension, she had to gasp to fill her lungs, to stay alive. He moved her away slightly, brought his hand up to pull her face to his.

"Don't," she whispered. "I don't think I could stand it if you kissed me right now." She touched his lips with the tips of her fingers and smiled. "Give me a moment to get used to all this. I'm dizzy. It's been awhile, you know. I wouldn't want to black out here in your living room."

"Definitely not," Derek agreed, smiling. "I have an idea. Why don't we have dinner?"

Barbara paused, debating. "I don't think I could eat anything right now. My stomach is in knots."

He touched her cheek and she turned her face into his hand, kissing his palm.

"Then let me make love to you first," he asked.

She agreed with her eyes.

"Now who do you want to be, Val? You can pick from any of these races." Scott pointed to the five racial types listed in the *Hobgoblin* handbook.

"Human," Valerie responded instantly, dismissing the other species.

"Okay. If you're going to be human, then you have to choose what kind of human to be." On the next page he pointed to a long list of types.

"Gad, this is complicated. Miller, bar maid, farmer's wife, sea captain, thief." She read a half dozen other names out loud, then said emphatically, "I want to be a damsel in distress."

Scott picked up the red trait cards and shuffled them. "You get to pick four cards. They will tell you your character's constitution, intelligence, luck, wisdom." He spread open the deck and leaned over the coffee table. "Okay, draw the cards but don't show me the numbers. In the game each one of your traits will be tested. Now, it's important that a damsel have a high virtue, or else she'll be seduced by the first wandering black knight or highwayman or even a wealthy landowner who finds her without protection."

Valerie drew her cards one by one and looked at them. "What's considered a high number?" she asked.

"All the trait numbers run from zero to 100. Anything over sixty-five is very good. She's not likely to get raped, for example, if her virtue card is that high."

Valerie took another peek at her virtue card. The number was 93.

"Now sometimes a damsel can have a low virtue card, but she'll save herself by being particularly cunning, or maybe by having enough magical powers. It depends on the Adventures and what forces this damsel comes up against. Now what do you want to call her? She has to have a name."

"Marie."

"Okay, why Marie?"

"It's my middle name, and I like it."

Scott paused. "They tell you in the handbook not to use your own name or a friend's name. Take a name that's Irish."

"Why can't I use Marie?"

"Because suppose something happens to her? If she gets raped by a gang of roaming dwarfs or is tricked into submission by a black knight, then you'll feel bad. It's better if you aren't too closely connected with your character."

Valerie shrugged. "Don't worry. I'll be okay. Marie can

take care of herself," she said, getting into the game. "Come on now, let's get started. What's my Adventure?"

Scott opened the Adventure handbook and flipped to the section on damsels. He had only played the role of Dealer a few times; he preferred to run Brian Ború, to have his character in an Adventure.

"I'll roll these cube dice," he explained, "and whatever number comes up, that's the Adventure. Understand? That way it's all chance, the Dealer isn't controlling the game. Except you always have to remember, the dice never lie."

"Throw the dice, Scott. Let's play."

He spun the two dice onto the plastic Battleboard.

"Three. Okay! Now here's the Adventure," he said, going to the correct paragraph in the handbook.

"The damsel Marie was orphaned at birth and sent to live in County Westmeath with a wealthy merchant who traded extensively on the North Sea with Scotland, England, Scandinavia and the low countries. At the time of Fin MacCunahail the trade ships were sequestered by the king."

"What does that mean, sequestered?"

"The king confiscated them, took them for battle," Scott explained. "The merchant's ships were seized without payment the subsequently lost in the Battle of Dublin Bay. Penniless, the trader arranged for Marie to be married off to Lord Monaghan, a wealthy landowner in County Westmeath.

"Reluctant to marry the aging lord, Marie agreed only because she wanted to help her foster father. She left Dublin by coach, chaperoned by two elderly aunts. If she arrives in Westmeath still a virgin, the marriage will be consummated and her foster father saved.

"However, less than six hours from Dublin the coachman loses his way in a shrouded mist and comes to a stop at Landman's Tavern, the only public house in the Black Bull Pass.

"Her aunts order rooms and Marie is sent to bed in the attic of the tavern. Tired, she falls asleep immediately, only to be woken several hours later with a knife to her pure white throat and a man's hairy arm wrapped tightly about her slim body. She is being held captive by Emmett, the owner's son, a dim-witted boy of twenty. Emmett has never possessed a woman, but he has fallen in love with Marie and is determined to make love to her."

"I'll scream," Valerie said as Scott closed the book.

"She can't scream," Scott said, picking up the tale on his own. "Emmett has his hand across Marie's mouth. He's too big, over twelve stone, and she is helpless."

"Well, what is happening now?"

"He's putting his hand under her dress."

"Oh, God, I can't believe this." She stacked her cards on the coffee table.

"Come on, you said you wanted to play."

"But I don't like what's happening in this game."

"I told you not to call your character by your own name."

"You're just getting even with me from before." She could feel herself getting angrier.

"Val, I didn't pick a damsel as the character. You did. I didn't roll this Number Three Adventure. You did. Now come on, run your character—see how she does. Remember, Emmett is dimwitted. You can outsmart him and get away."

"How then?"

Scott placed four cards on the table. "Here are his traits. Now I roll the dice for him, and you have to choose how you want to engage him, by strength, by wit, by magic, by virtue. But I wouldn't take virtue."

"Why?"

"Because he wouldn't recognize it. The odds are against you."

"I don't understand this," she moaned.

"Here, on this one I'll help you. Look at his cards. Emmett is strong—see, he's 83 in brute strength—but his intelligence is only 8. It's his turn so I'll roll the dice for Emmett." Scott tossed one of the cube dice onto the Battleboard. "Nine—that's added to his native intelligence, giving him 17. Now you roll." He handed Valerie the dice and she quickly flipped it onto the table.

"Don't tell me your intelligence total," Scott said, looking away from the Battleboard. "That's your secret. Now, Emmett could challenge you, demand to know your intelligence quotient, and if your number is higher than his, he would become your servant for life. But then I, as the Dealer, would also know, and it would influence me in how I run the game. It's better to keep all your traits secret as long as you can. Besides, Emmett isn't important. Okay, what do you do to free yourself?"

Valerie thought a moment. "I relax and he thinks I'm giving up and removes his hand from my mouth and then I scream. And my two aunts rush into the attic." She sat up straight, pleased with the solution.

Scott nodded, agreeing. "Good, but you have to roll both cube dice to see if your trick will succeed." He handed the dice to Valerie. "You need to score at least four on the roll."

Valerie flipped the dice onto the flat Battleboard.

"Seven," she said.

"Okay." Scott thought for a moment, deciding what should happen. "Emmett runs away," he said, picking up the story. "He climbs out on the roof where he slips on a wet tile and falls to the ground, breaking his neck on a horse post."

"Oh, God, you didn't have to kill him. All he was doing was feeling up Marie. I mean, she's not vindictive."

Scott shrugged. "This is a brutal and violent game," he said with some pride. "Only the good and strong survive. Now, Marie spends the rest of the night in peace and the next morning she continues her journey inland to the country of Lord Monaghan.

"Shortly before noon, while passing through beautiful Macross Valley, they are set upon by highwaymen who surround the carriage and kill two of Marie's guards. Again Marie is captured and her virtue is threatened." Scott set out three tiny horsemen on the Battleboard.

"What about my aunts? Why don't the highwaymen go after them and give me a break?"

"Because you, Marie, are the beautiful young girl. You are the prize. But don't worry. Help is coming." Scott grinned, thinking of how he would save Marie.

"Tell me if it hurts," Derek asked.

"No, darling, no, you don't hurt." He was much slower than Warren, much gentler. It had been almost a year since she had been with a man. Now she let him direct their passion, and she followed his bidding.

Derek turned her so that she was lying above him. She was very light. He could not even feel her weight. She buried her face in his neck, then curled her tongue into his ear. He moved his hand across her bottom, stroking the rich curve of her buttocks, and then he came. She grabbed his hair with both hands and waited a moment, felt him driving again and again at her. Then she caught his rhythm and her own body took off. It had been so long that for a split second she worried whether she could come, but her hesitation passed and tumbled into the tide.

She was crying and cold and he reached down and pulled the blanket over them without moving, without coming away from her.

"Are you okay?" he asked.

She nodded and kept crying. "I'm sorry," she said, afraid he would misunderstand. Her face lay near his and she could feel his tongue licking the tears from her cheeks. His tongue was rough on her skin, like a cat's. "I just thought that I'd never make love again."

He moved her gently, holding the back of her head as if she were a newborn baby, moving a pillow so she could rest gently. The pillow case was cool on her face. Then he turned back the covers and moved to get up.

"Don't," she begged.

"I have to." He smiled gently. "You may not believe this, but my beef burgundy is still in the crock pot. It'll taste like tennis balls if I don't turn it off soon."

"But you won't come back. I won't have you inside me again."

"Yes, you will. In a few minutes."

"You promise." In her life she had only slept with Warren, and only when they were younger, before Scotty, had they made love more than once in a single night.

Barbara turned on the bed so she could watch Derek cross the room. She had not realized what a fine body he had. Warren had been a huge bear of a man, with thick arms and legs and an enormous waist. She had taken his enormous girth for granted, as she had his graying, the receding hair line. It was a fact of their life together.

Now she marveled at the sight of Derek crossing the room, his white body moving in and out of the shadows like the moon. He had the fine, strong body of a dancer, she thought, wide shoulders, a straight back that tapered to his waist, his buttocks rolled into a tight ball.

He stepped into the hall, swinging the door halfway closed before he flipped on the light. A shaft of brightness cut across the floor of the bedroom and Barbara closed her eyes to it. Then she stretched, tore at all her muscles, perversely enjoying the aches she felt there. In moments Derek would be coming back to her. He would slip into bed next to her, the length of his body overwhelming hers. She could already smell him, the wonderful sweat of his skin. She could already feel his lips on hers.

Scott unwrapped Brian Ború from a soft cloth and placed him on the Battleboard.

"Oh, he's beautiful!" Valerie exclaimed, picking up the miniature. "Did you paint him?"

"Yes."

The paladin was dressed in an olive green tunic, tiny brown leather boots, and a golden cloak dropped over one shoulder.

"I wish Marie looked this good. What's his name?"

"Brian Ború. A twenty-fifth-level paladin with magical powers, and a defender of virgins."

Valerie glanced at Scott. "Oh, yeah?" she said. "Well, how did he get here? Are you allowed to just drop a new character into the game?"

That wasn't allowed, Scott knew. But Brian had to be in the game, or it wouldn't be any fun.

"He hasn't just dropped in," he answered. "He was hunting in Macross Valley when he heard the sound of fighting and rode over to investigate."

Scott picked up the square dice and shook them out onto the Battleboard. "I have to find out how tough these highwaymen are," he said and rolled the dice twice more. "Okay, they're all within average attack points. Brian can handle them."

"But what if they attacked simultaneously?" Valerie asked. "I mean, wouldn't they?"

Scott nodded reluctantly, then smiled, thinking she was beginning to play now, to work out the game.

"Brian might lose," he offered. "I would have to roll the dice to see if he can repulse the three of them. Let's see. Their attack points are 8, 4, and 12, equalling 24. Now we have to multiply 24 by the basic strength for highwaymen, which is . . ." Scott picked up the *Dealer's Manual.*

"This game is too complicated," Valerie complained.

"No, it isn't. You've just got to give yourself time to learn the rules. Okay, here it is." He ran his finger down a column of names until he found highwaymen. "All right, there are two types: highwaymen who are simple bandits and highwaymen who rob from the poor and give to the rich. We'll make these bandit types, meaning they have a basic strength of 72. That's very high. So three times 72 makes 216 and then that times 24 means . . ." He took out a small pocket calculator and totalled up the numbers.

This game would never work at Flat Rock, Valerie thought. She couldn't think of any students who would go to so much trouble. It was harder than homework, she realized, watching Scott manipulate the numbers.

"Five thousand one hundred and eighty-four," Scott announced. He drew a circle around the numbers. "That's the three highwaymen's total strength points."

Valerie stared at Scott. It meant nothing to her. They were just numbers.

"As a twenty-fifth-level paladin, BrianBorú only has 2040—not counting his sacred sword."

"What does the sacred sword do?"

"Well, at times of great injustice in Eire, or moments in battle when BrianBorú is being overwhelmed, he can use the sacred sword given to him by the king of Ireland. However," Scott raised his hand in warning. "Only the Dealer can allow BrianBorú to use the sword, and it only can be used once in a game."

"Then use the sword, get rid of the highwaymen, and let's get on. My damsel, Marie, is getting upset. She doesn't like violence," Valerie answered, getting into the game once more.

"We'll let the dice decide," Scott said, tossing the cubes in the air. "A number above six means Brian Ború can use his sacred sword."

"Four," Valerie said, reading the dice. "Try again."

Scott shook his head. "No. The dice never lie."

"Then Brian could be killed," Valerie responded, realizing the consequences.

Scott nodded. "It's the highwaymen's turn to strike back. The Dealer rolls the dice for them and any number means a direct hit. Brian Ború wears armor that can repel an assault up till six. After that it's fatal." Scott picked up the dice to shake.

"Wait!" Valerie protested. "What can I do to help?"

"What are you thinking?" Derek asked. He was wearing jeans and a blue shirt with the sleeves rolled up, and he was standing by the kitchen door opening a bottle of red wine as she came in.

Barbara shook her head. She was wearing a shirt of his, and it reached almost down to her knees.

"I never expected anything like this," she said. She walked slowly, her bare feet soundless on the hardwood.

"What?" he asked, expecting to be praised.

"You. This." She waved toward the table set with candles and crystal, framed dramatically by the big casement windows. "I sort of blocked all this from my mind once Warren died. Locked myself up." She reached out and touched his face, as if reconfirming he was still there. The simple touch of him made her feel warm and loved.

"Why?" he asked, leading her to the table. "I didn't think widows burned themselves on the suttee any more."

Barbara shrugged. "I married young. Got pregnant. Warren and Scott have been my whole existence. Warren was a very forceful man; I lived in his shadow all these years and it was safe. I knew I was giving up something, but I accepted the trade off—the house in Weston, my security. The good life. Warren was very successful, or so I thought.

"Then the heart attack." She was whispering and it made her story even more lamentable. "It wasn't that Warren hadn't provided for us; he had. But he—never considered that he'd die." She looked again into Derek's eyes and leaned forward

176

across the small table. "I'm sorry," she added. "I don't mean to be morose."

"Please, Barbara. You're not."

"It changes you," she went on. "You become stronger."

"Some people do. You did."

"When I finally realized he was dead, I felt this odd sense of freedom, recklessness, really. I decided not to worry about the future." She stopped to see if he understood. "You would have thought differently, wouldn't you? So did I. I kept expecting myself to be destroyed by his death, but I wasn't. That worried me. I thought if I wasn't vanquished by his passing I was being unfaithful in some way. It was only later, months later, that I realized it was because of Scott."

"What did Scott have to do with it?"

"I still have Scott. And in that way Warren didn't die." She paused, realized she had been talking continually about herself. "Well, what about you?" she asked curiously. "How did you end up at Ballycastle?"

"Well, I'm from here originally. New York, that is. My parents had a potato farm on Long Island. All the other kids' parents had duck farms, so I guess I was the lucky one. Most of my friends quit school at 16, but I stuck it out. Then I won a state scholarship so I was able to go to college. You know, the old story: poor family, no money, youngest son makes good.

"I had to go all the way to Oregon to get a teaching job, but I did okay—until my seven years were up and they wouldn't give me tenure. With declining enrollments, they just didn't need another Shelley scholar on the faculty."

"Shelley?" she echoed. He laughed at the surprise in her voice.

"Yeah, what's the matter with that? Don't I look like a Romantic?"

"You look like a potato farmer," she said sweetly, then leaned across the table to kiss him.

"That's what they thought at Oregon," he said. "Plus I hadn't published very much, so the only other offers I got were for one-year appointments in the Frost Belt. And that's when the Foundation came along and asked me to be the Director. It was like winning the lottery on my last buck."

"But you were perfect for the job," she said loyally.

"Thank you, staff," he said. "But actually, I was. Perfect, I mean. I was an Irish-American with a good academic background. And the Foundation was perfect for me: a new job, a new career. A chance to get back east. I was out of Oregon before nightfall," he added, laughing.

"Well, you've earned every break you've gotten. And I'm glad you didn't get tenure; otherwise, you wouldn't be here."

"I'm glad, too. Now all we have to do is figure some way to keep you around this mausoleum." He reached across the small table to touch her hand.

She looked away, not knowing how to respond. She had a flash of what life would be like if she started over again with Derek, living with him at Ballycastle, giving her son a family again. She and Scotty and Derek. But she couldn't hold the image.

"I think I should go home. Is that all right?" she said quickly, as if asking permission.

"Sure. It's late," Derek replied quickly, masking his disappointment. He shouldn't have gone to bed with her, he thought. He had pushed the relationship too fast, demanded too much. She had a son to consider; she couldn't go popping into bed with the first new man who came along.

"Derek." Reaching out, she held his arm, stopping him from leaving the table. "This wasn't a mistake." She smiled wryly. "I mean, I enjoyed myself."

He bent forward and kissed her lightly on the lips. She rose to her feet and came into his arms, let him hold her, enjoyed again the brief pleasure of being embraced. She could feel him stirring, becoming ardent and she flattened her palm against his chest and shook her head.

"I have to go. It's getting late. And Valerie has to be taken home."

"Okay," he agreed. Together they walked back to the darkened bedroom. "Do you want to call them before we leave?"

"We could. Why?" In the semidarkness Barbara stripped off Derek's shirt and found her panties, pulling them on in one quick motion. The black silk panties defined her small body, Derek realized, gave it mystery. He wanted her again. She picked her black bra off the floor and hooked it about her waist, then slipped her arms through the straps and pulled the small cups over her breasts.

Derek still stood watching, marveling at the sight of Barbara dressing in the dark. She was reconstructing herself, returning to adulthood as she added clothes.

"What is it?" she asked, pausing.

Derek shook his head. "Nothing." He found her even more desirable like this, the black silk against her white skin in the dark room. He wanted only to stand and watch her move, to see her slight body break the flow of light from the other room.

"Stop," she asked. "You're embarrassing me."

"I'm sorry." He began to unbutton the shirt he was wearing. "You're just so lovely."

She smiled, then stepped into her black velvet pants, zipping them up like a boy as she walked. She found her Cacharel blouse on the floor at the end of the bed, tossed away like a dust cloth. She shook her head, smiled at her own abandon. It pleased her to realize what still was possible in her life. It was like discovering that she had a secret talent.

"So do you want to call him?" Derek asked, coming toward her. He had taken out a clean blue shirt, and unfolded it as he came closer. Barbara could smell the laundry starch; it reminded her of Warren, of opening his dresser drawer in their bedroom and smelling his scent.

She reached out and touched Derek's chest, felt his flesh. It brought her back to reality.

"I could call—but why bother? We'll be back at Ballycastle in fifteen minutes."

"Yes, that's why. I thought you'd want to telephone and warn him." Derek was smiling as he buttoned his shirt.

For a moment Barbara frowned, not understanding. Then she said, "Oh, dear."

"I was only kidding," Derek backtracked, seeing her reaction. "They're really not old enough."

She was already moving toward the living-room. "They're old enough," she answered.

Scott shook his head. "How can you help? You're a damsel in distress, a helpless girl."

"I'm not helpless," Valerie insisted. "Don't I get a chance

to strike back? I mean, it's my body they're after."

Scott picked up the *Hobgoblin Dealer's Manual* and searched through the pages, pausing at the section on sacrifice. "There's only one thing you can do, and that's offer up your life."

"You mean kill myself?"

Scott nodded, then read from the instructions:

It is permitted in the course of a melee for one character or another to forfeit his life for the common good. Such a gesture is considered noble and praiseworthy. However, the player is not allowed to run another character and is out of the game.

"Not much incentive there," said Valerie.

"It may not be up to you, anyway." Scott went on:

The leader of the Adventure may choose not to allow anyone to give up his life, or may demand such payment from the character as would make the sacrifice worthless.

"What does that mean?" Valerie asked.

Scott shrugged and gestured toward the tiny lead figures. "Well, the highwaymen want Marie's virginity. As leader of the Adventure, BrianBorú could call upon you to sleep with him first, and then you'd be worthless to the bandits."

"But I can't sleep with BrianBorú. I'm marrying Lord Monaghan."

"Well, he won't want to marry you, anyway, if the bandits get you."

"But suppose I wasn't a virgin in the first place?" Valerie was now smirking.

Scott shrugged again. He had the dice in his hands and he kept flipping them nervously. "Well, if you aren't a virgin then you can't marry Lord Monaghan no matter what happens."

"What about BrianBorú?" she asked, pressing. She could see her questions were making him nervous.

"I don't know."

"Yes, you do. What would BrianBorú think if Marie wasn't a virgin?"

"He wouldn't sleep with her."

"He wouldn't?"

Scott shook his head, gestured to his paladin. "Brian's not like that."

"Like what?" Valerie pressed.

"He doesn't go around sleeping with girls for no good reason."

"Doesn't he?" she teased.

Scott shook his head. "Come on, let's play."

"We are playing. We're trying to decide if it's better strategy for BrianBorú to fight the highwaymen or sleep with Marie."

"What do you think?" Scott asked abruptly, sitting up and staring across the Battleboard at her.

Valerie hesitated. She had been egging him along, pushing him about BrianBorú, and then the emphasis shifted. Now she was cornered by the conversation.

"Well, Marie would much rather sleep with Brian than get raped by those highwaymen. I mean, it would be a gang bang. And besides, what girl wouldn't go to bed with BrianBorú?" She picked up the small lead figure and brought it closer, examining how carefully Scott had painted the knight. "He's cute," she said.

Scott edged around the plastic Battleboard and slid up close to her. "But BrianBorú wouldn't rape her, you know." He reached up and took the tiny figure from her hands, held Brian high, like a prize.

Valerie shrugged. "He wouldn't have to. It wouldn't be against her will or anything like that." She did not look up.

Scott was slightly behind her. The length of her neck was exposed. She had such small ears, he saw. They looked soft and dewy, like the inside of a tulip. Her eyes were open, staring ahead, waiting. He moved only a few inches forward and kissed her on the nape of the neck. Her skin was warm, as if she had been in the sun all day.

When he kissed her she leaned back against him and his arms swept around her body. She turned her face and this time kissed him back, holding him to her like a magnet.

That startled him. He pulled back in alarm.

"See, Brian, you don't have to rape me," she whispered, hooking her arms around his neck like a Yale lock.

Scott kissed her again and this time he eased her back onto the floor, held her against him until they were both breathless. She turned her face sideways, gasping.

"You've got to give me a chance to breathe, Scott."

"I'm sorry. I never kissed a girl before," he admitted.

"Never?" She lay back on the rug, giving herself some distance.

"Well, you know what I mean, never like this." He did not know what to say.

"Kiss me again," she said, as if it were a new experiment.

This time he slid his hand up under her loose sweatshirt and she reached down and seized his wrist, held his fingers away from her breasts. They kept kissing. He was afraid to break away from her lips, afraid he would have to withdraw his hand from the soft stomach.

They rolled over on the rug, away from the fire and the *Hobgoblin* board, and stretched out flat beside the coffee table.

"The light is shining in my eyes," Valerie said.

"I'll get it." Scott jumped to his feet and snapped off one reading lamp at the end of the couch, then went to the other side of the armchair and turned off the small lamp on the end table.

"What are you doing?" she asked, rolling over on the rug to watch him.

"You said the light was bothering your eyes." Scott kept moving around the living room snapping off lamps.

"Well, leave some lights on."

"We have the fire, Valerie."

"That isn't enough. I can't see. What if your mother comes home and finds us in the dark?"

Scott came back to Valerie, dropping down on his knees.

"We can see the headlights from the beginning of the drive. It's easy to see cars coming and I'll just turn on some lights, that's all." He sounded older, as if he had done all this before.

"I'm scared," she admitted. She looked up and around the room, at the shadows from the flickering fire leaping off the ceiling and walls.

"Oh, scaredy-cat." He eased down beside her and hesitantly took her back into his arms. She relaxed gradually, wrapping herself into his embrace as if he were a safe spot in the room.

For a few moments her eyes kept watching the shadows on the walls and then she realized she was frightening herself and she turned her face into Scott's and kissed him quickly, closing her eyes.

He moved his left hand under her sweatshirt, up her side and cupped her breast. Only when he touched her there did she gasp and then dart her tongue into his mouth.

He was going to come, he realized, and pulled away, rolled off her.

"What's the matter?" she asked, frightened by his suddenness.

"Nothing. I'll be right back."

"What's the matter?" she demanded, sitting up, straightening her sweatshirt.

"Nothing. I was going to get us some Coke." He was already across the room, away from the firelight.

"Does my breath smell or something?"

"No, Valerie! For crying out loud, nothing is wrong." He made it safely to the kitchen, snapping on the light as he let the swinging door close behind him. For a moment she sat puzzled, listening to Scott's movements, and then she realized what had happened and she smiled, feeling a sense of achievement. Shifting around, she stretched out in front of the fire, letting the heat lick across her face, and she closed her eyes, like a cat on a hearth.

Her eyes were still closed when she heard the tapping at the bay window of the living room. At first it was faint and irregular and she took it for the sound of branches brushing against the glass.

It stopped and she took a deep breath, trying to decide what should happen when Scott came back from the kitchen. He was making a production of it, rattling ice trays and running water. Then again she heard tapping at the window. It was louder and more persistent, a steady tapping on the pane of glass, as if someone were hitting his nails against the window.

Valerie did not open her eyes, did not move from the fire. Scott would be back soon. She would let him go to the window and see what was outside. The tapping stopped. Valerie lifted her head and looked up. She could see several squares of glass in the bay window, but nothing beyond the black night.

"Scott!" she called.

"Yes, I'm coming." He picked up the glasses, then pushed through the swinging door and into the hallway. In the moment before the door swung closed, a block of bright light fell into the darkened living room, pinpointing Valerie on the carpet.

"Scott, I think there's someone outside," she whispered, as he settled down beside her on the rug.

"What?" He raised up on one arm, started to stand.

"Wait." Valerie grabbed his arm. "When you were in the kitchen I heard tapping. It would start and then stop."

"Like a branch?"

"Yes, sort of."

"Hey, dopey, that's what it is." Scott drained his glass of Coca-Cola.

"Are you sure?"

Scott nodded. "I've got branches against my windows and sometimes on windy nights they're so loud I can't even get to sleep." He stretched out beside her.

"But it isn't windy," she whispered.

"Come on, Val, you're just getting yourself scared over nothing. Look, I'll go turn on the porch light."

"No." She grabbed his arm. "It's okay. I was only kidding." She smiled, trying to show it was only a game. She did not want him to leave her, or, worse, find anyone outside. They were safe in the house. And Mrs. Gardiner would be home soon. "Scott, just hold me, please."

He brought her into his arms, lay back so she was resting against his chest.

"I can hear your heart," she whispered.

Scott touched Valerie's face, then the long nape of her neck. He couldn't think of a time when he had been happier. Just having her in his arms and knowing she was depending on him sent a surge of pride through him. He felt like Brian Ború, a paladin to this damsel in distress.

When the tapping started again she clutched his shoulders. Her sudden fear swept across him, as if they were both caught in an offshore breaker.

"Valerie, let go!" He tried to spill her off his body, but she wouldn't move.

The tapping was louder, more insistent, as if whoever it was wanted to get inside.

Scott tried to raise his head, but Valerie pushed him down, struggling to hold him from sight behind the sofa.

"He'll see you," she insisted.

"Valerie, we still don't know that anyone is outside."

Valerie kept shaking her head. "It's not a branch. It's a person."

"No one is on the estate but Conor and the security guard. They're not going to come knocking on the window." He tried again to pull himself up, but she fought back, held him down with her body. She had his arms pinned with her elbows.

"It's Fergus's niece."

Scott shook his head, not understanding.

"They say Fergus kept his crazy niece locked up on the third floor of Ballycastle, but when he died no one could find her. She had run off into the woods."

"Val, you're only frightening yourself. I never heard about any niece. My mom never told me."

The tapping stopped.

They were both silent and alert, listening. Scott moved again and this time Valerie let him go. He crawled to the corner of the sofa.

"Scott!" Valerie whispered, grabbed his leg.

He kept moving, inching forward on his elbows, crawling between the coffee table and the sofa. He felt like Brian Ború on a commando raid, creeping into the village of Kilcolgen, attacking the Urisk, the hobgoblins who haunted lonely houses and terrified travelers at night. Brian had had to rid Kilcolgen of these spirits and send them back to Loch Katrine, using only magic and without killing any, for they were good spirits, turning evil only when harmed.

Valerie crawled after him with her hand in his belt, as if afraid she'd lose him in the dark room. But she refused to move out from behind the sofa, or to let him do so.

"Damn it, Val, I can't move." Scott reached back to pull her fingers from his belt and the small house shook. Someone was banging the outside wall. Scott rolled over on the carpet and Valerie could see that he too was scared.

"We'll call the police," she said at once. "The security down at the main gate." She looked up, chanced a glance at the front door. "Is the door locked?"

"No!" Scott shook his head. "Mom didn't lock the front door," he admitted, almost in tears. Valerie still had hold of him, her nails digging now into the flesh of his back.

"We've got to lock the doors, Scott. Now!"

"No, let's get into my bedroom. There's a lock on the door, and the phone in the kitchen reaches into there. Once we call the front gate, they'll be up to the house in a minute."

Valerie nodded. Her fright had lodged in her throat like a piece of meat.

"Ready?"

She nodded again.

Scott turned over and got to his knees, then hesitated, saying, "You go first." He had to raise his voice. There was more banging in the front; the sound was unrelenting, like a storm door swinging wildly in the wind.

Valerie hesitated, afraid to expose herself. It seemed safer there, crouched behind the sofa.

The banging stopped. Scott grabbed her shoulder, held her still as they listened. Perhaps the stranger had gone away. Perhaps there had been only the night wind. The outside storm door could have swung open and hit the house. He hadn't checked it after his mother left the house.

They thought they heard the door knob rattle and both of them tore from their hiding place, stumbling over lamps and furniture and themselves as they raced for the room under the stairs.

Scott pushed Valerie ahead of him and into the bedroom, then slammed and locked the door behind him.

"Get down," he ordered, "on the floor." His single bed stood against the wall, below the windows. He reached across it and, grabbing the cord, dropped the venetian blinds with a crash, then crawled into the small space next to Valerie at the head of the bed.

"They'll break the door down," she whispered.

"No, they won't. They can't."

"Can we shove the bed against the door?"

"That won't do any good."

"The chair. Put that chair under the door knob," Valerie directed.

Scott jumped up and pulled his desk chair across the small room, fitted the back under the knob, and jammed it tight.

"The phone, Scott. We forgot the telephone," Valerie whispered from the corner.

"Oh, shit!" Scott spun around away from the door. It was too late now; he couldn't go into the hallway. Whoever it was would be in the living room, perhaps walking down the hall to the bedroom. Scott leaned against the thin wall, listening for footsteps. Someone was in the living room. He could hear furniture being moved. He looked back at Valerie, motioned her to be silent, and pressed his ear against the thin, wooden door. For a moment he could hear nothing but his heart, and the blood pounding against his ear drums.

Coming out of the drive, the headlights of Derek's car pinpointed the guest house as if with spotlights.

Barbara bolted up in the front seat. The front door was open and the screen door hanging on one hinge. The lights of the living room were on; they blazed out onto the circular gravel drive.

"Something's wrong," she said quietly, already preparing herself.

Derek pushed down on the gas pedal and his car skidded up the gravel. Barbara's fear for Scott was distorting time, slowing her reactions. She saw everything precisely, in clean bright images, recording it all as if on film—the house blazing with lights, open front door, and Derek's car swinging into the cul-de-sac and skidding to an abrupt stop.

He slammed on the brakes and Barbara ran into the house, shouting for Scott. She saw at once the living room had been ransacked, with lamps tipped over and the couch pillows tossed across the room. Someone had gone to the shelves beside the fireplace and pulled down the library of books, scattering them on the floor.

"Scotty!" Barbara kept shouting, spinning around, searching. Her shock confused her. She did not know which way to run. "He's gone," she could only cry out to Derek as he came through the open front door.

Now Derek shouted. His voice roared through the small cottage.

Down the long hallway they both heard the bedroom lock tumble over and then Scott appeared in the shadows.

"My God, you're safe," Barbara whispered. Seeing him left her weak. She dropped helpless to the arm of the couch.

"Scott, what happened?" Derek went to him. "Where's Valerie?"

Scott gestured behind him, to where Valerie followed him timidly.

"Are you two okay?" Derek asked, glancing at them both.

Scott nodded. "What happened?" he asked, astonished by the sight of the upheaval.

"We have no idea, Scott. Why were you two hiding in the bedroom?" Barbara had recovered and gone to her son, to hold him by the shoulders. She could see the glazed look in his eyes, the traces of shock. She embraced him, used her touch to comfort and reassure him.

"We were playing *Hobgoblin*." He turned to Valerie, as if for verification. "And...someone was trying to get inside, then..." He gestured feebly, unable to explain. Someone had been after them. Someone had watched them and tapped on the window and come into the house while they'd been barricaded in his room. And then he saw his *Hobgoblin* game on the floor. The tiny figure of BrianBorú had disappeared.

Fourteen

They had painted his locker yellow. And recently, too; the paint was still sticky. Up and down the hall kids hung around, waiting for his reaction.

"I'm going to get blamed for this," Scott said.

"No, you're not." Valerie opened her locker, put away her coat and began to pull out her geometry notebook.

"Those fuckers." Scott kicked the bottom of his locker, leaving a mark in the fresh paint. At the sound, some of the kids burst into giggles. Others ducked behind their locker doors and whispered to friends, explaining what was going on.

"Just keep quiet," Valerie advised, speaking under her breath. "Don't make a big deal of it. Just pretend nothing is wrong."

"Borgus, that shithead."

"Come on, get your books and we'll go down and tell Mr. Carpenter. He'll have it painted over before second period. This happens all the time, Scott. It's almost a tradition at Flat Rock. Kids are always getting their lockers painted."

"But none of them ever ran the wrong way in a football game," Scott said. "I should've known Borgus would get me for that. This is probably just the start."

Valerie's mouth tightened and she spoke slowly, as if to a child.

"Scott, everybody does something dumb. I do something

189

dumb every day, almost. Look at Saturday night when I thought there was someone outside the house and scared us both to death."

Scott glanced at her as he locked his locker. "There was someone in the house."

"There was?" Valerie's eyes widened.

Scott moved away from the locker and Valerie followed closely, anxious to hear his explanation.

"I went along with Mom and Mr. Brennan about how we had just frightened ourselves. We did pull the cushions off the sofa, and I know I knocked a lamp over on the way to my room. But there's no way we could've spilled all those books from the bookshelves. And, besides, Brian Ború is missing. She ripped it off."

"Who? Scott, damnit!" Valerie grabbed his arm and made him stop walking. "What are you talking about?"

Scott shrugged, as if he wasn't supposed to say anything, and then began, keeping his voice low and backing Valerie into one of the classroom doorways.

"You know when you saw someone in the woods on Friday?"

Valerie nodded. "But you said it wasn't true . . . ?"

"Well, Mr. Brennan doesn't want anyone from town to know, but some crazy woman got loose at Ballycastle. One of those shopping-bag women. She got off the bus on 12 or something and got lost in the woods. After I dropped you off, I went back and tracked her down and she got me, but good. Look!" He pulled the sleeve of his sweater up and showed Valerie the bandages, told her about his adventure in the woods.

"You kept saying it was a Black Annis."

"I said she looked like a Black Annis. I mean, there isn't any such thing. They're only a character in *Hobgoblin*." They began to walk again down the crowded hallway.

"And that's who was tapping on the windows and knocked over all the furniture?"

"Yeah. They got her once, but I guess she got another bus back out to Ballycastle."

"Did Mr. Brennan tell you that she got off a bus on Route 12?"

"He told my mom."

"Well, I live on 12 and there's no bus. Maybe he meant a charter bus or something." Valerie looked up, then down the hallway to Times Square. "Oh, shit," she whispered.

Scott glanced up too. Over the heads of the other students he could see the banner, painted in yellow and taped across the busy intersection: "Wrong way Preppie beats Flat Rock," it read.

"Oh, God," he sighed. "Now everybody is going to be after my ass."

Valerie grabbed Scott's arm. "Let's cut through the library. They're waiting for you at Times Square."

"No." He shook his head. "Fuck 'em." He kept walking.

"Scott, it's only going to get worse. Keep away from them." She had grabbed hold of his hand and was holding him back. Now she was frightened. Scott was staring ahead, watching the football players. His eyes had hardened and he no longer looked like a kid.

"Scott, they'll hurt you."

"No, they won't." He moved forward, down the long hallway. The first bell rang and from both sides of the hall there was a flurry of activity. More locker doors were slammed, and the hallway jammed with students.

Valerie lost Scott's hand in the sudden press. She reached out again, stretching for his shoulder, but he dodged her neatly, and pressed forward.

"Scott, don't!" she pleaded. They had seen him. Ahead, she saw Borgus straighten up, glance around at the other football players who were leaning against the walls. They would get him between them, she knew. They would work him over like a ball, bounce him back and forth between them.

She turned away and pushed through the crowd of students, running for the principal's office.

They had begun to chant. Borgus had started it. Raising his hand, he had yelled out, "Preppie, Fairy; Preppie, Fairy; here comes . . . the Preppie Fairy." Lining both sides of the hallway the football players picked up the chant, clapping their hands in cadence.

Scott kept walking, thinking of Brian Ború. Once, crossing Galway Bay, Brian had encountered the Blue Men of the Minch. They had swum out from Inishmaan and Inisheen to wreck his ship, and he had kept them at bay by singing a rhyme, hypnotizing them with his voice.

Scott smiled, laughed at them and yelled back, "Flat Rock Flat Heads. Flat Rock Flat Heads."

Students in the hallway were giving him room, backing off as he got closer to Times Square. The crowd opened up, giving him a wide path through the intersection. And then he and Borgus were face to face, surrounded by a gauntlet of teammates.

"Flat Rock Flat Heads." Scott came in shouting and spun around the circle, shouting into each of their faces, the same way Brian had circled from the port side to starboard, shouting into the rough seas, keeping off the Blue Men of the Minch.

Borgus yelled back but Scott's voice drowned him out. The preppie was laughing at him, facing him down in front of the team. He was the leader; he had to do something.

Like a bull, Borgus lowered his head and charged Scott, butting him hard in the solar plexus. Scott gasped and bent over in pain. Borgus raised his hands, acknowledged the cheers of the team. Scott came after him then; using his armful of books like a ramming rod, he bowled Borgus over.

Furious, the senior came back at once, hitting Scott on both shoulders, knocking him across the hallway. Scott let himself fly, hurtling into the row of football players standing against the lockers. He had lost his books and as he flew backwards he swung his elbow into Hank Simpson's middle. As the tall halfback doubled over, Scott pushed away, running for an opening he spotted in the line.

"Get him!" Borgus shouted and dove after him.

He caught Scott behind the legs, clipping him, and Scott hit the cement floor.

The girls in the corridor were screaming, their voices echoing down the hallways. It had been worth it, Scott was thinking. He had hit both Borgus and Simpson; he had really showed them. He was in a tight ball on the floor, shouting, "Flat Rock Flat Heads" when someone kicked him in the head.

The personnel folders were waiting on her desk when Barbara Gardiner arrived that morning. She had left them there the evening before, when she left early to get ready for dinner with

Derek. It seemed like a century since then. She turned to the events of fifty years ago with a sense of relief. It was easier to concentrate on the past than worry why her home was suddenly under siege.

There were dozens of files, but she knew which names to look for—the ones on the scrolls at Steepletop. One by one she culled those from the pile, and when she had all ten she stacked the remainder on her windowsill.

Now, her desk cleared for serious work, she took off her coat and went into the kitchen off the first-floor office to pour herself a cup of coffee.

"Come and drink that in here," Karen DeWitt called to her. Valerie's sister was sitting with several other tour guides and secretaries at the staff lunch table.

Barbara smiled over at them and shook her head. "Thanks, Karen, but this is my week to be a grind, I'm afraid. The board is expecting an initial report from me."

Back in her office she closed the door, sat down and contemplated the pile of folders for a moment. Then she lifted up the one on top and opened it on the desk before her. The name on the manila tab was Carmel Burke. Well, she thought, why not start right off with a bang. Carmel Burke, whoever she was, had already caused them all enough trouble.

The file was a letdown. It contained very little: the carbon copy of a letter from Ballycastle to Carmel's parents, agreeing to accept her as an employee; instructions for her to take the Cunard-White Star steamship from Cork; and a note saying where she should obtain her ticket. Ten pounds also had been included in the letter, for pocket money. The letter had been signed by Helen Wilkinson, housekeeper.

Beneath this was Carmel's original letter, responding to an advertisement that Mrs. Wilkinson had apparently placed in the Irish *Times*. It was a studiously formal letter, written in simple, careful script on oilskin. Barbara held the fragile paper gently in her hands. Reading it was like looking at an old portrait, a black and white photograph from another age. She could almost see the young Irish girl, dressed in a high-necked, stiff white blouse, her face rosy with color, her eyes deep blue. A lass.

Barbara set the letters carefully aside and picked up the

girl's payment sheet. In 1931 Carmel had been earning ten dollars a week. There was little else in the folder except receipts—for uniforms, doctor's bills, etc. Barbara shook her head. She had seen the same pattern of information in other personnel files. Fergus had paid all his employees' expenses, as if they were his children. That had been common practice in the nineteenth century, but by the thirties it was a little passé. Barbara went on to Nuala O'Neill's file. It was as disappointing as Carmel's. She was skimming a series of weekly payment slips when the letter slipped out.

It was a heavy envelope, mailed from Ireland and still unopened forty years later. Barbara picked it up and read the addresses. From Mary O'Neill, Rock Road, Co. Donegal, to Nuala O'Neill, Ballycastle, Hamilton County, New York. Barbara squinted at the fading postmark. The letter had been received in Flat Rock on August 9, 1940.

Barbara didn't remember the exact date on Nuala's tombstone, but it seemed to have been around then. Perhaps the letter had arrived after Nuala was already dead. Creepy. Barbara dropped the envelope back in the folder, then reached for the next file. Her hand stopped in mid-air. The allure of the unopened letter was irresistible.

Once more she extracted the thick envelope and turned it in her hands, as if weighing its value. Mary O'Neill was probably Nuala's mother, which meant that she, too, was probably dead. A letter from the dead, to the dead, and opening it now would be a little like violating a tomb.

She tapped the letter against her nails, debating a moment more. Then she told herself she was being morbid and unbusinesslike, and she slit the flap decisively. Inside were half a dozen folded pages, covered in a large, awkward script. Barbara glanced up, checking her office door, as if she half-expected to be caught in the act. She took a deep breath and read the dead girl's letter.

Dear Nuala,

It has been a fortnight now since your last letter. I have not written in all this time because so help me God I haven't known what to say.

As you must know your letter caused us all a good

bit of worry. Your father hasn't slept a whole night since it arrived. He keeps thinking it was his fault for letting you go off to America in the first place. And since you didn't say what was troubling you, we have been imagining the worst.

I took your letter with me to Mass on Sunday and had a word with Father Kerwin. I was hoping he might have a notion about what we should do to get you home, but reading your letter put him in a foul mood.

He said it was a crying shame that you left Drumfree in the first place, and he blames your father for bringing the Irish *Times* into the house. I don't know if we can blame the *Times*. You always had a mind of your own, Nuala. It would be easier to catch a hare in my bare hands than to have kept you home with me. And now Michael, God help me, wants to go off to New Zealand. He'd be gone by now, if we had the money.

What can I tell you, my child? We haven't the fifty pounds. This place, as you well know, is back of beyond, and if you weren't sending home an odd pound here and there, I would never put a piece of mutton on the table.

It tears my heart not to know what troubles you. God willing, perhaps Mr. O'Cuileannain will change his mind and give you passage home. Sure, it would be a pittance to a man like him.

May God bless you, Nuala, and remember it would do no harm to hear a second Mass on Sunday. Prayer will help you find your way in America.

I wish to heaven you were with me now before the hearth. I miss you all the time. I think some days my heart will break with worry. God bless and keep you well. And grant us a way to bring you home to Ireland.

Please write us at once and say why you must leave America. Not knowing what troubles you is a great cause of pain.

Your father sends his love.

Barbara slowly folded the letter and tucked it away. There were tears in her eyes. The poor mother, she thought, breaking her heart for a child already dead. The daughter never returned

to Ireland. She would have to ask Conor; he would know why
Nuala O'Neill had wanted to leave Ballycastle.

"Who hit you, Scott?" the principal asked. "Who started all
the trouble?"

He was standing before the boy, rocking back and forth on
the balls of his feet. The principal was short and wiry and had
the quick moves of a bantamweight.

Scott shook his head. "I tripped." He was still sitting on the
nurse's cot, with a bandage on his temple. He looked like a
war casualty.

"All right. Have it your way." The principal had small
change in his pocket and as he rocked he fingered the coins
nervously. "Mr. Russell will drive you home."

"I have my own car."

"You can leave it in the lot today. I'm not going to have
you driving on the highway. If you can't remember who hit
you in Times Square, then you're not well enough to drive
home."

"I fell down, sir. Kids were pushing to get to class and I
bent over to pick up one of my books, and someone—I don't
know who—ran into me and I fell and I couldn't get up." As
he talked, his explanation slowly began to make sense, as if
it had actually happened.

The principal kept bouncing nervously. He knew the boy
was lying, and he was relieved. There would be no need to
take on Tagariello and start expelling football players. Besides,
he reasoned, this Gardiner boy would only be at Flat Rock for
the year.

"Go on home now. I'll have one of the secretaries call your
mother."

"No, don't telephone." Scott jumped up from the cot. "It
will only get her upset. She'll worry, you know, until I get
home. It's better if I just see her."

The principal nodded. "Fine, fine." He had Scott by the
elbow, ushering him to the door.

It wasn't until the fifth file that Barbara noticed the con-
nection. It wasn't explicit; it wasn't even certain. It was simply

a hunch, growing out of the accumulation of information in the various files, the similarity of the details, the medical prescriptions.

She shuffled the files together, then picked up the telephone and buzzed Derek to ask if she could come up and see him.

Valerie was waiting for him at the locker.

"Are you okay?" Her voice was very soft.

Scott nodded as he spun the combination. On his first attempt the lock wouldn't work and he slammed the door and swore.

She moved in immediately and took the lock away from him. "What's your combination?" she asked.

"Eight–Twenty-two–Twelve." He stepped aside and let her do it. "Why aren't you in class?"

"I told Miss Tinko I was having my period. She gets all hysterical, like you're going to bleed down your legs or something."

Scott glanced down at his feet. He couldn't think of anything to say to that.

"Where are you going?" she asked.

"Home. Mr. Russell is driving me to Ballycastle. I have to leave the MGB here. They think I'm going to kill myself on the highway or something."

"Ugh. Who said that? Carpenter?"

Scott nodded.

"What a turkey he is." Valerie jerked open the locker and stood aside, watching the hall for teachers. They would send her back to class if they caught her out in the corridor. "Give me your keys. I'll drive your car home."

"You can't drive."

"Yes, I can. I've been driving a tractor since I was eleven."

"My MGB isn't a tractor. I'm not going to let you or anyone touch it." He dumped his books into the locker and pulled out his jacket.

"Scott, if you leave the car, Borgus and Simpson will see it after football practice and take it."

"How?" he demanded.

"By hot-wiring it, Scott! Everyone knows how. It's something you learn to do on a farm."

Scott shook his head. "I'll get my mom to drive me back this afternoon, after work."

"Scott, I can drive the car." She followed him down the empty corridor, toward the front office. "I even have a driving permit."

He kept shaking his head.

Valerie stopped in the middle of the hallway and let him go. "Okay, I don't care. It's not my dumb car."

She went back to her class, smiled reassuringly at Miss Tinko and looked out the window. The dark green MGB was parked off by itself, in a corner of the lot. He wanted them to do something to his car, she thought, just as he had wanted them to hurt him. He wanted a reason to get even.

"What's butesin picrate used for?" Derek asked. He was sitting at his desk with his legs up, flipping casually through the small white prescription slips.

"I don't know, but look." Barbara took the slips out of his hands and went to the flip chart, to the sheet where the girls' names and dates were written. She began to read off the names, matching each one with a doctor's prescription. "We're talking about a ten-year span and they all were given the same prescription by the same doctor. Don't you think that's too much of a coincidence?"

Derek swung his legs off the desk and turned his chair around to face her. He was wearing jeans and cowboy boots, but he had taken off the boots, and now he tucked his leg up, braced it against the leather seat.

"It could be nothing at all, Barbara," Derek answered. "Look, all these girls worked hard. Housework in the '30s was real manual labor. What's prescribed here could be nothing more than a muscle relaxer."

"Why a New York doctor?"

"I'm sure Flat Rock didn't even have a resident doctor in 1930. Besides, this man was probably Fergus's personal physician, and naturally he would have been invited up for weekends. What's his name?"

"Smyth," she answered, checking one of the prescriptions.

"Old Fergus might have paid Smyth to take care of all his

198

employees. Conor would know that. You could ask <u>him</u>." Then he paused, frowning, "Why all this interest, Barbara? Believe me, the board doesn't care if the housemaids came down with influenza every spring."

"I found a letter in one of the files. In Nuala O'Neill's file, actually. It was still in a sealed envelope, but I opened it."

Derek's head jerked up. Barbara looked away guiltily.

"I don't think I was violating any federal laws," she said. "The girl has been dead for forty years."

"What about it?"

"It was from her mother but it came too late; Nuala was already dead. The mother doesn't say much, except that Nuala had written and asked for money to return to Ireland. Something was wrong here at Ballycastle but apparently Nuala wouldn't say what it was."

Barbara walked to the narrow windows that looked toward Steepletop. She could not see the grave site, but she had placed its position on the long ridge. She knew where the land flattened and where the graves were.

"Maybe she was pregnant, then. These were simple Irish girls, Barbara. Catholic farm girls for the most part. Maybe she got pregnant by one of the farmhands and Fergus was kicking her off the land. He was a religious man. You've learned that about him. He built the Catholic church down in town, as well as the Knights of Columbus Hall."

"What if all of them were pregnant, Derek? What if that strange, Gothic graveyard up on the hill is full of young, silent girls, barely out of their teens, who got pregnant out of wedlock. If Fergus was such a good Catholic, then why did he bury them together up on Steepletop and not in Flat Rock, in the cemetery next to his precious church?"

Derek tossed the pen away and stood. "What are you driving at? What do you have in mind?" He hesitated, then realized what was troubling her. "You're not saying that Fergus got all those girls pregnant?"

"Yes. It's possible. Remember those French epitaphs we found on Steepletop? I checked out the ones I couldn't translate and guess what they mean? *Ma cuissette folâtre*—my frolicsome thigh. Frolicsome! *Mon téton d'albâtre*—my alabaster breast. *Ma friande douceur*—my dainty sweetness. At first I thought he was just being possessive about his people, but taken together, in context, all these parts of the body have sexual connotations. These were his women, Derek. He was sleeping with all his maids."

Derek sighed. "Barbara, that was half a century ago. It doesn't matter now. No one is alive. No one cares. Fergus left us thirty million dollars and this estate all for the purpose of philanthropy. I think we should concentrate on giving that money away to good causes and not get obsessive about some ancient graveyard."

"I'm not obsessed," Barbara replied coolly. She was determined not to let his anger intimidate her. "I'm curious," she added, for lack of a better retort.

"You have a preliminary report to present the board."

"I'm nearly finished. Anita is already typing the final draft."

"Fine."

"Derek, this investigation isn't going to interfere with my work. I won't let it." She came closer to him, as if to make amends. "There's something else that's odd," she said softly. "When you first came to Ballycastle and saw that tiny graveyard on Steepletop, you must have been curious. Did you ask anyone about it?"

Derek nodded yes. "I asked Conor, of course. I asked him a thousand and one questions about this place."

"And?"

Derek shook his head. "Nothing. He explained that Fergus had allowed all his Irish employees to be buried on the estate. It was a holdover from the old country. It was done in this country, for that matter, on plantations before the Civil War."

"And you didn't think it was odd, all those strange headstones over the graves of young women? Didn't you wonder why there were no men?"

"Barbara, I didn't even know they were all women. I never bothered to decipher the names. Unlike you, I wasn't in the market for a conspiracy." He had begun to pace. He was wearing what Barbara called his office compromise clothes—faded jeans with a blue cotton dress shirt and tie—and he tugged at the knot, unbuttoned the tight collar as he circled the room. He was overreacting, she thought, and she tried to cool things down by being calm and reasonable.

"I wasn't witch-hunting either, Derek. It was Scotty who found Carmel Burke's name on Steepletop and you who suggested that we have a picnic there. But now that we know something's up, I think we have to investigate. We owe it to the Foundation."

Derek stopped pacing and threw his head back, inhaling deeply. "That's just it, Barbara. The Foundation. Now, I know you've been pretty sheltered all your life, so let me explain a little about corporate chain of command. There's just one rule you have to remember. The boss doesn't want to know. If it's inconvenient or potentially embarrassing, bury it. And if the truth happens to be that the endower of the Foundation, the fount from whom all funding flows, was a sex fiend who impregnated nearly a dozen teen-age cooks and maids—well, that is information that the boss particularly doesn't want to know."

"But you told me yourself there have always been stories about Ballycastle—the crazy niece, for one, and the women's bodies found in the bathtub."

"Those were only rumors. A few nice, creepy legends for the tourists. No one really believes them."

"Well, no one will believe this, either," she said, gesturing impatiently, "so what's the harm?" But as she spoke, she knew in her heart that she did believe it. And so did Derek.

Conor stirred up the coals of the forge and dropped Monica Healion's old letters into the flames. The fire blazed up quickly, fed by the papers. It was best this way, he thought; get rid of all the papers, everything he had saved about the girls.

He tossed in Nuala O'Neill's yellow blouse. That took longer to burn. Then her Irish passport and her working papers. The next item in the wooden locker was Peggy Connolly's olive wood rosary. Conor picked it up and laced it through his fingers. He couldn't burn the rosary, he realized. Pope Pius himself had blessed it in Rome. Instead he slipped the beads into his own pocket.

Next Conor leaned over the box and picked up Carmel Burke's small bundle of belongings—the pearl-handled mirror, her letters from the old country, the love notes left by Conor in her lunch basket or hidden beneath her pillow when he left her in the early morning darkness.

Their love had been a secret—or so they thought, until Himself had had a word with Conor.

He tossed the papers on the forge—the mirror wouldn't burn—then stood away as his memories of Carmel burst into brighter flame.

"And what will we be doing, Conor?" she had whispered.

"Ah, we won't be doing anything we haven't done before, my love." He had held her hand lightly in his. There was no need to struggle with Carmel, to force her into the castle; she came freely, obediently, trying as always to please him.

"We'll have the big room, luv."

"But Himself."

"He's away for the night. He told me not more than an hour ago. I saw the Bentley drive off myself."

"I'm afraid," she had said, clinging to him. Conor had wrapped his arm about her. "Don't you worry, lass." His hand came up in the dark to fondle her and the breath went out of her in a sudden rush.

"Oh, darling." Carmel pressed against him.

They went along the dark hallway of the north wing, past the bedrooms, the sleeping guests, and into Fergus's bedroom.

"See, luv," Conor whispered. "We have it all to ourselves." He led her to the postered bed. The full moon lit the room, coming through the tall, narrow windows in bright patches.

Carmel stood as still as a nun while Conor undressed her. She was puzzled, first by his insisting that they go up to the main house, and now by the elaborate care he took with her dress and slip. He laid them aside on a wing chair as if setting a scene. He was not that way, Carmel knew. He was always in a great rush to have her clothes off, to be on with it.

She reached up to unbutton his shirt and he shook his head, saying, "Wait, luv."

"What is it, darling?" she asked, feeling strange dressed only in her knickers.

"Hop into bed like a good girl," he instructed. He was different tonight, she realized. He was holding himself back. He wasn't his usual self.

"What is it, darling?" she asked again, seeing in the pale light the sorrow in his eyes.

"Quiet, my dear." He kissed her once and, pulling back the quilts, eased her small self into the bed. "Now close your eyes."

"What is it? Conor?" Carmel raised her white arm from the covers and touched his worried face. "I love you, sweetheart," she said to reassure him.

"And I love you, Carmel." Of all the girls he had brought to Fergus's bedroom, he loved only her, and he could feel his own heart wrench with pain as he slowly undressed, glancing quickly around the bedroom to see where Fergus had hidden himself.

"Oh, darling," she whispered. Tears blurred her eyes, and he knew she had seen Fergus move in the shadows.

"Now, now, lass." He climbed into bed beside her and she did not resist. She would cooperate, he knew; they both understood and accepted their place in life, their position at Ballycastle. It wasn't their right to have anything more, born as they were to the bogs of the west country, the endless poverty of Ireland. Himself had saved their lives and now they were paying the price.

"Conor?"

The old man jumped at the sound of the boy's voice.

"Jesus, Mary and Joseph. What has happened to you? Have you been playing football now?" Conor left the forge and the flaming pile of love letters. Scott was standing in the open barn doors and Conor had to squint to see him in the bright midday sun.

Scott shook his head. "There was a fight at school."

"Aah, a fight you say. And what happened to the other fella?"

"Nothing," Scott whispered. He had wanted to brag to Conor about how he had faced them down, but it didn't seem like such a triumph anymore. "There were a bunch of them, and they knocked me down in the hall and kicked me."

"A bunch of thugs?"

Scott shrugged. "Football players." He did not like talking about it. No matter how many there were, Brian Ború would have left at least one of them on the floor behind him. "What are you working on?" he asked, changing the subject.

"Aah, it's nothing much." He went back to his workbench and beckoned Scott over. "Would you be knowing what this is?" he asked, gesturing toward the object on the bench before him.

"An old pistol."

"Aah, it is that, but this is a real beauty—a Snaphaunce sporting gun from the sixteenth century. It was one of Himself's favorites. See here, this is the Snaphaunce; it fires by striking a piece of flint against steel. That was a new way of doing it in them days. See, you fire it this way." The old man pulled back the cock with his right hand, locking it into position, and aimed at the open doorway. "Now what you do is press the trigger here, and the cock will swing forward. It knocks the flint against the steel; a spark falls into the gun powder in the pan; then . . ." Conor pulled the tight trigger and the gun roared.

Scott stumbled back, shocked by the pistol blast, and banged his head on an overhanging lamp. Laughing, Conor lowered the heavy pistol and put it back on the bench.

"That's real gun power for you, lad. None of your little peashooters. It's an English weapon. Every landowner in Ireland had one in them days."

"But that was almost five hundred years ago, and this one still works."

"Aah, it does. There isn't a weapon in the castle that can't be used today. I've seen to that," he said proudly.

"Let me fire it," Scott asked, his fear gone.

"Aah, it's a dangerous thing, lad."

"Come on, Conor, just once." He reached over and picked up the long-barreled pistol. It was too heavy for him to lift with one hand and he almost dropped it.

"Don't touch the barrel," Conor warned. "It heats up, you know, from the shooting."

"Where do you put the powder?" Scott asked, turning the ornate pistol in his hands.

"Here," Conor instructed, loading it for him. Then he pointed the pistol out into the empty barnyard. "That fence post. Let's see, lad, what kind of shot you are. Let's see if you're as good as your Brian Ború."

"Brian Ború never fired a weapon," Scott said, carefully taking the weapon from the old man.

"Time enough you both learned. Now careful, lad, keep the gun pointed away from the buildings. Aim low now; the pistol will jump when you fire. And you best use two hands to hold it steady."

"Quit fussing, Conor. You're making me nervous."

"All right, lad, all right. Just look you don't shoot your mother by mistake. Or Mr. Brennan."

Scott closed his left eye, then holding his breath tugged at the thick trigger with two fingers.

The gun erupted, throwing his arms upward as it recoiled. Scott saw a puff of dirt a dozen feet beyond the barnyard fence. He had missed the fence post entirely.

"Aah, you didn't hold it steady, lad," Conor said, taking the smoking gun from Scott.

"It hurt," Scott said, rubbing his shoulders, feeling the pain in the length of his arms.

"Aah, indeed."

"But it didn't hurt you," Scott said, following the small man back into the barn. He looked at Conor now, watched him return to cleaning the pistol with an oily rag.

"Oh, I'm familiar with it, Scotty. I've fired these old weapons enough in my day. Himself had a thing about them, you know." He glanced at the boy almost furtively, as if he had just revealed a secret. "He wanted all his guns kept in working order, with ammunition and powder and all. Come with me now, lad, and I'll show you more."

"I don't know, Conor. I gotta go. I mean, my mom doesn't even know I'm home from school." Scott hung back. His mother would get upset if she saw him hanging around the old man.

Conor nodded, but he looked so wounded, Scott felt as if he had hit him. "Maybe I could come by later after Mom knows I'm home."

Conor just nodded.

"Well, where are you going?" Scott asked, reluctant to leave.

"Up to the house," Conor answered, jerking his chin in the direction of the castle. He had several days' growth of beard, white and bristly, like an old drunk's.

Scott shrugged. "Well, maybe I'll go with you. I mean, my mom's probably up there anyhow."

"Well, then, lad, give me a hand, would you? Take this." He handed Scott the Snaphaunce. "Have I ever told you about White Man's Island?"

Scott shook his head, following Conor out of the shop and up the hill to the mansion. Conor walked slowly, placing his feet on the deep slope with precision. He lost his breath before he reached the grass, but he kept talking, telling his story.

"Now White Man's Island isn't in your *Hobgoblin*, is it?"

"I don't think so. I never read about it, but I don't know everything about the game."

"Aah, well, and I thought you did, but you didn't know about Nuckelavee, now did you?"

"What about White Man's Island?" Scott asked quickly. The thought of the evil hobgoblins sent a shiver of fear through his body. For a moment he could see the foul-smelling creatures: their pale, flat eyes, and their pig snout mouths.

"Well, I've never been there myself," Conor went on, puffing between sentences, "and I don't, to tell you the God's truth, know anyone who has. But it's an island in the Irish Sea where the ancient druids lived. Now, they're in your game. You can't have a game about Ireland without druids, now can you?"

"No. There's a whole chapter in the guidebook about them. They're magic-users."

"Indeed, they are. Well, they lived on this island and whenever sailors approached, the island disappeared. They say a fog, a thick mist, the dragon's breath, would suddenly blow across the sea, hiding the land. Only one man has ever been there. He set sail on a tombstone from a cemetery near Dundaek Bay. But he never came back, so we don't know anything about his experiences."

"Wait! Wait!" Scott began to laugh. "That doesn't make any sense. Look, you said he sailed there, but never came back. So how do you know he actually got to the island?" They had reached the house and gone in through the kitchen door.

"Aah, because the stone came back. It reappeared in the cemetery." Conor led the way through the empty kitchen into the pantry. Then he stopped and opened a small door.

Scott glanced around. All this was unfamiliar to him. When they moved to Ballycastle his mother had told him not to make a nuisance of himself at the castle and he hadn't. The castle was where she worked, and he had resented it too much to enjoy it.

Conor continued to lead the way, up the narrow wooden back steps.

"How did anyone know that was the same stone this sailor had used to get to White Man's Island?" Scott asked, persisting.

"Aah, because of the writing. Words had been chiseled, you know, into the stone itself." They had reached the second floor and Conor, exhausted from the climb, pulled open the door with an effort and stepped into the dark study of Fergus O'Cuileannain.

"And what did it say?" Scott asked, coming into the room after him.

"What did what say, lad?" For a moment Conor was lost in concentration. He peered closely at the rows of weaponry, then looked around the study, making sure, as he did every day, that every one of his master's belongings was in its proper place.

"The graveyard rock. Words were written on it, you said, Conor." Scott fidgeted impatiently, realizing the old man's mind had begun to wander.

"Aach, well, no one ever knew what it said. The chisel marks were unintelligible. Druids wrote it, and theirs is a secret language."

"But, Conor, this doesn't make sense!" Scott slapped his arms against his sides, laughing at the old man despite his frustration. "How could the stone come back on its own?"

Conor went to the study door and unlocked it, letting the bright light from the corridor fill the room.

"Come on, lad, put a leg to it," he said, and disappeared out into the hallway. Scott tagged after, towering over the leprechaun of a man.

"But it's not logical," he kept insisting.

"Well, you know, lad, not much in life is. And that's the real pleasure of it." He cocked his head, glancing up at the boy.

"What do you mean?"

"The mystery of it. That's the pleasure of life, looking for the mystery."

Scott waited. He had learned the old man's ways, how he

took his time telling any story.

"What you see, lad, what you can feel in your hands and smell and see clear as day, well, only a fool thinks that's true. You need to look farther. You have to have, as they say in the old country, fairy vision to really know the truth.

"So don't go around trusting what you see. Remember, a person—even yourself—is like the writing on those druids' graveyard rocks, a secret language." He stopped walking, stared at the tall boy, then said quietly, confidentially, "Take myself. I'll be eighty-two next March, God willing, and my life is still a mystery to myself. I've done things in my day that make not a bit of sense to me today. It's as if it had happened to another person." He shook his head. "But that's life, lad, and don't be in such a hurry to understand it all. You won't, you know. Learn to live with the mystery of it, that's all. Learn to accept the mystery of yourself. Think of yourself," he added quickly, as if seizing on a new idea, "as the land of *Hobgoblin,* a country of marches and foggy mountains, of bogs and hidden valleys. You'll never know all this strange terrain, Scotty. A man is like the sailor's stone of White Man's Island— an unintelligible language, written by the druids."

Conor stopped in the hallway, pointed to a suit of heavy mail.

"Take this fellow. He was a Knight Templar in the twelfth century. See the flag behind him? That's called a Beauséant, half white and half black, because Knights Templar were friendly to Christ but stern and black to His enemies. This fellow fought beside King Richard at the Battle of Arsouf in the Third Crusade. He gave his life to God and his king, but what about his soul, Scotty? Would your Brian Ború claim him as a friend?" The old man shook his head.

Conor crossed the hallway to another piece of heavy armor. "And this ancient knight. He was in the War of the Roses. The armor is Flemish. But the man? That's the great mystery. You never know about the man. Can you trust him in battle? Can you trust him as a friend?" Conor moved down the long hallway until he reached the top of the stairs.

"We never know the hearts of men, Scotty, not even our own, and all we have left of the past is man's armor. The weapons he used to kill his neighbor.

"See the sling there?" It was lying on the top shelf of a glass display case.

"It's like the one you made me."

"Aah, it is. This here's from the thirteenth century. They didn't put stones in them pockets, though, like you do, hunting for birds. See that bottle? It's full of quicklime. I got it down by the river. Well, you'd put a tiny clay jar of that quicklime in your sling and toss it at the enemy, and when it smashed open, there'd be a choking and blinding dust. Like poisonous gas it would be. Those that were sailors, I'm told, would use soft sap. Sling it from one battleship to the next, and the enemy would slip about on their own decks.

"Come along now." The little man led him further down the long hallway, crossing to the south wing. Scott kept glancing around, looking for his mother. There was a tour forming downstairs. He could hear the voices from the entrance hallway, echoing off the marble floor and downstairs walls.

"Do you know what those are, Scotty?" Conor asked, stopping at a display across one section of the walls.

"Bows and arrows."

"Aah, true enough, but what kind?"

Scott shook his head, and Conor lifted one from the wall.

"Don't!" Scott whispered, grabbing the old man's arm. "We'll get in trouble."

"Trouble from who?" he said angrily. "And didn't I hang these up in the first place for Himself? There isn't an axe or matchlock in this whole castle that I didn't mend or polish for him." He waved his hand through the air as if dismissing the thought of someone challenging him, and then he went on, raising his voice as if in defiance.

"The Normans first used these longbows against the Irish in the twelfth century. They're made of elm, and their arrows could pierce an oak door four inches thick. At the siege of Abergavenny Castle, a knight was pinned to his horse by an arrow that shot through the armor on his thigh, his leg and his saddle and buried itself in the horse's flesh."

"Can it still shoot?" Scott asked, taking the longbow in his hand and fingering the unstrung linen cord.

"Aah."

"Then how do you string it?"

"You pull the bow string up like this," he said, bending the elm and hooking it into the cow horn groove, straining with the effort. "There, good as new."

Scott lifted up the heavy longbow, gripped it around the thick, four-inch middle.

"What about arrows?" he asked, hefting the weapon. This was a longbow worthy of Brian Ború.

"They're here as well. I keep everything handy, the way he liked," the old man said proudly.

Scott looked down the hallway. Axes, swords, all manner of weapons decorated the high stone walls. He had only been in the castle a few times and never paid attention to them.

"What's this?" he asked Conor, pointing to a short, wide blade.

"A falchion. They used those in the thirteenth and fourteenth centuries. With the weight of the blade near the end they had a strong shearing power."

"And this is a mace?" Scott said. He pointed to a wooden club attached to a heavy iron ball by a short, thick chain.

"Indeed it is. You've seen a mace before, have you?" The blacksmith's eyes lit up with his pleasure at Scott's interest in the ancient weapons.

"Brian Ború carries one into battle sometimes."

"And so he would. This one is from the thirteenth century. Some were just clubs with metal heads but this kind, with a ball and chain, was the great favorite of knights. It's called a morningstar. And what's this, Scotty my lad?"

"A crossbow."

"Ah, you're a smart one. This is Norman. Himself had a grand collection of Norman and Roman crossbows. There's another beauty in the billiard room." Conor darted a little farther down the hallway. "This here is a Norman shield." He pointed to the kite-shaped shield on the wall. "It's made of wood and wrapped with leather. There's leather straps at the back for holding it."

Scott nodded and sighed.

"Conor, I've got to go," he said. "My mom could be looking for me. The school may have telephoned to tell her they were sending me home." He followed the old man into the billiard room.

"Aah, well." The old man placed the Snaphaunce pistol on its wooden peg. "Come now. If you have to be going, I'll show you a short cut." He cocked his head and grinned mischievously.

"Huh?"

Conor nodded toward the paneled wall behind him in the billiard room. Pleased with having recaptured Scott's attention, he scurried to the corner of the room and stood before a wall of books. Scott followed, lured by the promise of a secret.

"What's this?" the blacksmith asked, toying with the boy.

"A bookcase," Scott answered, scanning the high wall. "No, it's a secret passage."

"Aah, you're a clever lad. Watch now." Conor leaned against the wood panel beside the shelf and a door-high section popped out. Conor opened it wider and, reaching inside, flipped a switch. It lit up the long, narrow passageway beyond.

"They don't know about it, lad," he whispered, nodding toward the front of the castle and Derek's office. He motioned Scott to follow him inside and then pulled the bookcase back into place.

"This is terrific." Scott grinned, glancing around. The passageway was low and he had to duck his head to clear the low beams.

"The maids used it, you know, in their day, to get about the house. Himself had it built, but he never told a soul, and you won't find it on the blueprints of the place. Come along now."

The passageway turned and twisted, hooking up with the other dark and hidden tunnels to make a maze. Scott was lost. He had no notion where he was in the big house.

"Conor!" he called, trying to slow the old man down. "Wait!"

Conor turned and signaled Scott to be quiet. "They can hear you," he whispered.

"Where are we? Are we lost?" He had a moment of panic, a fear that Conor would disappear and he would be trapped forever in the walls.

"Aah, I could find my way through this place even if the lights were out. Many's a time I've spent the whole day in these passageways, working for Himself. Now don't you mind.

Here, I'll show you where we are." He scurried into a shallow recess, beckoning Scott to follow quietly.

For a moment he pressed his face against the inner wooden wall, then signaled Scott to come closer, to look for himself. "This was once Himself's bedroom," he whispered.

Scott took off his glasses and, turning his face to one side, squinted into the tiny peephole.

He saw his mother in Derek Brennan's office. He could hear her speak.

"Please, I'm serious," she was saying.

"So am I." He took hold of her shoulders and tried to pull her toward him.

"Come on," he whispered, "just one kiss."

"What a great big baby you are." Laughing, she pulled away and picked up her folders off the table. The room was shining with bright sunlight and it hurt his eye, made it water. Conor tugged at him to come away, but Scott shook him off, watching his mother. Now Derek was wrapping his arms around her.

"Derek," she said, smiling as she warned him.

"I want you."

"This isn't the time or place."

"I don't care."

"But I do. Someone could come in here." She squirmed in his arms, pushed at his waist to get away.

Derek bent his head and kissed her neck, his hands slipping down at the same time to caress her. Scott's eyes blinked and watered, but he did not move away from the peephole. His cheek was still flush against the bare wooden wall, burning with humiliation.

His mother wasn't fighting anymore. She dropped the folders on the table, and quickly her arms went around Derek's body, her fingers sweeping into his hair. Lifting herself up on tiptoes, she pressed her body against Derek's.

Scott stepped away from the peephole, brushed by the old man and rushed down the narrow passageway. He was crying and he grabbed his handkerchief and blew his nose, wiped the tears from his face.

At the corner he stopped. Three passages intersected before him.

"Fuck! Which way, Conor?" he asked, angry at his predicament.

"Here, lad." The little man led the way down a length of hallway and down a flight of stairs. They emerged in a small anteroom off the main hallway. Conor slid open a section of panel, concealed by a two-way mirror, and they stepped out onto the first floor.

"Now are you all right, lad?" he asked, slipping the mirror back into place.

Scott nodded dully. His head hurt from the beating and ached with his crying. He turned away from Conor, embarrassed by his tears.

"Another time, I'll show you the other secret doorways, Scotty. There are passages down here as well; the whole house is honeycombed." He had Scott by the elbow, walking him out the side entrance to where the lawns sloped down to the birchwood and the guest house.

Scott was not listening to the old man. He was thinking of his mother upstairs with Derek Brennan. He was angry at her, at him, but the anger had no real focus. It kept swelling up inside him in waves.

"Now be off with you boy." Conor smacked him lightly on the rump. "And don't tell a soul about these passageways. It's our own little secret." He winked and grinned, trying to cheer the boy up.

Scott nodded and made an awkward attempt at a wave, then ran down the slope.

Conor stood a moment and watched Scott disappear into the trees. He was an odd one, all right, a strange child. In the old country, back home in Clooncoorha, they'd have said he was touched by God, and he'd have led the procession on St. Patrick's Day through the cobblestone streets of the village.

Conor grinned to himself. The boy was queer, all right, that anyone could see. But it wasn't God who had touched him.

Fifteen

Valerie knew she'd be sorry. As she cut across the students' parking lot, scuttling from car to car like a fugitive, she kept glancing over her shoulder, searching for Borgus and Simpson. She wasn't worried about Scott. He wouldn't really be mad if she drove the MGB back to Ballycastle. It was Borgus and Simpson who would get even with her.

The MGB top was down, and she opened the driver's door and slid down out of sight in the leather seat. Her heart was beating fast from racing to the car and she was out of breath. For a few minutes she sat still, trying to gain control, to ease her panic. She had time, forty minutes before Borgus and Simpson got out of last period. By that time she would have Scott's car back at Ballycastle.

She was warm, sweating from nervousness, and she leaned forward, struggling to remove her leather vest. Finally it was off, and she tossed it into the space behind the driver's seat. Feeling freer now, she crouched down into the small space between the steering wheel and the floor, searching for the ignition wires. There they were. Crossing them beneath the dashboard, she pressed the clutch. The engine caught and Valerie eased back up into the driver's seat, grinning at her own success.

Nick Borgus was sitting on the hood of the car, his face inches away as he peered over the windshield at her. In the rear mirror, she caught a glimpse of Simpson circling behind her.

"Hey, Dunn, we're driving the preppie's car home."

"Get off the hood!" she shouted and gunned the gas pedal. The MGB jumped from the parking space and Nick reached out, grabbed her long hair and jerked her head.

Valerie hit the brake and the car lurched to a stop, tumbling Borgus off the hood. Angrily, he and Simpson moved in. Simpson opened the passenger door and dropped down beside her, his long legs filling up the small space. Nick Borgus pulled open the driver's door.

"Get over," he ordered, squeezing Valerie into the narrow space between the two bucket seats. "Spread your legs, Dunn, so I can reach the gear shift."

"Spread them wide," Simpson added, grinning.

"Scott told me to take his car home," Valerie said quickly. She was afraid now, trapped between them as the MGB spun out of the parking lot.

"Sure he did. That's why you had to hot-wire his car." Borgus was grinning. "Don't give me that bullshit." He leaned forward and said to Simpson, "It's a good thing we came along, hunh, Hank? Girls out stealing cars; you just can't trust anybody anymore."

"Nick, where are you going? Where are you taking me?"

"Where would you like to go?" Simpson tickled her under the chin.

Valerie grabbed his fingers, bent them back.

"Goddamnit!" He dug his elbow into Valerie as if she were a lineman and she doubled over, hitting Borgus's elbow with her own. His arm jerked on the steering wheel and the car swerved sharply on the neighborhood side street, almost hitting a ten-year-old on a bicycle.

"What the fuck, Dunn?" Borgus shouted, pulling the tiny car out of a spin.

"Tell your creepy friend to keep his hands off me."

"Why, you getting all you need from that preppie boyfriend of yours?" Simpson laughed.

"Nick," Valerie implored, "tell him to stop."

"What kind of wang does that duke have?" Simpson went on.

"Hey, Hank, shut your mouth," Borgus ordered.

"Shut your own fuckin' mouth."

Nick reached across and hit Simpson on the leg, digging his knuckles into the flesh. Hank flinched and grunted in pain, then swung back at Borgus. "Stop it. Stop it!" Valerie screamed, caught in the middle. .

They were beyond the town limits of Flat Rock, out on the open country road. The car swerved, and Valerie screamed again.

Nick Borgus slowed down then, brought the car under control, but still kept speeding.

"Where are we going?" Valerie asked. She had begun to cry.

"We're taking your boyfriend's car home, Val. What do you think we're doing?" Borgus grinned up at her, catching part of her reflection in the rear-view mirror.

"I thought we were going to find out if Dunn's got a cherry," Simpson said, sounding alarmed.

"Shut your fuckin' mouth a minute, will you?" Borgus reached across Valerie and punched Simpson hard on the shoulder.

Valerie stared straight ahead. Her breath had caught in her throat and lodged there. She knew now that it wasn't Scott's car that they wanted. It was her.

"Are you going to marry him?"

Barbara had just begun to cut the pot roast and she stopped in mid-slice, the knife still buried in the meat. She was giving Scott an early dinner so he could get to bed. He was still shaky from his accident in the hall at school.

"What on earth made you say something like that?"

Scott shrugged. "I don't know. He's been hanging around the house."

"Derek has not been hanging around this house!" Angrily Barbara sawed away at the roast, then stalked off to the cupboard for a platter. "That's the silliest notion I've heard." She arranged the meat on its dish, grabbed a serving fork and went back to the table. Scott had already begun to eat his mashed potatoes, using a spoon.

"Would you have the good manners to wait for your mother? And please use a fork."

Scott dropped the big spoon on the table.

Barbara took one breath and held it, determined to say nothing more. He was pushing her, and she refused to be drawn into a fight.

"He likes you." Scott picked up his fork, but did not look up from his plate. "Not that I care. I mean, it's your life." He went back to picking at his food.

"It's your life, too, Scott," she said quietly, trying to make him feel how important to her he was. "We're a family, or have you forgotten?"

He didn't answer. He didn't look at her. Something had happened to him that day, she could tell. Something besides the accident in the hall.

"I haven't forgotten," he said meekly.

"But you think I have?"

It took a moment before he nodded yes.

"Oh, Scott, why would you say that?" Now she was hurt. He shrugged, keeping his eyes down.

"Scott, please look at me." She had set down her knife and fork and was leaning across the table, bending her head, trying to catch his eye.

"Do you really think I'm going to leave you? Run off with some man? Scott, I'm your mother. I'm responsible for you."

"I could go back to Spencertown and live there. I mean, I probably could stay there in the summer. Or go to camp. This year I could be a counselor."

"Scott, what is this?" Barbara shoved back her chair and went to her son, slid in beside him on the window seat. She wrapped her arm around him and hugged him. He had pressed both heels of his hands against his eyes, but the tears washed down his face anyway, falling to his mashed potatoes.

My God, what has happened to him? she wondered. Something serious had to have gone wrong at school; there could be no other reason for his being so upset.

"Scotty, now listen to me." Barbara pulled his hands away from his face and made him sit back. "Here." She took his napkin and wiped his cheeks. "Do you feel okay? Do you have a headache?"

He shook his head, still choking on his sobs.

"Now what's gotten into you? Why are you so upset?"

"Conor says you and Mr. Brennan make out in his office."

"Make out!" The wind went out of her. "Scotty, I told you not to have anything more to do with that man," she went on defensively. "I told you to keep away from him."

The anger in her voice frightened Scott and he sat back in the window seat, as if to get out of her range. Then he shrugged and said again, as if it were a scab he couldn't resist picking at, "Conor said you and Mr. Brennan were necking in his office today."

"Oh, God!" The door had been closed, she knew. It was impossible for Conor to have seen them. She could feel again the touch of Derek's palm on her breast, feel his lips against her ear. "Scott," she said slowly, "I was not, as you say, making out with Derek. Yes, I have been kissed by Derek, but that's not Conor's business, or yours. I don't ask you about Valerie."

"Come on, Mom, we don't do that stuff."

"Oh, no?" She raised her eyebrows.

Scott could feel the short hairs crawl up the back of his neck. How could his mother have known? For a few minutes they sat in silence, the room quiet except for the sound of Scott's silverware scraping his plate, the clink of his glass.

"Scott," she said softly, realizing she had to ease his anxiety, "if I ever decided to get married again, I wouldn't just spring it on you. You're not going to lose me," she whispered.

"Then you *are* getting married," he said triumphantly.

"I'm not," she cried, exasperated, "I mean, do you see a great long line of suitors? Do you see me dating?"

"You went out the other night," he answered coolly.

"Okay!" Barbara pushed aside her plate of food. "This is enough. Scotty, look at me."

He raised his face slowly, as if coming up from deep under water. There were still tears in his eyes and they made his eyes bright as windows on a wet night.

"You must know that no one would ever—could ever—replace your father. Not in your life, nor in mine. That relationship is very special to us both, and will be ours forever. But we'll both have new friendships. New people to care about and love. That doesn't change what we feel about your father, or about each other. Look at you. You've already got Valerie. . . ."

"For cryin' out loud, Mom, I'm not in love with Val," he protested, sitting up quickly. The mist was gone from his eyes.

"But she is a new friend. And she does like you, don't deny that."

"Well, I can't control that." He threw up his hands.

"It's all right, Scotty." She reached across the table and smothered one of his hands in hers, smiling at his objection. "There's nothing wrong with having Valerie fond of you."

"We just happen to have lockers next to each other, that's all."

"I know. I know." Barbara nodded, agreeing. "And I'm only here at Ballycastle working with Derek for a few months."

"So you know you won't have time to get married or anything?"

Barbara shook her head, saying, "I don't know. But I would never marry anyone you didn't like, Scott. That's what you've got to remember. You're my number one man."

"Yeah, I know." Scott squirmed in the window seat. "And Mr. Brennan, he's okay, I guess."

"Then will you please do me a favor?" she asked, nicely. He nodded.

"Will you try to be nicer to him? He's been very helpful to me, and to you." She nodded her head, making the point.

"Okay," Scott whispered. "But when you two get married, will we live here or what?"

"Oh, Scotty, darling, I haven't even decided I want to date the man. He's my boss. It isn't easy working with someone and also going out with him." She stood up from the table, too upset herself now to finish dinner. "Let's forget all this marrying stuff. It makes me nervous," she admitted.

Scott grinned, seeing her reaction. "Sure," he said, swinging his arm over the back of the window seat. "But he's got to have my permission first if he wants to marry you, like I was your father or something."

"It's a deal!" Barbara smiled, relieved that a crisis had been avoided. Leaning over she kissed her son quickly on the top of his head. "I love you, honey bear," she whispered.

"Ah, Mom, you promised you wouldn't use that jerky name anymore."

"Okay, I won't. If you'll do something in return for me."

"What?"

"Wash the dishes . . . please."

"I did them last night!"

"I know, but it's been a long day and besides I need to rest these old bones."

"You're not old, Mom. Valerie said you look beautiful."

"She did?" Barbara smiled, pleased by the compliment. "Well, Valerie is very pretty herself. You're a lucky boy, having her."

"I don't have her, Mom! I told you we only . . ."

"Yes! Yes!" Barbara stacked her dishes in the sink and walked toward the stairs. "I know . . . lockers . . . she just happens to be next to you. It doesn't mean a thing."

"That's right." He sounded smug.

At the doorway she paused and glanced around, smiling. "Not to pry, Scott, but if you and Valerie 'don't do that stuff,' then why was one of her little gold earrings on the living room floor the other day when I vacuumed?" She spun around and kept walking, not waiting for his reaction. Behind her, Scott threw up a dish towel in the air, protesting, "Ah, Mom, it must've just fallen off somehow. By itself. Or she put it there!" The small towel floated to the kitchen floor like a white flag of surrender.

"Okay, Dunn. Take your clothes off."

"Are you crazy, or what?"

Nick Borgus nodded toward Simpson. "You want Hank to do it for you?"

"Yeah!" Simpson rubbed his hands together.

Valerie backed away from the two boys and stepped up flush against the graveyard fence. Steepletop was deserted, and she was trapped between the two of them like a calf they wanted to grab and wrestle to the ground.

"You know, you're really gross, and if you think I'm not going to tell my Dad. . . ."

"Come on, Dunn, we don't have all day," Borgus said, moving closer.

"What are you hiding anyway, Dunn?" Simpson added. "Your body ain't worth shit."

"Cram it, Simpson," she shot back without looking at him.

It was Borgus she feared. He was sauntering straight toward her, grinning, amused by the situation.

"You don't have to take off all your clothes," he said, as if striking a compromise. "You can keep your panties on."

"Hey, man, I want her panties. I mean, I collect 'em," Simpson protested, laughing. He kept looking back and forth between Dunn and Borgus, puzzled by what Nick planned to do with the girl.

"Shut your fuckin' mouth, Hank. You're getting Valerie all upset. Look, she's crying. Come on, give me your jeans and your blouse. You can keep your shoes and socks."

"Nick, what are you going to do?" she asked, pleading.

"We won't hurt you. Not if you give us your clothes."

"Why? What are you going to do with them? I'm going to freeze, Nick. It's going to be dark soon."

"We'll leave your vest. Hank, get Dunn's vest from the car."

"Hey, I want her panties," Simpson called over his shoulder as he trotted back toward the MGB.

Valerie made her break then. There was a small opening in the cemetery fence, and she ran for it. If she could make it into the woods she'd be safe. She knew those woods better than anybody.

Nick dove for her, cut her down in the open field between the woods and the fence. She swerved, trying to avoid him, but he clipped her foot and she fell forward into a deep bed of leaves, then kept rolling, unable to stop and regain her feet. Nick crawled after her on his hands and knees, seized her right ankle, and held her long enough for Simpson to get there and haul her to her feet, struggling and furious.

"Strip her, Hank," Borgus ordered, then turned and headed back to the car. With any luck, the preppie would have a piece of rope stashed in the MGB's boot.

Simpson's sleeves were rolled up, and Valerie bit him on his bare left forearm. Her teeth broke the skin and he bled into her mouth.

"You fucker!" He released his hammerlock on her neck but slapped the side of her head, knocking her momentarily senseless. Her knees buckled and she staggered, then Simpson grabbed her again by the shoulder and, holding her, ripped open the front of her blouse. The row of white buttons popped off one by one into the leaves.

"No," Valerie moaned. She was dizzy and too weak to resist.

He pulled the white blouse away and reached for the hook of her bra, which was in the front instead of the back. She doubled over so he couldn't find it, but he grabbed her long hair and yanked it until, with a cry, she straightened up.

"Jesus, Simpson. Don't hurt her," Nick shouted from the car. Simpson held the bra high over his head like a battle trophy and they laughed.

Valerie turned her back on both of them, shaking her head and crying, her arms crossed over her nakedness. She realized now she wouldn't get away from them.

"Do you want me to take your jeans off?" Simpson asked, following her.

"No! No!"

"Okay, then you do it—now!"

"Come on, Valerie, take off your jeans. Let's see your pretty panties," Nick added, arriving with the rope.

"You fuckers. I'm telling the police. You'll go to jail for this. This is rape." She unzipped her fly.

"Forget it, Dunn. We'll leave your precious body to your preppie boyfriend—if he knows what to do with it. But this will teach him not to play games with us. Running the wrong fucking way. Shit, who does he think he is?"

Her back carefully turned, Valerie pulled down her jeans.

"Hey, Dunn, you've got a cute little ass." Borgus reached out and felt her bottom.

"Oh, God, please!" Valerie slumped forward, tripping on her jeans and fell down again. Borgus reached over and grabbed the jeans, ripped them off her ankles. Free of them, Valerie curled up her long legs and lay still in the dead leaves.

Borgus dropped them and pulled her arms behind her, then wrapped the rope around her wrists and ankles.

"Don't hurt me," she said again, choking on her tears.

"Hey, Hank, are we going to hurt her?"

"Are we?" he giggled and shook his head. He had no idea what Borgus was going to do next. Back in the parking lot at school, they had spotted Valerie running for the MGB and only then decided to go after her. Now Hank watched as Nick tied her arms behind her then pulled her legs up and looped the rope around her ankles, tying her tight, like a young calf.

"Please, Nick, let me go. I won't tell anyone." Her frightened young face was pressed against a brilliant display of large yellow maple leaves. Next to them her skin was white, almost transparent.

"Hank, give me her blouse," Nick ordered. He was working fast, grunting from the effort. A band of sweat had broken out on his face and made his face shine. He folded the torn white cotton into a swatch, then blindfolded her with it.

"Hey, man, what the fuck are we doing?" Simpson asked.

"Shut up. Give me some help." He moved around and grabbed Valerie by her armpits. Simpson took her feet.

"Where to?" Hank asked.

"The graveyard," Nick directed, nodding to a slab of tombstone. Between them, they lifted her up and then arranged her on the cold slab of marble, laying her flat on her stomach as if setting her on a high shelf.

Valerie knew immediately where she was and her heart leaped in her throat. There was only one slab in the graveyard. The square tomb of Fergus O'Cuileannain, guarded by its ominous black angel. It was the one spot in Steepletop that frightened her.

"Please, Nick, don't put me here," she begged.

"Bye, bye, Valerie," Nick whispered in her ear.

"Nick, you can't just leave me," she cried. She'd thought she could stand anything as long as they didn't rape her, but the thought of lying naked in the dark on Fergus's grave terrified her.

"I can't, huh?" Borgus was grinning. It was only then that he realized what he would do, how he would get the preppie. Grabbing up the rest of Valerie's clothes, he signaled Simpson and together they ran for the woods.

Upstairs, Barbara closed the door of her bedroom and went into the bathroom to turn on the hot water in the tub. Until she moved into the guest house, she had never had a bathroom of her own, but now it seemed a necessity rather than a luxury.

She promised herself that when she left Ballycastle she would never share another bathroom with a man.

She sprinkled soap into the steaming water and returned to the bedroom, stripping off her clothes as she moved. Her blue turtleneck she stuffed into the laundry; her tight jeans were returned to the closet. She took her blow dryer out of the bottom drawer and laid it on the bed, ready for when she wanted to dry her hair. Wearing only her black bikini underpants, she stretched luxuriously, then went back to the tub and tested the water with her hand. She peeled off the panties and sank with a sigh into the deep, sweet-smelling water.

Only then did she let herself think of him. It was like a small pleasure that she saved for her private moments. At the office lately she had to fight to keep herself at work. Keep her mind off him. But since they had made love, it was a struggle to concentrate. Several times she had found herself sitting motionless, gazing off at nothing while she replayed their night together in her mind.

She was like a teen-ager, she thought, consumed with lust. She cupped some water in her hands and splashed her face, as if to cool herself down. It would be all right, she decided. Everything between her and Derek. Everything between her and Scotty. Everything, she realized with pleasure, between all of them.

For a few moments Valerie heard them running, laughing as they went downhill. Then slowly her breathing began to level off. She was first thankful; they were gone and she had not been hurt. But immediately she remembered she was on Fergus's tomb, and somewhere above her was the evil black angel. Even on a bright, sunny day it was never cheerful in that part of the graveyard.

She struggled at once with the tight rope and felt a stab of pain across her back. If only she could see what she was doing. "Nick!" she shouted. "Nick, come back here, you bastard." Her voice sounded weak and lost and she started to cry again, sobbing with pain. They couldn't leave her like this, she thought. It was just too mean. She would freeze without clothes.

The hinged gate at the graveyard moved and she stopped

sobbing. It could have been the wind, she thought, but then she heard the rustle of leaves. Someone was coming toward her.

"Nick? Please, Nick, don't do this to me." She struggled again with the tight rope. The rustling leaves stopped. She lay still, listening, her cheek flat against the marble slab.

"Nick?" she asked, whispering, begging for a reply.

The leaves rustled again, the sound of something moving around the monument. It was an animal, she thought next. A deer looking for a salt lick. She had seen deer before on Steepletop but never inside the cemetery. Well, scaring him off would be easy. She yelled as loud as she could, paused, and yelled again. There was no rustle in the fallen leaves. It was not a deer. A deer would have bolted at the first sound.

"Who is it? Who's there?" she cried. The leaves were rustling again, and the sound was moving closer, but from a different direction. Whatever it was, it was coming up behind her.

"Nick? Hank? Oh, God, please say something."

She felt the two hands on her skin and screamed. Hysterical now, she tried to squirm away from the leathery touch of the fingers that caressed her shoulders and bottom. The bony fingers ran along her quivering side and found her small left breast, then continued down to touch the fabric of her panties.

Valerie's breath caught in her throat and she couldn't scream. Beneath the tight blindfold she closed her eyes and lay rigid as the hands lifted her, turned her over so her body was exposed.

Scott washed all the dishes himself, by hand. The roasting pan took the longest and he used up two steel wool pads before he was satisfied. Then the leftover meat had to be wrapped and put into the refrigerator. When all that was done, he wiped the table and counter and swept the kitchen floor. He wanted the kitchen to be spotless when his mother came down.

Still carrying a wet dish rag, he walked to the bottom of the stairs and listened. Behind the closed door of her bedroom, he heard his mother's hairdryer. That would take her half an hour, he knew. He had time to clean the downstairs bathroom.

The telephone rang as he passed it and he lifted the receiver, saying hello.

"Scott?"

"Yes . . . ?"

"Hey, Scott . . . this is Lou. You know, down at the gate."

"Yeah, hi. My mom's taking a bath. Can she call you later?"

"Well, I was calling you, as a matter of fact. You got your car there, Scott, your MGB?"

"No, I left it at school today. Someone drove me home. Why?"

"Sheet." The security guard sighed into the phone. "Damn, I think I spotted your car 'bout half hour ago. I wasn't sure, but it flew in by the gate, and then Ted radioed that he didn't see it by your garage when he made his rounds. With the trouble the other night, we've been watching your place."

"But it has to be at school," Scott protested. "I had an accident early today and . . ." Then he thought of Valerie. She had threatened to hot-wire the car and drive it back to Ballycastle.

"It was your MGB," he heard the guard say. "Ain't but one around here."

"That's okay, sir. I mean, I think one of the kids at school brought it. I think I know where it is."

"Okay, I'll tell Ted. We just wanted to be sure."

"Thanks. It's okay." Scott tried to sound positive. "Thanks again."

Hanging up the phone, he spun around and threw the wet dish rag against the wall. "Damn her," he swore and slammed the door and walked out into the dark night.

"Scott?" Barbara opened her bedroom door and stepped out into the hallway. Her hair was dry and she was wearing a white terry cloth bathrobe. For a moment she hesitated, listening for her son, then she called out again, "Scotty? Are the dishes already done?"

When he didn't reply she moved down the hallway to the stairs, a quick tremor of fear racing through her body. She was overreacting, she knew, but couldn't stop herself. She thought again of the strange woman at the kitchen window. "Scotty?" she shouted.

At the first floor landing, she heard the back door open and slam shut. Thank God, she sighed. "Scotty, I'm done with my bath," she called, then continued down the stairs and into the living room. Turning on the television set, she settled down on the sofa and waited a few minutes. When he didn't come inside, she called once more. "Scotty, dear, are you okay?" She got up and walked down the dark hallway to the kitchen, saying as she approached the lighted room, "I think there's some ice cream in the fridge." Then she stepped into the kitchen and saw that the man there wasn't Scotty. A moment later the screen door opened again and a second man joined them, grinning.

"Who are you?" she asked, "and what are you doing here?"

Valerie thought she would be killed, strangled to death on the marble slab.

"Please," she sobbed. Then she felt the fingers working on the rope behind her back. First they untied her hands, then moved down to tug at the rope around her ankles. She felt the pain of blood rushing to her feet as the rope was stripped from her and she straightened her legs.

"Ouch," she whispered, feeling the brief tear of her muscles. She lay still, unwilling even to raise her head. But the bony hands were insistent, pulling her up by her thin shoulders. Valerie grabbed at the smooth wet stone, scraped her nails on the hard edge of the slab, but there was no resisting. When she was upright, the blindfold was pulled from her eyes, and Valerie instantly covered her face with her hands. She was afraid to open her eyes, afraid to confront face to face the owner of the bony hands.

Whoever it was, he was moving again, circling around behind the slab. Valerie opened her eyes a crack and saw that it was dark; night had fallen on the hillside. She felt a stir of hope. If Old Bony stayed on the far side of the slab, she could bolt away and run straight downhill to Scott's house.

Bony was directly behind her. She heard him pause, felt him breathing. Then the leathery hands were on her, circling her body to cup her breasts. For a moment he weighed them in his palms, his thumbs brushing the nipples harshly. Then, slowly, he began to massage them, his hands moving unhurriedly in lazy circles. Valerie sat petrified, her eyes wide open, her brain racing. But no ideas would come, only the fear.

In the end, it was the fear that saved her. With the strength born of terror she threw her elbows backward where they met old Bony's body and, for an instant, broke his hold on her. In that instant she flew off the monument as if launched by a crossbow.

At the graveyard gate she glanced back, to see if he was gaining on her. But Old Bony hadn't moved, except to hop up on the slab that she had vacated. The figure was powerfully built, and for a moment she thought it was Borgus, come back to play an elaborate game on her.

Then the creature threw back its head and laughed, and at the sight of its long yellow hair Valerie suddenly knew. Sobbing with fear she turned again and ran, stumbling out of the graveyard, running naked, downhill toward the castle.

"Yes?" Barbara asked. After the first shock she had realized that they were boys, not men—but older than Scotty, stronger. "Why are you in my house?" she demanded, hoping her nervousness didn't show; knowing that it did.

"Mrs. Gardiner?" Nick came forward. He had Valerie's clothes in his hands.

"Who are you?" Barbara asked sharply.

"Well, we're on the football team with Scott, and . . ." Nick smiled and, wordlessly, held out Valerie's clothes.

Barbara recognized Valerie's brown leather vest at once. "What," she demanded, "is going on here? What are you boys doing with those things?"

"Is Scott here, Mrs. Gardiner?" Nick said politely, as if the answer were a secret he thought it best to keep from her.

"What's wrong? Why do you want to see my son?" She raised her voice, tried to sound parental.

"Well, actually, it's Scott I'd like to talk to," Nick stalled. He hadn't expected to meet the preppie's mother. She was ruining everything.

"No, you can talk to me." Barbara folded her arms, as if in a show of defiance.

Borgus shrugged, glanced at Simpson, who couldn't think of anything to say. Still Scott did not appear.

"I think you'd better leave," Barbara said next, advancing on them as if to push them physically from the kitchen.

"Would you give him these?"

Barbara was shaking her head. "Why? What are they?" She did not let on that she recognized the clothes.

"Coach Tagariello asked us to go through Scott's football locker, you know, to get his uniform from last week's game, and we found these." From the bottom of the pile Nick produced Valerie's bra, let it dangle from his finger by a strap. He caught the look of shock in Barbara's eyes, and realized at once that this was better than seeing Scott.

"I don't know anything about these clothes," Barbara began to protest. "I suggest that you take them back where you found them." Her face was flushed. She could feel the heat of embarrassment in her cheeks. Still, she stood her ground. She would not be intimidated by teen-age boys.

"Well, you know, we thought we'd do Scott a favor, getting these out of his locker before Coach found them." Borgus could not contain himself. The thought of the preppie trying to explain himself broke him up. "Besides, we thought maybe Scott needed his bra." At that, Simpson burst out laughing and Borgus joined him but kept watching Barbara to see how she would take it.

"Get out of my house," she ordered.

"Just tell Scott we brought him a change of clothes," Borgus answered, dropping the small bundle on the kitchen table.

Then he paused, his eyes scanning her body, lingering on the loosely gathered neckline of her robe.

"I'll have you arrested," Barbara said calmly. "I'll telephone the security guard."

"Mrs. Scotty, we ain't done nothing." He kept grinning. "We ain't even armed." He gestured, opening his arms to her. "See?"

Barbara moved toward the phone, then turned back again as she heard the refrigerator door open. Simpson was going through the shelves, moving things around as if he was looking for something in particular.

"Stop that!" Barbara ordered, automatically taking a step toward him. She realized that the refrigerator was not important. She had to phone Security. She turned back toward the phone, but now Borgus stood behind her, the receiver in his hand.

"Just calling my mom," he said. "I worry about her when she's home alone." Then he ripped the receiver from the wall.

He and Barbara stood face to face, eyeing each other warily. If she could just reach the hall, Barbara thought, she could run up to her room and use the phone there. Her eyes had darted in that direction, measuring the distance, when, smiling, Borgus moved to block the exit.

The screen door was unguarded, Barbara knew. She backed up, trying not to signal her intention this time, when Simpson shouted from behind her.

"Beer!" Tossing a bottle over her head to Borgus, he lifted the rest of the six-pack out of the refrigerator and headed for the door.

"Come on, Nick," he said. "Another minute, she's going to get crazy on you."

Borgus saluted Simpson mockingly, headed for the door agreeably, flicking Barbara's breast with two fingers as he passed.

Then the two boys went out, laughing, into the dark grounds of Ballycastle.

"Bastards," Barbara whispered. She would've liked to call Security anyway, to get Ted Ward to throw both of them off the estate, but she realized it would just cause Scotty more trouble. She went back to the pile of clothes, picked them up and, out of habit, folded the jeans and the leather vest neatly. The bra wasn't in the pile, she realized; the boys must've kept it. Disgusting. But was it any more disgusting, she found herself thinking, than Scotty stashing it in his locker? Immediately she dismissed the thought. There was no reason to believe those boys. They could have said anything to her; made up any story about Scott.

She went to the back door and stared out through the screen, listening. At night she was more aware of the woods, of the insect life that seemed to make the darkness come alive with noise. She lifted her head, poised herself to call again for Scotty, but realized that they might still be out there, watching her from the shadows beyond the arc of flood light, and immediately she stepped back inside and locked the kitchen door.

Well, Scotty would just have to knock if he wanted to get inside tonight.

She walked back to the table and almost compulsively felt the clothes, fingered the material, as if it would give her some clue to where they might have come from. The boys would have to have stolen them from Valerie, or.... Oh, no! she realized, they had taken them off the poor child. She spun around, tried to focus on what she ought to do.

Valerie was out there somewhere. They had stripped her, taken her clothes and left her. Barbara rushed to the door and, unlocking it, ran outside to the edge of the white birch woods. She called Scott's name, called Valerie. These children were out of control and somehow, she knew, they were after Scotty.

The branches tore at Valerie as she ran all-out toward the castle. Again and again she tripped on branches and went sprawling, scraping her knees and palms, but she would scramble up and keep running, too frightened to stop, to listen for the sound of someone behind her.

She reached the creek at the bottom of the hill, jumped it easily and sprinted across the lower lawn between the castle itself and the horse barns, running now in moonlight.

At that moment Conor came out of the mansion carrying his dinner basket, the evening meal. He saw the girl on the lawn before him, the bright October moon, low on the horizon, silhouetting her as she ran.

"Oh, Mother of God," he whispered and blessed himself. The sight of her, the cool, clear evening. He could hear again the voice of Himself, telling Conor to fetch the girl back to him.

"Maeve, wait!" The old man ran forward a few steps, waving and calling out. "Maeve Donnellan, my dear, we won't hurt you." But the woman wouldn't heed him and so, dropping the dinner bucket, he ran after her.

Valerie never heard Conor, never saw him. Her eyes were fixed on the guest house, on its bright display of lighted windows. She ran off the lawn and into the woods, following the old, worn path that looped down the slight slope to the house.

It was there that Conor caught her.

"Now, Maeve, we won't be hurting you." Valerie heard his

voice but didn't recognize it. A hand on her arm could only be one person and she wheeled around and shoved, determined not to be captured again so close to home.

Weak and breathless from the chase, Conor went down under Valerie's assault. He hit the ground, but before she could turn and run, he grabbed hold of her ankles and pulled the naked girl into his arms, trying as he did to soothe her.

"Aah, Maeve, there's nothing to worry about. It's just a bit of fun. Now don't be fretting about your immortal soul. There'll be absolution for you in the morning. Himself has arranged it."

The old man's grip was as strong as his anvil; Valerie couldn't break free, no matter how she squirmed and kicked. Crying with frustration, she took a deep breath and screamed. Scott was walking up from the river when he heard her.

Conor regained his feet and pulled her up beside him, whispering obscenely in her ear. "Come on now, lass, we'll have a fine time, and Himself will give you a nice present for your troubles."

Valerie understood nothing of what he was saying. All she knew, at that moment, was the feel of his rough arms on her bare skin, the smell of his filthy body and old clothes, and she started swinging at him, hitting at his head with both arms and crying to be let go.

Barbara heard her. She had heard the first cry only faintly and thought it might be Scotty, fighting with the two football players in the dark. She came through the screen door on the run and spotted Scott, ran up the slope and into the birch trees.

Scott pulled the old man off Valerie, wrestling him to the ground and pinning him with the weight of his body. It was only then that he looked clearly at Valerie standing shivering on the path, clothed only in panties, sneakers and white socks.

"Val," he asked innocently, bewildered by the sight of her. "What happened to your clothes?"

Valerie was hysterical, trying to speak and choking on her breath. She was saved by Barbara who burst out from the trees and ran straight to them. Embracing Valerie with both arms, she pulled the child's head down against her shoulder, let her bury her face in the warmth of her terrycloth bathrobe. Over Valerie's shoulder, Barbara spoke quickly to her son. "I'll go telephone for Security. Can you hold him that long?" They both looked at the old man, lying quietly under Scott's body.

"Yeah, I'm okay. I don't think Conor would hurt me. But what's going on here?"

"I have no idea, Scott. But we'll find out. Give us a few minutes to get downhill. I don't want this girl frightened again. All right, Valerie darling, come along." She turned the sobbing girl and led her along the path to the guest house.

Scott waited until he heard the screen door slam before he got up and helped Conor to his feet.

"Thank you, Liam," Conor said, fixing himself, straightening out his work trousers. He seemed to have forgotten what had just transpired.

"Conor, what was going on?" Scott asked, ignoring Conor's greeting.

"What's that, Liam?"

"Why were you fighting with Valerie? Where are her clothes?"

The old man looked confused. "Who would that be, then?" he asked, fidgeting nervously.

"Hey, Conor!" Scott touched him lightly, reassuringly, on the shoulder. He realized then that the old man didn't understand him. "Conor, who was that girl you were chasing?"

"Aah, that's Maeve Donnellan. She ran away from Himself and he sent me to fetch her back. She's only seventeen, you know, and she hasn't the good sense God gave her." He was grinning, displaying his mucky teeth in the moonlight.

"What are you talking about?" Scott asked, bewildered.

"Aah, don't be pretending, Liam. You know well enough, as well as me."

"Liam?" Scott laughed nervously. The old man was crazy. Or maybe he thought Scott was so dumb, anyone could put one over on him. Well, he'd show him you couldn't. "You know I'm not Liam," he answered back, his voice rising. "Conor, I know you know who I am."

Conor's head jerked, as if he were snapping out of a trance.

"Oh, Scotty, what is it, lad?" He looked around, confused by where he was. Where was his dinner pail? She'd be looking for it.

"Hey, Conor, are you okay?"

"I'm fine. Now, why wouldn't I be all right?" He turned

away, to walk back toward the castle. He seemed to be regaining strength, pulling himself back together.

"Conor, who's Maeve Donnellan?"

"Maeve Donnellan? Now what would you be wanting to know that for?" Conor paused on the path to look back at Scott.

"Well, you were shouting her name and everything. You called my friend Valerie by her name. I mean, does she work at the castle or something?"

"Maeve Donnellan is dead, lad. She has been dead now for forty years." He jerked his head toward the ridge beyond the castle. "She's buried up there with all the others—Carmel Burke and Maureen Leahy and that little lass from Tobermoe, Anne Kilferick. They're all buried there, lad." His voice choked up at the end, as if he were in tears, and Scott peered at him more closely in the dark.

"But what did they die of, Conor?"

The old man walked on as if he hadn't heard.

"Was it the Nuckelavees?" Scott asked, already feeling his fear returning.

Conor nodded. "Aah, the Nuckelavees," he whispered, then walked on slowly, fatigued by the long night, his run through the birch wood, by memories of the terrible past when Himself was still alive and the servants' hall was filled with girls just off the boat from home, all of them fresh as spring flowers, spirited as colts, and virgins all. Virgins all.

"Who's Maeve Donnellan?" Valerie asked. She was sitting cross-legged on the sofa, wearing her jeans and an old sweatshirt of Scott's with "Spencertown Academy" stencilled across the chest. With both hands she cradled a red Coca-Cola can.

Barbara looked across at her and then at Derek Brennan, who stood before the fire. After Barbara called Security, Ted Ward called him, and he had just arrived. He hadn't yet said a word, only warmed his hands as he listened to the long account of the evening. Now, under Barbara's gaze, he had to answer Valerie.

"Maeve Donnellan is a young woman who once worked here," he said. "There's a tombstone over her grave up at Steepletop. Conor, it seems, has gone senile. He must have thought you were Maeve."

"Was it Conor who untied you up in the graveyard?" Barbara asked.

Valerie shook her head. "It was the Black Annis." She glanced at Scott. "You know, that woman we saw in the woods on the south drive, the one you said looked like that *Hobgoblin* character."

"Our shopping-bag woman," Barbara said softly. She was watching Derek, saw how he suddenly moved away from the fireplace and took a chair.

"I'll have to talk to Ted about her again," he said quickly.

Barbara knew he was lying, but she kept still.

"And Conor was calling me Liam," Scott added. "Who's Liam?" That one Barbara herself could answer.

"There's a Liam MacMathuna on the employee rolls. He worked here with Conor during Fergus's days on the estate."

Derek left his chair and resumed his place at the fire. "MacMathuna was the manager of the farm, Scott, for almost twenty years. He retired and went home to Ireland. I believe he's dead." He took the poker and stirred up the logs, sending a shower of sparks up the chimney. "What we have here is the mental decline of an old man. For your sake, Valerie, I'm sorry I never noticed till now. I'm afraid I've been concentrating on Foundation programs and not paying much attention to the staff. We'll just have to do something with Conor—care for him more."

"But suppose he goes after Valerie again?" Scott asked. "Thinking that she's Maeve, I mean."

"Oh, I don't think you have to worry about that, Valerie." He smiled reassuringly. "I'd suggest that we keep this in the family. Conor's just an old man. He won't hurt you. There's no need to take this up with anyone else, is there?"

"Wait, Derek." Barbara jumped in before Valerie could agree. "Conor would never have gone after Valerie if those boys hadn't abducted her first. We have to do something about that."

"Valerie, what do you think we should do?" Derek appealed to her directly. "Do you want me to call the police about them?"

She shrugged. "I don't know." She glanced at Scott as if for help, then said softly, unevenly, "They didn't actually hurt me or anything."

"But, Valerie, they did!" Barbara insisted, incredulous at Valerie's hesitation.

"Things like that happen at school sometimes, Mrs. Gardiner," Valerie said. "You know, Scott getting his locker painted and having the kids jump him in Times Square. There's always something like that going on."

"What do you mean, Valerie? Did somebody attack Scott at school?" Scott looked at her nervously, and she understood. "Well, we can talk about that later. What happened to Valerie was more serious."

"Barbara, this isn't Spencertown Academy," Derek said quietly.

"Oh, come on, Derek, we're not talking about blue blazers versus denim jackets. This was a criminal offense. If Valerie won't press charges, I will."

"Please, Mrs. Gardiner, I'll only get into trouble at school." Her eyes had widened in fear at the thought of what Borgus's friends would do if she got him in trouble.

"Then I'll talk to your principal about what happened in Times Square. And about them stealing Scotty's car. They're probably still joyriding around, and God knows when we'll see it again. I think there are enough grounds for complaint."

"I told Mr. Carpenter I fell down, and that's how I got hurt," Scott reminded her. "He'll think I'm a liar if you tell him differently."

"And Nick will leave the car in the school lot tomorrow morning," Valerie added. "I'm sure of it. The tank will be empty, that's all."

"Oh, God, I don't believe this!" Barbara dropped back into the leather chair. "Do you kids think you're doing the right thing, standing up for each other? Well, who's standing up for you, Scott? And you, Valerie? You could have been raped by one of those two boys. They certainly looked capable of it."

"Barbara, I'll talk to Joe Carpenter," Derek joined in, being helpful, "and I'll make a complaint about those kids being on Ballycastle after closing. How did you get inside anyhow, Valerie? Weren't you stopped at the front gate?"

"No, Nick just raced through. The gate was open."

"Okay, I'll talk to Ted and Lou about that."

"Mrs. Gardiner?" Valerie spoke softly.

"Yes, dear, what?" Barbara smiled at the girl.

"Do you think I can go home? It's getting late, and I haven't had supper."

"Of course, Valerie, I'm sorry." Barbara was out of the chair at once, going into action.

"I'll take Valerie home," Derek offered. "Scotty, do you want to come along?"

"No, I don't want Scotty going out again tonight," Barbara answered sharply.

They all stood for a moment, looking at each other. Then into the silence Valerie said, "Scott? Can I ask you something— you know, privately?" She was blushing with embarrassment, but Barbara admired her determination.

"Scotty, why don't you and Valerie go into the kitchen," she suggested. "I have something I'd like to say in private, too."

She kept smiling as they left the living room, then turned at once to Derek. "All right. Enough of this bull. Who is this crazy woman?"

"Maeve Donnellan," he admitted at once.

"No, the woman in the woods. This alleged shopping-bag lady."

"Maeve Donnellan," he repeated.

"But she's dead. I saw her tombstone."

Derek shook his head. "She's alive. She lives at Ballycastle, in that small cabin back in the forest, the section beyond the river that's closed off to the public. She's sixty-some years old and completely out of her mind."

"Scott, promise me something," Valerie asked, whispering to him in the kitchen.

"Promise you what?" Scott asked.

"That you won't do anything to Nick and Hank."

Scott frowned a little, unsure of what she meant.

"Because of what they did to me."

"Val, are you kidding? They beat me up this morning. Painted my locker yellow. Stole my car. And you're afraid of what I'll do to *them?*"

Valerie came up closer to him, shaking her finger, getting

angrier. "But you wanted them to steal your car. You wanted another reason to get even with them. And now you have it."

"You lied to me, didn't you?"

"Well, if you want to see it that way...."

"My God, how else am I supposed to see it? You've known all along that she's crazy, yet you allowed me to move in here with my sixteen-year-old son. When she attacks my house and assaults my son, you tell me not to worry, that she came here on the bus."

"Listen, Barbara, give me a chance to explain."

She didn't answer, and he took her silence as permission.

He sighed, dreading the long explanation, wondering how he'd ever thought he could avoid it.

"Maeve Donnellan was here when I opened the house for the Foundation last year. She had been locked up ever since Fergus died, or maybe before, I'm not too sure. I have all this from Conor, who says that forty years ago she was a maid at Ballycastle, and a favorite of the master's."

"What do you mean, favorite?"

Derek shook his head.

"Were they lovers?"

"I don't know. But it doesn't matter. He arranged to have her cared for all these years. There's nothing in his will, but he set it up with Conor."

"Then the Foundation has no legal obligation to keep her here?"

"No, and I didn't even realize she was until we moved in ourselves last winter. We commissioned aerial maps of the property, all two thousand acres, and that's when I spotted the cabin.

"Conor was caring for her. Bringing her meals from the kitchen. I had just assumed those buckets he was carting off were for himself."

"This is incredible," Barbara whispered, astonished by the revelation. She slipped down onto the arm of the chair. "You mean this woman has been living out in the woods, being cared for by a crazy old man who brings her a bucket of scraps every evening, after dark, when no one is around the castle?" Barbara kept shaking her head. "What is her cabin like? What is she like? Have you spoken to her?"

"I've never seen the cabin. I mean, I haven't seen the inside."

"What about the board? What did they say?"

"I didn't tell the board. We were just beginning, and I thought I should take the initiative, solve the problem on my own." He stopped and laughed. "Actually, that wasn't really it. I knew what they'd say if I asked them, and I just didn't have the heart to send her off to some state institution. Conor took care of her. She was harmless. This had been home most of her life." He shrugged his shoulders, as if to admit his susceptibility to compassion.

"I'm sorry I've been so hard on you," Barbara said softly. "Keeping this a secret must have been a strain. Especially with me around, prying into things that are none of my business."

"It is your business when she attacks you and Scotty. You have to believe me; she'd just never done anything like that before." He stopped, as if a thought had just struck· him. "Maybe it was the lights. You're the first people to have lived here, you know, since Fergus's time. Maeve probably lived here herself, years ago. This guest house was once part of the servants' quarters."

"Oh, God, and that's why she came here. Of course." Barbara was swept with panic. She could feel her fear crawling up her throat, choking her.

"It's all right, Barbara. I've spoken to Conor," Derek said quickly.

"What good will that do? Conor is as crazy now as Maeve Donnellan."

That stopped him, but only for a moment. "You're right," he admitted. "She'll have to be committed, and maybe Conor should go into a nursing home. Although I must admit I can't imagine it." Barbara knew he wanted her to smile, but she couldn't. After a moment he went on. "It'll take a couple of weeks. They'll both have to be examined by doctors. And I'll have to find places that will take them. In the meantime, Ted Ward will check the house every hour after dark."

Barbara nodded, but she was not reassured. Her skin crawled at the mere thought of the old woman, out there in the dark, watching them. After Derek left she would go through the rooms and pull down all the blinds.

"Okay," Barbara said. "What do we do next?"

"I go home and we all get some sleep."

"Do me one more favor?" Valerie asked as they left the kitchen. "The sweatshirt."

"What about it?"

"Can I have it?" she smiled, trying to coax him.

"Why? I mean, what do you want it for?"

"Cause it . . . I don't know. . . ." She sighed, wondering why he always had to make things difficult. Then she stopped abruptly in the hallway, put her hand flat against his chest and whispered, "Because I like you."

His eyes blinked as she walked away.

Sixteen

Dressing for school the next morning, Valerie put on Scott's red Spencertown sweatshirt with her jeans. She wore it proudly, like a badge of honor in defiance of Borgus and Simpson. Still, as she watched the school bus slow down outside her house, she zipped up her jacket and hid the lettering. They would be on the bus, she knew, sitting at the rear, legs spread out, the two of them taking over the full back seat.

Her house was at the end of the route and, as usual, she was the last student to climb aboard. As she stepped inside the bus, she was met with cheers.

"What is this for?" she whispered to Tracy, slipping into the seat beside her friend.

"I don't know." Tracy had books on her lap and she drew her knees together, carefully collecting herself so she wasn't touching Valerie.

Valerie leaned closer. "What do you mean, you don't know? Come on, give." The other kids were all sneaking looks at her, giggling behind their hands. The bus started up again, bounced back onto the highway, when Valerie spotted Mrs. Miller, the bus driver, watching her in the rear-view mirror. The woman was frowning, her mouth set like a lock.

"Tracy, come on, what's the matter?" Now Valerie was

243

upset, realizing that it wasn't her imagination. Everyone on the bus was looking at her, whispering among themselves.

"Hey, Dunn!" Nick Borgus shouted from the back of the bus. "Are you wearing your pink panties?" The roar from the busload of students was deafening.

Valerie turned around in the seat and looked back the length of the aisle. Nick was sitting in the middle of the rear seat and when she spun around, he gave her a big wave. Then, over the noise, he shouted, "Hey, Dunn, let's see your appendix scar again."

"Ah, shit." Valerie looked back at the front of the bus. She could feel her face flush red. "What did he tell everyone?" she said quietly to Tracy.

"Nothing." Tracy turned her head elaborately and stared out the window.

"Tracy, tell me or I'll bend your fingers backwards."

"I don't think you're very nice," Tracy answered back, glancing quickly at Valerie. Her friend was at least five inches taller than she was and a lot stronger.

"What did he say, damnit!"

"He said that you gave him and Hank a ride home yesterday in whats-his-name's car and that you drove them up onto the hilltop instead."

"Tracy, that can't be all."

Tracy shrugged. "Well, then he said you did this crazy striptease, dancing on top of tombstones and playing the car radio, you know. And that you wanted to have a threesome with them on top of this slab of marble."

"And you believed all that bullshit?" That surprised Valerie more than any of Borgus's lies.

"Well, he said you wore pink underwear, and you do. I know you do."

"Tracy! Me and at least ten other girls in our gym class. Borgus could've guessed that easily, and you know it."

"Yes, but what about your appendix scar?" Tracy said quickly, anxious to defend herself.

"Everyone knew about that," Valerie answered. "I was out of school for six weeks when I had the operation. Tracy, I just can't believe you fell for this."

"But, Valerie, he described it," Tracy finished, almost in

tears. "He said it looked like a fish hook dug into your belly button, and you know, Val, that's exactly what it looks like. I was thinking the same thing the other day, when you were trying on clothes at my house."

Valerie dropped back into the seat. That bastard, she thought. What a dirty thing to do, spread stories around before she could tell anyone what had really happened on Steepletop.

From the rear of the bus, Borgus had begun to shout, "Take it off, Dunn. Take it all off." Simpson picked it up, as did the other football players. The chant grew louder and louder as more students joined in, laughing and shouting. "Take it off, Dunn. Take it all off."

Valerie slid down in her seat, as if to hide. She was the only one who rode into the schoolyard in silence, listening to the chant rise above her like a new school song.

Conor carried the two buckets of oats downhill to the small pasture near the barns. The horses still in his care were like him, he thought, too old to stray far from home. At the sight of Conor they raised their heads and trotted over to the fence for their morning feed. He grinned, pleased to watch them run. There was nothing, he thought, in all the world as lovely as a horse in motion.

He thought then, as he often did, of Nightfall, the colt he had broken for Himself in the spring of '31.

Conor had loved, then, to get up early in the morning, before the mist came off the river, and ride Nightfall out to the steeplechase field. Of all the horses at Ballycastle he loved Nightfall best, loved his lines and his spirit. It took all his strength to contain him as they took to the course, the stallion running full out, digging into the soft turf, leaping effortlessly over the high jumps. The loins of the animal moving with the smoothness of a woman's under his thighs. "Go, luv," he whispered, leaning forward, urging on the colt as they worked the course in the cool early morning.

"Good morning to you, sir," Conor said, speaking out loud in the pasture, "and how would you be today?" The years melted away, and it was as if Conor saw his master coming towards him once again.

In his day Fergus had been a bulk of a man, not tall, but

with strong arms and square shoulders that made him look like a peasant as he crossed the bridge and came up through the alfalfa field.

He still was not sober from the night before, Conor realized, seeing the man stumble on the uneven path. Conor swung his leg over Nightfall's back and slipped to the ground. The horse snorted jumpily, still edgy even after the hard ride.

"I'm fine enough, Conor, given my condition." Fergus smiled, amused by his own behavior. He had learned to live with his excesses, even taking a certain pride in his vices, the punishment he gave his own body.

"Maybe we should skip a day, sir. He's a bit randy this morning."

"Aren't we all, Nightfall?" He grabbed the reins from Conor and the big horse snorted and reared up, jerking Fergus off balance.

"Son of a bitch," Fergus swore, bracing himself, planting his feet in the soft soil.

"Easy there, Nightfall; easy, luv," Conor whispered, going to the big black horse, gently petting his neck, bringing him under control.

"Hold him steady, Conor," Fergus ordered and set himself to mount.

"Let me have another go with him around the course, sir."

"I'll break him down, don't worry about that." He swung himself up, pulling the reins into his own hands. Once astride the animal he seemed in control. The man fit a saddle well, Conor saw again; he looked handsome on the horse, as if he were born to it.

Nightfall bolted and raced for the open field and high hedges, taking them as easily as if they were part of the steeplechase. Fergus tried to turn him back toward the course, but Nightfall was running full out, as if he were a wild horse all on his own.

"Steady, boy," Conor whispered. His eyes never left the huge animal. Fergus swayed on the saddle, then gained his balance momentarily, before pitching forward. "Oh, dear God," Conor cried. Nightfall was jumping into the morning sun, the bright slice of orange that came out of the river upstream. It blinded Conor, yet still he saw Fergus reach forward, try to grab the stallion's mane, then pitch out of the saddle and into the high hedge, disappearing under the animal as Nightfall struggled to find footing, then scrambled over the hedge and away.

By the time Conor reached him, Fergus was lying still in the mud below the hedge.

Conor shook out the oats into the feed trough and turned away from the fence. It did no good, he knew, to dwell on the past, to trouble his mind with memories.

The telephone was ringing when he reached the barns. Barbara Gardiner was calling, wanting him to come see her at once.

Barbara Gardiner wrote "butesin picrate" on a piece of paper and handed it across her office desk to Conor Fitzpatrick. "Do you know what this is?" she asked, keeping her eye on him, hoping she'd be able to tell if he was lying to her.

"Why, it's a salve, ma'am."

"A salve? And what was it used for? Why would all the maids at Ballycastle have the same prescription in their files?"

The old man stared at the name as if contemplating the question, then he shrugged and replied, "I guess because of the beatings, ma'am."

"The beatings?" Barbara shook her head. Questioning Conor, she had come to realize, was like finding one's way out of an endless maze.

Conor nodded. He was sitting on the one straight-back chair in Barbara's office, wearing the clothes he saved for special occasions: an old black suit, a white shirt and a pencil-thin black tie.

"Why were the girls beaten, Conor?" Barbara spoke carefully.

"Ah, for any number of things, ma'am. Not making Himself's bed right, being late for tea, sleeping through Mass on a Sunday morning, or going off, you know, with one of the lads."

"And who would do these beatings?"

"Well, it would be Mrs. Wilkinson, mostly." He smiled when he answered, as if he had gotten a test question right.

"Mrs. Wilkinson—you mean the head housekeeper?"

"Yes, ma'am. She was English, the only English servant Himself ever had. He always favored English housekeepers. He thought they had a way with the girls, could keep them in line, you understand."

"And she'd beat them?" Barbara asked.

"Aah, with a switch."

"And they let that happen? Didn't they complain to Fergus?"

"Well, you know, it was a common enough thing in its day. They were only girls, seventeen and eighteen years old, mostly. They needed a lickin' now and then to keep them in line."

"And do you know how the girls died, Conor?" she asked next, still watching his eyes.

"Galloping consumption, ma'am."

"Consumption? You mean tuberculosis?"

"Aah, it was a terrible sickness in them days."

"Conor, there are nine graves up on that hillside, not counting Maeve Donnellan's, and you mean all of them died of T.B.?"

He nodded his white head.

"I just can't believe that," said Barbara. "We're talking about the United States in the '30's."

"The girls were from Ireland, ma'am, and she's a damp, dreary place."

"But still, nine of them."

"Well, you know, we had quite a few employees here over the years. Most of them made a bit of cash and then went back home again—to get married to some lad and settle down. Himself helped quite a few lads and lasses in his day." Conor smiled, as if remembering. "Nine wasn't really such a lot, compared to all of them."

Barbara shook her head, still disbelieving, but unable to articulate exactly what was wrong. Finally she said, "Well, thank you, Conor. I'm sorry to keep bothering you with all this."

The old man stood, donning his black cap as he went to the office door. The slight rise of his right shoulder seemed more pronounced, and he moved with the slow, careful step of a man who had lost the knack of walking.

She listened as the sound of his footsteps disappeared down the marble hallway, listened until she knew he had gone out the side door, and then she stood. A salve, she thought. A salve for the beatings dished out by Mrs. Wilkinson. Malarkey. She would drive into Flat Rock and show one of the old prescriptions to a druggist. He would tell her what butesin picrate really was.

Barbara checked the stack of files in her In Box, but none of them were the ones she needed to gather the prescription forms. Then she remembered. She had left the dead girls' files in Derek's office, on the windowsill behind his desk.

"Shit!" She went out of her office and upstairs to the second floor.

"He's not in, Barbara," Derek's secretary called from across the hallway. "He's in town at the bank. Can I help you?" She smiled through the open doorway.

"Oh, Marge, I forgot some files. Is it all right if I pick them up?"

"Of course. The door's unlocked. Call if you need me."

Barbara stepped inside and closed the door halfway behind her. She saw at once that the files weren't on the windowsill.

She scanned the top of his desk, then fingered through his In Box, checking to see if he had simply slipped them under some other papers. Finding nothing, she opened the top desk drawer.

The center drawer contained nothing but an assortment of paper clips, rubber bands, sugar packets and plastic spoons. She pulled out the other six drawers and found nothing. Puzzled, Barbara sat back and tried to guess where else he might have put them. They were old-fashioned files, too big for a normal cabinet, and she doubted if he would have given them to Marge.

The desk had to be the hiding place. All right, she told herself, one last quick look and then she'd leave. She leaned forward in the chair and started again, beginning with the wide bottom drawers of the old-fashioned desk. This time she pulled the drawer open and searched more carefully.

The bottom drawer was packed with brown manila envelopes, each clearly labeled in black magic marker. Barbara lifted a pile from the deep drawer and sorted through the large envelopes. Derek had marked the contents of each: Tax Returns; Ballycastle Survey Maps; Board Meeting Reports, 1981; Miscellaneous Correspondence. She kept flipping through the envelopes, then reached down and lifted out several more. It was then that she spotted the old blue photo album buried in the bottom.

She paused a moment, wondering what it might be, then reached in and pulled the album out. She set aside the envelopes and, leaning back in the soft leather chair, opened the old album at random. The first photograph she saw made her flinch.

Printed on thick, old-fashioned paper was the picture of a naked girl. She was sitting in a huge, heavy Jacobean chair with gargoyles' heads carved at the end of each arm. Her legs were thrown up over each of the arms, and a man was kneeling down between them. All that was visible in the photo, shot high and from the side, were the muscles of his shoulders and a sliver of his profile, which was in shadow. And the tip of his tongue, which was almost touching her, but not quite. Her head was thrown back and her mouth was wide open, in an expression very much like the gargoyles'.

In the next, a different girl was kneeling in front of the same chair, naked, with her wrists tied to the chair arms. A man stood just out of frame, with one leg planted forward, and he had just brought a whip down on her back.

Barbara quickly flipped through the thick pages. On each page was the photo of a different girl in a different sexual position, but something was oddly familiar about the photos. She paused a moment and studied them, looking for what it might be. Then she realized it was the background. In many of the photos were tall, narrow windows. She glanced up, looked across Derek's desk and recognized the same windows. The pornographic pictures had been taken right there in that room, the room that once had been Fergus O'Cuileannain's master bedroom.

Scotty slipped the note to Valerie in second period social studies. "Did you see Borgus on the bus?" it said.

They were sitting next to each other in the back row, and Mr. Russell was busy erasing the board. Valerie turned the note over and scribbled out an answer. As soon as Mr. Russell began writing on the board, she leaned across the aisle and returned the loose leaf to Scott's desk. At that moment Mr.

Russell turned back to the class and said, "Man loves war games almost as much as he loves war. War games go back to chess, which began, historians say, in Hindustan, then spread to Persia and Arabia before Christ was born. Chess reached Spain in the eighth century, and Benjamin Franklin brought it from Europe to America." The tall, red-haired teacher jotted the names and dates on the board, then turned back to the class.

"But, aside from chess, war simulation games did not begin as sports. In the eighteenth century, toy soldiers were used to plan battles. Prussia, for example, used them in the 1871 Franco-Prussian war." Carefully removing his rimless glasses, Russell rubbed the bridge of his nose, and Scott quickly scribbled, "Those fuckers—why don't you tell Carpenter?" He handed the folded paper back to her.

"By the twentieth century, simulation games were being played for fun. H. G. Wells, for one, published a set of rules for maneuvers to be fought with miniature soldiers. In our own century, a National Guard lieutenant designed a war-simulation game to teach tactics to his troops during the second World War. Later on he realized he could make money on his games and he put them on the market in 1958. The Gettysburg Battle was one of his first."

Valerie slipped her reply to Scott and he unfolded it, holding the slip of paper up behind the back of the student in front of him. "No! There will only be more trouble if Carpenter hears. I'm just forgetting it. Borgus is crazy anyway."

"Okay, then in 1973 two war-gamers, Dave Arneson and Gary Gygax began developing a new strategy game," Russell went on. He had begun to pace through the classroom, down one aisle and up the other, carrying a piece of chalk. Scott slid the note under his books.

"Instead of using historical wars, they added the element of fantasy. Their battles took place in medieval worlds with imaginary characters. Each player assumes the identity of a character he creates. The idea of the game is to send a group of these imaginary characters on an adventure. They might be told to find gold, or to free a trapped king, but they go through dungeons and forests filled with monsters, dragons, and so forth." Russell had returned to the blackboard and began to write quickly.

Scott pulled out the note and found space on it to write, "They took the MGB. I'm going to the police." He handed it to Valerie.

Russell stepped back from the board and said, *"Dungeons & Dragons* was the first. Then came *Runequest,* and *Traveller,* a science fiction fantasy game." The teacher stepped closer to the first row of seats, looked out over the class, and continued, "I understand we have yet another fantasy war game, this one called *Hobgoblin."*

Scott glanced up at the sound of the name. He had not heard a word that Russell had said, and now he paused to read what was written on the blackboard.

"If any of you saw the last school newspaper, then you probably read Valerie Dunn's article about Scott Gardiner and *Hobgoblin.* Since Halloween is on Saturday, let's ask Scott to tell us more about this scary fantasy game."

The teacher moved down the outside aisle, along the row of windows toward Scott and Valerie. "If we can get these two to stop slipping notes to each other back here, we might find out more about *Hobgoblin* from Mr. Gardiner."

Scott started to get up, then remembered that at Flat Rock students didn't stand when they answered in class. Several students giggled at his mistake.

"What about this *Hobgoblin,* Scott?" the young teacher said, ignoring the other students. "It's based on Irish myths, right?" He kept talking, seeing Scott's embarrassment.

Scott nodded without looking up. Being laughed at made him angry.

"Why don't you tell us more about *Hobgoblin,* Scott?" Mr. Russell spoke calmly, but he was watching the boy. He saw how Scott reacted, the flush on his face, the way he gripped the books on the desk. He would have to talk to the sophomore counselor, Russell thought. This boy needed some help. He considered dropping the subject, just going back to the front of the class and leaving the boy alone, but that too would draw attention to Scott. So he went on.

"Why do you play, Scott?"

The boy shrugged, glanced across at Valerie. She was smiling, nodding, urging him to talk.

"Well, it's like acting," Scott said softly, speaking only to the teacher.

Russell backed up slowly, forcing him to talk louder. "How is it like acting, Scott?"

"Well, you know, you become someone else."

"Brian Ború, right?" the teacher asked, lifting Valerie's article off his desk.

"Yes. He was a legendary king of Ireland."

"So you don't use real people?"

Scott shook his head. "That's the fun of it. You create the characters."

"What kind of characters? Historical figures?"

"Sometimes. Brian Ború might have been a real person. But in *Hobgoblin,* a character doesn't necessarily have to be human. He could be, you know, an Athach."

"A what?"

"That's a name for a giant or monster. Or maybe a Kelpie. Those are evil water spirits who come ashore and take the form of horses. That happened to Brian Ború once. He got this golden stallion from the king of Tullamone, but it was really a water spirit that threw him into the River Shannon. That's why it's hard to know whether you can trust your own horse." Scott was caught up in the game now and he spoke quickly, explaining.

"What happened to Brian then?" Russell asked. He saw how the class had quieted down to listen. Derek Brennan had been right. A few days before he had called Russell and told him about Scott's trouble with the other students. "He needs help," Brennan had said. "See if you can get him to talk about *Hobgoblin.* It's a game he plays."

"I saved him," Scott said.

"How? Could he just swim to shore?"

"Well, you see, all these characters have four traits—intelligence, luck, wisdom, and constitution. And each one has his own LOA. That stands for level of achievement."

"Mr. Russell, I don't know what he's talking about," complained one of the girls at the front of the room.

"That's because you have to be smart to play *Hobgoblin,*" Valerie said loudly. At school, in the classrooms and hallways, she was always on the alert, ready to defend Scott, to take on her classmates. She got a certain pleasure from it, this secret mission of hers. She felt like a guardian angel.

Mr. Russell was holding out the chalk, indicating that Scott should come up and use the blackboard to explain the game.

"Go ahead," Valerie urged. "Tell them how to play."

"It's too hard. No, I don't want to."

"Come on, please," she pleaded, leaning forward, hiding her face from the front of the class. "Maybe you can get a club started like at Spencertown."

Her smile broke down his resistance. It was a silly smile, sweet but off center. Scott pulled himself out of his seat. "It's complicated," he began, walking up the aisle tentatively.

"Well, give it a try," Russell said. "We're all listening."

"Well, first of all you make up this character, like I said, and you deal cards to see how much power he has, and how much strength. Then the Dealer—he's, you know, the referee—deals out the *Hobgoblin* cards."

"What are they for?" Russell asked. He had stepped away from Scott, giving the boy the front of the classroom.

"The cards are different colors, and each color does a different thing. But in general, the cards tell you what monsters you'll meet, what battles you'll fight, what journey you'll take. And before you draw any cards, the Dealer has to give you the Adventure."

"Well, give us one now."

"You mean just make one up?"

"Sure, or tell us one you've been on. Show us how the game works." This was Scott's chance, the teacher thought. If he could get them interested in the game, he'd establish his own clique.

"Well, this is an Adventure that Mr. Speier, my teacher at Spencertown, once gave us. It begins on the Isle of the Magic Maiden, in the Irish Sea off Carrickfergus. Now this island is only a steep crag that juts out of the sea and touches the clouds. In ancient times it was ruled by the daughter of Finetor, a Greek magician, and that's how the island got its name."

Scott lost his shyness as he retold the tale of the Island of the Magic Maiden. At Spencertown, it had been one of Brian Ború's best Adventures, taking three months of games to finish.

"Now Finetor's daughter, the Magic Maiden, was skilled in necromancy."

"What?" Half a dozen juniors shouted at once.

"Does anyone know the word?" Mr. Russell asked, surveying the class. "Scott, write it on the board, please. Valerie, do you know?"

Valerie shook her head. "I never heard of it, Mr. Russell."

"Okay, Scott, tell us."

"It means the secret art of communicating with the dead. Necromancers can predict what's going to happen in the future. See, in *Hobgoblin*, Mr. Russell, there's a lot of this stuff, premonition and augury."

Bill Russell nodded. No wonder Scott was having trouble, he thought. "What next?" he asked, encouraging him.

"Well, this Magic Maiden built a beautiful castle on the island. This was a time when many ships crossed the sea between Ireland and Norway, and the Maiden, using her magic arts, would pull them onto the rocks and rob them of their cargo. If knights were on board, she'd make them fight each other in battle for her amusement."

"Who else did that sort of thing?" Russell asked the class. "Pitted one knight against another?"

"King Arthur," someone answered.

"That's right." He nodded back to Scott, telling him to continue.

"One day the Maiden captured a knight from County Sligo and fell in love with him. He knew who she was but allowed himself to become acquainted with her charms."

"What does that mean, Mr. Russell?" several of the boys quickly asked.

"You know what it means," he answered, not looking at them. "Go ahead, Scott."

"Okay, then one day when they were sitting on this rock overlooking the sea, he leaned forward as if to kiss her—"

"Okay! Okay!" A roar of applause went up from the class.

"Quiet down!" Russell demanded, motioning Scott to keep talking.

"Well, instead of kissing her, the knight pushed her off the cliff and into the sea. Then he ransacked her castle, taking all the wealth, the gold and jewels and stuff, back to Ireland.

"But he was forced to leave behind the greatest treasure."

Scott hesitated, slowing down the story. He saw that everyone was watching him, listening. It was like Spencertown again, when Mr. Speier would be telling them a tale, setting an Adventure.

"What's the treasure?" asked one of the girls in the second row.

"No one knew for sure. It was locked up in the highest turret of the palace and protected by a magic charm that couldn't be released.

"The knight who killed the Magic Maiden returned to Ireland and told the story, boasting of his feat. Other knights followed, seeking the treasure left behind. One by one they went, but always in the winter, when they could be sure the poison snakes and water leapers were hibernating. Water leapers are gigantic toads, with wings and a tail instead of legs."

"Oh, gross!" one of the girls said. "Mr. Russell, this is silly."

"Be quiet, Mary Beth, and you'll learn something. What else, Scott?" he asked, hurrying him on. The story was too involved, he realized, and the class was getting restless again.

"Still, when they got to the rocky castle, they couldn't get inside the turret. But the knights did say, and legend tells us, that written on the door in blood, in a mysterious language, is the name of the knight destined to enter the room after having dislodged a sword imprisoned in the door handle."

"Like King Arthur," Russell added.

"Sort of." Scott shrugged. "That's where the Adventure begins. Your mission is to go to the rock of the Magic Maiden, open the tower door and seize the treasure. Then the Dealer plays the *Hobgoblin* cards and you see what happens."

"Do you have a deck with you?"

"Sure." Scott pulled them from his hip pocket.

"How do you go, by rounds?" Russell asked.

Scott nodded. "Each player first gets a green card. That tells where you are in Ireland. Then you get a blue card; that's your first Challenge. It could be some sort of monster that has to be defeated before you can reach the rock of the Magic Maiden.

"Now the Dealer can throw down more blue cards or a red

one, which means you have to do some special task before you reach the rock."

"Okay, do one round, Scott. It will be easier for everyone to understand if you show us. Deal a set of cards to, let's say, Terry."

Scott shuffled the deck, then dealt several cards to the girl. He turned over the green one.

"Okay. You are at the gateway to Inishbofin, in a fishing village called Cleggan. From here you must sail in a currach—that's a fishing boat—to the neighboring islands of Inishark and Inishdogga. On each island you will find a strong sailor to accompany you on your Adventure." Scott looked up and explained, "This would take at least three turns, and then the Dealer turns over the next card, the blue one, and she finds out her first challenge, the first monster she has to fight.

> *Type:* Hlanith
> *Frequency:* Rare
> *Armour Class:* 2
> *Moves:* Walk, fly
> *Size:* Immortal Spirit
> *Intelligence:* High
> *Alignment:* Evil
> *Magic Resistance:* High (Immortal)
> *Weapons:* Book of Spells
> *Special Attack:* Fishing Nets made of Fog
> *Special Defense:* Amphibian
> *Language:* Manx

At the bottom of the card was a paragraph of explanation that Scott read out loud to the class. "'These Hlaniths once lived in ancient Eire, but now live in Mag-Mell. They often return to Ireland by walking on the water, flying on the wind or sailing in ships wrapped up in the fog. On land Hlaniths adopt a human form. They are old and evil-looking people who carry with them always a book of spells. In this disguise they kidnap men and take them back to Mag-Mell where they too become immortal, but only as long as they remain on Mag-Mell.'

"So what happens is Terry and the sailors have to . . ."

The three girls in the front row began to giggle uncontrollably. They leaned forward, hiding their heads on their desks. Scott looked at them, unsure of what he had said. He was afraid he had mispronounced something or used a word that had a dirty meaning in the school.

"What's the matter with you three?" Russell demanded. "Peggy?"

"Nothing, Mr. Russell," the little blond answered, whispering, her eyes full of tears. Now more students were grinning, beginning to giggle. Laughter swept across the entire social studies room.

"Roger! What is it?" Russell demanded, singling out a boy in the middle of the class. Roger ducked down, looked away. "Come on, Cox, what's so damn funny?"

The boy looked up, but fixed his eyes on the bulletin board so he wasn't looking at either the teacher or Scott.

"Well, it's just stupid, Mr. Russell." He started laughing again, trying to talk at the same time. "It's weird, all this stuff about Mag-Mell and Inishbofin and the Magic Maiden getting off on some rock." At the mention of the strange names, there were more rolls of laughter. Scott grabbed the cards off Terry's desk and glared at the class. They were all laughing now, sneaking glances at him. Russell held up both his arms, motioning for the class to be quiet, but now the kids were shouting names back and forth, calling out:

"Hey, Kelpie? You want to ride my horse?"

"Shut up, Magic Maiden."

"Up yours, BrianBorú."

The names flashed up and down the length of the room like insults. In the back, Valerie got halfway out of her seat, tried to decide what to do. Scott had pinned himself against the front blackboard. He was watching the class, his eyes shifting back and forth, flinching at each mention of a name.

Slowly Mr. Russell brought the students under control. He walked down the center aisle, planting himself among the rowdiest students, and put his hand on their shoulders. Now he lowered his voice, kept speaking gently until the laughter and noise ceased.

"All right," he said calmly. "We have had our fun. I would

just remind you of the saying that only an ignorant person laughs at what he or she doesn't understand."

"Mr. Russell, we understand," John Pettit spoke up, "but it's stupid. I mean, it's like a game you'd play in the sixth grade." Another outbreak of noise swept the room and the teacher said quickly, "Well, ladies and gentlemen, you happen to be wrong. I've read that the majority of students who play this game have above-average intelligence. In fact, a lot of *Hobgoblin* players are college students."

"Weirdos," a voice declared from a corner of the room.

"Close it down. Close it down," Russell demanded. There was an edge in his voice that the class recognized and they immediately stopped talking.

"Scott, what do you think? You're the expert here." He was speaking nicely to Scott who still stood against the wall as if held captive. Russell smiled, tried to seem encouraging. "Can you tell the kids why you think they'd like to play *Hobgoblin?* For example, it's really helped you in math, hasn't it?"

"I don't care if they play it or not," Scott answered back.

"But it gets easier as you go along, doesn't it? It's not so hard once you get started—or so I'm told."

Scott shook his head. He felt detached. Removed from the class. He didn't know them. He didn't care about any of them. They were staring up at him, twenty grinning faces. They looked like a pack of Padfoots, the huge dogs with immense feet and saucer eyes that came after Brian Bóru when he was crossing the Hills of Ballyhoura. Brian had beheaded half a hundred of them as they came in waves, snapping at his heels, lunging for the flesh of his bare calves. Twice he had been hit. Twice the wild highland dogs had dug their white teeth into his flesh, but he had picked their bodies off like leeches, using the pike of his horseman's hammer to spear the beasts and cast them aside.

"Scott? Why don't you sit down now?" the social studies teacher asked. He was watching the boy closely and realized too late that Scott was past obeying.

"Brian Bóru will slaughter you all," he declared passionately. "Kill every one of you dogs."

"All right," the teacher said at once, coming between Scott and the first row of girls, who went off into new fits of laughter.

"He'll soak the woods with your blood and let the Nucke-lavees eat your entrails." Scott was yelling at them, shouting to be heard over the uproar of laughter and swearing. A dozen hands went up, giving him the finger.

"All right! All right!" Russell could not control the class-room. Scott kept shouting. "You're all turds. Big, fat, round turds."

"Scott." Russell grabbed him by the arm, and felt Scott shaking violently under his grip.

"Let me go." Scott ripped his arm from Russell's fingers. "Get away from me." He backed off, stumbling against the slightly raised platform on which the teacher's desk was set.

Valerie jumped up. "Scott, please!" she shouted from the back of the room.

Scott did not see her. Half the class was on its feet, ignoring the teacher, screaming at Scott. Now he was giving the finger to the class and swearing back at them.

Russell went for Scott. He had to get the boy outside, he realized. They'd be fighting next, tearing the classroom apart. Christ, how in the world had this happened?

Scott saw the teacher coming. He ran straight at him, catching the teacher unprepared, and stiff-armed him, sending Russell crashing back against his own desk. It lurched under the teacher's weight and slid halfway off its perch. Books and papers flew into the air as two of the legs hit the floor with a crash, and several girls screamed at the sudden explosion of sound.

Scott regained his own balance and ran for the door.

"Scott, wait," Russell pleaded, struggling to his feet.

Scott hit the empty hallway running. The long corridor was oppressively silent, the floor heavy with wax and the bright, hot reflection of sunlight. At the far end of the hall a doorway to the parking lot stood open. It was cooler out there. He could feel a breeze. He ran for the daylight.

"I found it in the first weeks after the Foundation took over the estate," Derek admitted, looking down at the leather album. "I was living here alone and looking for a house off the grounds. There was no one to talk to after six o'clock but Conor, and that, as you can imagine, wore thin pretty quickly."

Barbara smiled wryly.

"One night when I was foraging around for something to read," he continued, setting the album on the conference table, "I found this in the bookshelf against the wall. It was leather bound, and I don't think anyone ever realized that it wasn't just another volume in the Dickens section." Derek opened the album to the first photo. It was of a nude girl languishing on a big four-poster bed. The photograph had been shot from the foot of the bed and the teen-ager seemed to be asleep, her small, dark head resting on a lace-trimmed pillow.

"She's lovely," Barbara commented.

Leafing through the large, heavy pages, Derek began to remember how the album was set up. "There's a progression, see? Beginning with that simple, rather innocent photo of the girl sleeping, and leading into real perversion. Look."

He was turning the pages quickly, displaying the effect. It was like an old-fashioned nickelodeon—the stilted photos, the grainy black and white images. Each one was taken from the same high angle in the same soft light.

In the first series of a dozen prints, the girl moved on the bed, twisted and turned, exposed more of her body, fondled herself. Toward the end, Barbara saw the bruises and welts develop on the girl's body. Noticed the boots at the corner of the frame, spotted the thick black whip handle.

"There's another series," Derek explained. After one blank page the pictures began again. "This time it's different girls, and they're never alone."

The pictures had been shot with some skill, Barbara thought. The photographer had used late afternoon light to shade the image, to soften the girls' features and cast the bedroom into mystery.

"They're so beautiful," she said, marveling at the loveliness of the women, shot after shot of slender, adolescent girls all in the first years of their maturity.

"Who is he?" Derek asked. "Do you have any idea?"

"What?" Barbara shut the book guiltily and looked up.

"The man. It isn't Fergus—that's for sure. He was blond, and this man is very dark."

"Oh." She looked again, sifted through the album. She had not been paying attention to the male figure who was seen only from the back and only in some of the shots. He was like a prop, an extra, a part of the scenery. But now she studied him.

It was the slope of his bare shoulders that alerted her. She kept turning the old pages, studying the shape of the man. She could see only his bare back, his black hair, his muscular arms clutching the anonymous nude girls. His face was always lost in the shadows or buried in the flesh of the women.

"When would these pictures have been taken?" she asked at last.

"The thirties, maybe earlier. Since no one is wearing clothes it's difficult to tell."

"The man is obviously older than the girls—in his mid- or late twenties, say. So if the pictures were taken in the thirties, then he'd be about eighty now."

Barbara tapped the hard picture. The dark half-figure of the male. "That's Conor. I'd bet anything that was Conor Fitzpatrick when he was in his twenties."

She set the heavy album on Derek's desk and pushed back the chair, looking up at the director. "The shoulders give it away, really. See how one is a little higher than the other? That's Conor. You've seen him walking across the lawn. You know what I mean."

Derek nodded, suddenly seeing that she was right. He leaned forward, looked again at the man's back. His face was buried in the shallow arch of the woman's thighs. She was pulling him closer, her fingers laced into his thick black hair, and the man was grasping her buttocks with both hands, squeezing her tight. They were positioned sideways to the camera and she was looking up into the aperture. The shutter caught her at that moment, her eyes closed, her mouth gasping for air. Derek could feel her pleasure.

"Who was she?" he wondered aloud and then answered himself. "I guess we'll never know," he said, drawing back from the old photo.

"Yes, we will." Barbara stood and started out of the office. "Wait here. I'll be right back."

"Well, congratulations," Bill Russell began. The class had slowly quieted down after Scott Gardiner's dramatic exit, and one of the boys had come forward to help Russell maneuver his desk back up on its platform. The others pushed their desks back into rows, and settled down to a quiet buzz of conversation while the teacher rearranged his papers and decided what to say next.

"Congratulations on really making a new guy feel welcome in your school." Back in the tenth row, Roger Cox rolled his eyes at his friends, Bob Senese and Carl Gutterman. Russell was really going to lay it on; they could tell.

"I guess you all feel pretty sure of yourselves, don't you?" Russell continued. "You've known each other all your lives. You know what's cool and what isn't; you know exactly how everybody expects you to behave. Well, maybe at Scott's school you wouldn't know. Maybe you'd dress funny and feel uncomfortable and not know how to play soccer, or *Hobgoblin* or whatever it is those kids play. I want you to think about that. I want you to think about how it would feel to start at a new school and have nobody like you."

"Valerie likes him," one of the girls piped up, causing a ripple of giggles. Valerie's face flushed scarlet, but Mr. Russell acted as if he hadn't heard.

"I think some of you should go see Scott and apologize," he said. "Maybe you should offer to play *Hobgoblin*. Get a group together during sixth period. And I mean you, Senese, and you too, Gutterman. It'd do you a lot more good than standing out back by the trash bin smoking."

"We're building up our cancer cells, Mr. Russell," someone answered back.

"Well, why don't you learn something instead? For you, Senese, that would be a new experience."

"But Mr. Russell, you gotta admit, it's a stupid game."

"Senese, I don't gotta admit anything," Russell replied, angry enough to make fun of his student. "I'm always willing to learn something new. I'm willing to broaden my experience."

The bell rang, ending the period.

"Then you play the damn game and tell us about it," Senese shot back quickly, and bolted out the door.

Barbara set the framed black and white photographs on the conference table, spreading them out as she explained.

"These are old group photos of the staff from Fergus's years at Ballycastle. Conor gave them to me when I started work on my report. Look!"

The pictures had been taken in front of the castle, the whole staff dressed in uniform. Every year the layout was the same, as if they were class pictures.

They spotted Conor easily in each of the dozen old prints. He always stood to one side, at the far right edge of the frame, wearing either a black suit and tie or his heavy leather blacksmith apron. He stood ramrod straight, as if under orders, and squinted into a bright morning sun.

"I wish the faces were bigger," Barbara muttered. She had opened the album and was searching for comparisons. "Here!" she said immediately. In the album a small girl, barely out of her teens, was being sodomized. Barbara pointed to a girl in the framed photo. She stood at the front of the crowded group of employees.

"These two look alike, don't they? The same blunt features. She looks almost like a boy, doesn't she?" Barbara turned to the next page of the album, and then searched the staff pictures for a look-alike. "What about this one in the third row? They have the same cheekbones. Oh, if only there were names on the back of these staff photographs. Then we'd know if these are the girls who are buried up on—"

"Barbara, stop." Derek slammed the album shut and kept his hand on it. "This is all fantasy, sheer speculation. These servants all dressed alike and wore their hair alike. You can't possibly tell if they're the same girls as in the album."

Barbara stepped back, surprised by his reaction. He took the album, went to his desk and locked it in the center drawer.

"We've wasted enough time on all this ancient history, Barbara. I have a Foundation to run."

"Derek, let me ask you a question. If Conor is the man in these photographs, then who's taking the pictures?"

"I don't know. And I don't care. Finish your report, Barbara. Tell us about the furniture and the architecture and the armor. And forget about solving mysteries."

"Why?"

"Because it's beyond the sphere of your contract."

"Come on, Derek, don't give me that."

He paused, stood before her with his hands on his hips. It was shortly after eleven o'clock in the morning and he already looked exhausted.

"Don't you realize what all this might mean? What it's all leading up to? The graves, the pictures, the salve, the mysterious French epitaphs?"

"Yes, of course," she said haughtily. "Fergus was some sort of sexual pervert."

"And what else?"

Barbara looked him in the eye. She was wearing jeans and one of Scott's old blue cotton dress shirts, but she looked solemn and serious. "We're talking about mass murder," she answered flatly, without emotion. "I would surmise that between 1930 and 1940 nearly a dozen young girls, poor immigrants from Ireland, were forced to engage in sexual perversion with Conor certainly, and possibly Fergus, and in return they were murdered. Some ritual maybe, involving sex and beating. We've seen the progression of photos in the album. It was probably just a few steps further to murder. I certainly don't believe Conor's story about the cruel Mrs. Wilkinson. I went back again to the files and read that letter from Nuala O'Neill's mother. That girl must have been desperate to get out of here, trying to return to Ireland, trying to save her life." Barbara shook her head, incredulous. The enormity of the atrocity left her numb.

"But you have no proof," Derek said quietly. "Whatever you may think of the photos, today there are lots of people buying videodiscs so they can watch the same sort of thing in their own living rooms. You won't nail Fergus as a murderer with this evidence."

"Even if we fail," said Barbara, "I think we should try."

"Why?" answered Derek, "when the price of trying would be the destruction of the Foundation? There would be lawsuits. The money he left, all thirty million, would be tied up for years in court battles and legal fees and eventually would end up in the hands of distant cousins who never met Nuala O'Neill or any of the others. All the Irish-American scholarships we've just started awarding would have to stop. And, to be totally selfish—and honest—I'd lose my job and so would you."

"I'm finished here in April."

"Yes, but I've already asked the board to hire you full time." He shrugged, looked sheepish.

"So you don't think we should do anything more. Just carry this little secret with us?"

"What real good would there be in bringing out the truth? The girls are dead; they have been for forty years. The net result would be to destroy the Foundation and ruin the chance of anything good coming from his money."

"You've forgotten one thing."

Derek lifted his head, jutting out his chin. He had weighed everything, had forgotten nothing.

"Conor Fitzpatrick. If that was he in those photographs— and I'm convinced it was—then he, too, knew about the killings. He was involved in the deaths of those girls."

"And he should pay? Regardless of whatever else that means?"

Barbara nodded. "He's alive, Derek, and nine young girls are dead and buried on Steepletop. Yes, Conor should pay. They did, with their lives."

Seventeen

"Well, as the chairman of the Halloween dance committee, I think it's a good idea," Tracy declared, looking across the lunch table at Valerie. "Much better than the gym, where we always get stuck having it."

Shaking her head, Valerie sipped her Coke and scanned the cafeteria, watching to see how many students were huddling together, eyeing her, laughing among themselves. By now Borgus's version of what had happened at the graveyard had to have spread through the whole school. Nick would have seen to that.

"I'm in enough trouble," she said. "I'm not going to have everyone laughing at me again." It was better to just lay low, she figured. Keep quiet and let the whole mess pass.

"No one is blaming you for anything. I mean, you didn't run the wrong way in the game." Tracy tossed her hair back from her face, but didn't say any more. She knew better than to pick on Scott in front of Valerie, but it was no secret she thought he was weird and the source of all Valerie's troubles with Borgus.

Valerie shrugged and finished the soda in one long gulping sip. "No, but everyone on the bus this morning knew what color underwear I had on."

"Val, it's not your fault. Everyone thinks those two are creeps."

"They don't think so." Valerie nodded toward a table of football players. "They think Scott is a creep, and they think I'm a creep for hanging out with him. And they believe I wanted to have a threesome with Hank and Nick."

"Hey, I don't believe that," Tracy said defensively. "About the threesome, I mean. But if you're going to act all mean and weird, I guess I'll just leave." She stood up and reached for her Flat Rock Twirlers jacket.

"Would anyone come?" Valerie asked. She did not look at her friend.

"Sure. Why not? I mean, if we can have the dance at the castle, everyone would want to come. That would really be neat," Tracy answered in a rush. She sat down again, ready to talk more. "There isn't much time, but I think Carpenter would let us make the switch."

"Would any of the girls come?" Valerie asked next. "Do they really think I wanted to have a threesome?"

Tracy shook her head. "Half the kids don't even know what it means."

Valerie glanced quickly across at her friend. "Tracy?"

"Huh?"

"What does it mean, anyway?"

"Oh, God, you don't know?"

Valerie shook her head, her green eyes wide with innocence.

Conor kept to his routine. He had little enough to do around the estate but he kept himself busy. At four-thirty he went to the castle and picked up the dinner pail. Most days he would chat a bit with the cook, sit in the staff dining room with the secretaries and the cleaning girls, but today he was in a rush, afraid that Barbara Gardiner might nab him for questioning again, and he was in and out of the castle in minutes, returning to his own place in the barns.

On any other afternoon he would have stayed there until nightfall, or until the Foundation people had left for the day. But now he was too impatient, too troubled, and he set out immediately, lugging the metal bucket down to the bridge, across it, and into the woods beyond. In a matter of minutes he had disappeared into the trees. There was no path beyond the river, and Conor always approached the small log cabin by a slightly different route.

The cabin itself was hidden, built in the thick of the trees with no clearing to give the hut a glimpse of the sun. Himself had wanted it that way, saying rightly that the place would be better for hunting, blending as it did with the forest.

Conor stopped a hundred yards off to see that no one was about. He no longer trusted Brennan, not after what he had heard that morning, hiding in the passageway, watching him and the woman studying the old pictures.

When he was certain that no one was prowling about, he continued on, his feet kicking up the deep bed of leaves. He circled the small cabin and went up onto the wooden porch, his shoes thumping on the old boards.

Most days he just set the bucket outside the front door and went away. This time he knocked lightly on the thick door, whispering, "Maeve, are you there now?" His voice sounded loud in the silent forest. He tapped the door again with his bony knuckles and then leaned closer, listened with one ear up against the door.

He could hear her coming, her soft slippers shuffling across the bare floor. At the door she paused and unlocked the small wooden peephole, opened it and looked out, peering through the iron bars he had installed years before.

"And how would you be, Maeve?" He tried to sound cheery, to ease her loneliness.

"I'm the same as always, and why wouldn't I be?" The old woman glanced back into the room as if checking on something.

"Aah, you're a good soul, Maeve." Conor braced his arm against the door frame.

"What is it, Conor?" She was puzzled by his visit, his stopping to talk. It wasn't their way.

"Well, things are not good, Maeve." He shook his head.

She could see the worry on his face. He told her then of Barbara Gardiner, how she had seen the graves, and found the old album they had all forgotten. The old woman stared out blankly through the bars. She did not understand what Conor was saying, did not know why he was so troubled. Himself had told them years before that they would always be safe at

Ballycastle, that whatever happened in the world, here they were safely at home, among his things, on his property.

She remembered how he had come to her when she was a girl, brought her to his big bed and drawn her into his arms, whispering, "Never leave me, Maeve, never leave me." And she had asked him to swear that there would never be another woman in his life. He swore it, and in return she promised she would never leave him, and then she gave herself to him.

"Yeah?" Scott said, answering the kitchen phone.

Pause.

"Yeah?"

Pause.

"Oh, yeah?" he said quickly, angry now.

Barbara watched him as he paced the room, stretching the long extension cord.

"Yeah! Yeah!" he said again. Barbara bit her lower lip and went back to setting the small bay window table.

"I don't know. Maybe," Scott whispered in the receiver.

Barbara smiled. He was so secretive, as if his whole life were a conspiracy.

"I don't think it's a good idea." He glanced at Barbara. "Listen, can't we talk about this at school?"

Barbara ignored him. She put the string beans in the steamer and set them on the stove. Derek would be there within a half hour, and she wanted to eat dinner immediately and then get down to business.

Scott had stretched the telephone cord down the hallway and into his bedroom. She could hear him say, "God, that's really dumb," and she shook her head, wondering who was having the pleasure of this disagreeable conversation with her son.

He reappeared and hung up the phone, slamming the receiver down.

"Who was that, dear?" she asked, ignoring the display of temper.

"Ah, no one." He went back to the dishwasher and began his job of unloading the machine.

"You spent the last ten minutes being hostile to no one?"

"I was talking to Val, that's all." He banged one plate down on another, for emphasis.

"Oh. And how's Valerie?" Barbara asked sweetly.

"She's okay," Scott mumbled.

"Well, what did she want?" Barbara pressed.

"Nothing."

"Nothing? Really?" Barbara smiled at her son. "Then why are you so upset with her?"

"I'm not upset," he snapped.

Barbara folded three napkins and waited.

"She just called about some crazy idea of hers," Scott said at last.

"Hmm."

"She says some kids want to have the Halloween dance here at Ballycastle and have everyone come as a *Hobgoblin* character."

"Why, that's a great idea, don't you think?" She turned her full attention to Scott.

"Why should the dance be at Ballycastle? And why do they want to wear *Hobgoblin* costumes?" He was shaking his head. "They don't even like the game, anyway."

"But, honey, don't you think it would be a good idea? The castle is a wonderful place for a dance, and having everyone come as a *Hobgoblin* character would make it that much more fun."

"Well, we can't do it anyway," Scott answered, dismissing her enthusiasm.

"And why not?"

"Because the Foundation wouldn't let us."

"Oh, I think they would. Ask Derek tonight. It would be good for community relations, a way to connect Ballycastle with the town."

Scott shrugged, and she backed off. She knew better than to press him. It would only make him obstinate.

The phone rang again.

"I'll get it," Barbara said. "It's probably Derek saying he'll be late." She hung a towel on the refrigerator door and went for the wall phone. "Hello."

"Oh, hello, Mrs. Gardiner, this is Valerie Dunn." She

sounded timid, as if she hadn't expected Barbara to answer the phone.

"Why, hello, Val." She turned around and smiled broadly at Scott who smiled back, gritting his teeth.

"I'm sorry to be calling at dinner time, but could I please speak to Scott again?"

"Certainly." She motioned to Scott, then said quickly to Valerie, "Oh, I think your Halloween dance at Ballycastle is a wonderful idea."

"You do?" Valerie's voice brightened.

"Yes, of course. The castle is certainly large enough, and it really does look like a haunted house, doesn't it?"

"Well, I guess. I mean, it really wasn't my idea. My friend Tracy suggested it—she's the chairman of the dance committee—and I was just calling Scott to see what he thought. He doesn't like the idea, but now that everybody's hot to do it they'll all be mad if he turns them down."

"Oh, I don't know." Barbara lowered her voice. "I think perhaps you can talk him into it, Valerie. Now here's Scotty." She handed him the receiver, saying, "I'm going to put the car in the garage. Baste the chicken, please." And then disappeared down the dark hallway, leaving her son alone.

"Don't hang up on me again," Valerie said immediately.

"Hmmm."

"Come on, Scott, even your mother likes the idea."

"Yeah."

"God, you're impossible."

"Well, if I'm so impossible then why do you keep calling me back?"

"I don't know." Valerie sighed, then said all in a rush, "Because you're being so stupid about this. Because if you were nice for just a few minutes then the kids at school would like you better."

"Oh, yeah? Then why did they shit all over *Hobgoblin?*I was just trying to show them the game, explaining and everything."

"Okay! Okay! You think *Hogboblin* is so neat, but you saw how hard it was for me to learn the game. Give us a chance."

"Yeah, well, I gave you a chance, and you didn't like it. You've never asked to play again, not since that first night."

"Fine, I'll play the game. I'll play on Saturday night."

"That's the night of the dance."

"Right. The kids will play the game. All of us. It will be fun." She sounded excited, caught up in her idea. "Everyone will be in their costumes, so they can see everything and not have to imagine it. They'll like that a lot better."

"Why should I do anything nice for assholes like Borgus or anyone in social studies?"

"Because we'll play the game and everyone will lose. You can kill them all off, show Borgus and the other jocks how stupid they are."

It clicked then in his mind how it would be. Instead of using a little Battleboard they'd use the whole castle, the endless rooms and the long corridors. Brian Ború would run an Adventure against all the kids at school, everyone on his list.

"Scott?" Valerie asked. "Are you listening? Did you hear me?"

"Uh-huh."

"Well, what do you think?"

"All right. I'll ask Mr. Brennan."

Valerie sighed into the phone. "Thanks," she whispered. "Are you coming to school tommorrow?"

"Yeah, sure, why not?"

"Because you weren't there today, that's why. Where did you go after social studies?"

"Around."

"Around where?"

"Just around! For crying out loud, why do you want to know?" She was like his mother, he thought, always probing.

"Nothing. I'd just like to go with you the next time you cut, that's all."

"Oh." It surprised him that she wanted to do something with him. "I don't do much; I mean, I just hang around with Conor, that's all."

"Well, that would be fun," she answered. "Take me next time, okay?"

"Sure, I guess. Why not?" He tried to sound nonchalant.

"And can I have a ride to school tomorrow? I mean, if you're driving."

"Yeah, okay."

"And Scott . . . ?"

"What now?" He tried to sound put upon, exasperated.

"Don't forget to baste the chicken," and then she hung up.

Derek Brennan turned off the highway and stopped at the main entrance, waiting while the security guard came out of the gate house and raised the wooden bar. Then he pulled up beside him.

"Quiet night, Rick?"

"Yes, Mr. Brennan."

"None of those high school boys around then?"

"No, sir, not with the south gate closed."

"Good. Where's Ted?"

"Oh, he's out there someplace. Do you want me to call him on the CB?"

"Yes, let him know I'm going up to the castle in case he sees the lights on in my office. Then I'll be stopping by the guest house. The old lady hasn't gotten out, has she?"

The guard shook his head. "Haven't seen her."

"Good. I got on Conor's case, told him we'd have to put her away if it happened again. He's been too lax, I think."

"Mr. Brennan, I've been meaning to ask you. Did you see her the other day, when we were tracking her through the woods?"

Derek shook his head, looked up at the guard. "Why, what did you notice?"

"Well, I didn't get a good look. I was down by the truck and I had the binoculars on her. She was running across the ridge, and I couldn't see her clearly, of course, because of the trees, but she looked strange, you know, from the distance."

"How so?"

"Well, she didn't look much like a woman."

"What do you mean?"

"She had long yellow hair, all right, and she was small, but she didn't run like an old woman, sir." The security guard was shaking his head. "She ran like some kind of animal."

"Rick, the woman is crazy. She has been locked up in that cabin for longer than you've been alive, and I'm afraid she isn't really much better than an animal. I'm trying to find an institution that will take her but it's hard. The state is putting people like her back on the street every day."

"Well, don't worry, Mr. Brennan. It can't be long now."

"How's that?"

"She can't live forever."

Derek shook his head and laughed. "I don't know, look at Conor! The Irish are a hardy bunch, Rick. All that cold, damp weather keeps them healthy."

"Not all of them, sir."

Derek glanced up at the guard questioningly.

"Those girls buried up on the hillside." He nodded toward Steepletop. "There isn't one of them lived past twenty."

Derek's fingers tightened on the steering wheel.

"That was a long time ago, Rick. People died young in those days." It won't go away, he realized; the graveyard had become his albatross. The past, he thought regretfully, couldn't be buried. It kept coming back, not to haunt Ballycastle but to destroy it.

When Himself lived in the mansion there had never been a door locked, a room that Conor didn't have access to. He thought of that as he fingered through his chain of keys, looking for the one that would open the kitchen door and let him into the dark, silent building.

He didn't turn on the lights. That would only bring the security guard and though Conor always had reason enough to be in the castle, he didn't want anyone to know that he had been back in the building tonight. Besides, he did not need lights. Thousands of times he had made his way about the castle in the dark, leading one girl or another up the back staircase.

"But Conor, Himself won't want us tonight, what with the party and all those people," Carmel said, coming up with him across the lawns.

Conor shook his head and shrugged. "He just told me we should come along, luv."

"Oh, Conor." She clutched his hand. "It isn't right, all those pictures. I don't want anyone to be seeing what we do together."

She leaned close to him, and in the shadows of Ballycastle they embraced. The music from the ballroom on the river had already begun and they swayed slightly to the rhythm. Then Conor broke away, and led her to the castle by the hand.

Conor went up the back steps into the small study, moving slowly; the steep steps were hard on him. At the top he had to stop and rest. He was out of breath and wheezing.

"Should I undress now?" she whispered in the darkened room. That was what they always did, acting as if they were alone while the master took his pleasure. Sometimes he simply stood and watched, but even when he circled the bed, using that camera of his, they had to pretend he wasn't there at all. In all the times she'd been up to his room, she'd never heard the master speak a word.

"Ah, here you are!" Fergus said, before Conor could answer. He entered the bedroom in a rush, his voice startling them both. He had come straight from the party, dressed in elegant black evening clothes, and Conor could see he was already flush with drink.

"Thank you, Conor, my lad." Fergus set his champagne glass on the dresser and loosened his black tie in one quick, clumsy jerk. The first gold stud on his starched shirt front popped loose and shot across the floor. Carmel jumped for it.

"Let it go," Fergus laughed. "Let it go, my love."

Stronger now, Conor went quickly along the hidden passageway to Derek Brennan's office, then let himself into the dark room that had been Fergus's bedroom. Crouching down beside the desk, he took out his flashlight and beamed it on the locked drawer. Then he pulled the chain of keys from his pocket, all the keys he had collected over the years at Ballycastle.

"Should we get ready, Mr. O'Cuileannain?"

"No, not now." Fergus was calmly taking off his platinum cuff links, dropping them onto the top of his chifforobe. "Why don't you go along instead, Conor lad?"

Conor glanced at Carmel, smiled. It was all right. Himself

had changed his mind. He was too drunk to want them.

"Well, we'll be going then, sir." He reached for Carmel's hand.

"No, Conor. You run along and leave Carmel here with me." He was working on his shirt studs now, popping them out one by one.

Carmel turned quickly to Conor, pleading with her eyes.

"But don't you want me, sir? I mean, it's always Carmel and myself."

"Not tonight." Fergus stepped between them. "You go out to the north field and see about Nightfall. That left foreleg of his was swelling up this morning. Go on now. Carmel will be here when you get back."

Abandoning his keys, Conor pulled a screwdriver from his back pocket and shoved it into the crack, breaking the simple lock. He opened the drawer. The album was there. The past. All those nights that he had blocked from his mind.

Carmel's heart dropped when the door clicked closed and Conor was gone. "O dear Mother of God," she prayed.

"Listen! Can you hear that music?" Fergus asked. He bent down, fumbling with her blouse, breathing quickly, as if in pain.

"Please, sir." He would pull off the buttons and Mrs. Wilkinson would be after her, seeing the damage.

"Fucking clothes," he swore, then ripped the white blouse away. The milky softness of her breasts startled him. "Ah," he whispered, pleased by the sight. "You're a lovely lass, Carmel Burke." And he bent to kiss her. She shivered when his wet lips found her nipples.

"Please, sir," she begged again.

"Don't worry about Conor, now," he said, guiding her toward the canopied bed. "He knows all about it."

He was eager now, hurrying, directing her to lie face down and naked on the bed. Then he tied her wrists and ankles to the bed posts, pulling the velvet straps until she cried out with the pain.

Spread-eagled on the bed, Carmel managed to turn her head

and saw Fergus drawing his riding crop from the chifforobe. She had seen the crop before. Fergus had made Conor hold it in a couple of their photographs. But this time, she sensed, he meant to use it.

The first blow fell on her buttocks and she screamed.

"Oh, no, Carmel, you mustn't scream. Mrs. Wilkinson will beat you for misbehaving."

Gently he turned the weeping girl's face into the pillow and hit her again. Once, then twice, again and again, faster, harder. She sobbed into the pillow until the pain overwhelmed her and she fainted.

She woke when he entered her, crushing her pinioned body under his heavy weight. She tried to move, to turn her head to scream, but his hands had seized her long black hair and he held her secure, face down in the fat goosefeather pillows, as he drove against her again and again, pounding into her body. She fought to breathe but the hands were unrelenting, and as she died she knew that this had been what Fergus always wanted.

Conor lifted the large album from the bottom drawer and tucked it under his arm. He felt immensely better, safer, now that this final piece of the past was safely in his hands. Nothing now remained that could tell strangers what had taken place at Ballycastle.

Nightfall's foreleg was not swollen. Coming home, Conor followed the music from the ballroom, heard the women laughing and the sounds of silverware and glasses clinking together.

It had never been like this before, he thought. Himself had never wanted to be alone with the girls. He felt tears on his face and realized only then he had been crying.

From the top of the hillside Conor could see the ballroom, all lit up and sparkling. The staff had spent a week polishing every inch of glass, the roof and all, then prayed it wouldn't rain the night before the party. He could see the guests as well, the women in their lovely gowns, the men in evening clothes. It looked, he thought, like a movie picture, and he went on walking. In the tall birch trees by the river he stopped again.

The guests were coming out on the lawn, carrying glasses of champagne down to the cool bank of the river.

Dinner was over, he thought; they would begin to dance again soon. Himself would be returning to the party. He started to move on when he heard a noise from the opposite bank. Someone was creeping along in the brush hiding from the couples on the lawn.

Conor pressed his body against the birch behind him and held his breath. It would be prowlers, he thought at once, or anarchists after Himself. From where he hid in the woods he could see the bridge and the telephone at the boat dock.

He moved carefully, hiding in the trees, on a parallel course with the intruder on the other bank. Suddenly, when they were at some distance from the ballroom, Conor's quarry emerged from the underbrush, shaking dirt and mud from his clothes. Then he glanced around, making sure he was alone. It was Fergus O'Cuileannain.

Conor crouched motionless as the master peered across the river. Satisfied that he was unobserved, he set off toward the castle, and Conor straightened and stared after him. He could think of no reason why Himself should be crawling through the mud of the river. But if Fergus was down here it meant Carmel was at the castle, waiting for him. But he was wrong.

Crossing the bridge he saw Carmel below him, her body caught in the stone pilings. He grabbed the wooden railing and stared down at his lost love. Still buoyant, she floated in the river, her pure white face a water lily surrounded by the black waves of her hair.

"Carmel," he whispered. And her body broke free, slipped under the bridge and was swept away, as if finally she were free of him, of Fergus and Ballycastle.

Conor stood up straight, clutching the photo album. He had heard something—the sharp sound of a door being opened and shut. He cocked his head, listening. Someone was crossing the first-floor entryway, coming toward the stairs.

Conor stepped back to Derek's desk, replaced the album, and quietly slid the drawer closed. He crossed quickly to the fireplace and in the dark he felt the paneled wall until he found the latch and swung open the hidden passageway. He stepped inside, pulled the panel closed behind him, and waited to see who else had business in Ballycastle after dark.

"The album is gone," Derek told her. He had waited until Scott went into his room to study and they were alone, drinking coffee in the living room. Barbara bolted up on the sofa, surprised at the news.

"Did you call Security?" Barbara asked quickly. "Maybe we should call the state police."

"Barbara, I know who took it."

"Who? . . . Conor?"

Derek nodded. He set his coffee cup down and took out a pack of cigarettes, lighting one nervously as he continued to talk.

"He found out about it, that's all. You didn't say anything, did you?"

"Of course not."

Derek shrugged. "Well, he must have overheard us talking this morning."

Barbara flopped back in the sofa. "Well, what do we do?"

"There's not much we can do, is there? That album was the only real evidence we had. If Conor has it, and we both assume he has, then we're stymied."

"Can we have the bodies exhumed? That ought to reveal something."

"Not forty years later. Besides, it's a legal issue. We'd have to go to court, show some evidence that the women on Steepletop were murdered."

"And that's something you don't want," Barbara said quietly.

Derek nodded, kept sipping his coffee while she watched him silently, judging him.

He said then, in defense, "I'm not being heartless, Barbara. I'm not being irresponsible."

"Oh, no?"

"Fergus is dead."

"Conor is alive. And so is Maeve Donnellan."

"Maeve Donnellan is crazy and Conor is senile. What could we possibly learn from either one of them?"

"We have the graveyard. The album..."

"Now stolen."

"Stolen, but not yet lost," Barbara snapped. She realized then that they had drawn up sides.

"Nevertheless, we're not going to start digging up graves, or start accusing Conor of murder." Derek stood up. He too felt the new chill in the room.

"But he did steal your album."

"Yes, I'm assuming so." Then he added without thinking, "Unless you did." The minute he said it he regretted it.

"No, I didn't break into your office," she said haughtily. "I didn't jimmy your desk drawer. I wouldn't know how, even if I wanted to." Now she was on her feet, ready to rail at him about his responsibility to Ballycastle, but it wasn't her place. She was only an employee. Temporary help. Unlike the Irish girls, she would leave Ballycastle. She had a life of her own beyond these walls. She had Scotty. Her family. And then she remembered Scotty's request and asked about the Halloween party.

"I know you don't rent out the building, but this one time might be useful for community relations. The Foundation doesn't really promote itself locally." She could hear herself selling the idea and she stopped. She didn't want to be indebted to Derek.

"I don't see any problem," Derek said immediately. He seemed happy at the chance of ending the conversation on a pleasant note. "Tell Scott it's okay. I'll call Bill Russell tomorrow at school and set it up."

"Thank you. They'll appreciate it, I'm sure." She opened the door and waited. He wanted to smooth things over, she knew, but she was no good at masking her feelings.

He stepped onto the porch and took a deep breath of cold night air. Then he turned back and said, as one last word, "I think I'm being responsible, Barbara. Conor is the only one who knows, and no one will ever persuade him to speak out against O'Cuileannain."

She nodded, resisting the urge to argue. She had thought of a plan, but it would be foolish to confide it to Derek. She ushered him out in silence.

* * *

Derek swung his car around in the cul-de-sac and his head-lights swept across the cottage windows. Barbara stood in the doorway with her arms folded, watching him leave. She did not wave. He raced the car out of the drive, up toward the main building. He had planned to do an hour's work upstairs before driving home, but now he was too depressed. He drove right past the mansion, down the long curving front road to the main gate. Halfway there, in the middle of the woods, he hit the brakes and stopped.

He had just remembered what Barbara said when he asked her about the photo album. She hadn't jimmied the lock, she said; she hadn't stolen the album. But how did she know the desk drawer had been jimmied, the lock busted?

Derek sat staring ahead. The headlights glowed into the trees, casting a bright patch of light for a few hundred feet, then fading in the distant dark.

Eighteen

"Where are they, Barbara?" Derek asked calmly. He stood before her desk the next morning, his attaché case resting on the edge.

"I have them," she admitted. "They're safe." She was surprised at her own coolness. It pleased her, this new sense of confidence.

"Well, what are you going to do with them?" he asked, still casual, as if it were no big deal.

Barbara shrugged. "I'm not sure, really. I just don't want anything to happen to them."

Derek stepped away from the desk and loosened his tie, which meant he was nervous. She realized with some surprise that she had become familiar with his ways. It was like being married, knowing another person's habits.

"And what do you think might have happened to them?" he asked, as if he wanted only to know the weather. He had gone to stand by the windows, to look out across Ballycastle's lawns.

"I'm not sure. Maybe they would have been stolen."

"But they were stolen. From my desk drawer."

Barbara nodded, unsure for a moment of what to say.

"I'm the director here, Barbara." He left the windows and

came closer. "Dealing with those photos is my decision and my responsibility."

"But you aren't dealing with them, Derek. I'm sorry, but in my opinion you are not being responsible. I don't like saying that, but it's true."

"I disagree," he said sharply. "I made a mistake with Maeve Donnellan, yes, but I've already admitted that to you."

"Why did you?" she asked curiously. "Why didn't you keep me totally in the dark?"

"After she came into your house, I couldn't keep on lying about her existence. It wouldn't have been fair to you or Scotty."

"Well, what about those personnel files? You didn't have to make Conor give them to me."

Derek nodded. "I thought they would be enough to satisfy you." He smiled wryly. "I didn't realize you were a natural sleuth. In any case, I misinterpreted your commitment. You're obviously determined to find out the truth about those graves on Steepletop."

"And you?" She raised her eyebrows, poised herself for his challenge. He could stop her very easily, simply by firing her from her job at Ballycastle.

"Last night," he began, "when I saw it was you who had taken the albums, I was really furious, and for awhile I couldn't quite understand what was upsetting me." He smiled sheepishly, shrugged. "Yes, I admit I was angry because you'd outsmarted me. But that wasn't really the problem. Last night I also realized I didn't want to lose you." He paused a moment, waited until she looked directly at him. "I finally figured out that you and I were on a collision course, and that if I kept this up you'd hate me. Barbara, this job means a lot to me, you know that, but last night I admitted to myself that you mean more. Losing you isn't worth it. Hell, there's more than one foundation in the world, but I'm not sure there's another Barbara Gardiner."

She looked down, blushing from his declaration. Then she pulled herself up in the chair and, sighing, said, "Well, if Richard Nixon can reform, I guess you can."

Derek laughed, and reaching over, touched her cheek. Impulsively she kissed his fingers. "Thanks," she whispered. "It isn't every day that one gets such a vote of confidence. At least, I don't."

"Well, what do we do now?" he asked.

"God, I have no idea!"

"Okay, then, let me make an executive decision." He stared off, out her office door. Tourists had already begun to arrive at the castle and he could hear Karen DeWitt giving them directions. "How about lunch? We'll table all important decisions until then."

"A deal."

Derek stood and picked up his attaché case. At the doorway he paused again. "Promise me one thing. Don't go off investigating on your own any more. Before you take any steps, at least talk them over with me first, okay?"

Barbara nodded, agreeing, and gave Derek a brief salute. Still she did not tell him what she planned to do next. He wouldn't let her, she knew. He would say it was too dangerous. But there was still one person alive at Ballycastle who had been to Fergus O'Cuileannain's bedroom—and had been driven mad by it. And Barbara was going to find her.

"Are you almost ready?" Valerie asked from the door of the library. She had her jacket on and was carrying her lunch.

"In a minute." Scott continued to tap numbers into his pocket calculator.

"What's all this?" she asked, seeing the stacks of paper.

"LOAs. I'm doing them for the game."

"LOAs! You mean levels of achievement? I've never been able to understand them. God, Scott, it's going to be too complicated. No one will want to play." She dumped her books on the table and slid into a seat. Everyone would go crazy at the dance if Scott made them sit down and concentrate.

Scott kept working, mathematically determining the character of each player. "At Spencertown," he explained, "we used the school computer. If I had a program I could just rip through these LOAs."

"Scott, please don't make it too hard," she pleaded. "The kids are only going to get bored. Everyone isn't as smart as you. Besides, it's a dance, too."

Scott stopped writing. When he looked up, he was grinning.

"Hey, Val, I know. I know. There's no way seventy-five kids who've never heard of *Hobgoblin* before are going to play it for the first time at a dance. I've worked out characters for everyone, but that's really just for flavor. What we'll really play is a simple game I just made up, based on one of my favorite *Hobgoblin* characters, the Lady with the White Hand."

"Are we going to have to roll dice and everything, like we did the other night?" Valerie asked suspiciously.

"No. I told you it was simple. I've broken up all the characters into two teams, and the game is just a fancy, competitive version of Hide and Seek."

"Well, how does everybody know who they are and how they're supposed to dress?"

"Because this afternoon at homeroom everyone who buys a ticket to the dance will get one of these white sheets and a map of Ballycastle. That tells them everything they have to know. Here, look at Borgus's. I made him a Raging Banshee.

> *Type:* Banshee (A Death Spirit)
> *Frequency:* Common
> *Armour Class:* 3
> *Moves:* 60 feet
> *Size:* 5 feet
> *Intelligence:* Low
> *Alignment:* Evil
> *Magic Resistance:* High
> *Weapons:* Magic (Spells and Poisons)
> *Special Attack:* Teeth
> *Special Defense:* Shrieking, Screaming
> *Language:* English
> *Handicap:* Sightless in Daylight

At the bottom of the page Scott had written: "Banshees are wailing women with long, streaming red hair, dressed in gray cloaks over green dresses. Their eyes are fierce and they weep continually. They are death spirits that wail for family members and can foretell the death of someone who is either holy or very important."

"What am I?" Valerie demanded, curious now. "I don't want to be Marie again. People are always after her; it's creepy."

"You're much better than Marie; you're the Lady with the White Hand." Scott fingered through the stack of papers and handed a chart to Valerie.

"What about Tracy?" Valerie asked.

Scott ran his finger down the long list of students. "She's a Fideal, a water spirit. They look like girls, but they drag swimmers down and drown them."

"She's not going to like that. Can't she be someone nice? She'll be mad at me if she isn't."

Scott shook his head. "It's all worked out; if I change her it'll take hours to balance the teams again. Besides, she'll like the Fideal's costume—it's all gauzy, like the dress the White Rock girl wears."

"Okay, that's good. But what about Borgus?" Valerie glanced at the Raging Banshee sheet. "He's not going to want to wear a dress."

"Then he doesn't get into the castle. Mr. Russell promised me that everyone has to come in the right costume or he won't let them in. Not even onto the grounds. He's going to check everyone at the front gate."

"Well, what's my costume?"

"You have to wear a long gown, either white or pink," Scott answered, looking at the *Hobgoblin* book. "And you should wear a circle of green leaves on your hair. But you also have to frighten people, so I want you to paint your hands and arms white. . . ."

Valerie took her sheet and studied the costume description. This wasn't so bad, she thought. She could wear the pink bridesmaid's dress that Karen had worn three years before to Linda Pettit's wedding. It looked terrific on her, but there were never any formal dances at Flat Rock that she could wear it to. She began to get excited, thinking about all the possibilities. She would go up to Ballycastle after school and get Karen to start planning with her.

"What team am I on?" she asked next, getting herself organized.

"You're not on a team," Scott answered, keeping his voice low, as if not wanting to give away a secret.

Valerie frowned, looked puzzled.

"You're the Lady with the White Hand," he whispered. "If you catch a player by surprise and touch him, he becomes a zombie and not even a high-level cleric with arcane powers can resurrect him."

"But what about you?" Valerie interrupted. "Are you coming as BrianBorú?"

"Yes, of course."

"And which team are you on?"

"Neither," he answered happily. "I'll be the Dealer and you'll be the Hobgoblin. Together we'll wipe out every student at Flat Rock High School."

Conor Fitzpatrick could not keep his mind on his work. He started up the fire in his small forge, then forgot why. Lately he had found himself waking in the morning and not knowing where he was. He couldn't concentrate, couldn't remember what he wanted to do that day. He would make a list, something to help remind him, and then misplace it. Now he went back to the forge and stirred the coals, as if to jar his memory. Then he remembered. He had just finished the sword that Scotty had asked him to make—a sacred sword, the boy had told him, long and thin and light enough to carry into battle. A sword like the one given to BrianBorú by the first king of Erin. The old man smiled. The lad reminded Conor of himself as a boy, before he had left the old country, before he had ever met Fergus O'Cuileannain.

"Conor? Conor?" Scott appeared outside the blacksmith's shop, leading Valerie by the hand.

"Ah, lad." The old man tipped his cap to Valerie as if he'd never seen her before, then reached behind him into the shop and brought out the sacred sword.

"It's done!" Scott ran forward.

"It's worthy of any knight, lad," Conor grinned, pleased with his work and the boy's pleasure as he tested the long sword in the wind. "Now, let me go get the sheath." He went back into the shop, moving quickly, but with the short, jerky steps of an old man.

Scott turned to Valerie, slashing the long, thin sword through the air.

"Be careful, Scott," she asked. "You'll hurt someone."

"It's like a claymore," he explained. "Both edges can cut. But it's longer and lighter than a real claymore and much more elegant-looking."

"You didn't need a real sword, Scott," Valerie said. She set her books on the long bench outside the shop and sat down. The afternoon sun touched that end of the building, making it a warm spot on the cool day.

"Yes, I did. BrianBorú doesn't go into battle with a plaything."

"Boys," Valerie thought.

"It goes with my outfit," Scott said, still parrying.

"You already have a costume?"

"Sure. Once a year at Spencertown they have this big convention for games like *Hobgoblin*. Everyone dresses up. Mom made mine. It's an authentic paladin's costume, just like in the manual—a leather vest, green tunic and gray leggings. I also have this golden cloak."

"How neat. Scott, why didn't you tell me?" She loved the idea of Scott having a costume. They would look terrific together, he in his tunic and cloak, she in her long gown and coronet of leaves.

"Here you be, Scotty." Conor came back carrying the leather sheath. "You can cut the mist off the moon with a blade as keen as this, lad, so be careful with it, hear me?" He took the long sword from Scott and slipped it into the tight, homemade sheath. "There now, buckle it on, my boy. You're looking more like BrianBorú every day." He sat down on the bench beside Valerie and slapped his knees with enjoyment.

Scott whipped out the long sword and slashed the air, parrying and thrusting. The sun flashed off the bright metal.

"Be careful," Valerie cautioned again. She hated sounding like his mother, but the sword looked dangerous.

"Ah, BrianBorú could use a sword well enough in his day. There wasn't his match in all of Erin. Would you be knowing about BrianBorú, lass? Scotty, have you told your sweetheart about him?"

"She's not my sweetheart, Conor." Blushing, Scott busied himself with resheathing the sword.

"What about BrianBorú, Mr. Fitzpatrick?" Valerie asked, warming a little to the old man.

"Ah, Brian was a great knight in the old days, a great man, as fine as Jack Kennedy himself. But there was a warrior from Connaught, a man called Diarmuid Timcarna, who hated Brian for the great respect in which he was held.

"So one day off he went in his chariot to visit Brian Ború, and he took a wise old warrior from Ulster with him for protection.

"Brian Ború was playing draughts at the time. Now, that's like a game of checkers, and his back was to the road but nevertheless he said to his friends, 'I see two chariots coming here. There is a big, brown-haired man in the lead, wearing a crimson cloak with a golden brooch on it and a hooded tunic with red embroidery. His shield is ornamented with a rim of white bronze, and the sword that lies across his thighs is as long as the rudder of a boat.'"

"Is all this true?" Valerie asked impatiently.

"Come on, Val." Scott had squatted down on the ground before Conor, forgetting even his new sword in the excitement of the tale.

"Well, it's true enough, lass. True enough," Conor said, continuing.

"Now the two chariots arrived at Brian's castle and he recognized at once the good old warrior from Ulster. 'Welcome, father,' said Brian. 'If a fish swims into the river, you shall have a salmon and a half; if a flock of birds comes to the plain, you shall have a wild goose and a half; a handful of watercress, a basket of brook lime and a drink from the sands.'"

Conor glanced at the two teen-agers, adding, "That's the way one was greeted in the old days, no 'hello and good-by' and what have you. But then Brian saw this Diarmuid Timcarna staring at him, which was a great insult. 'What are you staring at?' he asked. 'Yourself,' Diarmuid answers coolly enough. 'I do not know why anyone should be afraid of you. I see in you no horror, no terror, no overpowering of odds. You are a pretty boy only, with weapons of wood and impressive tricks.'

"Brian thought about this a moment, for he wasn't a rash man, and then he replied, 'Even though you abuse me, Timcarna, I shall not kill you, for the sake of this good old warrior beside you. But if it were not for his protection of you, your stretched entrails and your scattered quarters would reach from here to Dingle Bay.'

"Now at this," Conor went on, "Diarmuid challenged Brian to combat the very next day and drove off in his chariot. But he hadn't driven three miles when he said to his charioteer,

'I have boasted to fight with Brian Ború tomorrow, but I cannot wait for it. Turn the horses back again.'"

Valerie's attention began to wander. She didn't understand the point of the story, or any of that old Irish stuff, and she tried to catch Scott's eye, to signal him that she wanted to go. But Scott never saw her, so enrapt was he with Conor's story.

"Now Brian says to his friends, 'Here comes Timcarna back again. Let us down to the ford to meet him as he deserves.' But Brian did not wish to kill the man, so he took only his long sword, like the one you have there, Scotty, and cut the sod from under Timcarna's feet and he fell on his back with the sod on his belly."

Valerie grinned, amused in spite of herself at the absurdity of the tale.

"'Go away,' Brian said, 'I cannot bear to wipe my hands on you.'

"'We shall not part this way,' said Diarmuid, 'but fight until I take your head or leave my head with you.'

"'That is what will happen,' said Brian, and struck Timcarna with his sword about the armpits, so that his clothes fell off him, but he did not wound the skin. 'Go now,' Brian said, dismissing the fool.

"Well, he wouldn't leave," Conor went on, shaking his head at the foolishness of Timcarna. "So Brian passed the edge of the sword over Diarmuid's head so that it cut his hair off as clean as if he'd been shaved with a razor. But still the oaf continued to be troublesome. And so, at last, Brian wheeled about and struck him so the man was split in half from his crown to his navel."

"Oh, gross!" Valerie cried. She had gotten herself caught up involuntarily in the story.

"And that wasn't half of it, missy," Conor continued. "Still angry with the boorish cur, Brian dragged the body back to the castle behind his own chariot, and as they drove over the rocky ground, the one half of the body separated from the other, and they buried him in two graves, side by side, so people would always know what becomes of men who challenge Brian Ború."

"All right!" Scott exclaimed, applauding the story.

The old man nodded, pointed toward Scott's new sword. "Many's a man will be wise and wary of coming up against that new sword of yours, Scotty. You can slice them into bits as well as Brian Ború with such a weapon."

"Oh, wouldn't that be great," Valerie said disdainfully. "Scott, I'm going. You can stay or not; it's up to you."

"Oh, come on, Val, it's only a story." Scott, too, stood up, fixing his sword so the blade hung easily at his side.

"But don't you think it's gruesome, all that killing?"

"Ah, they were violent in them days," Conor pointed out, moving into the shop. It was chilly outside, and he wanted to be inside, closer to the warm forge.

"Come on, Scott, let's go," she asked.

"Okay," he agreed. Then he unsheathed the sword once more and pointed it toward the blacksmith's shop in a salute. "Thanks again, Conor," he called, and the old man waved as he stepped inside. Caught up again in his toy, Scott pranced about for a moment in the dirt outside the shop, flourishing the sharp, thin blade.

"Would you please put that away?" Valerie demanded, angry with him suddenly for being so silly about the sword and *Hobgoblin*. She was glad none of her girlfriends could see him now, whirling the sword, parrying with imaginary warriors. One minute he seemed so smart and mature, the next he was acting like some grade school kid. She shook her head, not understanding.

"What's the matter with you?" he asked, coming over to where she stood in the sunlight. He was out of breath from his playacting.

"You look silly," she said.

"What do you mean, silly?" he asked, but he knew exactly what she meant.

"Playing with the sword. Like you were one of the Three Musketeers or something."

"You sound like my mother. If it isn't something you would do, then it's silly or childish." Again Scott raised his sword, fenced with it.

"That's right. I'd never do such childish things."

"What about your big dance? Isn't it childish to dress up like *Hobgoblin* characters and have a party? Or is that all right because you and my mother dreamed it up?" He raised the sword, pointed it at her.

"That's different." She backed away from the long, thrusting sword. "Put that away, Scott, please. It's dangerous. I can feel the point." She retreated another step, and found her back was up against the barn.

"Take it back," Scott demanded. The tip of the blade was pressed against her throat, hard enough to hold her to the barn but not hard enough to draw blood.

"Scott, this isn't funny." Her long neck was stretched, her head flat up against the boards.

"Come on, you boorish cur. I warned you once. Now I'll shave your hair off, cut the clothes from your stinking body."

"Please . . . ," Valerie whispered, beginning to cry. She dropped her armful of books.

"Lad! Good God, what are you doing? Let the lass go." Conor had come back into the doorway. "You'll hurt the poor child. If I had known you'd be carrying on like that, I'd never have made the sword for you in the first place. Now put it away, you little gypsy."

"Even though you abuse me, Valerie Dunn, I shall not kill you for the sake of this old warrior. But if it were not for his protection of you, your stretched entrails and your scattered quarters would reach from Ballycastle to Flat Rock."

Scott backed off, sheathed the sword in its leather case.

"Stupid!" Valerie answered.

"Hey, Val, I was only playing," Scott said, trying to be friendly now. He bent to pick up her scattered books.

"You could have cut my throat, Scott Gardiner, do you realize that?"

"No, I wouldn't have, Val; I knew what I was doing. It was just fun, that's all."

"Fun for you, not me!" She turned and walked away angrily, with Scott tagging after her.

"How was I supposed to know you weren't crazy or something?" she went on. "You're always threatening to kill Nick Borgus. Maybe you'd kill me too." She could still feel the sharp blade against her neck, see the gleam in his eyes, as if he were enjoying himself.

"Come on, Valerie, you know Brian Ború wouldn't hurt you. He's a twenty-fifth-level knight. A paladin."

Valerie came to a halt and turned to face him. "Scott, I'm

not talking about Brian Ború," she said. "I'm talking about you. You know, you do that all the time." They were standing in the open fields below the mansion, out of Conor's hearing, but still she spoke softly, as if what she had to say was secret.

"Do what?" Scott pushed his wire glasses up the bridge of his nose.

"You know what I mean," she insisted. "The way you're always saying Brian Ború this, Brian Ború that, as if you were the same person or something."

"Val, come on, it's just a game." He slapped his thighs impatiently. "I mean, give me a break. I know I'm not really Brian Ború."

"You just like to pretend you are. You like being him better than you like being Scott Gardiner."

For a moment they were both silent, embarrassed by her sudden insight. They began walking again, up toward the white birch woods and Scott's house.

"Sometimes," he began, not looking at Valerie, "it's more fun to be someone else. When I start pretending I'm Brian Ború, I get this feeling like I'm really strong and everything. It's cool."

"But you always know it's a game, don't you?" Valerie asked, still not convinced.

"Oh, sure. I guess." He shrugged and started down the hill.

"Hey, what do you mean: I guess?" Valerie stopped walking. "When you had that sword up against my throat, did you know you were just playing or were you really ready to cut me up and leave the pieces from here to Flat Rock? Did you know or didn't you?"

Scott tried to walk on, but she grabbed his arm and held him.

"Sometimes I know," he finally answered. "Sometimes I'm having fun, pretending, carrying on, and other times. . . ." He thought a moment, looking past Valerie toward the woods. Valerie had dropped his arm, letting him go.

"Sometimes I am Brian Ború. I mean, I know him. I made Brian. I rolled the dice, fought his battles, put him up against the Boobri, the Blue Hags of the highlands. We had to fight the Spottoggins, the Were-rats and the army of Klippes."

"Oh, Scott, stop!"

"It's true. I mean, you don't know because you've never played the game, not really. When your life is in danger and you have to keep Brian Ború alive, it's not a game." He was excited now, finally putting his feelings into words. "But when you win . . . when you roll the pyramidal dice and Brian slices a gang of Bugganes in half, or destroys the Deenee Shee, the fallen angels of Ireland, well . . ." Scott smiled, remembering.

"Let's go," Valerie finally said. But she wouldn't give up. She was determined to understand his obsession. Maybe she would feel it at the dance, when he dressed as Brian and she was playing the Lady with the White Hand. Maybe on Halloween she would finally understand *Hobgoblin*.

Nineteen

"I ain't wearing no fuckin' dress," Nick Borgus answered, talking back to the social studies teacher.

"Nick, I can't let you onto the grounds." Bill Russell leaned over and looked into the car full of football players. "I must say, this is a weird looking group. Where're your dates?" He kept smiling, trying to be friendly.

"Nickie's my date, Mr. Russell." Simpson reached over and squeezed Borgus's knee.

"Get your fuckin' hands off me, queer!" Nick wrestled with Simpson in the front seat.

"All right, everyone, let's keep it cool." Russell was already regretting his promise to man the front gate. It was getting cold and besides, these kids were just too tough to back down to him. Borgus and his gang were only there to cause trouble.

"Come on, Mr. Russell, let Nick go in. He's painted his face, hasn't he? He's wearing his old lady's wig, isn't he?" Jim Kohler asked from the back seat. Again the carload of students howled.

"What are you supposed to be, Jim?" Russell asked, avoiding Borgus for the moment. He glanced down the long list of characters that Scott Gardiner had given him.

"I'm a Ghent. A fourth-class ghoul. Don't I look like one, Mr. Russell?"

The teacher found Kohler's name on the third sheet. Scott Gardiner had typed out:

Kohler, Jim:
   Ghent, fourth-class ghoul. An evil spirit that plunders graves and feeds on corpses. Dress like a gravedigger with heavy boots, overalls, and carry a shovel. Face should be painted black with charcoal.

Russell glanced at the football player. His costume was right, and his face looked black. "You got a shovel, Jim?" he asked.

"In the trunk, Mr. Russell."

"And what are you, Tyrone?" Russell asked the only black student in the car.

"An Azmara, sir. That's some kind of holy man. I can cast spells, unlock doors, heal people, you know." He grinned.

"And you're wearing a monk's outfit?" Russell asked, consulting the lists.

"Yes, sir."

"That's why we call him Brother Tyrone," Kohler added. He stuck his head out the car window. "Hey, Mr. Russell, you got to check everyone, huh?"

"That's right." Another car had pulled up at the gate.

"How come you, Mr. Russell?" Kohler asked next.

"Because he's a new teacher, jerk," Hank Simpson said. "All new teachers get the shitty deals. Oh, sorry, Mr. Russell."

"I volunteered, Hank. Everyone is supposed to be in *Hobgoblin* costumes, and I told Scott and Valerie that I'd help out."

"I ain't wearing no fuckin' dress," Borgus announced again. His hands were clamped on the steering wheel.

Someone in one of the cars behind Borgus hit the horn. There were now four more cars waiting.

"Okay, Nick, go ahead." The young teacher stepped away and waved them in. Borgus hit the gas and sped forward. Russell watched the car for a moment, hoping he hadn't made a mistake. That was a carful of trouble, he thought as the boys disappeared from sight.

* * *

"Where's your mother?" Derek asked. All around him, Flat Rock students were arriving, dressed in gowns and tunics and monk-like robes, carrying staffs and lanterns and homemade lances. The entrance hall of Ballycastle looked like downtown New Orleans during Mardi Gras, but Derek was not in the mood for a party.

Scott shrugged, "I don't know." He was sitting at the reception desk in blue jeans, seeing for himself that most of the kids were in character and costume. "She went for a walk this afternoon, probably around four-thirty, five. Do you want me to go look for her?" He tried to sound willing.

"No, you're busy here. But if she turns up, ask her to come see me, okay? I'll be in my office."

"Sure. I know she's going to the dance; she promised."

"Good. Hey, how come you're not in costume?" Derek paused, remembering that this party was Scott's big triumph.

"Oh, I'm going home to change in a couple of minutes. I just wanted to be around for the beginning, you know, when everybody was first getting here, and see how they dressed."

"Well, you've done a great job," Derek said enthusiastically. "Everyone looks terrific." And I hope nobody breaks anything, he added silently to himself. Then he waved good-by and went upstairs to call Ted Ward.

"Ted? I'm in the office. Have you seen Barbara Gardiner?" Stretching the phone cord, Derek looked out the front windows, hoping he would see her crossing the lawns of Ballycastle.

"No. What is it? Her kid causing problems again?" The security guard sounded ready for business.

"I think she's gone into the woods, Ted."

"Shee-it." The guard sighed. "You want me to find her, Derek?"

"You better." He leaned forward, looked toward the sky. "It's going to be dark within the hour. She'd get lost in the woods easily enough during the day, let alone after dark."

"Do you know where she was headed? Back up to Steeple-top, do you think?"

"No, Ted, that's the problem. I think she's gone to the cabin. We've got to find her before she gets hurt."

From the bridge over the river there was a path through the woods. It was man-made, straight and clearly marked, and

Barbara followed it confidently. It was nice, she discovered, to be alone in the woods. Here was an available pleasure of the estate that she had not taken advantage of. Especially now, when the woods were brilliant with autumn color. Barbara walked quickly, feeling pleased with her excursion and with herself. Lately she had had the feeling that she was suffocating between Scott and Derek, that her days were consumed with their worries and problems. Just being off by herself felt liberating.

She lost the path then. Beyond the steeplechase it simply disappeared, the way water vanishes into sand. She hesitated, then kept going. She knew where she was, could even see one of the castle's high gray turrets. Also, she had a feel for where she was going. Her sense of direction, unlike Scotty's, had always been very good, and besides, she was determined. Maeve Donnellan, she was convinced, was not the utter madwoman Derek had portrayed her as being. If she were, Conor would never have had the patience to deal with her all these years, and Derek would never have consented to keeping her around.

If the two of them could talk to Maeve Donnellan, well, so could she. Maeve had been their prisoner. Now, Barbara thought, striding through the forest, she would see to it that after all these years Maeve's own voice was heard.

The woods simply swallowed her. Still inspired by being out of doors, Barbara went blithely ahead. Walking was not difficult. There were deer paths crisscrossing the underbrush and she kept choosing one at random, in the carefree way of people who aren't concerned with where they're walking. She showed no respect for the denseness of the forest and quickly, like a child in a crowded department store, she found she was lost.

Still she pushed forward, expecting that ahead, on the next slight rise, she would see some reference point. But the trees were enormous and blinding. Night was closing in, but she kept that fear from her mind. She would panic if she thought about being lost in the darkened forest.

She considered her situation. She was wearing jeans, a white Oxford cloth shirt, her green down vest, and loafers. She should have thought this through, been better prepared. For a few minutes she was just angry at herself, then she moved on, faster now, hoping to spot the highway. If she could only get home before dark, she would forget all about the log cabin and Maeve Donnellan.

Then from the top of a small ridge, indistinguishable in the denseness of the woods, Barbara spotted the cabin, hidden in the forest like the gingerbread house in *Hansel and Gretel*.

Saved, she thought. Weak with relief, she leaned back against a tree, exhausted but no longer frightened. If she could find her way in, she could find her way out, she reasoned, and she debated the best way to approach the house without being seen.

She slid down, stretching her legs, and relaxed against the tree trunk. It was pleasant there, quiet and calming, and Barbara closed her eyes and sighed. In moments she began to hear the forest. Gray squirrels were foraging in the fallen leaves, then scrambling up the trees with their morsels. She could smell the wet soil near the tree, smell pine and the medicinal scent of the imported eucalyptus.

She thought: I could go to sleep right here. Another squirrel scampered in the thick fall leaves and Barbara found herself tracking the sound, trying to guess in what direction the animal was going. She cocked her head, listening closely, and then she realized it wasn't a squirrel.

The rustling was coming closer, moving in a direct path toward her. She opened her eyes, looked straight ahead and held her breath, hoping the trees would hide her from sight.

The footfalls continued, steady, relentless. Barbara tried to remember if bears had ever been seen in these woods. There were brown bears, she knew, nearby on the Appalachian trail. It was possible. It could be a bear.

She closed her eyes as the animal went by. The sound filled her ears until she could not breathe. But the footsteps moved on, receding, and she opened her eyes to see that it was Conor. He had passed within feet of where she sat motionless. She watched as he walked through the trees to the cabin. She did not need to move to see him climb up on the porch, knock loudly on the wooden door. She crouched down suddenly, but the precaution was unnecessary. Conor obviously assumed he was alone, and never looked over his shoulder to scan the woods.

The door cracked open. Barbara could not see inside, nor from that distance could she understand Conor. His thick brogue was unintelligible. She only saw him pass the dinner pail inside the narrow entrance. Maeve Donnellan was being fed. The thought of the old woman's dismal life infuriated Barbara, confirming her decision to bring Maeve forward to bear witness, if she could.

Meantime, it was important that Conor not catch sight of her on his return trip. If he realized that she dared to visit Maeve, the old woman might disappear forever. Barbara rolled to one side, thinking, I'll crawl away, hide in the underbrush until he leaves. She glanced back at the cabin. The old man had disappeared; gone inside, she assumed.

Barbara got to her feet, ran in a low crouch away from the cabin. At twenty yards she straightened up and slowed as she went up the slope. She was all right now. Safe. She grabbed the low branches and pulled herself toward the crest of the slope, out of breath from the uphill run.

At first she did not realize why she fell. The hill was steep, with thick roots buried in the blanket of leaves. She stood up and kicked out, tried to shake loose the vine that had tripped her, but it held and she fell again, sliding backward on the muddy slope. The leaves were soft and wet and she couldn't grab hold.

She slipped further backward, and then coldness filled her as she realized she was not slipping at all, she was being dragged. Flooded with adrenalin she struggled harder, and had managed to gain a few inches when she felt the fingers close around her other ankle.

Sobbing with terror, she surrendered to the strength of those bony hands. They pulled her roughly to the bottom of the incline, then turned her over. At the sight of the face above her, Barbara began to scream, twisting her body to and fro and frantically scrabbling in the dirt with her nails. She had to live. She had to stay alive for Scotty. Oh, God, she thought, she should have listened to Derek. Ballycastle would not give up its past. And then it was too late. She shouted for Scott, shouted for Derek, as the large monogrammed handkerchief descended and filled her mouth, stifling all sound.

Conor Fitzpatrick heard laughter on the wind as he came back to Ballycastle. He halted on the dark path, unsure of what he was hearing or where it came from. He had been in the woods for the last hour, searching for Mrs. Gardiner. He had heard her scream and had understood why, but by the time he'd gotten out of the cabin she had already been carried away.

Conor resumed walking. He crossed the steeplechase field under a bright harvest moon, then plunged into more trees. It wasn't until he reached the last hilltop before the river that he saw Ballycastle, ablaze with lights, as he'd seen it so often in the old days. From his distance the mansion seemed to be afloat in the darkness, drifting under the passing clouds. He heard the sound of voices and music.

"Glory be to God," he whispered. "Now what in the world are we having?" The old man limped down toward the river, remembering the last party at the castle in the first weeks after the war.

It was September, 1945. The master wasn't right and had not been since that day years before when Nightfall had thrown him at the hedge. The passing years had only made things worse, but the war had brought some peace to Ballycastle. No weekend parties and hardly any passenger ships plying the Atlantic. Mrs. Wilkinson had made do with a skeleton staff, all wives and daughters from Flat Rock. But now the five-year respite was over, and once again Himself was ready to entertain.

"We'll have another grand affair, Conor," he had said, "like in the old days."

But this party was different. The guests were not the same ones from before the war, old friends from Ireland and Great Britain, and the very rich from Boston, Philadelphia and New York. Now there were generals and politicians from Washington, movie stars from California, even local people who owned big houses near Flat Rock. Himself had invited anyone at all, just to fill his castle.

Conor had stayed close to the house that weekend. He helped out in the kitchen and carried drinks out onto the terrace late on Sunday afternoon, after they had finished the hunt. He kept busy and stayed close to Himself, making sure the master was under control. In all the last five years Himself had been with only Maeve. She was the last girl to arrive before the Germans closed the seas to travelers, and Fergus had seemed satisfied, content to let her live. But now the house was full of women, all lively, all beautiful, most especially the beautiful Nina Millay.

Nina had visited the house before the war, with her family from Philadelphia. But she had been only a child then, unnoticed in her large family. Now she was nineteen and grown, a cool blond ingenue already starring in her first moving picture. Although she stood four inches taller than Fergus, she made it clear she found him fascinating.

"Do you see her?" Maeve stopped Conor in the kitchen that Sunday afternoon. "She's throwing herself at him. She hasn't the sense God gave her." Maeve's eyes burned with rage.

"She'll be gone soon, dear," he'd answered. "They'll all be out of Ballycastle by tonight."

They were safe, Conor thought. They'd made it through the weekend, and soon they'd have Himself alone again. But then Fergus sent word for him to saddle Nightfall and the filly, Roxane's Jade. He and Miss Millay were going for one last ride.

Conor followed them on foot. When they crossed the steeplechase and rode into the woods, he thought he knew where Fergus was taking her. The cabin was not luxurious, but it was isolated—as good a place as any to take a woman so no one could hear her. But this time, Conor realized, Fergus would not go scot-free. The woman was important, famous even, with a rich family to boot. She was no curtsying, fearful servant from the old country.

Conor had to stop him—for Fergus's sake and for his own, as well. For ten years he had helped Fergus with the women. In some savage way it had been his own revenge for Carmel. All of them, Monica, Nuala, Peggy and the others, they paid with their lives for what Fergus had done. But now Conor's rage was over, and with all his heart he wanted an end to the killings.

He was nearing the cabin when he heard the girl scream,

a hopeless cry of pain and fear. Running up onto the porch, he grabbed a club of firewood from the stack near the door and burst into the cabin's single room.

Nina Millay was cowering on the bed, her naked back and thighs already laced with bloody cuts. "Help," she pleaded weakly, and Fergus turned, raising the riding crop in self defense as Conor lunged forward and brought his club down on the side of Fergus's head. It was a weak spot, the same place that Nightfall had kicked him, and Conor felt the cranium give way as if he had struck a ripened watermelon.

The old man shook his head, remembering as he walked across the lawn uphill to the lighted mansion. At the top of the slope, in one of the wrought iron terrace chairs, he found Barbara Gardiner.

She was sitting up, facing the ballroom, as if enjoying the dancers beyond the French doors.

"Ah, Mrs. Gardiner, you're all right, thanks be to God. I was worried there for awhile. . . ." He stepped around the chair and stopped, seeing that Mrs. Gardiner was not watching the young people at all. Her head was slumped down, as if she had fallen asleep on the chilly terrace.

"Mrs. Gardiner," the old man whispered and reached out his fingers to feel her stiff body. She tipped forward, falling, and as he grabbed for her instinctively, her face turned up and stared at him accusingly. Her eyes were open, her mouth frozen in an "O," as if she had been trying to say something when she died.

Tears came to his eyes as he touched her white cheek. She was as cold as stone, as white and stiff as Carmel Burke had been the morning he reclaimed her lovely body from the river.

"You look beautiful!" Valerie exclaimed. Her mother had dropped her off at Ballycastle but she had run down to the guest house first so she and Scott could make an entrance together.

"Neat, huh?" Scott spread his arms, displaying the gold velvet cape. "I made the leather vest myself two years ago at camp. The paladin doesn't actually wear one in the manual, but I figured it looked cool."

"And those trousers!"

"Mom got this canvas material and made the pants. Then she laced up the outside of each leg with the shoelaces, see?"

"You look like Robin Hood or something."

"Brian Ború!" Scott insisted. Stepping back into the center of the living room, he whipped out the long sword.

"Come on, Scott, you'll cut yourself, or somebody." Valerie hated the very sight of the sword.

"No, I won't. I'll be careful."

"You're not taking that to the dance?"

"Yes, and my slingshot and my shillelagh. Conor made them, too."

"You can't dance, carrying all that on your belt."

"I can't dance anyway."

"Scott, you promised!"

He shook his head. "I never said I would."

"Yes, you did. Your mother heard you—let's ask her."

"She isn't here."

Valerie was disappointed. She had wanted Mrs. Gardiner to see her dressed up as the Lady with the White Hand. "Well, is she coming to the dance?"

"I guess." Scott was adjusting his cape, making sure it fell in a smooth, straight drop from his shoulders. He wished he had talked to Conor earlier about getting one of the horses from the barn. It would have been great, he thought, riding up the lawn on a white stallion, like Brian Ború at the castle of Kilkenny.

"Scott?"

"What?" He looked up.

"You're not listening. Is she coming to the dance or not?"

"Sure. She only went for a walk. Mr. Brennan was looking for her earlier when I was up at the castle."

"Aren't you worried?"

"About what?"

"I don't know." Valerie shrugged. "I mean, about something maybe happening to her." She glanced out the window. "It's really dark outside."

"Val, she just went for a walk. Come on, let's go up to the castle. She's probably there."

"How do you know?"

"Because where else would she be but in the castle? You said yourself, it's dark outside."

"Conor? Conor? Where are you, my lad?" the Black Annis was mumbling. It had gotten inside at the kitchen door and now stood in the dark pantry, distracted by the music.

In defense against the strange sound, the Annis cupped its hand over its ears, trying to squeeze out the noise. Then it stumbled on in the dark, searching for the old door off the pantry.

Ahead, through the entrance to the ballroom, the Black Annis saw the figures of dancers. The long, large shadows leaped off the white walls.

The Annis crouched down, felt with its old, strong fingers for the panel.

At the doorway to the ballroom, someone pushed through the crowd and came down toward the kitchen just as the Black Annis found the pressure point.

"Hey, man, what the fuck?" Hank Simpson squinted at the crouched figure in the shadows. "Hey, who's this?" he grinned, then reached out to touch the short, powerful figure.

The Black Annis swung wildly at the touch, clipped Simpson, then crouched down again.

"Hey, shithead, who do you think you are?" Simpson turned back to the other seniors and shouted, "Nick! Kohler! Hey, Tyrone." He walked down the hallway a few yards, trying to get their attention.

"Hey, Nick, have you seen Burns? I think it's him back here, dressed up like some weird freak with yellow hair."

"Burns isn't coming," said Borgus. "He told me. He's working tonight."

"Shit! Who's this, then? Look yourself." Hank moved to one side and let Borgus see.

"What are you talking about, Simpson? Goddamn, you're flying, man. Get your face out of here." Borgus stood in the pantry doorway, looking into the empty kitchen. There were no lights on, but he could see well enough to know no one was in the room. "What shit are you smoking?"

"I swear, Nick, I just saw him. I touched the fucker right

there." He pointed uneasily to the empty spot.

"Give me a jay."

"I don't have nothin'. Dave's got it, I told you." Hank kept looking around, searching. "Nick, you know, I swear to God I saw someone. A weird little fucker. Maybe it was McClintock. I bet my ass it was McClintock."

"Dave doesn't have it—I asked him," Borgus said, ignoring Hank's nervousness.

"Dixon, maybe. He's always got a stash. Come on, let's find him." He walked quickly back to the ballroom and the long flickering shadows of dancers.

Conor circled Barbara Gardiner. He couldn't leave her on the terrace, what with that gang of children less than twenty yards away. Someone had already opened the doors, they'd be outside soon, dancing on the flagstones. He knew that well enough from the old days.

Conor leaned over and picked up the body. Her legs had stiffened and he staggered slightly from her weight, the awkwardness of her position. Her head rolled to one side and hung limp, as if her neck had snapped.

"Jesus, Mary and Joseph," he whispered, and then he gained his balance and carried her down the steps of the terrace and into the darkness beyond.

"It's better than I had hoped," Scott said, smiling. He stood with Valerie upstairs, on the balcony overlooking the main entrance, watching Ballycastle fill up with students dressed as *Hobgoblin* characters.

"You think so?" Valerie beamed, pleased with herself. "I don't recognize anyone. The costumes are just so neat!" She bounced up on her toes and leaned over the wooden banister, looking down at the crowd of kids.

"There's a Morrigan," Scott said, pointing. "She's a war goddess but dressed like a raven."

Valerie checked Scott's list for the Morrigan. "That's Pat Bell. God, I'd never recognize her in that outfit. Oh, Scott, this is just a super idea! Tell me who the others are."

"See the guy with the green hair standing by the door? That's a Peg Powler." Scott pointed around the room, naming characters as he went. "Meg Moulach, the giant hag with one eye; a Jenny Greenteeth; Friar Rush; a Shriker—they wander invisible in the woods and give off fearful screams." Scott kept pointing. "That's a Gentle Annie, the governor of storms. She seems nice but underneath she's evil. Gentle Annies are very common, especially during the summer, and their alignment is always evil."

"You made Joe Higdon the Gentle Annie," Valerie said, looking again at the list. "Why?"

"Because his name is in my notebook."

"What does that mean?"

Scott shrugged. "I started this list of kids who weren't nice to me. Borgus is on it, and Simpson."

"How many kids?" Valerie was curious, surprised to learn about the list. Every day, it seemed, she learned something new about him.

"I don't know, maybe twenty-one or twenty-two."

"That many!" Valerie leaned forward over the banister to look up at Scott. "You mean that many kids were mean to you?"

"Yeah, sort of. In one way or another." He was being deliberately vague, not wanting to admit that her name, too, had been put on the long list.

"Gee." Valerie shook her head. "I think you're too sensitive," she said finally. "A lot of times, you know, kids say something, or do things, and they don't really mean anything at all. I know I do." She stopped and glanced quickly at him. "Am I on the list?" she asked quietly.

"Yeah, you were, at first."

"And you took me off?"

Scott nodded. Valerie looked down at the kids in costume. Several had spotted her and waved, shouted for her to come down. The band had started again and they wanted her to dance. She nodded, but before she left Scott, she touched his arm.

"Please, Scott, do me a favor, okay? Take them all off, will you? I mean, everyone is being nice to you now. This is going to be a great dance, thanks to you." She kept smiling. "Okay?" she whispered, gently squeezing his arm. For some reason, it seemed important to her.

Scott looked away, stared down at the students. They were

leaving the main hallway, going back into the ballroom. He spotted a Luridan, one of the goblins that lived on the Isle of Pomona, and Etain, the second wife of Midir the fairy king. Then behind her, standing alone in the hall leading to the Foundation offices, a Black Annis.

"Well?" Valerie pressed.

"Okay. I mean, it was just a game," he answered finally.

"Thank you." She reached up and impulsively kissed him on the lips, startling him. "Is this the first time Brian Ború has been kissed in costume?" she asked, teasing.

Scott nodded, too confused to speak.

"Good," she whispered and tapped his cheek lightly with her fingers. Then she was gone, running quickly down the wide staircase to the first floor.

Scott watched her skipping down the stairs. He could still feel the pressure of her lips on his. It made him feel great. Then he remembered the Black Annis. He didn't recall assigning anyone that character and he wished he had taken the list back from Valerie so he could check it. Once more he looked down the hall that led to his mother's office. Whoever she was, the Black Annis was gone.

Derek dialed the guest house a dozen times in twenty minutes, then called the front gate and asked for Ted.

"He's still out in the woods, Mr. Brennan," Lou explained.

"It's been almost an hour, Lou. Can't you raise him on the radio?"

"He walked into the woods, sir. Left the jeep by the river, he said." Lou paused, then realizing there was a problem, asked, "You want me to drive up and check out the jeep?"

"Who's at the gate with you?" Outside Derek could still hear cars arriving, swinging up to the front doors, then parking beyond the main building.

"Just myself, Mr. Brennan. Rick's off. There was one of the teachers here for awhile, checking on the kids, but he walked up to the castle about twenty minutes ago."

"Well, you better stay put. We can't leave the front gate open. Have Ted call when he gets back. I've got to go downstairs and check on this dance." He was furious now at himself for having agreed to let so many young people onto Ballycastle after dark. There would be a lot of problems if he wasn't careful. "Oh, have you seen Mrs. Gardiner, Lou? She didn't drive off the estate, did she?"

"No, sir, not in the last hour."

Derek hung up and again dialed the guest house. Barbara would have to go home first, he reasoned, to change before coming up to the castle. He let the phone ring a dozen times before he gave up.

Scott Gardiner jumped onto the small bandstand and stopped the music, then blew a whistle to get everyone's attention. "It's time for *Hobgoblin*," he shouted. "Whatever team wins has tomorrow off from school."

A cheer burst from the crowded floor and he let it die before adding, "Of course, tomorrow is Sunday."

A roar of boos came back to him.

Scott raised both hands, grinning. He was having a good time. "Okay! Okay! *Hobgoblin!*"

The kids roared again, began to clap. Everything would be all right, he thought. They really did want to play.

"Everyone has a map of Ballycastle, right?" he shouted.

More cheers.

"Now there are two teams, the Kelpies and the Spriggans, and everyone has been assigned to a team and a partner. When I blow the whistle, you and your partner go hide anywhere in the castle. In three minutes I'll blow the whistle again, and the two of you have to change hiding places. We'll do this ten times, so you have to think of ten good hiding places. At the end of the tenth round, come back downstairs to the ballroom— if you haven't been eliminated."

There was a murmur of confusion. "Eliminated by who?" someone called out. It was Tracy, the Fideal, wrapped in a gauzy see-through dress with a white body-stocking underneath.

"Good question," answered Scott. "But for the answer, you must listen to the tale of Ballycastle." Unfolding a sheet of notebook paper, he signaled the students to be quiet. When they were ready he began to read:

"We are not tonight in Ballycastle, five miles from Flat Rock, but in Ballycastle of yore."

"Yore who?" Borgus shouted from the floor. He was standing at the back, away from the press of students near the bandstand. A dozen voices shouted him down. "Fuck you," Borgus muttered back at them.

"We are in the first Ballycastle, in the mountains of Donegal." Scott paused and the audience waited. Everything was okay. He had their attention. He began to loosen up, to make his story dramatic, as Mr. Speier would have done at Spencertown.

"In the years before Tara became the home of Irish kings, there lived in the Land of Shadows, on the western coast of Erin, a beautiful woman called the Lady with the White Hand." Scott paused again and Valerie stepped forward. "After she died she became a spirit and lived in a laurel tree near her castle. But the lady was very lonely and sorely missed the gay companions of her youth. So every night, at twilight, she would rise up out of her tree and go drifting after travelers.

"She was pale as a corpse and her clothes rustled like leaves when she moved, but it was her long, white hand that strangers feared."

Valerie raised her hands over her head and the long sleeves slipped back to reveal arms painted dead white with theatrical makeup. The girls began to shriek excitedly.

Scott blew his whistle for silence. He wanted everyone to hear the wind blowing against the stone walls, hear the old building moaning. It was more fun that way, scarier.

"If the lady with the white hand touches a man's head, he is driven mad. If she lays her hand on a woman's heart, she dies." Scott furled his golden cloak over his shoulder dramatically.

"Tonight the lady is abroad in Ballycastle. She will seek you as you hide, and if she finds you and touches you with her white hand, you are no more. Forthwith you are a zombie, doomed to return to the laurel tree and keep the lady company for all eternity.

"If you elude the lady, however, you and your partner may return to the ballroom and your team will get two points."

Laughing and cheering, the crowd of teenagers pushed for the doors.

"Remember!" Scott halted them with a shout. "The lady's

312

cold white hand will be everywhere. Woe to you if it finds you!"

To avoid the students, Derek stayed away from the main staircase and the front entrance of the castle. Instead he went downstairs by the old servant's entrance to the south wing. Barbara might have taken all the teacher chaperones down there for a break. There was an office lounge in that wing and Barbara had keys to the liquor cabinet.

He skipped quickly down the narrow back stairs. He would check the lounge before he started searching the woods. It was the last possible place she could be in Ballycastle.

At the bottom of the steps he paused to flip on the overhead switch. In the blinking fluorescent lights he saw someone crouched in the dark a dozen feet from the stairway. Derek jumped involuntarily, then calmed down, realizing that the *Hobgoblin* game must have started. Barbara had warned him that Scott planned on taking over the whole castle.

"Sorry." Derek smiled, stepping around the figure. "I didn't plan on getting in the middle of the game." He caught a whiff of the costumed character as he passed. The smell was staggering. This was ridiculous. The kid must have doused himself in pig shit, he thought. "Is that odor part of your character?" he asked, trying to seem friendly.

"What's that? Bugger off, lad," the Black Annis mumbled, still not stirring from its position against the wall.

Derek stopped abruptly and turned back. "Say, the Foundation has gone to a good deal of trouble for this dance of yours."

"Piss off," the Annis said.

"Excuse me?" Bill Russell had told Derek how insolent these kids were, but this was too much. "What's your name, young man? It is a man, isn't it?" Derek was confused by the strange costume, the long yellowish hair. He still hadn't gotten a good look at the kid's face.

"Where's Conor? Where's my man?"

"Conor?" Derek backed off slightly, puzzled by the accent and the question. "My name is Derek Brennan. I'm the executive director of Ballycastle. What do you want with Conor, son?"

Before the Black Annis could respond, the rear door of the mansion burst open. Ted Ward was standing in the beams of the outside floodlights.

"Derek? Come here!" the guard shouted.

"Just a minute, Ted." Derek turned his attention back to the squatting student.

"Derek, now!" Ted Ward shouted. He was leaning against the open exit door, breathing hard, as if he had just run cross-country.

Derek started for the door then, realizing that something was wrong. "I think you better get back with your friends," he told the student, brushing by him. As he hurried toward the end of the hall, he heard the boy get up and shuffle down the hallway, back to the ballroom.

Ted Ward still stood in the open exit door, letting the cold October wind turn the narrow hallway into a wind tunnel.

"Close the door, Ted. Jesus!" He rubbed his arms, shuddering.

"She's dead," Ted whispered, stepping inside the hallway.

"Dead? Who? What do you mean?"

"The old lady. Maeve Donnellan. I went out there like you said to look for Barbara Gardiner and I found her." The fat man pushed his baseball cap up higher on his head. "Someone killed her, Derek. There's blood all over the cabin." He looked away, as if still confronted by the sight.

"Oh, Christ." For a moment Derek was stunned. This was something he hadn't expected, couldn't explain, and in that moment he felt events slipping from his control. "Okay. Here's what we'll do. First find Conor."

"I can't. I've already looked. And I can't find Mrs. Gardiner either," Ted confessed. "They cut the old woman up, Derek. Butchered her, for chrissake. What'll I do?"

"Did you find any kind of weapon?" Derek asked. He tried to make eye contact, to help Ted's mind focus.

"It must have been Conor," Ted went on, disregarding Derek's question. "Who else? He was the only one who knew she was out there."

"A bear, Ted. A brown bear. Couldn't it somehow have gotten into the cabin?"

Ted Ward walked off a few feet down the hallway, disgusted

by the question. "No fuckin' bear killed that old lady, Derek. Hey, listen to me!" He raised his voice, as if to assume control. "She's been murdered. We got to get the police out here fast. And we got to find Barbara Gardiner. Whoever did it—Conor or whoever—then Barbara, she could be in trouble too. I mean, he's not going after you or me."

What Ted was saying kept spinning in Derek's mind. For a moment, incongruously, he remembered the rumors about Ballycastle, the mad niece in the tower, dead women floating in bathtubs.

"All right, Ted, go back down to the gate and make sure no one gets off the grounds. When the police come, have Lou take them out to the cabin. Make sure everything is secure at the gate, then keep looking for Conor. He's around somewhere. I'll telephone the police now from my office, and I need to tell someone on the board. I don't want them to hear about this on the news." He sighed, exhausted by what he had learned. Now Ballycastle no longer had a secret to hide. Instead, he thought ruefully, it had a killer.

"This way," Scott said, grabbing Valerie's hand. The crowd of students had already rushed the staircase, running for their first position.

"Scott, I can't find all of them."

"You don't have to. Come on." He pulled her after him, out of the ballroom and into the deserted pantry. "This castle is honeycombed with backstairs and hidden passageways," he whispered. "We can go from room to room without anyone seeing us. Most of the secret entrances open up behind curtains or from bookshelves—I've checked. You can just slip out of the darkness and touch them, get them out of the game."

"It's like a horror movie, secret passages and stuff." She grabbed his arm, excited again.

"But here's the thing, Valerie." Scott was suddenly serious. "You can tag all the Spriggans you want. But don't touch the Kelpies—except for Borgus and his pals."

"I thought the idea was to send as many zombies as possible down to the ballroom."

"No. The idea is to get Borgus. And nothing will get him better than if he and the other jocks are the only ones on their whole team who get caught—and by a girl."

"Scott, that's great." Now Valerie understood the plan, and her eyes gleamed at the thought of Borgus's humiliation when he had to stand up in the ballroom and admit he'd been clumsy enough to get caught. Compared to what he had done to her, she was letting him off easy.

"Okay," said Scott. "Ready to go upstairs?"

"Ready!"

He felt along the paneling until he found the wooden knob, spun it slightly and the door swung open. "Go ahead," he said.

"There's no lights." Valerie looked up the long, narrow staircase to the second floor.

"There's some. It seeps in from the rooms and hallways. And I've got a flashlight."

"I'm scared," Valerie admitted. She shivered and stepped back against Scott.

He wrapped his arms around her, holding her from behind.

"It's okay. Don't be a scaredy-cat."

"I can't help it," she whispered. She bent her head, hoping he would kiss her on the back of the neck.

"Don't be afraid, Val. I'm going to be right with you." He pushed her forward and up the stairs, pulling the door closed behind them.

"Hey, come with me." Nick Borgus grabbed his friends and motioned them into a corridor, away from the crowd of students who were pairing off in the entrance way.

"What about the game?" Simpson protested. He glanced down at his map. "You and me gotta find our hiding place."

"Fuck our hiding place," Borgus answered.

"Shit, man, turn on some lights," Tyrone asked. Scott had lowered the lights before he left, and now Ballycastle was a warren of half-lit hallways and shadowy staircases.

"Shut up!" Nick demanded. He glanced over his shoulder, saw that the entrance way was emptying. Most of the students had filtered off into the huge building.

"But someone just grabbed my ass," Tyrone complained.

The football players broke into giggles. In the deep interior of the long corridor, they could see only the dim shapes of each other and a block of light from the entrance way. They glanced around in the pocket of darkness, uneasy in the strange building. They jabbed at each other, nudged shoulders and grabbed ass on purpose, their proximity giving them only a little comfort.

"What about the game?" Simpson asked. "Don't you want to beat Gardiner?"

"The game is to get Dunn, Hank. Forget all that other *Hobgoblin* shit."

"But that's not the game, Nick," Kohler interrupted. "That's not the way we're supposed to play."

"Yeah, and preppie's not supposed to run the wrong way in football either."

Nick glanced back down the long corridor. The main entrance was deserted. "Okay, let's go," he said. He led the football players into the lighted area.

"Here's what we do," he began, laying his map flat on the reception desk. "Simpson and me were going to hide in the pool room—'billiard room' they call it here. Where were you and Kohler headed, Tyrone?"

"This bedroom up on the third floor. I figure it'll take this girl awhile to climb that high."

"Yeah, it might," Borgus agreed. "Except the preppie's going to see to it that she comes looking for us first. She's just going to keep checking every room until she finds us."

"So we fool her. We don't go into any rooms. We hide outside in the hallways, two of us at both sets of stairs, front and back. And when she comes looking for us, we grab her."

"Hey, that's cool." Hank slapped Borgus on the shoulder. "But what if she touches us with her white hand? Then we're dead, man."

"Goddamnit, Simpson! Don't you understand? Once we get Dunn, we take her someplace nobody would ever look—the stables, maybe, or out in the woods. And then we make the preppie buy her back. After what happened in that graveyard, he'll give us anything we say. It's a great deal—we scare the preppie shitless, plus we make some money on the game."

"I don't know," said Tyrone. "I was kind of looking forward to playing."

"We will be playing, man," said Borgus. "Just not the way Gardiner figured. It's like the coach always says, right? Always make the other guy play your game."

Derek ran up the back stairs and headed for his office near the front of the mansion. There were students upstairs now, running through the halls.

He was two steps across the carpet in his office when he saw her, and he stumbled on the rug at the incongruous sight. She was lying on the conference table, her knees drawn up stiffly, her head not quite touching the table.

"Barbara?" he asked, but he knew that she wasn't asleep. He stepped closer and reached out to touch her, to let the warmth of her flesh disprove the evidence of his eyes. But she was not warm. "Please," he whispered, as if to talk her back to life with his voice. But the touch of her cold skin chilled him, left him shivering. In one single flash he remembered her at his house, in his bed. He kept thinking that they hadn't really had a chance, that everything between them had been just beginning. "Please," he said again, as if this time he were asking for forgiveness.

Then he thought of Scotty and the dozens of teen-agers filling the castle. He stumbled to his desk and grabbed the phone, dialed, whispered to the operator that she had to give him the police.

"State Police. State your name and address before proceeding to give any other information."

The flat, bored voice of the dispatcher shocked him. She didn't, couldn't understand what he had seen. "This is Derek Brennan, the executive director of Ballycastle," he began. He was too excited to know whether his voice was trembling or not. "Two people have been killed here tonight, two women, and we need the police immediately."

"Could you speak up?" the police dispatcher said. "I'm having trouble hearing you."

"I said we have two corpses here," he shouted angrily, then suddenly crouched down behind his desk, pulling the phone with him. Conor, he realized, could still be within hearing—watching, waiting.

"We have a deranged man here at Ballycastle," he said into

the phone more calmly. "He's already murdered two people. And there's a Halloween party going on for the high school students from Flat Rock."

"Hey. Is this some kind of joke?"

"Jesus Christ!" He shouted into the telephone. "I told you— I'm the director of the Foundation. There are two dead bodies here already, soon to be joined by half the class of '81 if you don't get some cops out here, sister!"

For a long moment there was silence, as if the dispatcher was debating what to do next. Then she said curtly, "I'll radio a trooper."

"I'd appreciate it," Derek answered. Then he hung up the phone.

The initial silence was comforting. It was as if he had fallen asleep.

He had done his job. The police had been called. Help was coming. Momentarily he remembered the board and the necessity of informing the chairman. That was unimportant now. He had to do something about the kids. The chaperones would have to find them all, get them together in one safe location. Then he would have to tell Scott about his mother. His mind faltered for a moment, then went on. And Conor. They had to find the crazy old man and stop him before he killed somebody else.

"No one's here yet," Scott whispered. He had opened the narrow door leading into the billiard room. "Okay, let's go." He grabbed Valerie's arm and pulled her after him.

"Where are we?" she whispered, looking around. At one end of the large, high-ceilinged room was a fireplace, at the other a billiard table covered with a white sheet, as if it were a body.

"This is where I figured some of the football players would be. They wouldn't pass up a crack at the pool table."

"Well, let's look somewhere else, then," said Valerie.

"No, I've got to blow the second whistle," Scott decided. "This is taking too long."

"Don't leave me." Valerie grabbed his arm. "I don't like this game. It's too scary."

"Come on, it's just getting to be fun," Scott smiled, pleased with himself. Everyone was just beginning to get frightened. In another round or two, he knew, they'd be too scared to leave one room and go to the next.

"You're okay," he told Valerie. "If someone comes in after I blow the whistle, just jump out. All you have to do is touch them. Then you give the person this and make him wear it." He opened his leather sack and pulled out a paper skeleton's mask. The painted white skull glowed brightly in the dark.

"Scott, how did you do that?"

"It's fluorescent, see? Once a person becomes a zombie, he glows in the dark. Then the zombie will go scare the shit out of everyone when they're changing rooms. I mean, no one is going to know who they are."

"You never told me about these." Curiously, she examined the illuminated mask. "Where did you get them?"

"In town. At the K-Mart. Look." He pulled the mask over his head. In the dark corner of the billiard room his head glowed like a skull.

"Oh, God, take it off," Valerie said. "It gives me goose bumps."

"Hide it away until you get someone." He gave her the sack of masks.

"What do I do then? Where do I go next?" She didn't like being left alone.

"Just send the zombies out into the hall and slip back into the hidden passage. I'll be back right after I blow the whistle." Scott stepped into the passageway and pulled the door closed, disappearing.

"Shit," Valerie whispered. For a few seconds she stood quietly, waiting for the whistle to send everyone scurrying. But it would take Scott time to reach the balcony.

In the silence she heard the sound of two girls giggling. Valerie recognized Tracy's voice and smiled. It made her feel better, knowing her friend was near her in the big house. She would get Tracy first, Valerie decided. Scott was right; *Hobgoblin* was just getting to be fun.

Conor Fitzpatrick did not know what to do. He had left the body in Derek's office—out of the way of the children, he thought—then gone back to his small apartment in the barns and put on a pot of tea. His hands were shaking and he had to calm himself down.

"I'll have a cup of tea," he mumbled. "And then, with the help of God, I'll put a stop to this." He spoke aloud, as if trying to calm himself with the sound of his own voice. "Oh, dear God," he whispered, thinking again of Barbara Gardiner, of how her head had flopped over when he felt her shoulder.

"Ah, Maeve," he sighed.

The tea pot was boiling and he went back to the stove, took out a bag of Irish breakfast tea and dropped it in the cup. "We shouldn't have done it, Maeve," he went on, mumbling again in the silence, but speaking now in Gaelic. He had lost his use of English. "It was a foolish thing, girl, thinking we could hide it from them all."

Conor stopped. He heard the barn door slide open. Someone was trying to be quiet about it, he realized, sneaking into the stables. Conor flipped off the apartment lights, leaving himself in the dark. He leaned against the wall, gasping for breath. He'll be the death of me yet, Conor thought. I should have killed him then, that day in the woods, and had done with it.

"Oh, Conor," Maeve had said when he carried Fergus to her. The master had lain between them, unconscious in the big four poster bed. Maeve had leaned over him, pressed a cold cloth to the wound.

"I'll take care of him, Conor. He'll be all right, wait and see," she whispered. "We'll keep him here with us; we won't let him run such risks again. They'll never know. Can't we just say the poor man died? They'll never find us here, Conor. Why, the woods are deep enough to hide a family of tinkers."

"Don't be daft, woman. Even if Himself agrees to it when he's well again, we'd need a death certificate, and a will, and a body to bury in his place."

"Himself could fix it, Conor—him and that New York doctor of his, Smyth. We'll say that Nightfall killed him, cut him up so awful no one but Dr. Smyth could see the body."

"And bury an empty casket up on Steepletop?" Conor tried to think it through. It was a reckless plan, but Himself would have to risk it or deal with Nina Millay and her family. She'd believe Fergus had died of Conor's blow, and her father would see the wisdom of the Nightfall cover story.

"Would you do it for me, Conor?" Maeve was asking. "Would you do it for my Fergus? Don't let them take Himself away from Ballycastle."

Outside his own office, in the small hall closet, Derek found the two girls hiding.

"I'm sorry," he said, standing in the door, "but I'm afraid the party is over." He did not explain why. It would do no good to have a bunch of screaming teen-age girls running frightened through the castle.

The two girls did not move. He was not sure they were girls; the darkness and their costumes hid their faces. But both figures were small and clinging to each other.

"Where can I find Mr. Russell, girls?" he was getting impatient.

The girls did not answer.

"All right, that's enough," he said and reached for them, to pull them out of the enclosure.

"Who are you?" one of the girls whispered.

"My name is Derek Brennan, and I am the director of Ballycastle." He spoke confidently, assuming the girls would do whatever he told them. "Go downstairs, please, into the ballroom and if you see anyone else tell them the game is over."

Then he walked away, down the length of the north wing. It would be best to proceed that way, he thought, to search for students room by room.

At the end of the long hallway, standing near the large windows overlooking the terrace, he saw a costumed figure. He was standing as still as the armored knights, watching the hallway. What light there was from the harvest moon caught his eyes, made them flash.

"Say, son, go downstairs. The game is over," Derek directed.

"Go downstairs yourself, son," the Black Annis answered.

"Oh, it's you." Derek kept his distance, yet even at half a dozen feet he caught the man's odor. "Let's go," he ordered. "The party's over." He tried to sound tough.

"I told you, lad—fuck off."

Derek stepped closer, tried in the semidarkness to make out who this student was. "Okay, that's enough bullshit." He reached out and grabbed the Annis's arm and the man swung at him, enraged. It wasn't a high school student, Derek saw. This was no teen-ager dressed up in long yellow hair and old, tattered clothes.

"Hey, what is this?"

The Black Annis swung his right fist and caught Derek in the neck, knocking him hard against a display case filled with Waterford crystal. The glass crashed like ice breaking.

Derek couldn't get his breath. The blow had jammed his Adam's apple up into his throat. He rolled to one side and tried to stand, his mind working furiously. He had been wrong. It wasn't Conor they had to fear. It hadn't been Conor Fitzpatrick at all, or Maeve Donnellan. And in that sudden insight before dying, Derek understood who this stranger really was. "You!" he exclaimed, raising his head to catch the mad eyes of the old man.

The Black Annis caught him by the shoulders, jerked him up and tossed Derek against the wall. When he hit, his spine popped. Whimpering in pain, he began a slow slide to the floor. He never made it.

The Annis turned, yanked the Knight Templar's lance from his armored fist and drove it into Derek's chest, slicing through his rib cage and clear through to the other side. Derek hung like a butterfly, pinned to the wall.

"Maeve, would that be you?" Conor asked in Gaelic. He opened the apartment door and looked into the blacksmith shop. The wide doors were pushed open. He could see moonlight beyond the entrance. "Maeve?" he whispered. She would have come looking for Fergus, he knew, just as she had that night at Barbara Gardiner's house. She had been sure Fergus was inside, drawn by the lights and perhaps a glimpse of the beautiful Mrs. Gardiner. He hadn't been there, of course, not then. He had waited till the night the children were in the house alone. He'd always liked the young ones, Fergus had.

Conor stepped into the dark shop and closed the apartment door behind him. He was safe here. He knew his way around the blacksmith shop. Maeve had not opened the door, he realized. It was Fergus who had come to get him.

"Mr. O'Cuileannain, now where would you be, sir?" Conor

asked, speaking softly in Gaelic. He moved toward the cold forge and lifted a set of long metal tongs from the hearth. The scrape of metal was the only sound in the shop. "Mr. O'Cuileannain, it's time we went back home, sir."

There was a man against the wall, a lump of a figure he could barely make out in the darkness. Conor raised the tongs with both arms and sidled toward the corner. He would have to strike at once, kill him with one blow. With Fergus he would have no second chance.

"God bless you, sir, and keep your soul," Conor said in prayer and using all his strength, swung at the figure. The shotgun blew Conor away. The short range blast lifted him up and drove him across the room. The shower of pellets devoured his stomach, ripped apart his chest. He landed against the opposite wall in a heap of flesh.

"Jesus H. Christ." Ted Ward came out of the corner. He had fired both barrels and the smell of gun powder burned in his nostrils. "Jesus H. Christ," he kept whispering. The sound of his own voice kept him stable. He would be all right, he knew, if he didn't choke on the smell of flesh and blood.

Like a swimmer breaking the surface for air, Ted stumbled outside and gasped. The night was cold and clear and he felt a sense of relief, realizing he was alive. Even with the shotgun in his hands, he had been frightened at the sight of Conor coming at him waving the tongs, mumbling in Gaelic, crazy out of his mind. But now everything would be okay, he told himself. Conor was dead. Maeve Donnellan was dead. There was nothing more to hide.

The whistle blew and Valerie stepped behind a wall tapestry, waiting for someone to enter the billiard room. She hoped it would be Tracy, but whoever it was the Lady would kill them, as long as they weren't Kelpies. She wanted to have tagged somebody by the time Scott came back looking for her.

She heard heavy footsteps in the hall, and the double doors of the billiard room opened.

"Shit, she's not here," she heard Borgus whisper.

"Come on, then," Hank said, "Let's get back to the stairs."

Valerie nerved herself to leap out and tag them. It was what Scott wanted; for him, it was the only reason for the dance.

But she was too frightened of the seniors. No matter what Scott said, it was dark and she was alone. They could do something to her again; they could hurt her.

Then her moment passed. The door closed again and they were gone, their footsteps lost in the rush of students in the hallway. Valerie could hear them running for their second stations, pushing and shoving to be in place before the whistle. Beside her, near the tapestry, the billiard room door opened again and someone else stepped inside.

"Tracy, don't leave me," a girl pleaded from the hallway.

"I'm not. Let go, Betty. I can't walk with you hanging on me every step."

Valerie bit her lower lip. She was grabbing her sides, keeping herself from giggling.

"Where do we hide?" Betty asked.

"Under the pool table, maybe. I don't know. I can't see anything in this damn dark."

The second whistle sounded and both girls jumped.

"Damn it, Betty, you're scaring me to death!"

Valerie reached out from behind the tapestry and touched both of them on the shoulders. They screamed together, making Valerie jump as well.

"I got you!" She leaped out and grabbed their arms, kept them from running.

"Oh, God!" Tracy closed her eyes for a second, afraid to even look behind her. Then Valerie laughed and the three teenagers hugged each other, all frightened by the surprise.

"Valerie, damn you!" Tracy pulled herself away, shivering. "What a mean thing to do."

"I'm sorry. I mean, God, it's only the game."

"But you didn't have to pick on us!"

Valerie took out two of Scott's masks. "Well, now you get to wear these. Aren't they neat? They're zombie heads." She held up the glowing skulls. "Put them on and go down to the ballroom."

Tracy pulled the mask over her head and the skull glowed in the dark. Mollified, she headed for the door, eager to find someone to scare.

"Oh, Val, it's great!" Betty said, reaching for her mask. The luminous head seemed to float in the night as she too carefully made her way to the hallway, closing the door behind her.

"Val!"

Valerie jumped at the sound of her name. Scott had returned to the billiard room through the hidden passage.

"Where's Borgus?" he asked. "Did you get him?"

"No. I mean, he was here looking for me, but I didn't get a chance..." she whispered, not wanting to admit her fear.

"Why was he looking for you?"

"I don't know."

"Well where did he go?"

Valerie shrugged. "I don't know."

"Damn it!"

"Scott, what's the matter? The game's working," she said quickly, pleased with herself. "I've already killed two people."

"The game is only ten rounds. Borgus could end up getting away. Come on." He grabbed her hand. "We've got to start looking for him."

"Wait," Valerie asked. She stepped closer to Scott. "I'm scared."

"Of what? You're the one everyone's afraid of."

She shrugged. "It's creepy in this house, and you're always running off."

"I've got to, Val, The only way everyone can hear the whistle is if I blow it from the front staircase. Let's go. We'll go upstairs and check a few rooms from the passage, then I've got to go blow the whistle."

"Scott, wait. Do me one favor."

"What now, Val? Jeez, we're wasting time."

"Oh, never mind." She brushed by him.

"What?" he demanded, grabbing her arm.

"You could be nice to me," she asked, whispering. "As if you liked me."

"I *do* like you. God!"

"You could show me then, like another boy would."

"How?" he asked.

"Well, you could try and kiss me sometimes."

"I did try once and you hit me."

"Oh, never mind!" She pulled away.

"Hold it." Scott touched her arm and she stopped walking. He pulled her into his arms.

"I can't touch you," she whispered. "I'll get all this white makeup on your costume."

Down the length of the hallway, from the other wing of the castle, came the roaring sound of glass crashing. Valerie jumped.

"Oh, Christ," he moaned. "Something just broke. Shit. My mom is going to kill me."

At the explosive sound of the breaking glass, Betty grabbed Tracy around the neck, clinging to the taller girl.

"Betty, please!" Tracy pulled away. The paper skeleton mask had only two small holes for eyes and it was difficult to see in the dark. She stopped at the entrance of the north wing and raised the mask to look ahead. At the end, she saw someone move. "Come on, Betty, get up against the wall and hide," she whispered quickly. "When he gets close we'll jump out and scare him."

"No, let's go downstairs. Zombies wait in the ballroom, Valerie said so. Come on, Tracy, we're supposed to be dead."

"Be quiet!" She pushed the shorter girl toward the stairs. "Go ahead down if you want, I'm going to scare him. I think it's Bob Senese; he always thinks he's so smart. I'll fix him."

She crossed the wide hallway to hide between two heavy suits of arms, then turned and waved frantically, motioning Betty away. Flattening herself against the wall, Tracy listened to her prey come down the hallway. Now she was sure it was Senese. He came slowly, banging his fist against the furniture and weaponry that lined the walls. It made a ferocious noise, and she inched forward to peep out from behind the knight's armor.

It was not Bob, she realized, seeing the Black Annis. Bob had come as a woodsman, she remembered then, carrying a bow and arrow. Whoever this person was, he smelled like rotten eggs. He deserved to be frightened. She pulled the mask down over her face and jumped into the hallway.

Fergus saw first the glowing skull floating freely in the dark, then the body of the girl, the white skin wrapped in a flimsy dress, and he grabbed her.

"Aah, love, I've been looking for you, lass," he whispered. The paper mask shifted on Tracy's head, blocking her vision. She could not see who had her, but she swung at him with both fists, shouting for him to let her go.

"Aah, love, it will be all right." He twisted her right arm and she screamed. The shrill, desperate cry rippled through the quiet halls of the castle.

"Love, please." His bony hands clutched the thin white neck and squeezed, lifting her easily off the floor. He held her like a glittering snake, and she twisted in his grip. Inside the paper mask she struggled for air, and his hands tightened each time she gasped for breath.

Then he dropped her, and she fell to the floor with a thump, blood filling her mouth and nostrils. She pulled at the mask, struggling to see better, and it came away with a rip. She was all right, she told herself. Whoever it was wouldn't kill her.

She was trying to stand when he saw the Viking axe handle on the wall and grabbed it. She turned to run and he struck her, clubbed her hard behind her ears like a helpless baby lamb. Her skull crushed, Tracy collapsed, near death, on the carpet, while he fingered the axe handle admiringly. It had been found in Limerick, he remembered, a relic of the Viking kingdom there, and it had always been one of his favorites.

The scream could be heard, distant but clear, even in the hidden passageway.

"It's Tracy," Valerie said at once.

"How do you know?" They both stopped to listen.

"I know. She's hurt or something. I've got find her."

"She's not hurt. She's just scared, that's all. It's the game."

"I don't care. I'm going." Valerie reached out in the tight, dark passage and felt the wall. "How do I get out of here?"

"Come on, Val, you're going to ruin the game. We've got to get Borgus."

"Let's go find Tracy first, then we'll find Borgus. Come on, Scott, I'm serious."

"Shit!" He leaned back against the cool stone outer wall of the castle and thought for a moment, trying to decide where in the rambling mansion the scream had originated. But it was impossible to tell. The hidden passage distorted every sound, either muffling or magnifying it. Tracy might be out in the second-floor hall, or in a different wing. "Where did you send her?" he asked Valerie.

"Downstairs. To the ballroom."

"Come on." Scott turned abruptly, scanned the narrow passage with his flashlight, then went ahead quickly, ducking his head under the low beams.

"This is Fergus's old study," he explained, opening the hidden panel door. "There's a back staircase that leads downstairs into the kitchen. Go down and look for her, then come up the main front staircase. I'll meet you there."

"Where are you going?" she whispered, upset that he was leaving again.

"To blow the whistle. This is the third round already and we haven't gotten any of the football players." He sounded furious.

"All right! All right! We'll get them in a minute. Don't get so mad."

"I'm not mad," he declared.

"Fine." Valerie pushed ahead of him and stepped into the study. "Where do I go?" She glanced around, looked for the doorway.

"Here!" Scott pulled back the heavy curtain and opened the door, watched until she reached the first floor safely. Then he went across the room and carefully unlocked the study door. There could be kids outside, he knew, hiding behind any of the suits of armor.

He moved quietly, but at his first step into the hallway, glass crunched loudly under his foot. Glancing around he saw the shattered display case, and the shards of Waterford sparkling in the moonlight.

"Shit!" he whispered. Now he was in trouble. This must have been the breaking sound he had heard earlier. Those assholes, he thought, they had done it on purpose.

Treading carefully on the scattered glass, he tiptoed toward the windows to see what else had been broken. Up ahead he spotted the end of the Knight Templar's long lance sticking out of the wall. Then he stepped around the bulky trunk of the knight and saw Derek dangling motionless, his eyes wide open, the ancient lance buried in his chest.

Scott screamed. A sharp cry of fear and pain. He couldn't look away from the hanging figure. He thought only of his mother. He had to tell his mom, he thought. She would take care of him; she would know what to do. He stumbled down the hallway, back to Derek's office and a telephone.

"Jesus Christ, what was that?" In the darkness near the back stairwell, Hank Simpson jumped at the sound of Scott's cry.

"Shut up, Hank," Borgus ordered. They were both crouched down, hiding near the head of the staircase.

"Who was that?"

"Some silly girl. What the fuck do you care?"

"Well, she sounded like she was in trouble or something."

"Who are you, rent-a-cop? Just get your ass out of the light."

Ignoring Borgus, Hank moved around the exit door and looked down toward the intersection of the two wings.

"Someone's coming," he said. He could just discern a shape at the end of the hallway.

"Is it Dunn?" Nick jumped up.

"I don't think so. It looks weird. Hey, let's get out of here."

Intrigued, Borgus took his place at the door. The strange shape was coming down the center of the hallway, moving slowly, one laborious step at a time.

"Who the fuck is it?" Borgus whispered, puzzled by the figure. "What's he doing?"

"Come on, Nick," Simpson urged. He grabbed Borgus's arm, tried to pull him away.

"He's dragging something," Nick answered. Jerking his arm free, he stepped into the hallway to see better.

The figure paused.

"Hey, what's up?" Borgus asked out loud. "Is that you, Senese?"

"Get out of my house, you blackguards," the Black Annis answered.

Borgus grinned. "What is this shit, Bob?" He stepped forward, still laughing.

The Black Annis let go of his victim's hair, readying himself to do battle. When he released her, her head bounced on the hallway carpet and Nick saw that it was a girl; it was Dunn's friend, Tracy.

"Hey, asshole!" Nick pulled back, stunned. The man had been dragging her down the hall by her hair.

"Get away," the Annis shouted, lunging at Borgus.

Nick dropped down into a crouch and caught the Black Annis with his shoulder, as if the old man was coming at him through the line. Fergus flew off Nick's shoulder and hit the wall.

"He's killed her!" Nick shouted, then kicked at the old man, tried to smash his head against the baseboard, but in the dark and his excitement, he misjudged and only kicked his shoulder blades. "Hank! Help me get this fucker!"

Regaining his feet, the Annis kicked Borgus in the groin and, without waiting to see the result, ran for the billiard room. Simpson dove after him, tried to catch him with a flying tackle in the doorway, but Fergus slammed the heavy wooden door shut and caught Hank on the side of the head. The big teenager yelled with pain as he tumbled to the floor.

He needed a weapon, Fergus knew. Any weapon at all to fight off these anarchists. His hands groped along the billiard room wall, searching. Then his bony fingers touched a wooden peg and he grabbed the Norman crossbow and turned on the two of them.

Simpson was on his feet, but staggering. "Jesus, Nick, I'm bleeding."

Fergus held the heavy bow with both hands. The arrow lay in the groove; he had only to wind the bowstring back and notch it. Borgus was coming at him as he fired.

At first it only felt as if he couldn't swallow, but when he tried to speak the blood gushed from his throat. He was choking, he realized, choking on his own blood. He tripped forward, smashing against furniture, and fell.

"Oh, shit!" Hank cried, seeing the short crossbow arrow. It had entered Borgus's thick neck and come out the other side.

Now the old man was coming at him. Fergus had tossed away the crossbow, useless without a bolt, and grabbed a morningstar, the thick-handled mace from the wall. He whipped the iron ball around his head.

"Hey, lad, you want a fight, do you?"

The heavy lead ball whistled in the air.

Hank ran backwards, too frightened to turn his back on the

man. All along the hallway, kids crept to the doorways of rooms to watch Hank Simpson run for his life.

"Where's Tracy?" Valerie asked, grabbing Betty in the almost empty ballroom.

Betty shrugged. "I don't know. Upstairs, I guess."

"Didn't you hear her scream?" Valerie shook the girl's arm. "And take off that stupid mask."

"Well, you gave it to me!" Betty complained, yanking off the paper bag. "Anyway, we can't play any more. The man who runs this place just told Tami and Judy that we had to quit." She turned away, as if to leave.

"Wait!" Valerie grabbed her arm again. "Is Tracy upstairs or not?"

"I guess so. I left her there. She was going to scare Bob Senese."

"Valerie, where's Scott?" Bill Russell came into the ballroom from the small office next to the reception room.

"He's still upstairs, Mr. Russell. He's about to blow the whistle for the next round."

"Well, we have to quit, I'm afraid Mr. Brennan told some of the girls the game was over."

"Why? We can't quit now." Tears of frustration flashed in her eyes. Scott would just die, she knew, if he couldn't get the football players. She had let him down, too, running off looking for Tracy when she should've been after Borgus.

The teacher shook his head. "I don't know, Val," he answered nicely, seeing she was upset. "I haven't spoken to Mr. Brennan myself yet. But let's find Scott. It's time to start dancing again anyway, right?" He tried to sound positive.

And then they heard Hank Simpson yell.

Scott saw his mother at once. "Mom!" he said, then stopped, baffled at the strange sight of her curled up on the long conference table. Then he realized what had happened and for a moment he couldn't focus his feelings. It was as if his nerves had overloaded and burned out, and he gasped and vomited on the office rug.

Slowly he went forward, circling the body, looking for her face, afraid to touch her and unable not to, needing to know for certain if she, too, was gone. He thought of the day the headmaster told him his father was dead. He had thought then that nothing else in life could ever hurt as much.

Her body was cold and his hand jumped away, trembling from the touch. He stepped back to the door and shut his eyes, willing himself to blot out what he had seen. But the image of his mother's body could not be evaded, no matter how his mind twisted and retreated. For a long moment he stood helpless, searching inside himself for a strength he did not have. And then, almost with a feeling of surrender, he remembered. He was Brian Ború and his task was vengence. The Nucke-lavees had killed his mother and turned her body to stone.

The boy who called himself Brian Ború unsheathed his sacred sword and went to do battle at Ballycastle.

Brian stepped onto the balcony and saw that a melee had begun. Knights, sea monsters, Bugganes and ladies-in-waiting had rushed into the hallway, shouting, wailing, running for safety.

A Giant Troll stood on the second-floor landing, fighting in single combat with a Black Annis. The troll had borrowed a shield from the Lombard knight and he held it high, trying to protect himself from the whirling mace.

It was useless, Brian knew. The Troll did not have enough armor class to withstand single combat against an Annis. He would be killed before the next round.

Behind the shield, Hank Simpson called for help, shouted to the students who lined the second-floor banisters. The crazy man had driven him to his knees, and he didn't know how many more blows he could withstand. His attacker moved in and swung. The mace struck the metal shield with a crash. It sounded as if the house itself was being wrecked.

"Get back, you Annis," Brian Ború shouted, pushing through the crowd, his sacred sword held high. "Get back to Groagh Patrick or your entrails will stretch from here to Dingle Bay."

"Ah, it's another of you terrorists," Fergus shouted in Gaelic. Spinning away from Hank, he turned to face his chal-lenger.

Brian Ború circled the man on the wide balcony. "Listen,

you boorish cur," he shouted, "I'll cut your yellow hair from your head, and strip the clothes off your back."

Around the perimeter of the circle students began to cheer Scott on, rallying him against the Black Annis. Brian lunged forward, aiming at Fergus's neck, when the old man slipped, weary from hauling the heavy mace, and Scott tumbled over his shoulder.

"Ah, there you go, lad." Out of breath, Fergus leaned against the wooden banister as Scott went sprawling. "Conor, where are you?" he gasped, speaking in Gaelic. "Where is Maeve, my lad? I'm tired of all these people." His head hurt. The pain began in the spot above his ear, where Nightfall had kicked him, where Conor once had struck him, that last grand party after the war. He had survived them both, but oh, the pain was worse than it had been in all the many years.

Then his eye caught Valerie Dunn. She had run halfway up the stairs, hoping to reach Scott, when the Annis suddenly lurched toward her.

Bill Russell called out, "All right, that's enough. You kids have taken this fantasy stuff too far. We're calling it quits."

As he spoke, he tried to mount the stairs and pull Valerie back, but Fergus was there before him, whirling his mace to keep everyone at bay. Amazed by what was happening, Russell was forced back into the wide circle of students out of range of the heavy ball. The two other chaperones, Arlene Banks and Kristin Chase, ran to his side, both at a loss to know what they should do.

"Now what's your name, lass?" he crooned. "The picture of Nuala O'Neill, you are."

Valerie stood poised, confused by the melee. She felt the danger, but didn't know where it came from, or why. Then she remembered where she had seen this creature before. She recognized the long yellow hair, the strange dress and the foul smell of the Black Annis.

"Scott!" She looked wildly around the tight circle of students.

"Ah, lass," Fergus lowered the mace, let the ball drag across the hardwood steps as he came for her.

"Don't," she pleaded, backing off. "Scott!" She had backed herself up against the wall when Fergus grabbed her arm in his bony fingers, seized her before she could flee.

"No, please!" Over the Annis's shoulder, Valerie saw Scott push through the students. He was brandishing his sword, thrusting it forward, as he had done down by the barns.

"Stop him, Scott!" she pleaded.

"Surrender, you recreant," Brian Ború demanded, placing the point of the long sword at the back of the Black Annis's neck.

Fergus felt the sharp blade beneath his ear and swung the mace wildly. The chained ball whipped around, taking Scott by surprise. His heavy cape absorbed much of the impact, but the lead ball still struck his wrist hard enough to send the sacred sword flying.

At the sound, Fergus was off and down the stairs, dragging Valerie behind him, his fingers like iron on her slender wrist. Bill Russell leaped forward, but before he could reach Fergus, the circle parted and he was gone, out the front door and onto the lawns of Ballycastle.

As if released from a magic spell, the crowd of students on the second floor unfroze and came streaming down the stairway, shouting to their teachers. Mrs. Chase went up the steps to Hank Simpson, to see if he was all right. He got to his feet shakily and came with her to the first floor.

"Mr. Russell," someone shouted, "he's not leaving. He's running around the side of the house."

"Lock all the doors, front and rear," Russell told Arlene Banks. "Don't forget the French doors in the ballroom. We've got to keep him outside. I'm calling the police."

He went into the front office and dialed nervously, wondering how the hell he would explain what had happened at Ballycastle that night.

"State Police. Please state your name and address before proceeding to give any other information," the dispatcher said.

"Ah... This is... My name is William Russell. I'm telephoning from Ballycastle off Route 12. We have a deranged student... a deranged man threatening the lives of students."

"Sir, we have that report," she interrupted. "A state trooper has been dispatched. The nearest available vehicle was several towns away, but it should be arriving shortly."

"Oh." Russell stopped, confused. "You mean someone already telephoned?"

"Yes, sir. At 8:06. Derek Brennan, executive director...."

"Fine! Okay!" So Derek knew. Russell sighed, "Thank you." Already, faintly, he could hear the police siren. They would arrive in a few minutes, he realized. All he had to do was keep the kids safe until then. He rushed back into the front hallway, shouting for everyone to get into the ballroom, into the brightly lit room overlooking the lawns and the terrace.

The boy who called himself BrianBorú dropped to one knee and clutched his injured hand. All around him flowed a stream of villagers, all crowding to the main floor of the castle now that the danger was past. He had lost his sword and now he was in pain, but they did not pause to offer comfort. No one would help him, he thought. It was like that day in the Hills of Ballyhoura, when he had had to fight the pack of Padfoot dogs alone.

His sword had slid to the foot of the stairs and he ran for it, wiped it clean on his canvas pants and sheathed it. He would need more than the sword to kill the Black Annis, he thought as he ran back up the stairway. She had magical powers and would disappear in the woods, change herself into a rock or a tree. Even a twenty-fifth-level paladin could not find her in a forest of other trees.

At the head of the stairs he turned and began to lope down the hall toward Fergus's study. As he ran, he glanced at the glass display cases, eventually stopping at one and catching something up from the shelves. Then he continued on to the study.

He would take the back stairs, the short cut to the side lawns that Conor had showed him. The Annis had to be cut off before she reached the river and disappeared for good. The Nucke-lavees would help her, Brian knew. They'd set the long grass on fire to keep him from crossing the bridge and going into the woods. And the Lady with the White Hand would be dead. Before morning, they'd turn her body into stone.

On the flagstone terrace, Valerie seized the leg of a heavy lawn chair and held on. The old man stumbled against the wrought iron furniture and fell, too exhausted to drag her further. He would never get to the woods now, not without Conor to help him carry the maid.

"Nuala, my love, please come along," he asked.

Valerie bit his hand and the old man let go, swearing at her in Irish. She spun around, tried to find an escape. The huge terrace was flooded with lights and behind the wide windows and French doors of the ballroom, Valerie could see dozens of her classmates, their faces pressed against the glass.

"Open the doors," she yelled. "Open the doors and let me in."

Faces turned to Mr. Russell and the other teachers. Grim-faced, Russell shook his head. His helplessness made him sick, but he couldn't take the risk of letting the maniac back into the ballroom. He'd have to go outside himself and help the girl.

Fergus seized Valerie's ankle, tugged her back into his grip. "It's all right, Nuala, it won't hurt you at all." He folded her in his arms.

"Scott!" she shouted, twisting away, throwing up her arms to hide her face, to keep the old man from kissing her. "Scott, please help me!"

Brian Ború ran out through the kitchen door and raced around the mansion to the terrace. As he ran he unhooked the slingshot from his belt and made it ready. He knew now how he would stop the Annis.

Leaping up on the thick terrace wall, he spotted the Black Annis. Behind the locked doors and windows the kids had seen him and begun to shout. He could hear their cheers as he whirled his slingshot in the air, whipping it faster and faster. Nestled in the leather pouch was the small glass bottle of quicklime that Conor had showed him.

With a mighty battle cry, Brian Ború snapped his slingshot. The bottle flew the length of the terrace, sailing through the flood of light and smashing within a foot of the Annis. The quicklime exploded; the fumes mushroomed in its face.

The students cheered. Brian could see them in the windows, jumping up and down, shouting for him. He grinned, sure of himself. He was a twenty-fifth-level paladin. No Black Annis could defeat him in single combat. Disregarding the pain in his hand, he unsheathed his sacred sword and charged the monster.

Choking on the quicklime, Fergus released the girl. "Conor," he coughed, trying to speak. He fell back against an iron love seat, stumbling away from the fumes. He could see the anarchist on the wall, running toward him. Fergus grabbed a chair and raised it in self-defense.

Brian Ború's thin sword struck the iron at an angle and snapped. The long blade bounced away, shattered into pieces. He halted and Fergus lunged with the chair, striking his face with an iron leg.

Brian cried out in pain and covered his face. The wrought iron had dug a deep cut into his cheek.

"Had enough, have you?" Fergus shouted. He raised the chair again and brought it down on Brian, knocking him to the terrace floor.

The old man stumbled as well, exhausted by the fight. As he dropped to his knees, his hands reached out to steady himself and he seized the mace handle.

"Ah, I'll have done with you for good." He pulled himself up once more and turned to Brian Ború. Using both hands, he raised the iron ball, whirled it above his head. "Here you be, you scum." The studded ball gleamed in the floodlights as Fergus stepped forward, came within range of Brian.

Brian Ború had no arcane knowledge left. He could not use magic on his foe, nor roll the cube dice and reverse the game. And if he died this time, Brian Ború could never be resurrected.

"Scott, look out!" Valerie shouted. She came at the old man, tried to grab his leg and stop him.

Brian rolled to one side, and the ball of the mace whistled by him, shattering a flagstone. In that instant, Brian Ború jerked the knobbed shillelagh from his belt. He had never wielded it before. "Use it only in time of great danger," Conor had told him, "and your knight will be a true son of Erin."

He saw Fergus kick Valerie away, doubling her over with the pain. "Run, Scott, run," she sobbed. "It's not a game this time; he's crazy!"

Scott saw then that there was no Black Annis above him, but only a strange looking old man. He saw the crowd of students behind the ballroom windows, and then Valerie on her knees, only inches away from him. His mother was dead, he realized, and the Nuckelavees of Donegal had not killed her. Then the madman raised his arm once more, and Valerie began to scream.

338

HOBGOBLIN

The ball of studded steel was floating toward him, straining at the end of its chain. Desperately, Scott rose up on one elbow and swung the shillelagh at the old man. The mallet struck Fergus where he had been struck before, dug deep into the old man's weakened cranium. Then the morningstar sailed harmlessly away as the dying body of Fergus O'Cuileannain fell on the golden cloak of Brian Ború, the legendary knight of Erin, the last paladin of Ballycastle.

Epilogue

Dear Val,

Well, I got to say you really made a hit at old Spencertown. About twelve guys have already asked me if you really won the Hudson Valley Hang-Gliding competition. God, did you tell that to everyone, or just the gullible types? Okay, I know some of the guys are jerks, but no worse than the crowd at Flat Rock. How is that asshole Simpson, anyway?

I've been thinking over what you said, about staying at your house over spring break. I can afford the trip, I guess. I got a letter yesterday from Mr. Kyle, my parents' accountant in Hartford. He says that with the insurance settlement and everything, I can afford to finish boarding here at Spencertown and also have money for a good college, if any of them will take me. (That's a joke. I hope.)

Anyway, I've got the money, and we get ten days off at Easter. And I'd really like to see you soon. I didn't tell you when you were here, but having you down last weekend was really okay. The headmaster's wife said if you wanted to come back, they'd put you up again any time.

But going back to Flat Rock—I don't know. I talked it over with Dr. Frisch. He says I'm doing real well now and accepting my mother's death, and my Dad's, which is good, I guess. I mean, I know it is. But it still hurts, Val. I guess what I'm saying is, I just couldn't stand to see Flat Rock, and Ballycastle, again.

I'm glad you liked McNulty. He and Evans have been really great to me, especially about school. They lent me their notebooks from last term, and Evans talked a friend of his who's a senior into giving me special math tutoring so I can catch up. Between the time I spent at Flat Rock and all the time I lost after that, seeing Dr. Frisch, going to the inquest and having all those tests, I'm really going to have to work to pass the SATs. (Dr. Frisch said the state spent over $10,000 deciding I wasn't crazy after all. He said they should have asked him. He'd only have charged $5000, and split it down the middle with me.)

The guys are really hot to have me play *Hobgoblin* again. They just started running a game after midterms, and there's a brand new monster manual that just came out. But I told them I can't. Between regular homework and extra English make-up stuff and the math tutorial, there's no way I'll have enough time to spare.

But that's not really why I don't want to play. I love the game, and I loved BrianBorú. But the game just goes on and on; it never ends. First the Black Annis is the enemy; then the Brobdingnagians; then the fallen angels of Ireland. You go right on from one to the other, and the only thing that happens is you just get stronger. You think that fighting against evil is an Adventure. A great fantasy Adventure. But it's not. It's really not.

For me, *Hobgoblin* was the beginning and what happened at Ballycastle was the end.